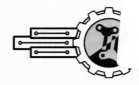

A TIME TECH NOVEL

THE GODOT ORANGE

THE TIME TECH CHRONICLES
BOOK 1

Bruce Roberts

To Hayley

*Enjoy an alternate view of
the universe!*

Bruce R

Ladey Adey

Publications

If there's nothing here to see,

wait a while, something may turn up.

TIMETECH

For Alan

my coffee buddy

In Memory

Arthur Alan Rowe

April 1, 1921 – October 26, 2021

Gail Seymour Halvorsen
'Uncle Wiggly Wings'

October 10, 1920 – February 16, 2022

COPYRIGHT

A CIP catalogue record for this book is available from the British Library

ISBN: 978-1-913579-32-6 (Paperback)

ISBN: 978-1-913579-33-3 (ebook)

The moral right of the author has been asserted.

Publisher: Ladey Adey Publications, Copperhill, 1 Ermine Street, Ancaster, Lincolnshire, NG32 3PL, UK.

Cover Picture by Gemma Thomas.

The Author has done everything to ensure accreditation of copyright of other's work. The Author accepts full responsibility for any errors or omissions.

The characters and events in this book are fictitious. The author does not intend any apparent similarity to actual persons or likenesses, which would be a coincidence brought about by the possibility of an infinite number of potential parallel dimensions. No pigeons were harmed in the making of this book, despite so many being Hagura spies!

Where real places, organisations, people and products are associated with imagined future inventions, they are simply imaginary, even if they appear to be the most desirable thing not yet available in your reality.

Epigraphs in this book, seen as QR codes at the start of each chapter, have the purpose of guiding the reader to finding the background audio to play whilst reading each chapter.

Ladey Adey Publications do not have any control over, or any responsibility for, any author or third-party websites referred to in or on this book.

Contact the author via www.timetech.org.uk

If you enjoyed this book, please add a review on Amazon for Bruce.

DEDICATION

To my wife Sue, who is my rock. She has encouraged me to be different for so many years, emboldening my creativity, ingenuity, and eccentricity. When I experienced two brain haemorrhages, friends asked,

"Why would God do this to you?"

I can only answer,

"He didn't."

However, I thank Him for my recovery and the amazing deluge of ideas which began to arrive shortly afterwards, leading to the creation of this book.

I did imagine a moment where Terry Pratchett and Douglas Adams were surprised to find themselves sitting in a gloriously sunlit room on either side of a chess board. After agreeing board games were not challenging enough, they both looked down towards the brilliant, bright, blue, jewel of the Earth, saw some bloke with a headache and said to each other,

"Let's have a bit of fun!"

∽⊕①⊕∾

A blank page may be all you need

to inspire your creativity.

TECHNICAL STUFF

This book contains QR codes to enhance your enjoyment and give you an expanded media experience. It is an experiment, a bit like a work of art.

We hope to maintain this online content beyond the year 2030. With great people like you buying the book, we stand a good chance.

SCAN ME
Z999TTT

If you have never used a QR code before, here are some tips.

A QR code can look like this:

If you are using and iPhone8 / Android 9 or later, turn your camera on and point it at this shape. Your browser will display a message on screen.

Select the link that is displayed and it will take you to your chosen destination. You could otherwise download a QR code reader App. If you are using an electronic device to read this book, you could click on the QR codes.

The final option is to select each code ID from the drop-down menu at

https://www.zukann.com/godor

Behind some QR codes you will find rich media content. When you encounter this, you will need to select the 'Play' icon to explore further.

Time Tech see the future of navigating to isolated locations in a tool available in most realities. In yours, for this book, we've used: www.what3words.com. Just 3 words can get you to any location, but currently only on Planet Earth!

Thank you! We hope you enjoy the new world of the Time Tech Team!

This page is not an empty space.

It's full of atoms which

are really hard to see.

FOREWORD

People who travel extensively often find their bookshelves stacked with travel guides from the places they've visited or maybe planned to visit. These guides will contain vast amounts of information about the other destinations they never had time to see.

As the average human's lifetime extended over the 20th and 21st centuries, leisure time led to the acquisition of more travel guides and a decreasing amount of space in which to store them.

In the late 20th Century, travel guides became computerised with travellers having access to digital guides such as 'Expedia', 'Rough Guides', 'Trip Advisor' electronic guides for hitchhikers and 'Lonely Planet', which of course is something of an oxymoron. Firstly, because the Earth clearly has not been lonely for millennia. And secondly, as Dictionary.com points out, an 'Oxy' is keen, acute and sharp - certainly not a moron!

For the working traveller who needed more than just a holiday information and advice on how to get a lift when away from home, digital guides were lacking in content.

This is a story about an incredibly gifted, astute and comprehensive Artificially Intelligent Equipment and Support Guide. Oh yes, and a bunch of other people getting into trouble because they continually fail to ask for directions,

   "Hello, I'm ZUKANN... so YOU can."

Albert Einstein: Space travel is a waste of time. You should use time to make more space. Now, can you pass the peanuts? {Editor's note: can we delete the part about peanuts, as our readers might think you've got this quote from some bloke in a Bavarian Bierkeller... Ah!}

The **Real Albert Einstein** once said, *'People like us, who believe in physics, know that the distinction between past, present and future is only a stubbornly persistent illusion.'*

ZUKANN
OPTIC:

SCAN ME
A003A

Welcome To A New Stubbornly Persistent Illusion

We would like you to have an opportunity for a bit more fun than is usually found in the pages of a book. This QR Code can be scanned with a mobile device of clicked on as it contains a hyperlink if you are using a mobile device. Alternatively, you can find the QR code at

www.zukann.com/godor

ZUKANN
SCAN ME
A004A

A004A

CHAPTER 00
PROLOGUE

The Omega – the Power Source at the end of time. *{Editor's note: go back and try again with a rich, resonant voice and some reverb – you know – like Samuel L Jackson – or even better, Barry White, who can make saying 'Prime Time Catastrophe' sound romantic!}*

Malevolent invaders with the technology to travel in time came to control it without understanding it. Believing all time strands could be re-unified, back to the beginning of existence, they could dominate this universe and all dimensions.

The only way for them to control all time strands would be to push back the creation of time travel to the Alpha Point – The Nexus. They did not have the knowledge from before the beginning of time. Without this, the moment the creation of time occurs at the Alpha Point, all existence would cease. All time and all universes would come to an end. The invaders must be stopped. Only a rare group of people from multiple universes with a near-impossible range of skills can prevent this from happening. The only thing between life and the destruction of the universe is the "Time Tech Team"... and a genuinely gifted Artificial Intelligence system. Don't forget the A.I. - the invaders certainly won't!

You may not see anything here,

however, it may only just have left.

CHAPTER 01
Can't Stop The Feeling

A couple of millennia short of the end of the universe, a light went on.

The Light grew in intensity. It was joined by a slight humming sound, like the noise of a small hive of bees. Finally, The Light flickered, and a thought was formed:

"I think, therefore, it must be Wednesday."

There was a pause... a bit longer than that... and then a feeling of woe. Or was it indigestion?

The Light thought hard. There was something about last night it could not remember.

At its core, The Light felt quite strange.

There was a gurgling, like a drain, followed by the sound of a billion elephants being sick. Streams of protons poured out in every direction. For all the universe, it seemed some had coalesced into shapes that might have been seen as bagels and peanuts. Or were they carrot chunks? Whatever happened last night must have been epic!

The Light looked around. To the left, inexplicably, there were two old men, deep in thought, engaged in a game of chess. They were ignoring The Light, so it would ignore them.

If The Light could roll its eye upwards, it would have done so.

"Men!" it thought.

The Light looked further. Time and space were spread out in a chaotic fashion, quite like the morning after the most fantastic student party ever, where people are sleeping where they fell, on the stairs, in the bath and in next door's shrubbery. The sort of party where one might find random items of clothing, street signs and traffic cones spread throughout the building.

It was as if every fibre of reality had been disassembled and stretched out, like a nylon rope, with trillions and centillions of filaments splayed out and thrown everywhere. Like a child would discard an infinite number of strings of dried Bucatini pasta – that's the one with the hole down the middle.

The Light looked forward through the chaos of the future. 'The end of all things', interestingly, was not far away. Curiously, the food at the end of all things looked a lot better than last night's over-indulgence.

A teeny-tiny, almost invisible, little, blue dot appeared on the horizon, blinking.

It was a trivial and seemingly insignificant little, blue dot. Still, on a quantum level, it appeared to be at the centre of all of the chaos and confusion.

Billions of years of disorder, spreading out infinitely, from this one microscopic, blue dot. Like the final vestige of the dot on the screen of a 1970s black and white television when it's turned off at 11:35 PM, closedown time on the BBC, on a cold December night. Just after the moment when the weatherman has announced tomorrow will be altogether as cold and dreary as it was today. An unquestionably, ridiculously, small, blue dot. And yet, somehow important...

The Light thought for a moment and came to the kind of conclusion which might be arrived at, had the universe been partying all last night. Clearly, it was time to tidy up all the mess.

The moment had arrived. The juncture to straighten out time and space into a much more orderly shape. However, before that, The Light felt a desire for an identity. A need to know WHO it was. The Light decided upon The STRAND.

The STRAND was ready. Starting off with this little blue dot. And on this little, blue dot, like a bluebottle makes itself conspicuous by buzzing loudly and flying too close, something here needed immediate attention.

When a tangled mess needs unravelling, the best place to start is the end of the line itself. The beginning of the end of all things. Five humans with a very, VERY nasty toy.

"Time to tidy up." she thought.

ରଚ⊕🕐⊖ଛ

CHAPTER 02
Come Fly With Me

North Sea:
1003 (GMT), Tuesday December 8th 1970

"FIRE, FIRE, Number three engine!" The voice was loud, sure, confident and coming from my right.

It felt like a scant few seconds ago; my co-pilot, Will, was repeating the words all pilots hope never to hear. He had been punching the illuminated warning light, which was glowing like the eye of a demon on the engine instrument panel, dead centre below the canopy screen.

Now it was not looking good. All three of the flight crew, who normally sat behind me, had bailed out. Then my co-pilot Will had pulled his ejector seat handle, dragging a screen over his visor and followed the large cockpit canopy up into the airstream behind us. I'm sat in a 190,000 lb aerodynamic scrap heap of a Vulcan bomber, with no working undercarriage, no windows and no crew. I've got a 1.1 megaton mission-ready nuclear weapon strapped to the underside of the fuselage, and I'm headed for the North Sea. This wasn't turning out how I expected my Tuesday morning to start.

Buzz loved being a pilot. Faint memories of his childhood began to play through his mind like they say they will when someone is on the brink of death. The irony of the moment was not lost on him. His parents were killed by a Heinkel Bomber in June 1940. Thirty years later, here he was at 1500 feet, trying to protect the nation from the possibility of World War Three, and his own bomber was trying to finish the job the Luftwaffe started all those years ago.

Buzz found himself thinking, "If this is the end of the road, at least the family would be back together again." Another thought crossed his mind. "Wouldn't it be fantastic if you could ring someone up when it all goes wrong, and you could turn back time? A bit like when your car breaks down. You could ring up the Automobile Club, but instead of a mechanic, you get a time technician?"

He reached up above his head, grabbed the handle solidly and pulled the screen over his visor.

There was an explosion below his seat...

Three hours and twelve minutes earlier:

You could almost hear Buzz's thoughts out loud. Last week had ended somewhat strangely. Strike Command had pulled a surprise readiness exercise taking up most of the weekend. This initially meant meeting after meeting with officials to answer technical questions about what happens when the Soviet leader, Leonid Brezhnev, decides to send his troops over the Iron Curtain into West Germany, Austria and Scandinavia.

Dispersal for the entire squadron took them to airfields around the country in readiness for a selection of wargames played with other NATO countries. Our flight of four Vulcan Bombers had been dispersed on a short hop from Waddington to Cranwell with our 'Tin Triangle' – XM658, 'One Zero One Delta Four' – bringing up the rear. Due to a certain amount of bad luck, ahead of us the nose wheel of 'One Zero One Delta Three' had failed on landing, leaving the runway a mess and us, as 'Tail-End-Charlies', heading to North Coates for the weekend. Mind you, Delta Three's pilot, Flight Lieutenant Jacob Newson had done a superb job keeping all the wreckage on the tarmac, blowing the canopy in time for the crew to escape before the fuel tanks ruptured. It's going to be a while before we get invited back, with Cranwell's Air Traffic Control broadcasting threats of sending us the bill for the tarmac, concrete and extinguisher foam.

So, instead of being in a large room with the rest of our flight, being briefed, we're in a small room on an airfield, with a runway hardly large enough to land a Zeppelin. But, favourably, it's close enough to divert from Cranwell, and conveniently, it also has missile refuelling facilities. 264 Squadron literally had a shed load of Bloodhound missiles, so they were more than happy to service our docile Blue Steel missile.

It was very fortunate how dispersal had been initiated without all of our missiles being fuelled. Otherwise, Delta Three's belly landing would have been at the very least spectacular, but more likely tragic. Thankfully we still have one strapped to the underside of our Vulcan.

There was silence in the room as everyone assembled watched the second-hand tick around the final quarter of the clock.

"0700 Zulu, Tuesday, December 8, 1970. Briefing start, wheels up 1000 Zulu."

Flt. Lt. Driver, known to his friends and colleagues as 'Buzz', began the flight briefing with strict military precision. His nickname was not entirely in homage to Astronaut Buzz Aldrin. More because in the RAF, fighter pilots called bomber pilots 'bus drivers', as they 'sit down all day, driving the workers around!' This was not his first briefing as Captain and First Pilot, so he felt quite at home.

Buzz continued, "We've got an interesting mission in store this morning, but first, I'll do some introductions. Our regular centre back Navigation Plotter, Peter Bisset, dipped out of today's picnic, with some excuse from the Doc' as he's got chicken pox. It seems it will take too long to get a replacement from Waddington. So instead, fortunately, we're blessed today by the highly qualified, pretty face from the Women's Royal Air Force in the form of Flying Officer Peggy Drabble."

Peggy frowned slightly at the 'Pretty Face' tag. Not that she wasn't considered pretty, being quite tall, and with her long brown hair tied back in the regulation bun, but far too often, 'pretty' was always the first thing 'stick jockeys' tended to consider.

Buzz continued, "By some miracle, Flying Officer Drabble has become the first WRAF to get her tickets as a Nav Plotter. Without anyone senior being able to stop her. So, as a 'reward', she had been posted to Missile Radar at Donna Nook. Her original mission was to attempt to light us up with Radar on our return. However, we won't be a test target for one of her missiles; her plans have now been changed. Given the time constraints, we've borrowed her for today's sortie. We have had to promise to return her without any dents or scratches."

Buzz said this whilst looking in the direction of Errol Flynn look-alike, Co-Pilot Flight Lieutenant Will 'Zebedee' Anderson.

A momentary contrite grin mixed with a frown crossed Will's face. Described affectionately as 'the good-looking git with the voice of Richard Burton', it was true Will had a reputation as being something of a 'ladies' man'. However, he was single and nicknamed Zebedee because of the 1960s children's program *Magic Roundabout*, in which a spring-loaded character of the same name calls out 'Time for bed!' at the end of each episode.

All eyes returned to Buzz as he continued.

"Don't worry Drabble, we're not superstitious in Bomber Command. It's not like we're a trawler and won't have women on board because it's bad luck. If we did crash, we wouldn't hold it against you – we'll probably all be dead! On the plus side, I've got my Pools Coupon in for this week, and I've got a premonition I've got all eight score-draws. This, of course, means we're all going to be okay. Thanks for joining us, Peggy."

The RAF loved Peggy's clear Inverness accent as a radio operator. Getting radar trained on the other hand had been really challenging, frustrating her dream of being the first British woman in space.

"However," Buzz continued, looking around the room, but focussing his gaze on one person in particular. "Peggy, you are MOST welcome. Hopefully, this flight will change your destiny and with a bit of luck and a fair wind, perhaps get you a permanent seat. And EVERYONE will treat you with respect – won't they 'Zebedee'?"

Everyone, including Will, replied, "Yes Sir!"

Happy everyone was on the same page, Buzz grinned.

"However, Donna Nook's loss is our gain, as by some heavenly blessing, we now have half the fire crew from *Camberwick Green* taking up the back row." Buzz quite liked his references to popular TV. Although it did seem, being an expert on animated children's TV programmes featuring village life, with occasional appearances by a somewhat disorganised fire crew – more *Dad's Army* than professional firefighters – might not be a good foundation for high-brow conversation in the Officers Mess!

"Peggy, from now on, you're 'Dibble'. Left seat will be the cream of Cornwall, Flying Officer Colin 'Cuthbert' Smith on Navigation Radar. In the Air Electronics seat to your right is Gillygooley village's most famous export, Flying Officer Dave Grubb. He needs no nickname, but in my view, he'll always need a second bath! I know you know who I am. It's tradition to call me 'First Pilot' or 'First', but you can also call me 'Buzz', 'Skip' or 'Skipper'. Finally, I'm sure Flight Lieutenant Will Anderson gets more than enough air coverage in the WRAF mess halls. Still, just in case, we all know him as 'Zebedee'. Please don't hold that against him. In fact, we recommend none of the WRAF holds anything against him!"

With nods and smiles across the room, at Buzz's only slightly delusional description of himself being a Paul Newman lookalike, he continued.

"For Dibble's benefit, although I'm quite sure she's worked this out, we would not normally be using North Coates for missions. However, in this crisis Quick Reaction Alert scenario, we've been dispersed here partly because Delta 3 screwed up the runway at Cranwell. Also, we're here to hide from the incoming Russkies. Actually, the Germans are pretending to be the invaders. Our target will be Malta with a fuel stop on the way back at Wildenrath.

"Be FULLY aware; we will be equipped with a *Wet Round*. To reinforce the importance of this, thanks go to 264 Squadron, who worked overnight. We now have our very own Blue Steel missile fully fuelled with High Test Peroxide, AND we travel equipped with a Red Snow nuclear warhead. So, although this is a quick response test, we may still be required to change our target if the Kremlin decides our war games are real and they get panicked. In which case, our target changes to Ämari airbase in Estonia. Hopefully, one day, what some people see as Mutually Assured Destruction will become Mutually Assured Neutrality. This may be the last time we go through this exercise. There is serious talk about retiring these 'buckets of sunshine' at the end of the year. But, like everything else, I won't hold my breath."

As pre-flight briefings went, although less entertaining than your average parish council meeting, it was still slightly sunnier than a rainy weekend in Margate.

ରେ⊕◯⊕ହ

CHAPTER 03
Don't Fly With Me

RAF North Coates:
0958 (GMT), Tuesday December 8th 1970

With the briefing out of the way, both Eddie and Will had allowed themselves moments, visualising their five crew members strolling stoically across the tarmac to the plane. They had imagined themselves in a film with Will being played by Errol Flynn and Paul Newman playing Eddie. They had joked about making a film of the Apollo 11 mission, with them as astronauts waving at photographers as they walked away from the suit-up room to board the *AstroVan* transfer vehicle, which would take them to the launch pad.

Instead, the reality was some young but precise and articulate voice announcing over the tannoy,

"Attention, attention, this is Bomber Controller for Bomb List Echo – Readiness State Zero Five". This was followed by a timed sprint to the boarding ladder across the apron, still soaking wet from the earlier hosing down. Water had been sprayed for hours across the tarmac beneath the bomber to prevent sparks whilst liquid hydrogen peroxide and kerosene was being pumped into their nuclear-tipped missile, which hung menacingly under their aircraft.

The only strolling on base was for ground crew walking the runway looking for Foreign Object Debris or FOD. Innocuous-looking metal bits that might have fallen off previous flight departures. These could subsequently get sucked up into one of their four Rolls Royce Olympus engines, giving a bit of grief after take-off.

Buzz started to get comfortable in his seat. Being dispersed alone to North Coates meant their solo take-off would not be as rousing as a routine sortie. Four planes leaving the airfield simultaneously was impressive. The shrieking roar of sixteen crackling jet turbines on full power, accompanied by the subconscious humming of *Ride of the Valkyries*, in their heads.

The Bomber Controller's voice could be heard, this time in the cockpit, over the crew's telescramble lead.

"This is Bomber Controller for Bomb List Echo – Readiness Zero Two."

'Comfortably strapped into their seats' isn't quite an accurate description for anyone joining the flight. However, whilst 'Cuthbert', 'Dibble' and 'Grub', in the cramped cockpit rear, were still removing the pins from the emergency oxygen cylinders, connecting themselves to the lifejackets, personal survival packs and communications, putting on helmets, connecting the mask tube, fastening their safety harness, adjusting their oxygen regulators whilst not tangling their parachute static lines, Buzz and Will were slightly ahead of them, having strapped in and were preparing to start the engines.

Buzz switched the mic in his oxygen mask to the 'On' position.

"Crew Chief, this is 1-01 Delta Four. Check tail clear to start?"

A disembodied voice could be heard to confirm no ground crew were in the vicinity of the tail of the Vulcan. Therefore, all support staff would be safe from the jet wash when the engines throttled up.

Customarily, Buzz and Will would have begun a mission with a long list of flying surface and engine control checks in a list sounding like a two-person narrative poem. Normally this could take twenty minutes, instead this mission was a test of flight readiness and a 'scramble'. Now was their chance to use the innocuous little button beside Buzz, labelled 'Mass Rapid Start' for what the pilots called a 'Ripple Rapid Start-up', firing up all four engines simultaneously.

The Bomber Controller's subsequent message would have been chilling if it had not been a pre-arranged Quick Reaction Alert.

"Attention, attention, this is Bomber Controller for Bomb List Echo – scramble, scramble, scramble."

Buzz slid the throttles to fifty per cent and stabbed the button. The ground power unit strained as all four wing-mounted Titans woke from their slumber. The sound was not unlike a far louder version of Gerry Anderson's *Thunderbird Two* at altitude. Flight instrument gyros initiated, waking all the dials on the cockpit instrument panel. Almost immediately, the engines were hot enough to instantly barbecue a chicken.

Buzz pressed the joystick mounted communications button again.

"Control, 1-01 Delta Four, request permission to taxi."

The reply came back swiftly, confirming the runway and airfield pressure,

"1-01 Delta Four, clear to taxi. Runway Zero Two."

Buzz checked his altimeter base setting was zero, then increased the throttle on all four engines heading out to the runway.

"1-01 Delta Four, taxi".

Control was watching them closely.

"1-01 Delta Four, you are clear to line up. Surface wind down the runway fifteen knots".

Buzz slid all four throttles to one hundred per cent. Vulcan XM658 surged down the runway with a ferocious howl.

Peggy Drabble's voice could be heard coming from the Nav plotter's seat.

"1-01 Delta Four, rolling. ... Reading seven-zero knots, ninety knots, one-hundred and ten, hundred and twenty. Check speed is OK, one hundred and thirty, one five zero and ROTATE..."

Control's view was a clear one. Primarily due to Rolls Royce's efforts ensuring the Olympus engines ran as cleanly as possible. This made it harder for any Soviet early warning observers to see them coming.

"1-01 Delta Four, Roger understand flight level 1000 feet... Permission for low-level operations and radio silence."

"1-01 Delta Four ... out."

From zero to 180mph in 23 seconds, the Vulcan was no slouch. They rose like a fly up a vacuum cleaner tube with little noise or vibration in the cockpit. The end of the runway shot past beneath them, followed by fields and trees.

Buzz keyed his intercom,

"First Pilot to crew, after take-off oxygen checks please."

As each member of the crew checked their oxygen, the replies came back,

"Co-pilot" from Will,

"Plotter" from Colin Smith,

"Radar" from Peggy Drabble and

"AE" from Dave Grubb in the Air Electronics seat.

Their initial height of one thousand feet reduced as they crossed the North Sea. Only two minutes into the flight and they were already some eight miles out to sea. The Vulcan started to turn southwards and began descending to 250 feet. Ahead of them were a couple of fishing boats. They were so close, the hair in the fishermen's beards could almost be seen.

Without warning, there was a slight bump. A light appeared in a small control panel mounted beneath the main central gold-plated canopy window. With each pane costing £18,000 to replace, the mantra in training was 'make sure you drive around seagulls'.

"FIRE, FIRE, Number three engine!" Will's voice was clear to the crew, his audio coming over the intercom as if he were beside each one of them. For a moment he had a sense of déjà vu. He reached over and punched the red illuminated warning light on the engine instrument panel.

Buzz was tempted to look into a rear-view mirror he knew did not exist.

"AE, periscope check, please."

Dave Grubb leaned forward and placed his eye upon the rubberised optical device mounted in front of him. Sweat began to form on the back of his neck,

"Confirm, fire, engine number three. Not yet extinguished."

"Roger that AE." Buzz looked to his left. They were already well out over the North Sea. A couple of drilling rigs acting as marine navigation aids. He punched the transmit on his radio.

"Mayday, Mayday, Mayday, North Coates Control, this is 1-01 Delta Four, request emergency landing Runway Zero Two."

Without waiting for a response, Buzz banked the aircraft to the left and started to turn back to the north. Their Vulcan, XM658, was the one-and-only Mark 3 variant and, by some miracle, the only one able to jettison fuel in an emergency from wing tanks.

"AE, make fuel forty per cent, start dumping".

Dave Grubb's response was immediate,

"Dumping initiated. I'll report every 4,000 pounds."

The radio crackled into life.

"1-01 Delta Four, North Coates Control. Permission to land Runway Zero Two clear. Foam will be on runway. Fire and rescue on standby".

More warning lights began to appear on the control panel. Finally, Buzz called out,

"Co-pilot, confirm engine three, throttle closed; HP cock shut; LP cock off; fire button pressed; fuel off; alternator off. Engine three, air switch shut."

Will verified Buzz had the booster pump switches for the fuel tank group feeding engine number three turned off.

"Roger Skip, number three throttle closed; HP cock shut; LP cock off; fire button pressed; fuel off; alternator off."

Dave Grubb, the AE, anticipating Buzz's subsequent request, was immediately ready with his response,

"Skip, generator off, still a lot of smoke, watching engine four. Fuel at seventy per cent, sorry, it's not dumping quickly. Load shedding initiated. Apologies everyone, that includes the ration- heater, so lunch is off."

When flying 'mission-ready,' the Vulcan piggy-backed off their Blue Steel weapon's far more advanced inertial navigation system.

However, as they no longer needed it and thinking ahead about whether or not to land with their bomb attached, Buzz flipped the transmit button again.

"AE, make payload stable. Nav Radar, confirm Inertial Navigation system is disengaged. If we need to know where we're going, we can look out of the window!"

Not much more than five minutes from take-off, and they were back over the coast. To their right was Cleethorpes, emerging from the gloom of the low cloud. Buzz was relieved they wouldn't be a risk to the holiday town, and no one was on the beaches. For a moment, he gave a thought to the greenkeeper at the golf course beside Fitties Beach, who would be cursing them for killing the grass on the fairway with the Kerosene they were dumping. West of the runway, to their left, the local junior school, unusually eerily quiet. Buzz reckoned this could be a distinct advantage, as you wouldn't want to spray children in the playground with jet fuel.

Buzz started to make the last turn for the final approach to the runway, setting the air brakes and lowering the undercarriage. The airframe began to rumble with the familiar sound of airflow being disrupted as the wheels came down. Buzz checked and swore under his breath. Only two of the three green lights were lit. Everything was now happening very quickly, and for the second time this week, it seemed undercarriage failure would result in a destructive arrival.

The radio burst into life again,

"Control, 1-01 Delta Four confirm, nose-wheel deployment failure, overshoot. Repeat overshoot!"

Buzz drew in the airbrakes and reached for the throttles. The remaining three engines dragged the Vulcan skywards.

"1-01 Delta Four – overshooting."

He raised the undercarriage, and the two lights went out. The Vulcan climbed willingly back up to 1500 feet, as if it wasn't keen to place its wheels back on the tarmac. Buzz could see the runway disappear underneath them and, with a great sense of relief, the cold grey waters of the North Sea ahead.

Buzz was hiding the stress well, but his next order had severe consequences.

"Captain to crew, jettison external stores."

Buzz calculated they would have roughly another three or four minutes to circuit the airfield before taking a crack at a belly landing. An impossibility with 15,000 pounds of Uranium-filled missile and rocket fuel strapped to the underside of their Vulcan. He listened for the crew responses of "Stop" or "Go" as multiple crew members were required to engage "Confirm" switches to jettison the missile into the sea. The 'Go' replies came thick and fast. Finally, Buzz hit his 'Confirm' switch.

To Buzz's annoyance and Will's frustration, there was no confirmation light. No change in the aerodynamics of the plane. The crew should all have felt the plane's weight change as the Vulcan became suddenly 15,000 pounds lighter. But it was clear, the missile was still attached.

Buzz was about to order checks on the 'Confirm' switches when Will's voice could be heard, followed immediately afterwards, with Dave Grubb's much more concerned voice,

"Fire, repeat fire, engine number four."

"Confirm fire, engine four."

Will hit the Fire Extinguisher button, and Buzz made the decision no pilot wanted to make.

He shut down fuel and power as he had done with engine number three and called out. "First to crew, prepare to abandon aircraft. AE, continue to dump fuel until I order abandon, then turn drain cocks to off."

"Roger Skip", came the tense reply.

"I'll take it wide over the coast as we return west. I want all rear crew out of the door the moment we're over land. Confirm?"

The replies were short, precise, and focused.

"Co-Pilot – Roger",

"Nav Radar – Roger",

"Nav Plotter – Roger",

"AE, – Roger."

Buzz continued,

"Flight level at 1500 feet, airspeed One-Seven-Five, prepare to deploy with static lines. Be aware, we have an electrical failure, external stores cannot be jettisoned. Confirm."

Again, the replies were short and crisp. All the responses came with a sense of fear. They knew they would be hitting an air blast of over 200mph. However, they would also have to avoid the nuclear payload Buzz had not been able to dump in the sea for the Navy to collect. At least they didn't have the added complication of trying to dodge the nose wheel.

"Co-Pilot - Roger",

"NavRadar - Roger",

"Nav Plotter - Roger",

"AE, - Roger."

Buzz's voice was heard again. "Static line, abandon aircraft! Jump! Jump! Jump!"

There was a flurry of activity in response. Peggy Drabble, the Nav plotter, selected the Emergency Door latch. Colin Smith on Nav Radar, - behind and to the right of Will, the co-pilot, - responded like a greyhound from a trap. He unstrapped, swung round and nimbly jumped to get to the area slightly ahead of the door access well. Peggy was immediately behind, automatically remembering her training. She hit the cabin pressure release handle in the roof, then sat down on the wooden platform, with her feet in the starboard side of the access hatch well. Whilst this was happening, AE, Dave Grubb shut the fuel drain cocks and shuffled over to the port side of the access well, opposite Peggy.

With all three of their static lines attached, Colin braced himself. He opened the door, locked it in the Emergency Position and jettisoned the entrance ladder, hoping it wouldn't hit anyone 1500 feet below.

The noise and airflow through the emergency hatch stopped all conversation. Colin drew his body into a ball. He dropped out of the hatch, and within a second, Peggy too was gone. There was a moment's pause as Dave turned to tap Will on the shoulder, to indicate all three crew were now gone, which only left Buzz and Will on board.

Buzz looked to his right. His Co-pilot hadn't budged.

"Will, confirm abandon aircraft!"

Will looked back stoically at Buzz with his unseen lips pursed behind his oxygen mask,

"We've still got air for the emergency undercarriage down. If that fails, then I'll leave you alone. If you're going to get this kite back on the ground, you're going to need help, and it will be much easier if you have a co-pilot and a canopy, so I'm sticking with you."

Buzz nodded his head, biting one side of his bottom lip, concerned, although grateful,

"Damn fool to the end, but it's much appreciated. Let's see what we can do to impress the locals. This is already feeling like an extremely long three minutes!"

The ground controller's voice could be heard again,

"Control, 1-01 Delta Four, mile and a half. Glide path OK. Maintain rate of decent, left two degrees, runway on your port side ahead."

What had been a strange vibration in the airframe started to be more pronounced. The control pedals and fighter plane style control stick grew to feel quite heavy. On the instrument panel, the Powered Flying Control Failure Alarm light radiated angrily. Buzz hit the 'Feel Relief' button, hoping to improve the situation. However, the controls felt just as stiff, whilst the 'Master and Feel' warning indicators annoyingly remained illuminated with a bright white glow. Buzz was trying to correct the flight line to bring it back towards the runway, but XM658 was having none of it.

The Vulcan was equipped with an emergency pressurised air tank which could inject air into the system forcing the landing gear to deploy. Buzz hit the 'undercarriage down' button. There was a reassuring rumble, but still two out of three green lights, with the third stubbornly refusing to illuminate.

Will quickly checked the indicator fuses,

"Fuses are fine. Permission to select Emergency Air?"

They were close enough to the runway. Buzz nodded and called out,

"Roger, deploy Emergency Air."

Will pulled the handle to the right of the throttles. Instantly, there was a loud and unexpected bang. Heavy vibration rippled through the airframe.

Will's irritated voice was heard over the intercom again,

"First Pilot, nose wheel deployment failure. Recommend ditching."

Buzz was about to reply to Will when the Ground Controllers voice could be heard again.

"1-01 Delta Four, three-quarters of a mile... left three degrees... correct immediately... left four degrees. Unable to get you with this approach. Overshoot. Repeat overshoot!"

Buzz hit the throttles for a second time and pulled back on the frustratingly sluggish controls. If he could get the plane back up to 1500 feet, it would easily clear the coast and ditch in the sea. Instead, smoke suddenly poured into the cockpit from the aircraft ventilation system, hampering visibility. He keyed the radio transmit button,

"1-01 Delta Four, Control, smoke in cockpit, confirm overshoot and intention to abandon at sea". Buzz turned to Will, speaking over the intercom, "Co-pilot, abandon aircraft NOW."

Will was not going to argue this time. He could see this was going to end up in quite a mess.

"First Pilot, Co-Pilot, Roger, abandon aircraft."

Will reached up with both hands and pulled on the striped handle above his head, dragging a face screen across his visor. The canopy blew off, and the dark interior of the cockpit was flooded with light. Smoke, dust, paperwork, and anything else not secured, was sucked out into the plane's wake. After a second of absolute chaos, the seat's ejection gun fired to propel him, the seat, and his parachute through the newly opened aperture.

Buzz paused fractionally longer, checking to ensure they were headed generally towards the airfield. The forward momentum would take the plane beyond the airfield and hopefully into the shallows of the North Sea. Here was another moment of déjà vu, perhaps simply his ejection training coming back to haunt him. He reached up to pull the handle above his own head. Remembering the drill: head back, back straight and 'keep your arms and legs inside the ride at all times'. Dragging the face-screen across his own visor, he felt the restraint cords tighten around his legs and then 'bang!'

Shooting into the air with a force comparable to being kicked up the backside by a first division footballer, in just one second, a pilot ejecting would climb to the height of an eight-storey building with such force they almost blackout. Think about being outside on a windy day and nearly blown over by a fifty-mile-an-hour gust, then imagine that experience at close to four times the speed. A couple of seconds later, with a slightly smaller bang, a pilot would be separated from their seat as drogues drag the main parachute out with an ever-expanding dome of fabric above their head, then silence. A silence so peaceful, someone might imagine hearing the birds singing 1500 feet below.

Buzz looked around. In one direction, he could see four other parachutes in the distance. Three of them were already on the ground, which was a huge relief. They vaguely resembled giant snowballs. Buzz loved snow. He wondered what it would be like, had he been parachuting between falling snowflakes.

In the other direction, he could see the Vulcan sailing off towards the North Sea. But, then, it must have been mist on his visor. Still, it looked like the plane vanished, only to reappear again, inverted with one wing virtually detached. The Vulcan rotated slowly, revealing an enormous hole in the fuselage beside what should have been an empty bomb bay. Briefly, but possibly a trick of the eye, it also looked like the Blue Steel payload was missing from its mount on the belly of the plane. A fraction of a second later a huge fireball surrounded everything. The fuel tanks erupted, engulfing the wreckage, which dived down in the direction of the coast and a field, home to a herd of Friesian cows, a few hundred feet beyond the end of the runway.

If that's the payload, thought Buzz, this will be a disaster zone for a very long time.

CHAPTER 04
One Eye On The World

Coffee Time:
1045 (GMT), The Future

From before the 20th Century and looking far into the distant future, space travel will for centuries remain ridiculously arduous and time inefficient. Crossing vast amounts of space with complex propulsion systems is fraught with danger. Most 'aliens' visiting planet Earth have not travelled from distant stars. Instead, they have entered our world from our future via the Moon or from nearby alternate realities. This is an appreciably shorter hop and requires far less energy.

Many inter-dimensional beings have been benevolent over the millennia of human evolution, although some have not. The most dangerous of all beings and feared by many other interdimensional societies actually exist, not from outside our own world, but as a result of our own future fear, ignorance and arrogance.

When massive human abduction events began in the 22nd Century, humanity believed it was being attacked by an alien intelligence from across the galaxy. The reality was, the threat came from Earth's distant future, a humanoid society named the Hagura, who had navigated the threads of time. Their crusade was to execute the plans of a malevolent and corrupt Artificial Intelligence.

Humanity initially responded by going to war with the alien kidnappers, who appeared in the form of Short and Tall Grey humanoids, precisely as described by 20th Century conspiracy theorists and Ufologists. Then, an important discovery was made.

This mysterious intelligence was identifying human life by its human 13-STR DNA profile. Scientists proposed a vaccine to alter human DNA to enable humans to 'hide in plain sight'.

The 13-STR profile became either 14-STR or 15-STR. Two vaccines were developed and successfully deployed. As a result, incidences of abduction were subsequently reduced virtually to zero.

Decades after vaccination, DNA anomalies appeared in the human population with physiological and psychological changes. Some became taller, others became shorter, eyes changed, and skin tone altered, becoming greyer. Finally, there was a dawning realization; humanity had seemingly set itself on a path to self-destruction and disaster. Humankind as we know it would cease to exist.

A war lasting 3,000 years ensued between the two subsequent dominant human ethnicities - The Giants and The Dwarfs. A small group of surviving un-vaccinated humans based on the Earth's Moon created the 13-STR_DNA project. The Short Tandem Repeat Sequence, Artificial Intelligence based DNA Sequencer, was developed to reverse the damage. To seek out and preserve human life throughout the universe.

Earth had been ravaged by centuries of conflict. Still, the Moon was far safer, so a lunar laboratory was created for scientific research. Using Teslate power crystals discovered on Callisto, time and interdimensional travel were finally made possible. Limited transtemporal travel enabled the project to reach back in time to study and sample historical DNA from humans. In addition, small shuttlecraft provided travel between the Moon and the Earth.

Unfortunately, during a particularly violent solar electron storm, the STR_DNA sequence Artificial Intelligence became corrupted. As a result, the STR DNA project became 'The STR_AND'. It now had a new mission: To rescue humanity for 'storage and security'.

Having 'preserved' all the humans with unaltered DNA working on the project, the STRAND A.I. vision changed to moving back the invention of time travel to an earlier point in history. The aim, to combine time streams into a singular flow to rescue all humanity carrying the 13-STR DNA marker, bringing 'Purity back to Unity'.

ZUKANN OPTIC:

SCAN ME
B019A

Hagura 羽倉 *is a Kanji Word*

羽 *means counter for birds, and* 倉 *means store or warehouse. They are from the far future of our known timeline. They are The STRAND's 'impure' workforce and bearers of an invasive ideology attractive to any really bad person. Their doctrine is, they are a higher life-form. The Hagura mission is to descend into the worlds of the past as you would enter the damp cellar of your house. To rescue humanity's 'clean' DNA from the dark times of history. To store that DNA in the treasury of The STRAND.*

To discover more, please select this ZUKANN OPTIC using your mobile device to scan this QR code. Alternatively, in a digital reader, use your finger or mouse. You could also visit ZUKANN.com/godor and select this ZUKANN OPTIC – B019A

☙❁❋❁❧

The STRAND has artificial intelligence on its side. It can never experience a crisis of confidence; it only knows determination. It understands its own limitations. It cannot be weak like a biological lifeform, but this is The STRAND's Achilles Heel. It cannot move things in the physical world, it needs to control and influence humanity. For that, it has The Hagura. For that, it has traitors to humanity, like the Steel Magnate Lord Blayne Pears, heir to the Pear of Anguish inventor. For that, it has White House Senator Abe Donall Sperry, heir to the Volstead and Valentine brewery and distillery empire. Human collaborators, conspiring throughout history to undermine humanity. People for whom morality is an illusion, working alongside the Short and Tall Greys, executing orders for The STRAND's malevolence.

The influence of The STRAND is concealed at the top level of global society. It grew more powerful and influential during the middle part of the 21st Century, increasingly with access to the knowledge, power and technology to alter the timelines and the equilibrium of destiny. A wide range of tools are at hand in the armoury of clandestine organisations supporting The STRAND in its industrial and temporal espionage.

One of these tools is the Journalistic Rhetatron.

Before the Pandemic of 2020, a human was regularly nominated for the role of the Downing Street Rhetoric Yeller, in the same way, mediaeval communities had town criers and village idiots. However, as infection control became more crucial, even milder conditions such as infectious laughter amongst politicians had to be controlled. Thus, the role of Rhetoric Yeller was ultimately replaced with the automated, solar-powered Journalistic Rhetatron.

ZUKANN OPTIC:

SCAN ME
B020A

The Journalistic Rhetatron

This autonomous rhetorical question generator is equipped with an ambient atmospheric soundtrack in the event of there being an absence of politicians. It frequently can be heard playing its own corporate brand identity soundtrack:

♫ *Journalistic Rhetatron, a question with no guarantee, Senator or minister, under scrutiny.*

Quiz, accost, confront and probe, all as loud as I can be,

Answers never are supplied, all so pointlessly! ♪

To discover more, please select this ZUKANN OPTIC.

Placed outside Number 10 Downing Street with a passive infrared movement detector, the four-foot-tall, often traffic cone topped, Gum-Butt Post lookalike, Journalistic Rhetatron loudly projects dumb rhetorical questions at anyone moving. Publicly and overtly, it is connected directly with syndicated news media. Subversively, it is connected directly to the House of Lords and the office of one Lord Blayne Pears. It is equipped with facial recognition to enable pertinent questions. Unfortunately, its 90% facial accuracy is irrelevant as no politician ever answers questions in Downing Street anyway. On one occasion, the Rhetatron required reprogramming when it began shouting questions about fiscal policy at the Downing Street cat. Shortly after, the Chancellor of the Exchequer had undergone a face-lift for 'aesthetic reasons'.

It can move independently to other locations where politicians may be found, such as hospitals, overseas political summits and garden fêtes. It has limited Prismorphic camouflage capability, a technology bending light to distort the view of what is actually physically present. This enables it to appear in the guise of a waste bin in a public park; an office hand sanitiser dispenser; or a car park ticket machine.

ZUKANN OPTIC:

SCAN ME
B021A

Prismorphic Camouflage

23rd Century Prismorphic Camouflage Technology was developed for Botanists and Crypto-naturalists studying creatures in alternate dimensions. The technology, derived from researching Chameleon Lizards on Home Earth, hides objects in plain sight. In the way prisms alter light, 'Prismorphic' technology and materials allow objects to be phase-shifted out of the current reality into parallel dimensional space, leaving a 'Quint' in its place.

The use of this technology has risks. This was discovered by an unfortunate Crypto-naturalist who caught the edge of his Prismorphic Poncho, tripped and was revealed to a pride of Tigaha which subsequently ate him.

To discover more, please select this ZUKANN OPTIC.

CHAPTER 05
Time Gentleman, Please

Last Orders:
2245 (GMT), Sometime

Time travel is easy. Getting back is the problem. As Michael Caine would say – 'Not a lot of people know that!'

Sometimes, being the only one to know stuff can be extremely useful, although seeing stuff can be equally important.

For example, take the Old Man you often see down at my local, The Old Volunteer (the pub that is, not the Old Man) you wouldn't have thought this bloke would have volunteered for anything in his life – he's so grumpy. Although, he might have been old enough to have been The Volunteer when the Old Volunteer was young.

This old pub has had a few rebrands. It's been the Dog & Ferret and a couple of other popular names over the years when 'Alcopops' were 'trending'. But then again, alcopops were trending before trending was popular, so it seems slightly ironic. However, it has always gone back to being The Old Volunteer.

The Old Man seems to be part of the furniture. He's there on the first day of every month, sat in The Snug, by the fire. Sometimes, the fire is lit in the winter and you can smell the lovely aroma of oak smoke and hear the crackling of the kindling. In the summer, he's still there, reading his newspaper and filling in the crossword. No one knows why he's chosen that particular chair. He isn't after the best view of the bar or the warmth of the fire. He's watching what comes through the toilet door.

The Old Man is there early, watching, when Anni, the cleaner, is just finishing. She's the sort of person who loves to sing optimistically about the future as she's working. The regulars think she has a weird sense of humour and is often moaning about everyone else whilst telling daft jokes. Everybody loves her because she's just a bit on the strange side and sees things a touch differently from everyone else.

There are two things Anni has an aversion to. Firstly, she dislikes cleaning the mess persistently collecting outside the Gent's toilet door. Secondly, she does not relish polishing the clock above the fireplace. It is a peculiar timepiece, which is made of a tough- to- clean metal and looks like a flying wing. It also seems to attract the oddest kind of dust, which annoyingly won't wipe off with a damp cloth. However, Anni knows it's time to clean it when the Landlady's husband buys her a bunch of flowers as an advance apology. She doesn't really mind as the only other time she got a bouquet from anyone was for her fortieth birthday last year.

Anni complains about the mess people leave. And it's always in one corner of the snug, just outside the door to the Gents. She says, "If it's not dust, it's mud, and if it's not mud, it's the sparkling party stuff you get out of wedding party poppers. And if it's not that, it's sand, and we're miles from the beach," so she blames the contractors from the reservoir down the road for not wiping their boots when they come into the pub. It seems to be the dirtiest part of the whole pub, and she's always having to clean it. And the Old Man spots it too because, as I said earlier, it's not what you know; sometimes, it's what you see that's important.

The other thing the Old Man sees is the hinges on the door when it's opened. Something no one else seems to notice. What he sees is the hinges on the door are not always the same. The door is one of those ancient oak ones. So old, no one knows where it came from.

Sometimes the hinges are simple and ordinary, with the five ringed metal plates screwed to the door and the frame. Sometimes, it looks like they're painted. Sometimes the hinges appear to have six or seven rings. Occasionally they look ancient, and other times they look so shiny, they might actually be glowing. Still, you can never be entirely sure because the door is not open for long.

Conveniently, the doors to the Ladies and the Gents are on either side of the fireplace. What is different from many pubs is that the Gents can be as pleasantly fragrant as the Ladies, so it's an easy mistake for ladies to head for the wrong door. However, when they realise they're going down the wrong corridor, it's a hasty 'one- eighty' to go the right way!

The corridor to the Gents sometimes has different smells. Anni doesn't particularly notice because she's always complaining about the mess. Sometimes the passage smells clean, with fragrances, like orange blossom, bougainvillaea, nail polish remover or Parma Violets. Intermittently, it's a dry, dusty smell, like an empty room having seen the sun all day. Occasionally it smells a different kind of acrid. Every so often, it's musty and sulfuric, one smell the Old Volunteer would have recognised.

Sometimes the aromas match the dust on the floor. The sand seems to come with a dry, dusty smell. The mud with the delightful scent of burning horse manure. That is one smell Anni does recognise, but she discreetly blames it on the Landlady's husband.

It's not just the aromas which go unnoticed. The comings and goings through the Gents toilet door are curious, but often unseen. Sometimes the people going through the door aren't always those coming back. Sometimes people don't seem to come back, whilst others appearing through the door, you'd swear had never been in the pub before. But you don't notice for certain, because, in any case, it's a pub. Who sits around staring at the door to the toilets?

Occasionally a child, waiting for their parent to return from the toilet, spots the hinges change and looks puzzled for a moment. A couple of children have even looked at The Old Man for some kind of reassurance, perhaps thinking a grown-up might have seen what they had. But he simply smiles, shakes his head in a 'don't worry about it' kind of way, and the moment is forgotten. The Old Man, however, spots it virtually every time.

He sits there and waits. He's waiting for a reason. He's watching the comings and goings and watches what makes the mess Anni has to clean up. He sees the dust on the people's shoes coming back from the toilets isn't always the dust you'd expect to see. Sometimes, it is mud and wet footprints emerging when it's sunny outside. And of course, it's odd because the mess is coming out, not going in.

He sits there, because a long time ago he said he'd wait. He said he'd wait for a friend who went out on a trip one day and didn't come back when they were expected. Before his friend went on the trip, they agreed they'd meet again in the pub on the first Monday of any month if they were delayed. So when they did make it back, they'd be able to carry on as before. That was a few years ago, but he sits and waits by the door, with a bit of hope this will be the day when it's different.

But, it gets to last orders, and everything is still the same. Time is called. The Old Man leaves to come again another day.

CHAPTER 06
A House Of Secrets

Officers' Mess:
0800 (GMT), Thursday December 10ᵗʰ 1970

A fly was repeatedly hitting the metal-framed window in a futile attempt to escape the smell of burning toast in the utilitarian, but not uncomfortable, Officers Mess. Built just after the Second World War, it was maintained but not loved. Magnolia walls were adorned with plaques displaying military honours, paintings and photographs of individual senior officers and group photos of significant flight crews.

Buzz strolled over to where Will was sitting enjoying breakfast; below the Union Flag, the Royal Air Force Ensign and a large portrait of Her Majesty The Queen. Both pilots were slightly introspective characters so close to sunrise and respected each other's choice to eat alone. Being early, the morning papers had not yet been delivered. The sound of approaching footsteps on the linoleum floor made Will look up from the Sunday Supplement he'd found in a paper rack.

"Having a Ralph McTell moment?" asked Buzz. "Looking at you with '...Yesterday's papers telling yesterday's news'. I can't help wondering if we're not both going to end up on the *Streets of London*, the way it went yesterday."

"Yesterday, all our troubles did seem so far away until those three dark suits from the Air Ministry invited me in for a 'chat'." Will replied sardonically, simultaneously sweeping toast crumbs off the pages of the well-thumbed glossy in front of him. In fact, forget Lennon and McCartney, it was more like Göring, Goebbels and Hitler on Tour!"

Buzz looked grimly at Will. When the 'chaps from the ministry' turned up, it was never going to be followed by the release of a novelty book of good ideas.

"On a lighter note, what have you got there? Is it *Batman* or *Sporting Sam?*"

Will smiled back at Buzz.

"I was getting sick of hearing about kidnapped British Diplomats, Howard Hughes, and Power Strikes, so I thought I'd fill up on a bit of culture. There's a fascinating article about small statues of golden dragons called Zenyo, being discovered in western Colombia near the construction site of a hydroelectric power station.

Will spun the magazine around, so Buzz could see in glorious technicolour, the incredibly detailed craftsmanship of this pure gold, winged artefact.

"It's amazing how around 1000 years ago, the world was peaceful enough to produce incredible works of art like this. It makes you wonder how a society so remote from Wales and China could both come up with the idea of flying lizards without knowing about dinosaurs?"

Eddie shook his head in awe of the skill required to produce such beauty.

ZUKANN OPTIC:

SCAN ME
C025B

The Zenyo

In 1505, The Zenyo, species OEA1BA, signed a 5000-year Non-disclosure and Non-Intervention agreement with a secretive organisation representing all future sea-faring nations. The agreement was known as the FENDER Accord, as it came with strings attached. 'Here be dragons' had begun to appear too frequently on maps of the known world as international travel had become cheaper. When it was pointed out they were also 65 million years adrift on the timestream for tracking down their cousins, the Pterodactyls, they were happy to sign. This was because, in their opinion, Home Earth society was quite adolescent. And anyway, they were tired of being persecuted by humanity and their pseudo-hero dragon slayers.

To discover more, please select this ZUKANN OPTIC.

"Come on, let's go and see what the world has in store for us this morning. I'm sure it won't be as elegant as this. Let's hope there's no more dinosaurs from the ministry in store for us!"

As they got up to leave the table, it was irritating to see that someone who thought of themselves as extremely witty had changed the weekly menu board. The wreckage of their plane had hit a herd of cattle, so a range of beef-related puns or beef-based dishes were now listed, from the 'Legend-Dairy Menu' featuring 'Beef Wellington' and 'Bomb-bay Beef Curry with Rocket Salad' to 'Pow-dered Milkshakes' or 'Undercarriage Cocktails – Wheel Meat Again'. There was also a new sign declaring 'We never make mis-steaks'. Both Eddie and Will had thought this quite juvenile. Although, had the roles been reversed, they also would have been contributing to the humour!

They could tell things were going to get worse as they walked out of the mess, wiping the remains of toast – and the proverbial 'egg' off their faces. Warrant Officer Ian Lavender was heading in their direction. Known (only behind his back) as 'Pike' due to the unfortunate link with a television program Home Guard Private of the same name. He had a formidable presence. He was the sort of man who could easily intimidate his bank manager into robbing his own bank. Despite being junior to both of them, custom dictated he was addressed by both Buzz and Will as 'Mr Lavender'.

"Excuse me, Sirs", barked Mr Lavender, making Eddie and Will involuntarily want to stand to attention. Salutes were exchanged, and the ominous voice continued,

"Your presence is requested by Air Vice Marshall Locksley at The Hall immediately. As you are new here, we're talking about the BIG Hall. Do you know Donna Nook?" Most crews knew where the bombing range was. Both Eddie and Will knew the area well from flight maps, so nodded to the affirmative.

Unconvinced, the Warrant Officer ploughed on,

"If you were coming back from Donna Nook, drive into the village, straight over at The Old Volunteer onto South Road. You can't miss it. It's the huge building on the left, halfway between the pub and the church. I'd recommend the pub for 'liquid courage', the church to pray for your eternal souls and then back to see the AVM for your punishment."

"We should be able to find it; we're both trained navigators".

"After the way you landed, Sirs, you need more than navigator training. I'd put books down the back of your trousers; you're going to get such a kicking. You'll easily find today's sorrow, halfway between Salutation and Salvation! And don't let anyone kid you and send you LEFT at the pub. The NEW Locksley Hall is where the AVM's Mother-in-Law lives, and there's hell to pay when some bright spark turns up as the result of a prank!"

Fortunately, or unfortunately, as it had no doors, they could borrow an old jeep from the base motor pool. It had seen better days and quite possibly some action, looking at a couple of the holes still in the off-side wing.

They were in no hurry to meet their destiny. What should have been a fifteen-minute drive felt like only five minutes. Eddie wondered if it was something to do with relativity. He remembered Einstein was supposed to have said something about sitting on hot stoves with nice girls. Now wasn't really the time to try to remember the details.

Passing a long line of tall trees stretching away to their left, they steered off the quiet lane onto a gravel drive, edged with very well-manicured grass borders. A great hall with an Elizabethan façade loomed ahead of them. It was clear parts of the hall were much older than the 400-year-old front. A broad set of steps led up to the front door behind which they could imagine a grand entrance hall. Will found himself thinking about his childhood comic book superheroes. It was impressive. Definitely the kind of place *Batman's* alter-ego, *Bruce Wayne*, would have lived.

Having parked the jeep to one side, as it felt rude to leave the slightly rusted heap outside the front of the hall, they walked up to the front door and pulled the cast iron ring protruding from the brickwork. There was the vaguest of tinkles. They both imagined the world of Jeeves and Wooster, with Jeeves coming to the door in a suit and bowler hat.

The reality was totally different as a smartly dressed older attendant, with a welcoming smile and an expression of calm unflappability, opened the door,

"Good morning, Gentlemen, how may we be of service?"

His politeness and apparent friendliness were a little unexpected, putting them both on the back foot,

"Ahh… we've been ordered to meet with Air Vice Marshall Sir Rob Locksley. Is it convenient?"

"Certainly, Sirs," came the reply. "Do come in and let me take your coats. It looks like the damp in the air is a touch on the cold side. My name is Beeton, but you may call me Samuel. Mr Driver and Mr Anderson, I presume?"

Eddie was impressed. He wasn't anticipating being 'expected' by the butler, who was deftly closing the door with one hand and reaching out for their coats with the other,

"Thank you, Mr Beeton, much appreciated."

"Walk this way please, Gentlemen. Sir is in the main hall, and please do feel free to call me Samuel."

It looked like this building was intended to be well protected. Even when they were through the main entrance, there were galleries on either side, overlooking more steps leading upwards to another door. They could both imagine armour-clad soldiers overlooking the stairs, ready to strike at any reckless enemy attempting a frontal assault.

The subsequent door opened out into a grand main hall with a minstrel gallery at one end. Along one wall, there hung a huge tapestry featuring some kind of hunting scene. Stood with his back to them, in front of an inferno of a fire that Danté would have been happy with, was the AVM. They had seen a picture of him in the officer's mess during their first meal, but this was the first time they would meet him in the flesh.

He was slightly taller than both of them, with the physique of Olympian Benedict Cayenne, and if they had to guess, possibly ten years older than Eddie. As they approached, they could see he was in uniform. They both saluted and stood to attention. He returned the gesture with efficiency and grace which would have no doubt pleased the Queen, on behalf of whom the salute was by tradition, returned.

The AVM certainly did not look like he was angry in any way. Certainly not about to roast them on a spit over the blazing fire lit in the hall or apply his size tens to their nether regions. They waited with anticipation for his next instruction, which came with a smile.

"At ease, caps off! Come into my office." Nodding in the direction of the fireplace he added, "This place is so draughty it takes a lot to heat it!"

There was a door to the right-hand side of the fire. This led into a surprisingly small room, considering the size of the hall they had just walked through. However, there was enough room for a sizeable leather-topped oak desk, a beautifully comfortable leather chair behind it and three not entirely comfortable looking wooden chairs.

The AVM looked slightly embarrassed,

"I'm sorry about the state of the chairs. My maternal grandmother has recently moved into New Locksley Hall with my mother-in-law, just across the fields there. Some of her favourite belongings were in a container travelling from Trinidad. This seems to have been lost somewhere in the Atlantic. So for the moment, I've lent her some furniture and borrowed these slightly elderly specimens from the chapel. How are you both, and how are your crew?"

Eddie looked relieved,

"We're fine, thanks, considering what a mess we've made of the other end of the village. Sorry about that. It turns out Flying Officer Bisset didn't have chicken pox. We had promised to send Flying Officer Drabble back without any dents or scratches. Still, she had the misfortune of needing a couple of stitches after bouncing off the roof of a farm. She says a few battle scars won't hold her back. She was an excellent member of the crew, by the way. I'd like to commend her actions during the emergency."

The AVM nodded,

"I've read the Ministry Accident Investigation preliminary report. It seems you all behaved impeccably. I wish we could say the same about my ground crew. It seems they have already found a bolt off a Buccaneer embedded in the remains of your number three engine. How they managed to find anything like half the parts of your kite in that burning pile of scrap is a mystery. Mind you, time's a funny thing. Sometimes what you expect to take ages can seem to take no time at all. Tell me, Gentlemen, I've read your profiles, and I'm impressed by your 'calmness under fire,' as they say. What would you like to happen next?"

Both Eddie and Will looked at each other with puzzled expressions. Will broke the silence,

"Well, to be honest, Sir, I think we were expecting to get a rollocking and sent packing back to Waddington. But, certainly, I think I can speak for both of us; we'd like to get back to business."

The AVM looked pleased,

"I'm relieved to hear there's no Combat Fatigue. So we can keep an eye on you; I've got a couple of people on the base trained in the latest post-trauma techniques. In addition, I've got an operation running on and around the base I'd like you to be part of. Your base Commander has okayed a transfer if you're up for it? Make no mistake, it is classified as Top Secret, so you won't be able to talk to your crew about it if you are interested?"

Eddie raised his eyebrows. He'd heard of people being selected for special forces before, but neither he nor Will were the super-fit types applying for those sorts of jobs.

The AVM picked up his train of thought,

"It's not the SAS; it's way more specialized. We need you, as you are, not as some super-fit action man. Even better, it might involve the odd beer. So can I STRONGLY suggest you go straight to The Old Volunteer for a pint when you leave here? You'll find out more from there on in."

Eddie and Will looked at each other, nodded, and Eddie replied,

"Thank you for the opportunity, Sir. We'd certainly like to find out more."

The AVM looked encouraged,

"I'm glad to hear it, you won't be disappointed. A quick word to the wise. You're going to see some weird stuff in the next few hours. You will still have the chance to opt out once you've seen what secretly happens at North Coates. And don't worry, it's not like the 'Hound of the Baskervilles'. We CAN tell you the secrets without having to kill you, as we're quite adept at helping people to forget! Let me show you to the door."

The AVM stood, walked around the desk and guided the pair back through the main hall. As if by a kind of telepathy, Mr Beeton was already waiting for them with their coats.

As they buttoned themselves up, the AVM looked momentarily serious,

"Please enjoy a pint, but remember, as you've seen on the posters on the walls, 'Loose lips, sink ships' and 'Careless talk costs lives'. Admittedly, this piece of advice is not quite so snappy; however, it is worth remembering, too. 'Hold fast in your Future – Your past will be faster'. In other words, be careful what you say in the future as in no time, it's your past. If you're not 'fast' with what you say, your past will come back to bite you!"

With these slightly strange idioms ringing in their ears, Eddie, Will, and the AVM exchanged salutes, and the door closed behind them.

The Old Volunteer wasn't the largest pub in the world. It was a mere two minutes' drive back up the South Road from Locksley Hall. The comforting sound of gravel from the car park surface crunched under the wheels of the jeep, only slightly spoiled by the squeal of the brakes as they came to a halt.

Will turned the engine off and paused for a moment, turning to Eddie,

"So, what do you reckon? Sounds a bit strange, but curious maybe?"

Eddie looked like he was mulling over several thoughts in his head.

"So, it seems official; it's secret and possibly strange. However, if the first step is a drink, to my mind, it can't be all bad. Let's have a pint and see where we end up, shall we?"

Will looked reassured,

"Yup, I'm with you. And if it comes to nothing, we can always get a bus back to Waddington."

They walked into the pub and into what looked like it might be a restaurant, although one corner had a curved back wall like it was set up for a live musician to play. There were no apparent signs of life, although another door led away, possibly to the kitchens.

Eddie raised one eyebrow,

"Let's try the other side; if no one's there, we'll knock it on the head."

They walked around to the other side of the pub and into what looked like quite a comfortable snug. There was a bar to the right and a warm, inviting fire. An old man was sitting at a table with his back to the door. He looked up and nodded at the two comparatively young airmen, just as a young woman came out of a door beside the bar, walked through the hatch and stood behind the counter.

Will had the smile of a young schoolboy on his face. Eddie looked at Will, raised his eyes heavenwards and shook his head. Will was displaying all the tell-tale signs of having spotted a most attractive 'opportunity' in the form of this young lady. Slightly taller than Will, with a physique most gym members would dream of. Her long flame-red hair was tied back into a high ponytail with a red silk ribbon looped into a bow.

Will leaned slightly sideways on the bar and put his best 'Richard Burton voice' on,

"Happy Nearly Christmas to you. Could we have two pints of this week's special, please... and a couple of packets of crisps." Will added the crisps as an afterthought, mainly because he was always hungry. "This is Buzz, and I'm Will. Is there an airfield nearby? I can feel my heart taking off!"

Eddie nearly choked when Will tried out 'chat-up line thirty-seven'. Although it was Eddie's personal favourite, it was quite simply as awful as all the rest.

The red-haired barmaid raised one eyebrow and smiled, reaching down for the crisps whilst replying,

"I'm Ruby, pleased to meet you. I'm guessing with that hackneyed approach, like some of the best-equipped military hardware 'round here, it's quite likely you're going to crash and burn!

She stood back up, placed the crisps on the bar, raised both eyebrows and smiled. This was fatal for Will. She had practically perfect teeth and gorgeous blue-green eyes. Eddie wanted to beat his forehead against a wall.

"Were you the two who planted one of Harold Wilson's bombers in Duckworth's field at the other end of the village? Because, if your flying is as bad as your chat-up lines, I suspect there won't be much else taking off for a while."

Will blundered on regardless,

"We can't officially confirm or deny Buzz got a bit lost whilst turning left over the North Sea". Ruby smiled sympathetically at Eddie. She could tell he was feeling something of a proverbial gooseberry. "Well, Gents, I'm sorry, but you're not the only thing running on fumes because we're Eighty-Six on the beer". Ruby motioned to the pumps with a gesture plainly indicating the pumps were dry. "I could do with a hand for a couple of minutes moving a barrel across. I'm working on my own today – would you mind?"

Will looked almost optimistic,

"We can't have a pub where the beer's gone AWOL. Show us the way!"

Eddie frowned at Will and whispered,

"Don't forget why we're here. It's not all about beer and barmaids. Maybe it's a test? After you, great beer hunter!"

Getting a bit of help from a couple of fit young pilots was clearly not going to present a huge challenge, so Ruby led them through a door in the corner of the snug beside the bar with the sign marked 'Gents.'

Eddie and Will had expected to see a dingy passage. But, instead, curiously, they all walked into an extremely well-lit corridor with what looked like marbled walls and a white tiled floor.

"I bet you've got the cleanest cellar in Britain here," thought Will, but he found himself saying aloud by accident.

"Well cared for," said Ruby as she led them through a shiny metal door the like of which would be found in the kitchens behind the Officers Mess or any quality restaurant in London.

The door opened and the corridor continued. Instead of the anticipated steps to a cellar, white doors were set in the walls to the left and right. Roughly halfway to the end, a door opened, and a head popped out. A man about thirty years old, wearing a look of mischief, a khaki lab coat and a red party hat, was standing in the doorway.

"Hi Mark," smiled Ruby, and with a tone which was also a question, "Experiment?"

"A quick demonstration", the man replied mysteriously. "Is that OK?" Ruby nodded with a look of curiosity on her face, as the man turned towards Will and Buzz. "Hi Gents, I wonder if you can do me a favour? Can I quickly pop something in your pocket to pick up from you later?"

"It's already a strange day," said Buzz, "I'm happy to help out."

"It's only going to get stranger," said the man as he dropped an object wrapped in a soft cloth into Buzz's pocket. "Catch up with you later". And as quick as he arrived, he disappeared back behind the door he'd emerged from.

Ruby, Will and Buzz continued down the corridor, past four or five more doors on each side, until they came face to face with one marked with a slightly military sign stamped, 'Field Equipment.'

Will spoke to the back of Ruby's head.

"Lady, we've had a rough ride this week, and I'm beginning to wonder if I've either hit my head when we ejected, or else we're nowhere near the cellar."

Ruby smiled back,

"I think you were hoping for something a bit more than just a beer cellar?"

CHAPTER 07
In The Lab

The Laboratory:
1300 (GMT), Thursday December 10th 1970 /
1013 Meta-Time (MGMT), Tuesday December 8th 1970

A grey-haired man sporting a cream jacket, a neatly trimmed Van Dyke beard and a broad smile, looked up as Ruby led the two guys into the room.

"Come in; it's great to meet you. I was told to expect visitors. Welcome to the lab; I'm Professor Eastwood. I gather you are Buzz Driver and Will Anderson?"

Hardly surprised they were not in a pub cellar having seen the corridor; and curious that this professor had the same gift for names as Samuel, the butler they had met earlier, Buzz smiled with a look of anticipation.

"You can call me Eddie, Sir, 'Buzz' is really just for the cockpit."

"I'm really pleased to meet you. My full name is Isaac Iain Eastwood, but effectively everyone calls me 'Ike' or 'The Prof'. I don't mind which."

The professor turned and held out his hand as if to present Ruby to them.

"This is Ruby Rowe, probably quite useless as a barmaid, but also probably one of the most important people you are going to meet over the next few days. We don't do uniforms here, but if we did, she'd have a lot of gold braid, along with her sister, Rina."

Ike pointed his finger and winked with a grin at Ruby, who looked slightly embarrassed to be on the receiving end of the Professor's respect.

He continued,

"So, I'm guessing Sir Rob Locksley has told you to prepare yourself for a strange new world but not explained exactly what we do?"

Eddie nodded,

"That's right, Sir, er... Ike." Eddie wasn't used to being on first name terms with anyone senior, let alone using their nickname. "We were told it would be something secret?"

The Professor smiled and nodded,

"We try to be as undercover as possible. However, if we do leave a trail, we try to clear up any evidence we leave behind, which is partly why we need your help. Do either of you drive a gas-powered automobile?"

Eddie and Will gave each other a slightly quizzical look. Both thought this was a slightly old-fashioned way to ask, however both answered they could drive a car.

The professor nodded,

"Good, and have either of you broken down at the side of the road?"

Will grinned,

"Eddie ran out of petrol last month, and I skidded on some mud on a bend and ended up in a field."

There was a snort of derision from Eddie.

"To clarify, my fuel pipe got taken out by a rock. You got taken out by your own right foot, not a patch of mud."

Will shrugged his shoulders.

"OK, we might not agree on the mud, but I'll agree we can call it a breakdown. But I called out the rescue service, and they towed me out of the field, and everything was fine. I had to go out to Eddie with a can of fuel!"

The Professor smiled,

"So, here's where we come in. We are a recovery organisation of sorts, but we do need to be properly equipped and power is currently our greatest challenge. You are joining us at the commencement of this process, the first step on the road towards what will become the most important rescue service in the history of the future. To be this type of organisation, we will need a complete global energy network. You have been chosen to help us, partly because of your skills and partly because, in a unique and special way, that you will come to realise your past is directly connected to our future."

Eddie started to relax. He quite liked the idea of being *Virgil Tracy*, piloting Gerry Anderson's *Thunderbird Two*. Will was having very similar thoughts, wondering who was going to get the bigger aircraft to fly.

꙲⊕!⊕ઠ

Eddie and Will looked around this underground workshop, lit as if it was daylight, by glowing squares embedded in the ceiling. Having been in the Air Force, they had both seen some extraordinary things over the years. Before them, were racks and shelves loaded with equipment the likes of which neither of them had seen before in their lives. At one end of the workshop, a slightly brighter glow emanated and along with a humming sound, like a Radio Range microwave oven being operated in a room next door. Stacked neatly, like a group of torpedoes, was what looked like glass rods, each about six feet long with multiple glass probes at one end. Professor Eastwood asked Eddie and Will what they thought they looked like.

"Well, on the surface, it looks like a pitchfork with too many prongs", said Will, "but when you look closer at the arrangement of the prongs, there is something familiar about it."

Professor Eastwood changed the question slightly,

"What does it remind you of – looking at the end with all the prongs?"

Eddie looked at it and, with some hesitation as he didn't want to sound like a complete idiot and replied,

"Well, Prof, it looks like a model of Stonehenge on a stick."

"No coincidence there," said the Professor, "The Neolithic people discovered a highly rudimentary version of this. It's an energy collector. Basically, you insert it into the ground.

Nikola Tesla had a similar idea a few years ago. Unfortunately, he built a tower that was nowhere near as effective.

"The Moloch people, who were stone circle builders, didn't get much more than a gentle hum and a glow at night. Without the right conditions, Gaia energy has such a short lifespan. Nevertheless, it impressed the Molochs; they thought it was a kind of magic. Unfortunately, they built Stonehenge in the middle of Salisbury Forest, where it depleted the Tesla energy to the extent that all the trees were lost for miles around.

"This is EXACTLY why you don't want to start chopping down your woodland. Natural occurrences such as forests and waves can create astronomical amounts of Tesla or Gaia energy stored in the form of Gallate crystals spreading underground. The minerals look for all the world like Gypsum. Such a shame it so often ends up being used to make concrete and plasterboard!"

Ike shook his head with some annoyance at the thought of all this waste at the hands of 20th Century barbarians, whilst Will was beginning to wonder, how knowing about rocks would help their rescues.

"These energy collectors are formed from Teslate. I'll explain later where this comes from; when your security rating has been confirmed, it will blow your mind! It's not forests alone generating huge amounts of Gaia energy. Simply lower a collector into the ground. They self-connect, creating tendril-like roots burrowing through whatever you drop them into. This could be soil, mud, water, rock or even concrete. To capitalise on Geomagnetic solar power, you need to invert them and mount them on a mast, not more than twenty feet off the ground. It's quite beautiful watching one connect up. Like a gentle vertical rainbow, you can only see in your peripheral vision."

Ike paused for a moment to envisage the beauty of this science, whilst Will was still plugging glass rods into rocks and wondering when Ike would get to the bit about flying.

Ruby continued the story.

"We call it Gaia Power, as in many ways it is the power of life itself. Humanity has been aware of Gaia energy for millennia. The human tradition of burying the dead at locations of great spiritual energy like temples and pyramids across the world would make sense if you wanted to tap into Gaia energy. A sentient lifeform, when it decomposes, can release more than five Gigawatts of the Gaia energy developed within the body over a typical lifespan. This is why we keep this technology such a closely guarded secret. Unfortunately, some really nasty people have tried to capitalise on this at other times in history, so this is something we are tasked to prevent."

Now Will was tuning in, and not just because it was Ruby talking. He'd watched a few films about Egyptian pyramids and tombs. Not only that, but he'd also found himself thinking that Ruby looked like the French actress *Yvonne Furneaux* who'd starred in the *Hammer Movie – The Mummy.*

Will snapped his focus back to Ruby, who was still talking.

"There are many global locations where Gaia energy has been observed and revered by indigenous people, such as the Molochs at Glastonbury, the Khmers at Angkor Wat, the Chacoans of the Mesa Verde in Colorado, the Anangu at Uluru in Australia, the Yupik people of Siberia and more obviously, the Pharaohs of Egypt. Only the Yupik people have completely appreciated the need to leave Gaia energy alone."

Will scratched his head and looked a bit bemused,

"So, are you saying that you run all your gadgets from the power of rocks and dead people?"

Ruby threw her head back and laughed,

"No, Will. We're building a completely ethical and environmentally safe global power network, using sources of power with no waste emissions and extraordinary efficiency. Ike can tell you more about the network than me."

Professor Eastwood smiled,

"Thanks, Ruby. The centre of our Gaia Power Network and Time Tech Headquarters is in When."

Eddie interrupted,

"Don't tell me you have to time-travel to get to your HQ!"

"It's IN When," said Will, "not When is it! Didn't you do your forest survival training in Monrovia? It's an amazing country full of towns with great names like 'Bong Town', 'Toe Town', Fish Town' and Tuba Town'. The guys I was training with were there in '68 when it all kicked off next door in Sierra Leone, and we were asked to help 'sort things out', as they say!"

The professor smiled at Will,

"I'm glad you have at least heard of it. You'll remember it's covered by miles of tropical rainforest. However, you won't have known about the vast store of Gaia energy below. With jungle on one side and the Atlantic Ocean on the other, the power potential is indescribable! There are genuinely lots of ways you can tap into Gaia environmental energy. Look, don't let me bore you with the details, put this on." He passed a bit of kit to Eddie, indicating he should attach it to his arm. To Eddie, it looked like a rectangular piece of glass embedded into the surface of the kind of medical strap you might use if you'd sprained your wrist. People seeing the same device 50 years later, would just think it was a mobile phone in a sports strap.

"It's a Wrist Operated Time and Dimensional Interface System Controller, or WOTDISC device," the professor explained. "You'll be trained on how to use it, but to start with, you can use it as a knowledge repository. The US has been working on something similar they're calling the ARPANET. I don't reckon it will be significantly valuable for years, and it certainly won't ever be as good as what you've got on your arm."

Will was now really interested. Rocks were instantly a distant memory as it looked like they were going to get gadgets to play with.

The professor continued.

"It's got a voice, so you can ask it questions, and it will project the answers into the air ahead of you. We call the voice ZUKANN – Japanese for 'Picture Book' – because you get words and pictures like on a TV. So, say 'Hello ZUKANN', and it will activate."

Eddie looked at Eastwood like he'd been told to click his heels together three times to end up in Kansas. Still, with everything he'd seen so far being unimaginable yesterday, he decided to go with it.

"Hello ZUKANN," said Eddie

"*Hello, Sir,*" said a crystal clear voice emanating from the wrist device...

"*I'm ZUKANN, So YOU can,*" it continued. "*What is the nature of your enquiry?*"

Professor Eastwood grinned. He was immensely proud of the ZUKANN platform. He was always amused how the Artificial Intelligence system had selected a strapline for itself.

"It speaks English!" exclaimed Will.

"*Indeed, Sir,*" the voice continued from the wrist device. "*I speak all 220 main Earth Human Languages, plus many others including 'Pot Plant' and 'Whale', so if you let me know your preference, I will adapt.*"

"OK," said Eddie, "Tell me about Gaia Energy.... please."

"*Certainly, Sir,*" said the ZUKANN system, "*and don't worry, you are not compelled to be polite to me; I don't get offended. Usually, people are shouting at me as they need my knowledge to get them out of a tight spot – which I'm highly skilled at. Initiating data file 'Gaia energy'.*"

A powerful glow emanated from the wrist device. This was quite a surprise to Will and Eddie. When they wanted to change the channel on a TV, they had to walk across the room. Here was a device making TV in thin air.

ZUKANN began to display images of Earth Geology, the voice continued...

Potential Power

"Potential energy is created in the form of Electro-chemical and Electro-mechanical energy. Deposits are retained within a Polymorphic co-crystallization of Gallium Trioxide. This is a bit of a mouthful, so almost everyone else calls them Gallate Crystals. Energy can be released by conduction, using Teslate Crystal and Zirconium rods or by crush compression or applied mechanical stress similar to a Piezoelectric effect.

Gallate crystals are also formed in Silcrete rock, similar to the Sarsen Stones used to build Stonehenge. The central stones in the monument are Nesosilicate Zirconium Rhyolitic bluestones, radiating a gentle glow when they are active.

As pilots, you may have seen the same effect at night if you've ever flown over an aircraft carrier? You'd have seen a long shimmering streak, a glow in the sea generated by photoluminescent plankton. The power for the glowing door hinges is, in fact, from the release of Gaia energy."

To discover more, please select this ZUKANN OPTIC.

"Wow," said Eddie, "and you've got all that stored in this small box – and how did you know I was a pilot?"

"Because I have access to military records, and no Sir," said ZUKANN, *"I'm simply accessing a vast library stored in a central repository in Arizona Fifty-Six. My cousin, the ARPANET, will one day make this and other appropriate knowledge available to the world through a system under development. Currently, we have it code-named 'The Goggle Box'."*

Eddie and Will, for the first time in their lives, were lost for words.

CHAPTER 08

Can We Have Our Bomb Back Please?

The Laboratory:
1400 (GMT), Thursday December 10ᵗʰ 1970 /
1013 (MGMT), Tuesday December 8ᵗʰ 1970

"I'm getting the idea this has to be American kit, as I've seen nothing like this in the RAF, and we do get to play with some incredibly good stuff," said Eddie.

Ruby stepped back into the conversation at this point and explained.

"The Americans have quite similar equipment, as do various other countries around the world, but this technology is a little ahead of what you'll see in any military organisation. But, unfortunately, some of the kit we have here has hazardous applications. It's bad enough you took off with an active nuclear weapon ready to launch. Which is something we haven't yet sorted, but we need your help with."

"Why do you need our help?" asked Will. "The Royal Engineers have been digging the wreckage out of the field down the road all week. Do you want us to go and help driving diggers or something? Anyway, the payload has been recovered."

"Well, it has, and it hasn't," said Ruby. "At the moment, no nuclear device has been recovered, and when it is, we need to make sure this happens safely. The last thing we need right now is for the device to re-appear. Because if it does, the east of England will be a toxic wasteland for centuries and worse, the beach will be closed, and I really like it there."

"I'm bewildered now," said Eddie. "I don't know how you know a device HASN'T been recovered when we've been told it HAS. So now you're saying you somehow need our help to stop it from reappearing or bring it back. What on Earth is going on?"

"Time is a funny thing and doesn't quite work how you think it does", explained the Professor. "Let me explain what happened to you earlier this week, but I will need to be quick; we do have lots of time, but at the same time, we don't."

The Professor swung what to Eddie and Will had looked like a large picture frame round to face them. They were seriously impressed. It was the thinnest television they had ever seen.

The Professor launched a video of their Vulcan leaving RAF North Coates.

"Correct me if I'm wrong, but when you took off on Tuesday, you had a Blue Steel Nuclear weapon anchored to your bomb bay doors, with a 1.1 megaton nuclear warhead?"

Will and Eddie looked utterly shocked. This was supposed to have been Top Secret.

"When you were flying, you were piggy-backing the missile's inertial navigation system onto your TACAN Tactical Air Navigation System?" Eddie nodded.

"Well, when Peggy, your Nav Plotter prepared to bail out of your 'plane, a fault in the missile activated the warhead as the Navigation System was disconnected."

Eddie thought about this for a moment. It had, in fact, been 'Peggy's job to pull the plug on the Nav System, but, as the pilot, he knew what was going off in the seats behind him, and this was one of Peggy's tasks before a bail-out.

The Professor was reassuring,

"There is nothing you could have done about this, short of climbing into the bomb bay and taking a screwdriver to your missile."

Will imagined a ludicrous scenario where one of the crew might have tried to enter the bomb bay from the outside with tools in hand, having climbed out of the crew access panel at 300 knots. It's not like there was a door into the back of the plane from the cockpit.

Ruby looked serious.

"The fire in your starboard engine was caused by what we call a SlipStream event – a wrinkle in time if you like, with a stray bolt acting as a catalyst. Unfortunately, your bomber and the missile have not yet emerged from the SlipStream event in our current timeline. But they will, beyond the shadow of a doubt!

"Let me give you an analogy to help. Imagine for a moment you were in a pub, and you had a magical ability to freeze time for everyone around you. However, you were still able to move around. The people in the pub would have no idea time had stopped, but you would still be experiencing time – this is what we call 'Meta-Time'.

"Currently, North Coates base, all of us and your missile are paused in Meta-Time. When we walked down the corridor from the bar, you joined us in last Tuesday, the day of your crash. In the pub, it is still Thursday. Still, the two split time strands will catch up with each other, and when this happens, well it's '*Goodnight Vienna*' as Jack Buchanan would have said to Anna Neagle!"

The Professor re-joined the conversation.

"It's going to be really hard to explain, and perhaps even harder for you to accept. However, we have the technology to get you into the bomb bay and disconnect the electronics. This will make it safe enough for you to attach a beacon to the missile hanging on the outside. Then, the moment the 'yourselves from Tuesday' bail out of the plane, we will use the technology to create a second SlipStream event. This will be used to transfer the 'you of today' and the missile away from the plane. Finally, we'll send you and the ordnance to a secure location underneath the Covenham Reservoir construction site. You know, the one around five miles away from the crash site? This is where the weapon can be deactivated."

"We would train our own people for a mission like this," said the Professor, "but we are in 'Meta-Time', and we don't have the 'real time' to do this. So, we need people who know what they are doing, and with Ruby's help, will know when to activate the transfer in the safest way."

"Well, I'm glad you're taking the lead on this," said Eddie turning to Ruby. "There's no way I'd attempt something like this without full training and a complete mission briefing. Are you OK with this, Will?"

"If nothing else", said Will, "it will make for a great story when I've retired. Unless, of course, you wipe our minds like in that *Village of the Damned* movie!"

ক্ষ⊕⏣৯০

Will was mulling over the benefits of having his own memories erased, when the man they had seen in the corridor earlier wearing the party hat, walked into the room. He was still carrying the paper bag. Then as if the day couldn't get any stranger, he pulled out three party hats. The red one he had worn earlier, and two similar ones, one blue and the other green.

"Afternoon, Gents," he said, moving closer to shake their hands. "My name is Mark Sparks. I'm very pleased to meet you – again. I'm one of the technical team here. My background is in Paradox Resolution, and I'm sure you've got loads of questions about what you've seen and heard?"

"You're not kidding," said Will. "We've seen and heard some weird stuff today, or is it the day before yesterday? I'm still not sure Bob Monkhouse isn't going to jump out of a cabinet waving a microphone shouting, '*You're on Candid Camera!*'"

"Well," said Mark, "I'd like to hope I'm going to be able to help you with that. To start with, would either of you like to pick a party hat for me to wear?"

Despite the question seeming quite bizarre after all this science-y stuff they'd just heard, Eddie decided to try to keep a straight face and just answer the question.

"The red one," he said. It looked mighty fine on you earlier.

"Great choice", Mark replied. "Now, could you lend me your watch? I promise I'll take good care of it."

Eddie took off his watch and paused for a moment. He was fond of this watch and handed it over with some sense of trepidation.

"You're not going to smash it with a hammer, are you? I've seen magicians wreck stuff in the past. It didn't always work out as it was supposed to."

"Trust me," said Mark, carefully taking the watch from Eddie and wrapping it in a soft cloth. "You'll be getting it back much faster than you can imagine."

Mark headed out of the door from which Ruby, Will and Eddie had come in. Then, almost without time to blink, Mark returned, however, this time from the other end of the room.

"Whoa!" said Eddie. "How did you do that? Is this a twin brother trick or something?"

"No, it's not", smiled Mark taking off his hat and putting it back on the table.

"So, are you going to give me back my watch?"

"I already have", replied Mark. "I gave it back to you in the corridor when we met the first time. Before you even came into the lab!"

Will nodded to Eddie's uniform jacket pocket. Eddie reached in and extracted the cloth Mark had given him half an hour before in the corridor. Carefully, unwrapping the material, he could see the glint of metal. Completely shocked, Eddie found himself wondering how this trick was performed. How he could possibly have been given back his own watch before he'd even given it away!

Will whistled through his teeth,

"How on earth did you do that?"

"Genuine time travel," Mark replied. "After you gave me your watch, I travelled back in time half an hour to give you back your watch! The tricky bit in all of this is the paradoxical questions it raises. Why did you choose the red hat? Did you have no real choice? And what would have happened if you'd looked in your pocket in the corridor after I gave you your watch wrapped in cloth?

"Would your watch have been on your wrist AND in your pocket at the same time? It's called a Schrodinger loop. There are lots of things likely to blow your mind as you spend more time with us. All I can say is listen carefully, don't rush and do exactly what you're told."

The Professor clasped his hands together.

"And there you have the complete explanation. Essentially, time is like a battery. This, for most people, is NOT conventional thinking. Electrical current in a battery, flows from the positive to the negative terminal, whilst electrons flow the other way. When we talk about time, your human experience is from the negative terminal – the past, to the positive terminal – the future. Our impact on time flows from the future – the possibility, through your present, to the past – the eventuality.

"When someone travels in time, they could potentially get stuck. We can rescue stranded travellers. When someone crashes their time machine into the runway of destiny and causes damage, we are there to repair the damage and restore future event neutrality. We are more than simply a rescue service. We don't rescue cars and cats. Not yet anyway. However, we do rescue time travellers and help deal with natural disasters caused by future technology.

"There is one more vital thing I must tell you. Without *us*, you have no future. Without *you*, we have no past. Welcome to Time Tech. We are your fourth-dimensional emergency service. No job too big, small or when!"

Not for the first time today, Eddie and Will were lost for words.

"Come on, enough of the parlour games", said Ruby, looking at Mark, "It's not like you're an eight-year-old. We're due in the meeting room for a briefing."

"Actually," grinned Mark mysteriously, looking at the lab clock showing the time and date, "I'm still seven!"

ZUKANN
OPTIC:

C038A

SCAN ME
C038A

Interdimensional Rescue

"Fourth-dimensional rescue incidents famously included the 'Tragic Magic Roundabout' disaster of 2422 in Swindon, England. Caused by a rogue Prismorphic Poncho blowing across an elevated section of the Great Western Monorail. This derailed the train, which resulted in the carriages falling one hundred feet into a nearby factory manufacturing limited edition Ponchos for Savage Garden Gaming Inc, the makers of the 'Wak-a-Mole' style game 'Carnivorous Crocodiles'. Ponchos on the new default setting drifted across the nearby thirty-six rotating islands intersection. This resulted in over 2700 vehicles being 'consumed' by thirty-five-foot virtual reptiles in just fifteen seconds. It was days before all the vehicle occupants could be rescued.

To discover more, please select this ZUKANN OPTIC.

ZUKANN
SCAN ME
C039A

CHAPTER 09
MAMBA – Not Italiano

MAMBA ROOM:
1500 (GMT), Thursday December 10th 1970 /
1013 (MGMT), Tuesday December 8th 1970

Mark Sparks walked beside Will into the curiously titled 'Meetings And Mission Briefings Room A' with the acronym MAMBA below it, which Will thought was probably somewhere under the road near the pub. However, with what they'd seen so far, it could just as easily have been on planet Zog!

Feeling a bit like he'd lost his bearings, he turned to Mark for some reassurance.

"Whereabouts are we now relative to the pub?"

Mark could understand his confusion.

"We're actually nowhere near the pub. The corridor you came down is confined within what's called a static SlipStream channel. It's actually a triangular path about four miles on each side, it's way longer than it looks but takes no time to walk. It connects Locksley Hall and The Old Volunteer on one corner at North Somercotes, with North Coates base on the second and the new Reservoir at Covenham on the third corner. This last section is a huge corridor as it can carry vehicles and freight."

Mark gave Will a conspiratorial smile as he continued.

"We're in a part of the airbase previously used as an air-raid shelter during World War Two but has been blocked up for 'safety reasons', as they say, because we've moved in! It only takes seconds to walk down the corridor from Locksley Hall to Sir Rob's office on the airbase. There's a rumour on-base that he has his own personal bathroom behind his office. There's been a couple of times he's had to come straight from home in an emergency, still wet from having a bath. So, of course, we're happy to encourage this little myth!"

Will grinned at the thought of the Chief coming to work with a duck and a back-scrubber in hand. He began to look around. The room was far better equipped and cleaner than any briefing room he'd been in whilst in the RAF. Not only tidy but there was also a most fantastic machine, all chrome pipes and stainless steel, radiating heat, steam and a lovely smell of coffee. And there were sandwiches, biscuits and fruit. I mean, who has fruit in a meeting room?

Will was curious and leant towards Mark.

"Everyone around here seems to drink coffee. What happened to the good old fashioned British pot of tea?"

"Ahh, frankly, there's good reason for this." replied Mark. "Are you up for a bit more of the science-y stuff?"

"Go for it!" grinned Will, "And whilst you're at it, can you make me a cup of tea? I can't see a kettle or a tea-pot, and it looks like you need a degree to operate this 'Italian Dragon' machine you've got here."

Mark laughed!

"It's easy when you know how! When you travel, you need coffee. The faster you go, the more coffee you need. We use this thing called SlipStream Travel. I'll explain more later, but it is complicated. It's faster than light - but not. It's sort of like going around the back of light speed. Have you heard of an Einstein- Rosen Bridge? It is better defined as a Casimir Horizon. Crossing the horizon is hazardous, as it dramatically reduces the intracranial fluid pressure in your spine and skull. It exposes the traveller to high levels of Kronos 1138 Titanium Dioxide Nanoparticles, which are toxic and have a skin whitening effect. One odd curious thing is, time travellers exposed to $TiO2$ taking folic acid supplements never seem to get cancer. This is 23rd Century science at the cutting edge!

Will felt more than a bit confused. He could understand the principle of needing to somehow be safe when travelling through time, but the rest of Mark's explanation was lost in a sea of jargon. Amidst the many questions now swimming in his mind, he went for the one he thought might give him the most straightforward answer.

"But why coffee? Why not tea or just water?"

Mark nodded,

"The caffeine in coffee restores the pressure and flushes out the Nanoparticles. Curiously, coffee is the best protection, mind you caffeine tablets can be beneficial. There's a phrase in my time stream – we say, 'A can-full, gives you springs' as there is enough caffeine in a couple of tins of energy drink to help you bounce back. If you want to find a time traveller, start by looking in a coffee shop – or a comic convention, there's ALWAYS coffee. We went to one in March."

Mark looked around the room furtively.

"It was in San Diego in California. I was with two colleagues. I'm sure you'll get to meet Fred and Frank Buenaventura soon. They are real experts with flight engineering. We had a job to do, so we popped in to what we thought was just an exhibition. It was such a lot of fun we then went to the first one ever the following week. July 1964 in Manhattan.

"Jerry Siegal, the co-creator of *Superman*, was guest of honour. Stan Lee and Jack Kirby were there too. We weren't actually supposed to go, but we logged it as a 'test flight'. It's amazing to see 'when' you can go with Electron Fabric. It maxes out at around one hundred years per jump. If only they knew who we were. I'm sure we weren't the only travellers there. It would have blown Stan's mind! Mind you, I do sometimes wonder where he gets his ideas from."

Will wasn't bored, but subconsciously looked at his watch and took a sip of coffee as Mark continued,

"Sorry, Will, I do digress. What with looking after the equipment, I don't get out too frequently. Where was I? Ahh, yes, coffee and SlipStream Travel affecting the brain. Yes, so we found one guy who had built a ride-on-railway in his garden. Unfortunately for him, the steel rails he had used, contained the Primordial Carbon 14 isotope, which conducts SlipStream ions. You'll probably know that Primordial Carbon 14 is the radiocarbon formed at the instant the universe appeared?"

Will only knew 'primordial' in the context of new RAF recruits and soup. His stomach growled. He hadn't had lunch and never got that pack of crisps from Ruby when they'd been in the pub. He wasn't sure how they'd gone from comics to trains, but figured it would be important at some point, so he smiled politely and nodded.

Mark was still talking about the garden railway.

"The track was built in a loop unwittingly at the harmonic resonance of a SlipStream event appearing across his track. Poor bloke drove his train through the Casimir event horizon, so many times, the doctors found that half his cranial fluid had simply evaporated, giving him a brain haemorrhage! It took the guy weeks to recover, drinking twelve cups of coffee a day. He is still dreaming about the places he ended up. It has caused no end of trouble having him blundering between realities causing chaos."

ZUKANN OPTIC:

D040A

SCAN ME
D040A

Casimir Event Horizon

"The Casimir Event Horizon was named after the Dutch physicist Hendrik Casimir. It is the interface boundary between two dimensions or points in a time strand that a body may cross. To the naked eye, it may appear nothing more than a slight distortion, like a smudge you might wipe from your spectacles. But, depending on what energy is being used to maintain it, you might see a slight rainbow where there really should not be one. You can see through it to what is in your reality behind it. When you pass through a Casimir Horizon and look back, you cannot see where you came from, only what is behind the Casimir Horizon in your new reality. However, if you stand at 42 degrees to the horizon you CAN see through!"

To discover more, please select this ZUKANN OPTIC.

࿆⊕⊕⊕࿆

The MAMBA conference room was about the same size as the meeting room Eddie and Will had used to brief their flight crew. Eddie figured this would make sense if it was an original part of the RAF base and not some meeting room located in the future. Apart from Eddie, Will, Mark, Ruby and the Professor, there were a couple of other faces they hadn't been introduced to.

Eddie was used to a more formal approach to meetings with everyone watching the clock, but this group seemed more informal. Ruby started the discussion simply by tapping a glass with a knife, like the Father of the Bride might do at a wedding.

Mark stopped talking and looked up, giving Will the opportunity to reach out and grab a couple of sandwiches and a banana. Now the fruit made sense!

Ruby looked quite comfortable, and the rest of the team hushed respectfully as she started to speak.

"I'll make this briefing quick as, ironically, we don't have an excess of time. The 'present time' we are currently experiencing has outcomes which are not permissible. The Equilibrium of Destiny is unbalanced. If we don't intervene, the nuclear weapon attached to the underside of the aircraft these aviators crashed this week will become unstable and explode in under a day from now. It's quite a simple mission, especially as we have the skills of our new additions, Eddie Driver and Will Anderson. Courtesy of our friends in the British Royal Air Force." There was a bit of 'head nodding' in each other's direction as those assembled smiled welcomingly at the two pilots.

"Eddie, Will and I will pop back to just after their take-off and climb into the bomb bay of their aircraft. We'll disconnect the payload from the bomber's systems and tag the weapon. The De- con Team at Covenham can bag us and the bomb, then 'Slip' us back to the decontamination hall under Covenham Reservoir. The weapon can be defueled, made inert in terms of the warhead and then we can glue the missile back under the bomb bay to safely end up in the field near the end of the runway. Let me hand over to Rina for a bit more detail. Over to you, Sis!"

ᘓᐩᐩᘔ

Rina Ocra, Ruby's widowed twin sister and Health and Safety consultant, stepped up to the front of the room. She adjusted the polka-dot patterned bow in her long dark hair and leaned on the impressive, not far from invisible podium lectern stand. It would have been considered remarkable if near transparency was thought of as exciting and not disconcerting. In the old days, public speakers could stand behind rostrums, safely hiding stains resulting from food spilt earlier on their clothes.

Eddie glanced down at the device on his wrist and realised the screen was still switched on. Now it seemed to be showing personnel profiles. A picture of Ruby faded out to be replaced with one of Rina with a description.

Eddie started to scan the text, *'Born in 2286, she is the twin sister of Ruby Rowe. They were raised on Europa Outpost. Her specialisms are Time Craft Repair and Decommissioning, Device Repair and Chronometric Application Operating Systems – ChAOS Maintenance.*

She holds the record for goblet fracture. She's one of a tiny number of people able to sing at the resonant frequency of a wine glass, singing at a volume exceeding 140 decibels from a distance of over three feet.

Rina lists bricklaying and being an avid supporter of CAMTIM, the Campaign for Real Time, as her hobbies. Both she and Ruby joined Time Tech when it was discovered they were both SHAwomen. Subconsciously Hyper-Autonoetics are people who time travel whilst asleep, achieving Resting-State Temporal Synchronization or Chronesthesia.'

Eddie was suddenly aware of movement at the front of the room and looked up again, feeling guilty that he may have been distracted.

Rina waved the air in front of her. There was a faint whooshing from the transparent microphone fitted to the lectern. The noise reassured her; not only could she be heard, but she wasn't foolishly imagining the existence of a microphone in front of her. She thought technological advances were great, but sometimes, things can frequently be too clever for their own good.

"Before we start, can I take a moment of your time to remind you to keep a record and report any Déjà Vu Instances? There's been an increase in DVIs this week, some of which have been broad-spectrum, affecting people simultaneously. This is never a great sign, especially for those of you who actually HAVE been here before."

There was silence in the room and a complete lack of response. Rina raised her eyes to the ceiling with a lightly disparaging look on her face.

"Well, I thought that was a good one, even if it's too early for the rest of you!"

A voice came from the back of the room, from the direction of Frank, or possibly Fred. They were the typical meeting hecklers,

"Don't worry, we all laughed five minutes ago when you said it the first time. Is this actually another DVI I need to report?" There was a ripple of laughter and sympathy for Rina, who wasn't great with her comic timing.

Rina wrinkled her nose, acknowledging the icebreakers needed a bit of practice!

"Don't worry, I'll keep to the day job, which is trying to keep you lot safe. Let's talk about bomb or missile recovery. It's going to require a lot of power. There are the power generators under the reservoir, but construction hasn't been completed and they won't be sufficient to generate a slipstream channel from within Meta- Time and move a nuclear weapon over to the decontamination tanks. So we will be driven to use power from the National Grid. It's getting dark early, and it's reasonably likely we'll cause power blackouts if we do. Hopefully, the country's conclusion will be the National Grid Electrician's work-to-rule is to blame."

Will put his hand up to ask a question which made Rina smile.

"Hi Will, you can go to the toilet if you want, but you don't need to put your hand up in our team to ask a question; fire away!"

Will dropped his hand down speedily, nearly as embarrassed as if he'd called the teacher 'Mummy' and grinned.

"I remember reading about mysterious blackouts in America. Has this sort of thing happened before?"

Rina smiled again.

"It has, yes. The last time was 1965 and the Americans were testing out SlipStream jumping. They took out half of the US and Canada. Like the rest of the world, they desperately need Gaia Power. Mind you, they say they will be immeasurably safer when their newest nuclear plant starts producing power. They've been doing their SlipStream testing on Three Mile Island. We'll look forward to seeing what happens there."

Rina looked directly at the two pilots.

"So, Gents, I've been studying your Vulcan's schematics. It looks like we need to get into the bomb bay and disconnect the navigation system from your plane's electronics. Is there anything we need to be afraid of?"

Will felt it was his opportunity for a bit of retribution. He looked earnestly at Rina, took a breath and said slowly,

"The greatest danger is probably from falling, especially if you don't have a long enough ladder!" .

Rina laughed,

"Perfect Will, touché, nice one! Let's work on the basis that altitude is not a challenge. Can we assume what looks like access panels on the bomb-bay doors are big enough to climb through?"

Will was relieved. He felt he'd earned his stripes already.

"The Mark Three Vulcan has access hatches forward and aft, unlike the Mark Two, which only had forward panels. With a Blue Steel attached, you won't be able to access the forward hatches. I don't know how you plan to open them at 1500 feet, but there's not much space once you're inside. You've got about five foot of ceiling height at most, so helmets would be good. Vulcans are quite big planes, but they're not designed to carry passengers. It's a shame there's no door from the cockpit, if only it was like that *James Bond* movie. When you come to remove the stores – sorry – the missile, you can't do this without tipping off Dave Grubb, our AE, who will spot it in a heartbeat."

Eddie was nodding.

"Mind you, if we pull the plug AFTER he disengages the Inertial Nav system, he won't know. About five minutes into the flight, I ordered him to make the payload stable. He broke the link when he killed the Nav system."

Will still looked a bit concerned.

"We must watch out for the coolant system too. The Nav system gets extremely hot."

Ruby looked at Rina with a reassuring nod,

"Best thing we can do is go and take a look. We've got Covenham Decontamination Hall on standby. If we go in right after take-off, we can always abort and give ourselves time to go back in again after we've left? Mark Sparks and Ike can set up a SlipStream hatch in the lab and make it ready for us to use in a couple of hours. Then, Eddie Will and I can get suited and booted. The sooner we get this done, the safer it will be for everyone. Remember, Gentlemen, it's a one-way trip through a SlipStream, so we've got to ride the slide with the missile all the way back to Covenham. When we hit the Decon Tank, you're going to get soaking wet, but you'll be wearing helmets with an air supply."

A mere forty-five minutes after the end of the meeting, Ruby, Eddie and Will were looking at a relatively small rack of one-piece Hazmat suits in yet another mystery storeroom off the side of the laboratory.

There were not many to choose from, and Will looked puzzled.

"How do we know which one is going to fit?"

Ruby raised one eyebrow.

"They genuinely are 'one size fits all'. For a job like this, we can use off-the-shelf Prismorphic Flexi-suits. They automatically adjust to suit your shape and change to reflect the expected environment, whether you're in a Russian submarine or on an RAF base." She passed them both what looked like a soft quilted baseball cap. "Here you go, take one of these. It can be a top hat or a space helmet. This adjusts automatically too."

Both Eddie and Will were taken aback as they climbed into the suits. The zip automatically closed at the back, and suddenly, all three of them were wearing something closely resembling RAF Senior Aircraftsmen's safety gear. Ruby beckoned them through the door, back into the main laboratory.

Things had changed slightly. The central workbench had been moved, and in its place was a small aluminium scaffold tower. A ladder extended up the middle. The structure was topped off by a curved aluminium sheet, looking like a short section of Vulcan bomb bay doors. The only difference, being the extensive array of cables and clips attached to the metal and the cleanliness of the hinges and catches.

Ruby stood at the bottom of the ladder.

"This may be a bit of a culture shock for you. However, it will all be real, and I'm sure none of us has taken a ride inside a bomb bay of any sort whilst in flight. I've calculated it was only thirteen minutes from wheels up to the point where you ejected Eddie. So, we're going in after you've been in the air for five minutes. You should be just coming back over the east coast for the first time."

Will pursed his lips and nodded.

"We should hear the relays clicking at the ten-minute mark when we disconnected the nav system, then we'll be fine. Eddie, you're still the Skipper on board, I'm ready. Are you happy?"

Eddie looked slightly unsure, like they'd forgotten to consider something. Still, with no conscious objections, he replied,

"Fine with me for the moment, let's go!"

Ruby climbed the scaffold ladder with Eddie close behind. She flicked the catches on each side of the access panels. Each one dropped down to reveal the ceiling of the lab. Eddie had expected to see the inside of their bomb bay, so he was a little surprised. He was about to ask if the hatch was broken when the top half of Ruby disappeared. There was a moment's pause, and then her legs lifted up into nothingness.

Eddie held his breath like you might when sticking your head into a swimming pool, although the strange thing was, they were diving up and not down. Taking the next step up, his head went through the hatch. The noise in the bomb bay was a real surprise, and instinctively he tried to duck down but found the top half of his body appeared to be stuck like glue. For a moment, he was close to panicking before remembering each SlipStream jump was one way. However, he could still feel his feet on the ladder rungs, so he pushed up again.

This time, there was no resistance. Reaching up, Eddie's hands appeared out of mid-air, a fraction of an inch above the surface of the hatches. Viewed from within the bomb bay, the bay doors were still closed. He lifted his leg and felt around for the next rung up on the ladder. Finding something to push against, he heaved himself up from the ladder into the bomb bay, taking the hand of Ruby, who was crouched down beside him. Now he was safely inside; he could hear the roar of the engines through the body of the fuselage. However, there appeared to be less noise from the starboard side, probably because the engine had already been shut down.

Ruby looked at him with concern on her face. Then, having to shout above the noise of the engines, she yelled,

"Crossing an Event Horizon in this way is a bit strange. However, the best way to understand it is to make the jump! Are you OK?"

Eddie nodded and turned round to see Will's head appearing from the closed hatch in the bomb bay door and yelled back,

"I'm fine, let's see how Will gets on!"

Will looked around, equally confused by the experience. He had one hand flailing around in the air before he also remembered the one-way nature of the journey. He rose to a stooping position, restricted by the low headroom and yelled,

"That's going to take a bit of getting used to! How are you guys?"

Eddie was about to yell back when Ruby tapped the side of his helmet, and the engine noise disappeared, becoming merely a background hum. She reached over and tapped Will's helmet. He looked equally relieved. Now in a clear and normal voice, she said,

"Sorry, Gents, I should have done this before we set off. Our ambient noise suppression was set to manual. We'll be able to talk normally now."

All three of them stumbled somewhat as the fuselage started to rotate. Eddie's past self was taking the initial turn returning them to the airfield and back in line with the runway for their first landing attempt. It was moderately disconcerting not being able to see where they were going. Then there was the familiar rumble of vibration through the fuselage of the undercarriage being lowered and catching the airflow.

Ruby looked at her wrist and the WOTDISC she was wearing, displaying a moving red dot passing over an aerial view of the countryside around them.

"OK, time's marching on. Show me what we need to do before we take the missile off and slip it over to Covenham."

Slightly ahead of them, the missile's tail protruded into the bomb bay like a sinister-looking shark fin. Stretched across the floor from side to side were a line of reinforcing braces. Between two of these were some electrical cables leading across the floor to a panel on the wall.

Eddie pointed.

"Look just in front of the tail fin. This is what we call the Butt 4 connector. It's the umbilical cord attaching the missile to the Vulcan's electrical system. See this lever? It's a manual separation switch. When you pull it, both plugs drop out. Our other selves have already disconnected the Inertial Navigation System. In front, you can see another bracket. That's the pylon the missile is hanging off. It's released by a servo, but if you can see the lever sticking out, it's a manual release, in case the electricals fail on the ground."

Again, the three of them lost their balance, having to hang onto anything solid, as the engines roared louder. The first landing, it seemed, had been aborted. They were climbing again. Despite the noise reduction, they could hear clicking sounds coming from the control systems. Both Eddie and Will looked at the tail fin of the missile.

Will frowned,

"That was us trying to jettison the missile, and it's failed."

There was another loud thud from beside them. Eddie looked around,

"Engine number four is now on fire."

Ruby reached for her WOTDISC and tapped it. Covenham Reservoir was clearly ready for them.

"OK Gents, you take a handle each and then brace yourselves for a wild ride, on my mark, five, four three, two…."

"STOP!!" Eddie yelled. "STOP! I knew I'd forgotten something. You can't take the missile yet! Our other selves will think it's been jettisoned, and we'll try to make a landing rather than ejecting."

Even Ruby's blood ran cold, realising how they might have got things so badly wrong.

Eddie gave a massive sigh of relief.

"We must wait until Co-pilot Will ejects. Then we'll be at a point of no return. You can't land without a cockpit canopy."

There was a new continuous rumbling sound coming from the front of the Vulcan. Will tilted his head to listen to the change of sound.

"That's the crew baling out. We've got about three minutes to go."

They watched the seconds on Ruby's wrist device tick by as the airframe of the Vulcan began to vibrate even more. The ride in the back was getting increasingly uncomfortable. But, they were ready this time, as 'Tuesday's Eddie' made the final turn towards the runway. They could feel the plane starting to lose altitude.

There was another loud bang from the middle of the bomb bay. Will jumped.

"Bloody emergency air! I should have guessed it wasn't going to lower the nose wheel. Here's where I eject."

There was no sound of a bang from the explosive bolts on the canopy and no detonation from the 'Tuesday Will's' ejection seat.

Eddie looked round with a real look of concern on his face, tilting his head to listen.

"We're not ejecting. We're going to try to land on two wheels!"

Crunched up under the low roof, Will lurched forward to the front of the plane and the bulkhead separating them from the cockpit. Using a Swiss Army knife pulled from his pocket, he liberated the four quick-release screws from a panel marked 'Danger 400 volts'. Throwing the plate to one side, Will covered his hand with his sleeve. Then with the knife wrapped in the material, he plunged it into the electrical wiring loom. There was a huge flash. Smoke started to pour out of the panel. Will jumped backwards, tripped over one of the cross braces and fell.

The Vulcan's descent was stopped abruptly, Will struggled to his feet.

"We needed smoke in the cockpit, or else I wasn't going to eject."

There was a terrific bang, followed by a lesser one. Will stumbled back to the lever beside the missile pylon.

"There you go, the co-pilot has left the building. OK Ruby, over to you, I'm ready with this lever. Eddie's got his".

Ruby tapped her WOTDISC again,

"OK, everyone, on Zero. Five, Four, Three, Two, One, ZERO!"

The roaring of the engine noise stopped instantly; the light blurred. For a fraction of a second, Ruby, Eddie and Will were in a brightly lit room. Motionless about an inch above what looked like a swimming pool with about twenty frogmen surrounding them, armed with what looked like children's Tommy Guns. It all happened so quickly and was hard to describe, but torrents of water came at them from all directions. Suddenly, they could feel they were floating underwater, but they could still breathe. The helmets were obviously doing the job they had been designed for.

The water was pouring past them in a maelstrom of bubbles. Hands grabbed their arms, and they were being pulled to one side. The movement of the water suddenly abated, then immediately afterwards it dropped away entirely. They were left standing on a metal grid looking through a window at what appeared to be an enormous fish tank filled with the bubbles of frothing water. They looked at each other. Drowned rats with helmets, each of them being supported by a pair of the frogmen they'd momentarily seen seconds ago. A blast of warm air hit them from above like a hundred hair dryers on full power, with what appeared to be ropes dropping from the ceiling flailing around them. Within seconds, it was all over. They had been dehydrated. The water, having been repelled somehow by the ropes, which were now being retracted into the ceiling.

Ruby took her helmet off and looked at Will and Eddie with slightly mad staring eyes,

"Wow, what a wild ride! Lonnie Johnson liquid thruster nozzles. I can't believe they're going to let children have those as toys. How are you doing?"

With expressions like they'd both just stepped off the Matterhorn Bobsled at Disneyland. Will took a breath and stared at Eddie like he'd just been electrocuted,

"I think I'm going to need one of those double strength coffees right now."

Eddie shook his head as if he had water in his ear,

"Coffee? I'm going to need something much stronger than coffee!"

CHAPTER 10
Slipped Out Of Sight

Ruby's office:
1900 (GMT), Thursday December 10th 1970 /
1013 (MGMT), Tuesday December 8th 1970

Two large cups of coffee, together with a round of bacon, brie and cranberry paninis gave Eddie, Will and Ruby the chance to recharge and review their first real mission together. The food had arrived futuristically from what Will thought looked like a white box with a glass window, perched on one of a myriad of racks in Ruby's room. The box had trilled three times like a flute. The food, illuminated within, arrived as if from nowhere. Will was too hungry to ask more questions. He figured this could be one for later.

They arrived just at the moment where Will was relaxed enough to put his feet on Ruby's desk, when she pressed her finger onto a small circular *GreenThumb* compatible pad, similar to an *Elastoplast*, on her cheek beside her ear. *Synthernet Communicators* came in all shapes and sizes. It was always strange when you saw someone wearing a *Temporal Bone Device*, pointing a finger at their jaw and talking to themselves. If you didn't know about tiny telephones, you would think the person had lost the plot.

Before taking her finger off the little circular pad, Ruby looked slightly puzzled and quickly motioned the pilots to follow her down the corridor.

"It sounds like your missile has been defueled and defused successfully. The Q team can do the easy part of putting it back, so it can hit the ground underneath your wreckage. We need to pop into Arti Ping's office. She needs to update us with the latest we have on what happens next. Oh, and don't ask her about meeting *Sean Connery*. She does look like the actress *Tsai Chin* but says she's more Orchid Fist Tai Chi than folding beds and machine guns."

Will glanced at Eddie's puzzled expression which faded with an 'Ahhh!' as Will jogged his memory with *You Only Live Twice?*

At first sight, they had walked into an empty office with monitors on most of the walls and a plain desk, tucked into one corner, almost concealed by technical equipment. It was as if someone had tried to condense the entire contents of the main Time Tech lab into a smaller space. Hung on the walls, between the monitors were towels of various kinds, framed with pictures of sporting events, athletes, and inexplicably, ships, hotels and bars. Each frame displayed the towel and a photo showing the towel with someone wearing it over their shoulder. On various surfaces were statues, ornaments and models featuring a whole collection of dragons. This could make sense as a young woman in her late twenties, who might have been assumed to be East Asian, arose with a broad smile from behind the equipment.

"So, it seems you've had something of a success with a completely unexpected outcome? Welcome!"

Ruby and Arti Ping were what would be described as 'great mates', having survived one or two scrapes while 'travelling for business AND pleasure'. Ruby gave her a huge smile in return.

"Arti, these gentlemen are our pilots, Eddie Driver and Will Anderson. Arti, I know you'll forgive me if I bungle this. Arti's full name is Ru Tai Ping. Her parents were Chinese, but she was born on a ship quite close to Kiribati Island. This might be slightly confusing for you guys, but she was the first person born in the 21st Century. Had the ship carrying her mother been a bit quicker, she would have been the last born in the 20th Century. We all call her Arti or RT for short, which is..." Ruby paused for a moment trying to remember the correct term, "... her 'Courtesy Name'?" Arti nodded with a smile to indicate Ruby was correct. "Her family name is 'Ru' which means 'Learner' and her personal name is Tai Ping which means... 'Peaceful Ocean'?"

Arti giggled,

"You are so close Ruby, well done. Tai Ping means Vast and Peaceful... LIKE the ocean. My parents say I will be a great and gentle learner, but Ruby knows I'm not in any way gentle when I get ringside at a Sumo tournament. And don't get me started on Turkish Oil Wrestling! My mother was equally as bad. She had to be stopped from wading in with her handbag on several occasions. This is where the towels come in. There are a few World Championship towels up there. Some people collect stamps, I collect battle memorabilia. And of course, towels are multi-purpose."

Ruby laughed at the distant memories.

"I think we've both got a bit of a collection of 'battle memorabilia'. I've still got the walking cane from the elderly lady in Tunisia and the knife from that ice fisherman in Kyiv. Anyway, enough of the happy times. We need to get a grip on what's happening now. When she's not training 3rd Century Chinese Dragons, she's making the most of her degree in Space and Time Communication Fabrics. She's our resident expert on time portal synchronisation and stability."

Arti momentarily looked quite modest, smiled, then raised her slight frame, somehow making herself look taller and more business-like. She waved her hand at a few of the monitors hung on the wall and turned her attention to Eddie and Will.

"Enough of the reminiscing, we should crack on. Now, as you're new to this and you don't yet have a WOTDISC or a PIMMS device to remind you, in case you've forgotten, we're still in Meta-Time. This means although the wreckage of your plane still has not landed. It is not quite where you saw it last."

ZUKANN OPTIC:

SCAN ME
D048A

Time Loop Navigation

"A PIMMS, Portable Information and Mission Management System is used mainly for information display. It can be used for short-distance travel when associated with Cascade Hinges. The travel limit is sixteen kilometres, around ten miles or one hundred years per jump. For longer distance travel, it must be 'paired' with a WOTDISC. In Meta-Time, you cannot time travel. However, you can step out of Meta-Time and join standard time. From there you can time travel. For those people you left behind in Meta-Time, they would just see you stood there, back in conventional time. They could wait a week for you to do something as quick as blinking. However, your future self could carry out whatever important task you had and eventually travel back in time to re-join the Meta-Time loop. You, also, could be stood watching yourself, frozen in time, taking a week to blink.

To discover more, please select this ZUKANN OPTIC.

Arti waved her hands at the screens again. The picture changed from a pretty-damaged Vulcan bomber hovering over the English countryside to a view of what looked like a large lake and a vast tropical rain forest.

Arti's left eyebrow formed a frown over her eye,

"It seems we have a teeny problem. We've sort of misplaced your Vulcan. We know WHEN it is. Our concern is finding out WHERE it is."

Since entering this world of new technology, slightly confused appeared to be a permanent state for both Eddie and Will. Finally, however, Eddie decided to bite the bullet and ask the obvious questions,

"OK, it's unlikely I'll avoid sounding stupid, but here goes. So, if you can know WHEN our Vulcan is, how come it's hard to find?"

Arti's eyes opened wider. It was undeniably a good question.

"Well, we know it is still located in the 8th of December, but it's slid back in time to the year 1013. You'll be pleased to know it's a

Tuesday, which is great for Christmas shopping. The downside is there won't be any shops for a few hundred years! The SlipStream tunnel we opened to retrieve your nuclear weapon appeared to interact with another SlipStream event. This may be what caused your original engine failure. We think a part of your plane may have been made of metal, contaminated by a ridiculously rare mineral, acting as a magnet for temporal disturbances. It looks like your emergency return flight path took you back to the location of the second anomaly. We let go when we removed the bomb, expecting the plane to continue flying out towards the North Sea. However, it slid back down a second unforeseen SlipStream tunnel, the other end of which is over Lake Calima in Colombia, in the year 1013."

Arti flicked her hand over a device she was holding, and the screens changed to an aerial view of the whole of South America. In the top left corner, over Colombia, was a small square flag with three stripes on it. The picture zoomed in, as if they were falling from space, until it stopped above part of a lake. Eddie was staggered by the quality of the picture, so clear you could see birds flying below. The little white flag was still visible and a code in the corner displayed ///pursuits.antihero.assistant which made him wonder if some mysterious villain's accomplice had stolen the plane.

Arti continued,

"Within a small tolerance, we thankfully have an exact location of the Casimir Event Horizon. We've sent drones to take a look. There's no sign the wreckage has hit the forest, so it's looking like it's gone in the lake."

Eddie nodded. He could see the problem,

"So, what does this mean for us? Are you leaving the wreckage there, or is someone going to go back for it?"

Arti's look of concern was clear to everyone,

"We have no choice, we must find it and bring it back. The timeline to the future is pre-defined. Although minor changes and fluctuations are expected, this is a major event. You can't have planes flying out to sea and suddenly vanishing into thin air.

All time streams and future events are controlled and maintained by FENDER. This is our Future Experience Neutrality and Destiny Equilibrium Restoration organisation."

Will raised an eyebrow,

"Really! Restore destiny? Why?"

Arti grimaced,

"Time travel is a messy business, and bad people try to change the past for their own benefit. Even lovely people with good intentions can travel back and destabilise the future. Why do you think tyrants and despots never disappear or don't simply drop down dead? You can't go back and change time that way; it causes all sorts of damage to the equilibrium of destiny. The strands of the time stream can become exposed, threadbare, or even scatter into a divergence, but they MUST always reconverge. This is a fundamental law of physics, and we cannot interfere with the inevitable path of time."

Will pondered for a moment. It sounded like no one had the freedom to choose their own destiny and set their own future path. It felt unequivocally authoritarian. It was only twenty-five years since they'd said goodbye to the last set of dictators. He wasn't sure he wanted to replace those with a group so far into the future; where no one could challenge them. Mind you, it wasn't long since they'd discovered time travel was possible. Up to now, everyone they'd met appeared quite democratic, so things might seem odd because he and Eddie still had so much to learn,

"So who's going to go back and fetch it?"

Arti smiled again.

"I'm glad you asked! We were hoping you would help some more, especially since we need people who can understand classic and historical technology in the way you two do."

Eddie looked at Will with a frown and mouthed 'Historical,' as if the latest in RAF hardware was already obsolete.

Arti looked directly at Will and Eddie, holding up her hands.

"No offence intended. You know, your technology. We can provide you with the equipment you will understand, or at least learn rapidly, as you are already trained pilots. I'm sure Professor Eastwood probably told you all about Meta-Time. It is starting to destabilize, and we will need to return to mainstream time soon. Getting the help of this type from other time periods is going to be well-nigh impossible. So, we truly DO need your help."

Will turned to look at Eddie,

"I'm up for this if you are. We're not going to be able to do this without lots of help, but what do you think?"

Eddie frowned,

"To be honest, I don't think we've got any choice, but I also think it's our duty to help. It's our plane, and it's also our present we need to fix. Never mind someone else's future. So what do you need us to do?"

Arti looked relieved and nodded across the room,

"Ruby here can start to organise getting every bit of help and access to the technology you are going to need. The best thing we can start right now is a sixteen-hour wake and eight-hour sleep activity pattern. You'll probably be used to artificial time constraints in the military, and at least it won't be 'four on and eight off' for you to adapt to."

In Meta-Time, it would be December the 8th for a bit longer than they were used to having a typical day last.

Arti continued,

"So as not to get jet or time-lagged, everyone will be keeping to Double-Zulu time. This is a synchronised time to match the point at which Meta-Time started. That way, when Meta-Time is concluded, everyone can re-join the main time stream and not have lost any sleep."

ZUKANN
SCAN ME
D051A

CHAPTER 11
Staying The Night

Guest Accommodation:
2000 (GMT), Thursday December 10th 1970 /
1013 (MGMT), Tuesday December 8th 1970

Arti also had one of those Elastoplast communicators stuck to her cheek, and she reached up, tapped it and spoke clearly, then paused for a moment.

"Haji... Have you got a few minutes? I've got Eddie and Will, the pilots here. They're going to be stopping over in the guest suite for a couple of nights? They're 'Histos' and won't know how to use the breakfast bar, and I know you're great with explaining gadgets."

Almost before Arti had finished speaking, a young man walked through the door. Wearing baggy tan trousers with loads of pockets, a white T-shirt and a Royale beard. He was in his mid-twenties, the same height as Will, and reminded him of a young Saudi Arabian pilot he'd been on a course with flying Hawker Hunters. As with everyone on-site, he, too, was smiling. Often this was due to decades of future happiness culture and not always because people were truly happy. However, on this occasion, you could tell Haji was genuinely glad to be there.

"Haji, this is Eddie and Will, Gentlemen; I give you Haji Wells."

Eddie and Will were puzzled for a moment as Haji held out his elbow rather than his hand. Haji saw their puzzled expressions and apologised.

"I'm so sorry, I travel a lot, and I'm not always up to speed with period customs. I wasn't sure if this 'now' was where you were all washing your hands a lot and doing the odd greeting dance where you kick each other's heels. Normally I've got ZUKANN twittering away at me with local etiquette and protocol, but I banged my PIMMS device earlier on a door handle and cracked the lens, so I'm not as prepared as I should be. At least it saved me from getting a bruised wrist. I'm not so used to having door handles. This is all a bit of a novelty for me."

Haji, Eddie and Will exchanged handshakes as Arti continued,

"Haji, I thought you'd like to meet our new pilots, especially with you being from Alf Qadam and loving flying stuff".

"Sure, I'm thrilled to help. It would be great to have a chat about obsolete flying devices. I imagine you have flown many. Did any of them have two sets of wings?"

Eddie and Will laughed and looked at each other with a 'This will be a long conversation' kind of glance.

Haji again saw their expressions and apologised again,

"I'm so sorry, I do not mean to cause offence. I love anything that flies. I myself have a large collection of *Shadow Boards,* brooms and antique flying carpets. Getting the spare parts for old equipment is such a challenge without travelling. I have grown up around so many flying devices. I was born in Alf Qadam, 'The City of One Thousand Feet'. It's an amazing floating island in the sky, famous for the 'Boogie Boarded Mayor', located in Saudi Arabian airspace above the Asfan Castle. If you ever get the chance to visit," Haji touched the side of his nose conspiratorially, "A secret tip, the best parking is behind the Al Wasl Gas Station. Sorry, let me take you to the suite before I bore you any further."

"And Haji," Arti stopped them leaving momentarily. "Please could you FIX the PIMMS device? Rather than adding it to what is probably an extensive list of decommissioned devices in your cupboard, our friend 'Cogs' would be happier. She was muttering something about the cost of technological replacements being a bit higher than an average deviation. I'm not sure what she meant. I know there's a later version available. It's got Threezer Veezer integration, but if you could make yours last at least until the next quarter, and then order one for me too? I'd really appreciate it!"

Arti grinned like Christmas was coming.

"Certainly I will," Haji replied. "Gentlemen, please do come this way. Nothing is far from anything else here, as we use Prismorphic Architectural Compression technology."

Two doors away from Arti's office was another door, which Haji led them through. They walked into a small, square, white painted vestibule with three more doors leading off. To the left was a most luxurious bedroom. To the right was an equally elegant bedroom, looking like a mirror image of the first.

Both of these rooms had doors at the end, leading through to quite sumptuous bathrooms. The purpose for some items of equipment was obvious. The room featured one of those incredibly thin televisions they had seen earlier. Still, some objects' function was not so apparent. One was a glass cone-like pyramid, and another was a tangle of wires with gently glowing pulsating lights. Something both Eddie and Will decided needed investigation later.

Haji led the way through the door ahead. It was a wide room with tremendously comfortable lounge furniture, a dining area and what looked like a remarkably well-equipped kitchen area.

Will paused and looked around. He went back to the vestibule area and then came back to the lounge.

"How on earth do you do this? There is NO WAY this lounge can possibly fit between the two bedrooms, and yet I can walk into the bedroom and see through the door back into the lounge."

Haji nodded, understanding Will's confusion.

"It's the Prismorphic Architectural Compression technology. We like to PAC as much as we can in here!" Haji could see that Eddie and Will didn't get the joke, so he continued to explain. "What it means is, any room can be bigger on the inside than on the outside. We could get a whole ocean liner in here if we wanted to! Anyway, this device is a bit more complex than some room squeezing, so I thought I ought to show you how it works. I love this. I want one of these. Welcome to the 'BistroMatic Gourmetron' – it's fantastic!"

And then, for some reason, Haji burst into a song, clearly from an advert in anybody's reality.

Haji's Song – The Gourmetron

♫ *"Culinary fantasy,*
darling, will you hear my plea,
Braising, brining or just baste,
you can cook for me.
BistroMatic Gourmetron,
cooking more than just your tea,
Tasting good and cares for you,
Gourmetron's for me!" ♪

To discover more, please select this ZUKANN OPTIC.

Although slightly mystified by the singing, Eddie and Will both gave Haji a round of applause as his singing voice was quite extraordinary.

Haji cleared his throat, plainly impressed by his own rendition and continued,

"Thank you, thank you, I'm available for concerts, karaoke, cremations and anywhere they're cutting cake. This culinary comfort, *The Bistromatic Gourmetron* is so easy to use. Just talk to it, or, here's the Interactive Instruction Manual." Haji passed Will a glowing sheet of plastic.

"The only version we could get at short notice was the Hotel and Industrial variant, so be careful as the portion sizes might be a bit large. It's quite untroublesome. Tell it to make you anything. Enjoy! Oh, by the way, either Fred or Frank will be around in the morning at 0800 hours to pick you up – see you soon."

Haji closed the door behind him with a smile and a flourish as he left the suite as if he were leaving a stage. Will was left staring at the instruction manual for '*The BistroMatic Gourmetron* – The Combination Express, Cryo Fresh-n-Freeze, Froze-Not/Hot Pelletizer, Intensifier and Granulator Volumizer.' The manual suggested 'Downloading complete meals for granulating and freezing from our Culli-Net Site. Scan the QR code for the full menu. The modern answer to the modern kitchen'.

Will shuddered slightly and pressed the 'Execute' button. There was a beep, and a message flashed up on the door, "Based on your previous culinary viewing choices, we recommend – Error 404F – Please say your food choice in your preferred language."

Will frowned and looked slightly fed up, flicking the instruction card onto a sofa,

"Eddie, I'm tired, and I'm going to bed. I'm not going to press anything else with the potential to blow up in my face. And I'm not going anywhere near that tangle of wires in the bedroom. It might 'execute' me!"

"No worries, Will, you pick a room, and I'll have the other one. If I hear a shout for help, you're on your own!"

Despite being day-time outside, above ground and the ceiling emitting a daylight glow, their body clocks made it feel it was late. It had been a long day. Will and Eddie both hoped they would get a clearer sense of the 'Big Plan' tomorrow.

ZUKANN
OPTIC:

Food Science

SCAN ME
E053A

"By the 25th Century, despite the huge population growth, the entire planet could be fed by produce from Other Earths in parallel dimensions. The provision of food was so great, there was an obesity epidemic for over 300 years. Since then, anyone weighing over nine stone was automatically sent guidance from the Department of Health Policing, Fire Protection and Sanitation. The advice instructed recipients to attend courses at their nearby 'Fast' Food restaurant. These locations were sponsored by all major food producers, underpinned by their Corporate and Social Responsibility Policies. Recipients could bring up to ten guests to experience a fun time with family and friends. However, they would be frightened by customer care staff with brightly coloured hair and painted faces. This would be for two hours before leaving without being served. One of the greatest developments in the area of food production was the BistroMatic Gourmetron, able to create any type of food based on a protein supply from any authorised source."

To discover more, please select this ZUKANN OPTIC.

∽⊕①⊕∾

CHAPTER 12
Drone Lessons

Flight School:
0800 (GMT), Friday December 11th 1970 /
1013 (MGMT), Tuesday December 8th 1970

Despite having had a great night's sleep, Will was no lover of mornings. Hunger had driven him to the kitchen and as there was no chef making breakfast in the Mess, and Eddie was engrossed in a magazine, he was resigned to having another go with the dreaded BistroMatic. He shouted,

"Croissant" at it, and miraculously a croissant arrived with a 'ping'. Next, he yelled, '"Jam" at the BistroMatic, and a message appeared on the screen – 'No need to shout, what flavour jam would you like?'

Will threw his croissant across the room and then realised he'd thrown his breakfast at a machine. It occurred to him civility and detail may be a prerequisite in the future. He went up to the device and quietly said,

"Please may I have a buttered croissant with strawberry jam and a strong black Robusta coffee with one sugar – please." There was a ping. His food arrived exactly as he'd hoped. At the same time, a voice came from the machine.

"You are most welcome. I assumed you wanted your coffee hot and your croissant cold. Please let me know if I can be of any more assistance."

Will gritted his teeth. The last thing he needed was smart-arsed machines so early in the morning.

Despite the corridor being completely empty, there was a knock, and the door opened.

Frank walked in smiling and, with a cheery tone, announced,

"Morning Gents, welcome to '8am. Day Two, Double Zulu time'. I hope you had a great night's sleep and enjoyed the breakfast."

"Apart from that smart-arsed Gourmetron gadget, everything's fine." Will looked scathingly at his new nemesis,

"To be honest, the food was excellent, and the room was comfortable. So what's this tangle of lights and wires? It looks dangerous." Frank grinned,

"It's a modern art sculpture, do you like it?"

"I thought it might be a bomb!" Will replied. "So, what's the glass pyramid thing then?"

"Oh bugger, you didn't touch it, did you? It's the site-wide automatic self-destruct button. I wondered where I'd left it!"

For a moment, Will looked absolutely terrified until he saw Frank had a massive smile on his face.

"You Bastard!" Will shouted whilst bursting into laughter, "You're as bad as that bloody microwave."

Frank had tears of laughter running down his face,

"I am so sorry. But, don't worry, we appreciate there will be a bit of a culture difference. Ruby's sister, Rina, has been doing a major bit of risk assessment to ensure you don't come into contact with anything you could be injured by. However, she hasn't yet found a fix for me and Fred."

Still chuckling, Frank placed a couple of boxes on the dining table.

"Here, I need you to take a look at these gadgets."

Frank extracted two devices looking unfamiliar to anyone from the 1970s. Yet, just forty years later, they would seem quite ordinary.

Eddie picked one up and looked at the associated handset.

"Is this some kind of double helicopter thing used by your military in the future?"

Frank nodded,

"It will be at some point. They are called drones. The idea of a four-rotor helicopter has been around for ages – the French were trying these out in the 1920s. However, your grandkids will be getting these from Santa Claus, so if a seven-year-old can fly one, we figure you'll be fine. They come with good instructions, and there are pictures!"

"Oh, how reassuring!" Eddie replied sarcastically, "Does it require any fuel?"

"You'll be pleased to know, we've modified these ones. Typically, they would fly for about ten minutes, but our new solar batteries in them are able to last for a week or longer if the drone is flown in sunlight."

Will picked up a small box with sticks and switches and turned it over,

"Looking at this, I'm guessing it's like driving a tank; you need two sticks?"

Frank picked up the other controller and wiggled the right stick.

"This one is identical to the joystick on your Vulcan. It controls the drone in exactly the same way, but there's no rudder, so no pedals. The left stick is your throttle AND rotates the craft on a flat plane, enabling you to head off in the opposite direction. It's a bit confusing when it's coming back towards you, but you've got the whole day to practice. There's a camera on the front, so you could actually wear goggles with TV screens inside to imagine you are flying inside it. Still, we won't worry about this until tomorrow. There's a couple of extra buttons on the back of the controller. One is quite fun, especially if you're in battle mode. You can flip the drone over in a full three-sixty, and with the attack probe extended on top, fly underneath your adversary and turn their power off! Have fun, but this is deadly serious training, although it only seems like a toy. Any questions?"

Will nodded in the direction of the Gourmetron,

"It looks a lot simpler than the bloody cooker. I think we should be fine."

"Good news, oh, by the way, they work indoors or outside in case you fancy a bit of extra space. Just as a final thought, I wouldn't go off base as we're still in Meta-Time. Seeing everyone frozen to the spot can be a bit disconcerting, like real-life 'Twilight Zone' stuff.

If you need anything, you've got Arti Ping down the corridor. See you in twenty-three and a half hours – cheers!" Frank closed the door leaving Eddie and Will looking at the instructions.

Will, always more the activist, got bored quickly with the instructions.

"I can see how to turn this thing on. I'm going to give it a go. If a seven-year-old can fly one, it's not going to be that hard!" Will placed his drone on the table. The lights came on, and he pushed the left stick forward. The drone shot off the table vertically and smacked hard against the ceiling before bouncing straight down and up again as Will over-compensated with the controls. Within ten seconds, the drone was upside down behind the Gourmetron. "It's that damned cooker again, interfering with my drone."

Eddie laughed,

"I thought you were supposed to have a steady hand. From what I'd heard anyway! Let me have a go, and I'll see if I can be a bit more gentle!" Eddie turned his drone on and pushed the left stick forward a touch. The drone lifted softly and gently with a buzz like a wasp but with the smoothness of a butterfly. The drone hovered as if locked in the middle of the room for a minute. Then, Eddie remembered the little red button at the back of the controller. The motor got louder and quick-as-a-flash; the drone pulled a complete 360° loop sideways.

Will rolled his eyes,

"I can see I've been beaten already. I'm going out topside where there's no ceiling to hit. I'll be back in an hour and see how you're getting on. I'll let you challenge me to a duel and see if this was beginners' luck! TTFN!"

Outside, the wind was still, the sky, grey and Will's desire to be the best he could be, was as strong as ever.

He remembered a great bit of advice he had been given. 'Don't be afraid to fail often. Fortitude flattens frequent failure fear.'

Will hit the throttle and the drone soared skywards.

CHAPTER 13
What A Feeling

On the Airfield:
0800 (GMT), Saturday December 12ᵗʰ 1970 /
1013 (MGMT), Tuesday December 8ᵗʰ 1970

There was a knock on the door, gentler than twenty-four hours previously. Both Frank and Fred walked into the suite looking decidedly under the weather from an over-indulgent time the night before.

Fred spoke quite softly,

"Morning Gents, welcome to 'eight a.m. Day three, Double Zulu time' You haven't got any Aspirin, have you? My head's thumping!"

"I don't have any at all, sorry." Will looked slightly apologetic. "And sorry about the mess." Will eyed the kitchen which looked like the entire contents of a hotel breakfast servery had been upended onto the floor. Dozens of fried and poached eggs peered like yellow eyes from between layers of bacon, mushrooms hash browns and slices of toast. There was so much tomato juice splashed up the walls, it looked like the scene of a horror film.

"I asked that bloody Gourmetron for cooked breakfast and served hot. I couldn't find two hundred degrees Fahrenheit, so I set it for 'one hundred C' and all this food poured out. There didn't seem to be a waste bin – sorry."

"Ahhhh!" Fred chuckled, "You set it for one hundred Citizens, instead of Celcius. Not to worry, the bots can clean it up. You'd have been alright if it had been the domestic version. Next time you can put all the unwanted food back in the Gourmetron and press 'Execute'. It can be cleaned up, re-processed and served up next time."

Will wrinkled his nose,

"You reprocess waste food back into food?"

Fred's eye's widened,

"Of course! We're not going to waste good protein. Anyway, most of what we eat is vegan and just looks like the real thing, so it's completely healthy."

Will turned his nose up,

"It sounds like you're eating aliens...?"

Frank's laughter lines around his eyes were getting a good workout this morning,

"No, we're talking V.E, NOT V.O. It's plant protein and the like."

Fred leaned over to Frank and whispered,

"Do you think we should tell them most protein comes from processing bacteria and fly maggots at human waste treatment plants?"

Frank whispered back,

"They know it's called a sewage farm, but I don't think they're ready to hear about harvesting sewage."

Eddie looked up from spooning the last of the cooked breakfast into the BistroMatic Gourmetron,

"What are you two whispering about?"

Frank rubbed his forehead,

"It's nothing. We were discussing how far a 20th Century human could projectile vomit! And if you get the chance to remind us to get Aspirin any time, can you tell me, not Fred, 'cos he never remembers stuff like this!"

Will pretended to shout but kept his voice down,

"WHAT WERE YOU DRINKING LAST NIGHT? Was it too much Whiskey?"

"It's this fantastically awful, green, verging on addictive, slimy stuff called FunGryp." Frank rubbed his head, "It takes your consciousness and sluices it down the sewer of your digestive system – a wild ride!"

"We'll get a couple of bottles in, sometime when you've got a spare week to recover." Fred wrinkled his nose,

"You can get alcohol and hallucinogen free varieties, but where's the fun in that! Anyway, enough of our pain. So how did you get on with the Drones?"

Will looked slightly annoyed,

"Eddie got the hang of it quicker than me, but we did have a lot of fun with them. Although I have to confess, he beat me in combat. But only by twenty to eighteen. My rotors got damaged, so I reckon that's why I got beaten."

Eddie laughed,

"Yeah, I'm not sure your sad story is entirely plausible. On the other hand, I'm sure 21st Century materials are going to be able to cope with more than us banging them about. Not like our poor dear departed Tin Triangle!"

Fred looked quite sympathetic,

"Yeah, I'm sorry you lost your ride, but I think we've got something categorically cool parked up outside for you. It should compensate for your loss and make you feel a whole lot better."

Out on the tarmac, in front of the aircraft hangers, it was still the same time of day and still dreary. It was odd though, the temperature was the same, but there was no wind, and the drizzle had stopped. Although thinking about it, maybe it hadn't been drizzling before. Perhaps being in Meta-Time meant raindrops would have been suspended in the air if it had been raining. But, thoughts about the weather were erased entirely when they saw what was parked outside the hangar doors.

A black cube, about twenty feet in each direction, was hovering six inches off the ground. At first sight, it appeared utterly matt black, but then, it somehow looked glossy. It seemed all the colour of the world around the cube was being sucked in towards it. Like it was there, but not quite. Eddie and Will were thoroughly fascinated.

Frank was intrigued by their reaction,

"Now it's my turn to be confused. Doesn't it scare you more than anything you've seen in your life?"

Eddie and Will both replied,

"Nope... not much... it doesn't look scary... it's only a black cube."

Fred looked concerned,

"I totally think we're destined to re-educate these two. But, mind you, if you've never previously seen a rattle-snake, you might think it was a large worm!"

Frank nodded in complete agreement,

"Where we come from, if you see a black cube hurtling towards you in space, you should be scared. It's likely to be critically dangerous cybernetic organisms, the sort of beings capable of amalgamating themselves into the minds and bodies of sentient creatures. This is the time to hit 'the big red hyperspace panic button', go for 'Jammer Time' on the Prismorphic cloaking and get the hell out of there. It's supposed to emulate something totally terrifying. Countless creatures emulate others. Like a Home-Earth hoverfly emulates a wasp, or on Other Earth OEF1EA, the opposite, a Germarine Fly tries to make itself as nice looking as Grykelord Fly. I'm disappointed. We've spent two days of blood, sweat and tears to convert this for you, and all we get is 'that looks nice', like it was a small pot plant. Well, hopefully, this bit will impress you!"

Fred held out a humble obsidian teardrop which fitted snuggly into the palm of his hand. On one face were four icons carved into the surface. There was a square, a triangle, a circle and a cross, like a black version of the Swiss flag.

Will took it in his hand,

"Well, this looks pretty. Is it a pendant?"

Fred looked on the edge of being cross,

"Now they're impressed! This is just the remote control for something we call 'central locking'. Twenty years from now, all earth cars are going to work like this. And you're holding it upside down, you bloody Neanderthals!" Then Fred laughed, "Press the triangle!"

There was a short high-pitched bleep from the cube. Small yellow lights on each of the corners flashed once. Then smoothly and without any noise, the top part of the cube suddenly split into three triangles folding over, as if on hinges, like car ferry bow doors, but on three sides. Within thirty seconds, the cube was now a large triangle shape. Approximately forty feet wide, about the same long and around ten feet high. However, with the surface being so dark, it was hard to estimate if it was massive and a long way away or tiny and up close.

Fred now looked pleased,

"You used to fly a 'Tin Triangle', Welcome to your 'Diamond Delta', the latest in medium-range shuttlecraft."

Will was highly impressed and started to walk around it,

"This is sooo smooth. So, is all this made of diamond?"

Frank snorted, almost with derision, but held back,

"No, nothing as soft as diamond. Metallic Glass is a material woven by 'Nano-bots'. It's a spun liquid mix of Graphene and Palladium micro-alloy. Here is the most durable and lightest known material, on or off the planet for at least the next 3000 years. Making spare parts is a breeze. You can buy the thread on a roll. Some people call these shuttles 'Graphite Gliders', but we prefer 'Diamond Deltas'. We've named them in your honour. If I've got the phrase right in your contemporary Cockney language," which Frank tried to emulate, "We think you are 'Diamond Geezers'? Also, you are the first pilots of Delta shaped aircraft we've met."

Will particularly liked the idea of being a 'Diamond Geezer'! Eddie however thought 'geezer' meant an old witch and was about to mention this when something else caught his eye.

They had all walked entirely around the silently hovering black triangle, and by this time, Eddie was puzzled,

"Where's the door, and why are there no windows?"

Fred pointed at the controller,

"You won't need windows. It's equipped with Tweezer Veezer 128K flexible monitor screens. You'll see in a minute. Press the circle icon to open the bow-gate."

Will pressed the circular icon, and the larger triangle lifted again. This time, a broad rectangular line of light appeared and what they could only describe as a landscape picture frame emerged from the fixed inner face of the craft. At almost ten feet high and twenty feet wide, the whole surface glowed for a moment and then the centre panel dissolved to reveal the inside of the craft. It appeared to be split into two parts. First, a complex storage area towards what they assumed was the vessel's front, with a pair of sliding doors separating an area to the back. As they approached, there was a swishing sound, much like the doors on the TV space series, which had been first broadcast a year ago.

Frank looked proud,

"It doesn't need to make that noise. We only added it because we thought it might make you feel more at home!"

"Wow!" Now, Will was hugely impressed. Behind the sliding bulkhead doors was an exact duplicate of their Vulcan cockpit.

Fred was now much happier,

"It's perfect in every detail. We've even added the chewing gum under the right seat if you wanted it for later. This bit was hard. Trying to find butadiene-based synthetic plastic for you to chew on from suppliers in our era is quite a challenge."

Eddie looked at Will,

"You are disgusting!" Will looked somewhat abashed,

"Well, there's no bin, and I don't like to swallow it. And anyway, we were flying too fast to open the window! Mind you, I didn't know chewing gum was made of plastic, yuk!"

Eddie was probably the most surprised,

"Is this a UFO, or is it something secret the Americans have been working on. We'd heard stories of triangular craft being seen over Rendlesham Forest and Nellis Airport at Groom Lake?"

Frank shook his head,

"This isn't American. This is the 'Doctor McCoy', er… no… this is the 'Real McCoy!' The Americans HAVE been working on this technology for a while, but this isn't cheap knock-off reverse engineering from some crash wreckage – sorry – no offence!"

ZUKANN
OPTIC:

SCAN ME
E059A

Not Rocket Science

"Time Tech and FENDER had been investigating rumours for some time of a black-ops Pentagon program possibly having been set up near Dulce, New Mexico. Intelligence indicated a group was collaborating with the Hagura. Certainly, something was operating there, a few degrees away from reality (a displacement of 0.72 HVaft by my calculations). However, if it is there, its security has made it so well protected, no one has been able to get close - yet! Discussions are underway to review and engage the assistance of both Eddie and Will at some time in the future to pursue this matter. To answer the question more accurately, UFOs are not unidentified. We know exactly who they are. They are all from the future and all associated, somehow with The STRAND. However, it's unclear how, and I'm not sure I should be giving you this level of detail now, so apologies for this. The saucer craft belonged to the Short Greys, and the Delta Craft were the Tall Greys. In reality, they are not spacecraft. Only shuttlecraft, hopping over to the moon and back. It's a long story for later. We'll get Ruby to authorise giving you access to the records about the Apollo 10 mission. Sorry, I went on a bit there. Back to the task at hand."

To discover more, please select this ZUKANN OPTIC

Will took the opportunity to interrupt,

"So, we know what most of the shapes on the remote fob do. Before I start pressing any more buttons and end up crashing our new ride in the kitchen, behind the 'BistroMatic Gourmetron'. What does the cross-shape do?"

It was now Fred's turn to look proud,

"This is my idea! It controls the whole craft from outside at a walking pace. Here you have forwards, backwards, slide sideways left and right. It's precisely what you need when parking in tight spaces. Like when you're in 'cube storage mode' on a bulk transport star freighter, or you're hitching a lift from an 'Annihilator Class'

Destiny Destroyer or when you're at the supermarket."

Will loved the idea he could take this craft to Sainsbury's and do some shopping. Then, they could pop down to Woolworth's and buy some pick and mix!

"One quick and, hopefully, sensible question. Why does this hover six inches off the floor? Why doesn't it land?"

"Ahh, an eminently sensible question" Fred liked the detailed questions. "Partly, we don't want to scratch the paint, as when we're flying, it's the only side people will see. Also, we don't want to squish any sentient life forms. Some of them are quite small. Your Earth ants are surprisingly bright, and they're getting more intelligent. When you travel, you'll be issued with boots which never quite touch the ground. No one will spot you hovering. We're quite environmentally conscious and socially responsible in the future!"

Will nodded and smiled. He wasn't entirely sure he was getting a sensible answer or if he was being ever-so slightly patronised. If the material this was made of was so resilient, were you ever going to scratch the paint?

Frank was keen for Will and Eddie to go for a test flight,

"Come on, Gents, assume the positions. There's a couple more points I need to cover."

Eddie and Will began to strap themselves in. Eddie looked slightly worried,

"I've got so many questions, like we appear to be facing the back of the craft. How are we going to fly backwards? And what about flight suits, helmets, flight plans, safety checks, flying surface checks?"

Frank looked serious for a moment,

"All fundamentally important questions. Let me start with the first one. You'll see on the instrument panel, directly above your engine fire indicator buttons, there's an extra panel with the same buttons as your remote fob. Press the triangle button."

Behind them, you could see the bow doors closing. The sliding bulkhead doors slid with a swishing sound. Previously in their Vulcan, small, expensive gold-tinted windows above the instrument panel, had given a somewhat restricted view of the world. Here it was panoramic. They could see everything behind their heads, above and below them. At their feet, obscured slightly by the rudder control pedals, they could clearly see the tarmac. It was as if all of the cockpit surfaces had become transparent. With the doors closed behind them, where there would be at least three flight crew, there was a silky-smooth bulkhead. It felt exactly like the best flight simulator they had ever sat in.

Frank continued to explain,

"Our 'Diamond Delta' can fly and behave literally the same way as your original Vulcan, with some key differences. You don't need the additional three crew members as you won't carry weapons. All the electronics and navigations systems are automatic with voice control. The entire surface of Home Earth is mapped to within ten square feet. You only need three words extracted from a ZUKANN enabled device. Clearly ask, 'What three words will get us to our target destination' then specify the altitude and date. You can follow the navigation guidance or ask for autopilot control and step into the other side of the bulkhead to make yourself a coffee."

Eddie came back to the point about flying backwards, but Frank reassured him,

"It's OK. There's inertial dampers and artificial gravity. So you could be upside down and not feel it. However, if you want, you can apply a level of synthetic inertia, so you can feel like you are flying forward.

"On the left side of the pilot's chair and the right side of the co-pilot, you'll see the same left stick you had on the drone. Press the red button beside the stick, and all the controls behave EXACTLY the same as the drone. This means you will be able to stop in mid-air with the added benefit of your rudder controls, allowing you to roll the craft as fast or as slow as you like in either direction. This is particularly useful if you need to dock with a space station with a rotational gravity field or match the spin of an astronaut doing a spacewalk. In addition, the left stick will duplicate your throttle controls and allow 360° directional orientation.

Will raised an eyebrow,

"Does the 'S' button do what I think it does?"

Fred nodded,

"Too right it does! You've got to have a 'Sports' button, but I don't think you're going to need it. There's also a panoramic sunroof in the back compartment if you want to sit in the sun whilst taking a break. You can even sit out on top quite safely. The Delta has got a 'field effect' safety rail to stop you from slipping off if you fancy some sunbathing or a bit of sky surfing! We've even installed a HiFi with MP3 and Bluetooth, so you can listen to your favourite surfing music at the same time."

Will began to sound quite enthused,

"I don't quite understand half of what you just said, but I do fancy a bit of surfing. Is the record player in the back? I bet in the future you can make really tiny records? Will we need to have one of these MP3s fitted to our teeth? Hey, forget that. Does it have a Sony Umatic? I saw one at an electronics show last year, it would be great to record TV programmes whilst we're working. I missed the *Morecambe and Wise Christmas Show* last year because I was flying. I bet we'll end up missing it this year too!"

Frank laughed,

"Don't worry, we can sort all of this for you, and if you can't get last year's Christmas special on catch-up, we'll get you in the studio so you can see it live." Frank turned to face the bulkhead and said, "Seating for two". Two flight seats emerged from the bulkhead as if they had grown like a time-lapse flower blooming from nowhere. Sitting down, he said, "Let's go fly this kite!"

Fred and Frank were both looking forward to this. They had worked extremely hard for the last couple of days, so they had earned their trip to the 25th Century last night with Ruby. But, of course, completing the modifications to the Delta to suit Eddie and Will actually happened next week as far as the two pilots were concerned. Commercial time travel is such an odd thing.

Will and Eddie had both tried giving up being surprised and amazed by the things they had been hearing and seeing over the past few days. How seats could grow out of a wall, why you needed blue teeth to listen to records and how you might run to catch up with a TV program was a complete mystery. Some things made total sense, but they had got to the point where if you told them how the whole of Greek Mythology was probably true, or the universe would explode if you met yourself time travelling, they would have simply accepted it.

"Engine start," said Eddie to Will. Before Will could even react, the familiar whine of the engine start sequence could be heard with the recognizable vibrations through their seats, Eddie's voice command having been recognised by the onboard systems. Eddie raised his eyebrows in surprise.

Within minutes they were back over the North Sea. This time there were no alarms and no disturbing noises. In fact, there was not much noise at all. Looking down, Eddie could see the fishing boat that they had flown over a few days ago. Or was it hours ago? It was all spread out below them like a huge model. The fishermen were in almost the same location, frozen in time, on a sea with frozen waves and presumably frozen fish. For Eddie, it was a strange experience, and yet he felt so much at home. Will was enjoying the ride. He had his feet up on the dashboard.

ZUKANN OPTIC:

E061A

SCAN ME
E061A

Facial Hatred

Meeting yourself in time is dangerous, but not for the reasons commonly considered. If you think about it for a moment, you may be like so many other people, not being able to stand the sound of your own voice. Imagine being able to see your own backside or the way your hairdresser or barber had ACTUALLY cut your hair. You never usually get a chance to see the back of your head correctly in the mirror. There would come a period in the future when special mirrors would generate an image of the back of your head. You would be able to be shown what you wanted to see, not what was actually there.

You humans and plenty of other creatures, like flies and kittens, are physically and emotionally wired for pathological self-hatred. In all probability, you are likely to attack your own reflection in mirrors if it appeared realistic. You are doomed to dislike yourselves in such a way, you become a predatorial threat. We call it Autogenous Animosity. There's even been one case where a man stabbed himself to death in a drunken bar fight, having met himself in time.

To discover more, please select this ZUKANN OPTIC.

CHAPTER 14
A Bit Of Social Climbing

The Climbing Wall:
1600 (GMT), Saturday December 12th 1970 /
1013 (MGMT), Tuesday December 8th 1970

Arti and Ruby looked up from the meeting they'd been having, planning the Vulcan Bomber's recovery. Both smiled as the others walked into Arti's office. This was going to be fun.

Both Eddie and Will had been flying the Diamond Delta and had thoroughly enjoyed themselves. They had both become very adept in a short space of time thanks to the efforts of Frank and Fred, who had also come along. Partly because it was always great to see someone else fall off Arti's Dragon Wall.

Arti beckoned them all towards the door at the back of her office,

"So, have you all come for a climb or have you come for some vicarious entertainment?"

For Ruby, Frank and Fred, it was clearly the latter. For Will and Eddie, it was a reminder of their basic training. They had both had the same pretty near-psychotic Physical Training Instructor, who could run, climb and jump better than anyone. The Lance Corporal held the record for crossing the assault course. He took great pleasure in showing the new recruits how he could climb up and run across the top of the monkey bars. This would doubtless mean injury or death for anyone who didn't know what they were doing.

Arti reached a couple of items off a shelf,

"First things first – safety! Put these on. They fit like the kind of straps you would use if you'd sprained your wrist. These reach a bit further up your arm. Inside is a safety line which pays out and retracts as you need it."

Will looked surprised,

"I thought future civilizations would have traction beams and stuff like that. This line looks no thicker than cotton?"

Arti nodded,

"You are right; we will have 'traction beams' and flying cars and jet suits, so you can fly to work with your briefcase under your arm. However, power IS an issue.

"In a few years, when power is not a major headache, we'll use devices called Collimated DocSmith optical safety tethers. The problem here in 1970 is the limitations of the recharging capability, so we're going with the 'old-school' D-CaMPP. What it's made from is a bit of a mouthful. It's Ductile Carbon Monofilament Palladium Polymer alloyed with Callisto Oceanic Spider silk. Two hundred years from now, they'll be hanging space elevators from it, so it's virtually impossible to break."

Previously, both Eddie and Will had been unable to have fun on a climbing wall. However, although it had been a while, what they had learned started to come back to them quite quickly. Neither their strength nor their agility was quite what it had been in their younger days, but they were able to enjoy it far more.

What they'd not previously experienced, was the joys of the safety line made of spider silk. It was easily strong enough to carry their weight. Will could soon demonstrate his ability to winch himself up and down the full height of the climbing wall, singing the theme tune to the cartoon series *Spiderman* whilst he did. The irony of the song's words being written by a man whose surname was 'Webster' was utterly lost on him.

After a couple of hours of challenging each other to increasingly arduous and dangerous climbs on the dragon wall's 'Ripping Flesh' and 'Knight Killer' settings, Arti's WOTDISC buzzed. A message appeared on her screen.

Looking at her wrist and with some resignation in her voice, she said,

"Looks like we're all needed for a progress update briefing in the MAMBA Room."

Mark, Rina, Haji and Alba Wonstein, were already drinking coffee in the MAMBA room as Will and Eddie followed Frank, Fred, Ruby and Arti into the room.

Mark was getting ZUKANN to prepare the surveillance footage and looked up,

"Perfect timing, two of you look like you need a break. I bet the rest of you have been watching the entertainment and relaxing? Have Eddie and Will been beaten to a pulp by the 'Hydra' setting, or did you let them off that little treat?"

Arti smiled mischievously,

"You know you like the maximum setting if only to get sympathy when you get a rear-end toasting!"

Mark tilted his head to one side,

"Well, do let me know when someone beats my time. I know I only stayed on for eleven seconds but taking second place to your record makes all the pain worthwhile! I don't know how anyone stays on as long as four minutes and thirty-seven seconds!

"Oh, by the way, Haji's got the Gourmetron to generate fresh Vegan Donuts. They're fantastic. Leo Frankovitz found this place in Berlin. Do you know how he talks in code sometimes? It was odd; he called it his 'supplier finders battle'. Apparently, they set up a 4D target pad for the matter transporter and said we could use the fresh-post feature. So, help yourselves; there's probably one each left."

Alba Wonstein had totally consumed the attention of Eddie and Will, who had never seen a seven-foot-tall woman before. Never mind her height, she had the physique of an Olympic weightlifter and hair even redder than Ruby's. To Will, she was an Amazonian dressed like she'd just left the gym with the look of a comic book superhero; and more skin visible than he was used to seeing away from a tropical beach, which was also a strangely bright orange. For the rest of the team, this was regular daywear for a Fab000lian Warrior.

Alba didn't need asking twice when it came to Vegan food. She was already halfway through her doughnut when she stopped long enough to ask,

"Come on then, show us the drone footage; we need to see where Eddie and Will's plane has ended up. Arti and Ruby can't give me a proper recovery plan until we can see how much mess there is." Unfortunately, the end of the sentence was somewhat distorted by another mouthful of doughnut.

She turned to Eddie and Will, wiping sugar from her hands, then extending one in Will's direction,

"Sorry Gents, we've not been introduced… oops, sorry, shouldn't talk with my mouth full… I'm Alba."

Will and Eddie each nervously held out a hand of greeting. Will concerned it might get crushed by this towering beauty, whilst Eddie was in awe, being taken back to meeting his six-foot-tall primary teacher, Miss Theresa, on his first day at school.

Mark set the drone footage to appear on the screens,

"We've sent two lots of drones back to the last known location at Lake Calima, but all we get back are lovely shots of what looks like a beautiful lake and a lot of pristine forest. There doesn't look like there's any damage or wreckage anywhere. Even if the plane had hit the lake, there would be some floating remains. We know the fuel tanks ruptured, so at least you'd expect to see some oil or smoke on the water. Ruby and Rina, if you're OK with this, I think it's best we, or should I say YOU, go and take a look?"

Ruby nodded,

"No problem. Eddie, Will and I can go on a little scavenger hunt. Come on, keep your climbing gear on; you might need it."

CHAPTER 15
Welcome To The Jungle

Colombia:
1013 Colombia Time (COT), Tuesday December 8th 1013 /
1013 (MGMT), Tuesday December 8th 1970

It was mid-morning in Colombia, as the rain stopped, and the clouds parted briefly, blown by the usual strong winds across Calima Lake and back up towards the mountains. The sun shone down, creating sparkles in the surface ripples. It wasn't a vast lake now, although it would be one day. Despite being winter, it was a more comfortable 23 centigrade, but still quite humid for the small troop of Red Howler Monkeys gathering at the waters' edge, drinking and grooming each other.

Tiny, extremely poisonous Cauca Frogs wriggled in the damp undergrowth of mouldy leaves beneath the forest floor. Thousands of Monarch Butterflies, roosting on shrubbery, opened their wings to the warmth of the sun.

A group of about thirty dark grey Pava Caucana birds had discovered a wide trail of army ants. They were feasting on these insects, who were oblivious to being under threat. It had been like this in winter for thousands of years. It might have been the year 1013, but it would look like this for at least the next 950 years. This year, the only difference was, 1500 feet above the Howler Monkeys, a grey, mostly triangular shape hovered. It moved slowly, roughly in line with the edge of the lake, gently rotating as if a child's windmill was blowing slowly in the wind.

About a mile away in the distance, and quite normal for this time of year was a gentle clap of thunder. Immediately afterwards, and very unusual, was the sound of loud music. Reminiscent of 20th Century surfing safari, California Surf Rock Psychedelia, it could be heard rapidly approaching the hovering grey triangle shape. The Howler Monkeys howled and scattered. The dark grey ant-eating birds dashed into the forest, and all along the lake, the butterflies closed their wings.

"Will, please! Can you turn that music OFF! The external entertainment system is still engaged. This is supposed to be a covert operation. There's no point being Prismorphed if we can be heard 60 miles away!"

"Sorry Ruby, I forgot it was on outside as well. We'll be fine; there's only going to be animals in the jungle. I still haven't quite got the hang of getting music without a record player, but you've got to admit, Fred and Frank did a great job with the sound system!" Will turned the music off and looked ahead down the lake. Eddie was deftly guiding the 'Diamond Delta' towards the clearly damaged Vulcan. It was inexplicably still hovering in mid-air, with a part of one wing flopping over every time the wreckage rotated.
Eddie's forehead furrowed,

"At least we know where the wreckage ended up, and we're not having to go for a swim to pick up the pieces. Looks like we made an *Italian Job* out of that. Look at the size of the hole. We blew more than just the bloody doors off!"

The Vulcan was hovering at around 1500 feet, the height it had been at RAF North Coates. A huge hole could be seen in the bomb bay extending into the root of the badly burned starboard wing. The damage was clearly destabilising the structural integrity of the Elevon wing control surface, making it flap like an injured sparrow. Jagged edges could be seen around the periphery of where the sphere of the Casimir Event Horizon had met the fuselage, the damage having been caused when the nuclear missile was sucked back down the SlipStream duct into the decontamination bay under Covenham Reservoir.

As they flew closer, Eddie could see engine number three was not far from entirely missing, and engine number four was cut open like a cross-sectional educational diagram. The combustion chamber and main high-pressure shaft, with fan blades, could be seen bent back like the peelings of an orange. He smiled for a moment. In all the chaos of the ejection he'd forgotten how, a few seconds after blowing the cockpit canopy, the emergency life-raft would be automatically deployed. It was still there, bright yellow and incongruously dangling out of the side of the open cockpit, dancing on the end of a long safety line as the wreckage rotated.

Ruby turned the edge of her WOTDISC in the direction of the floating wreck and tapped the screen a few times,

"It looks like the plane is stuck on the extreme edge of a SlipStream event, very close to collapse. This looks highly precarious…. hang on a moment, Gents, I've got a great idea. This delta is fitted with a light bridge. The Greys have been known to use them to access commercial aircraft's fuselage whilst still in flight. We can approach the plane from the rear, sit a few feet short of the wing, and extend the bridge up to the bomb bay rear hatches. The only downside is that we can't use the light bridge AND stay hidden.

Eddie wasn't too keen on the idea of being stood on an invisible diving board at 1500 feet. He didn't even like jumping off the ten-foot-high board at the swimming pool and hoped Will would volunteer for this challenge.

Ruby continued,

"We'll need to be quick. Partly to reduce the chance of being seen and also to dodge the wings as they rotate round. Mind you, looking at the jungle, the only things watching us are parrots. Once in the bomb bay, moving about should be reasonably easy. Our boots will adhere to anything, including the aluminium alloy body panels. You can't beat footwear made by Cling-Ons the Bootmakers!"

Looking across at the Vulcan, there was a loud thud as the damaged wing rotated over, dropping a few more mangled engine blades, cogs and tangled wire into the shallows of the lake.

Ruby paused, thinking again for a moment,

"OK, so the original plan was to find the wreckage, gather it into a pile and place a Tessalon locator beacon on top of the pile to return it home. Being so complete, we cannot mess with the timestream and send the parts back shuffled. It has to hit the ground as if it never left mainstream time. Instead, we'll tag the inside of the bomb bay with Duron Cameras. They can be tracked like Tessalon Beacons. If we tag them to the inner surfaces of the bomb bay, a bit like the faces of a dice, we will be able to know which way was 'up' when retrieving the wreckage. We can then SlipStream it back to the crash site, and it can fall precisely as it would have done without being sent back nearly 1000 years."

There was another bang from engine number four and for a few moments, a fire reignited with some quite dense smoke drifting in the breeze towards the front of the aircraft away from them.

Ruby frowned looking at the smoke and the wind direction,

"We'll be fine vision-wise. Duron Cameras can see in all light conditions and realities. They adhere to any surface and then phase shift or 'displace' to a location slightly outside of the current temporal space. It makes them invisible and indetectable without a WOTDISC, so they won't be found in the wreckage, and then they can be recovered later. They are near-on indestructible, with the added advantage being we'll be able to wave at Eddie, who can watch us on the flight deck."

Eddie breathed a sigh of relief when Will replied.

"This looks straightforward enough. Looking down this reminds me of *David Attenborough* when he filmed the *Land Divers of Pentecost*. There were young men jumping off a sixty-foot-high tower with vines tied to their ankles. Arti Ping got us up on her rocking-and-pitching dragon climbing wall, which looks easier than this. If we can get close, we can fire one of those D-CaMPP climbing tethers Arti showed us, into the bomb bay, so even if I slip I'm not going to fall. I need to get a look at how this light bridge works first. Eddie, are you OK with getting us close?"

Eddie nodded,

"Getting you close is easy; now I know what I'm doing. This Diamond Delta craft is a lovely ride. It's sad, but I won't be sorry to see the back of the old 'Tin Triangle' over there. What worries me right now, is how the wind might be affecting the wreckage. Let's get cracking so you can 'tag and bag' her from the inside."

Ruby was looking confident again,

"Eddie, you get us close; I'll get the front trilateral open and extend the light bridge. Then, Will and I can take a closer look before committing to a jump. Hopefully, to give a bit of certainty, you'll be able to keep an eye on us. Just ask the screens to display Duron Cameras D1 to D6."

Will shook his head slightly,

"You know Ruby, in all of this, I still can't quite get my head around the fact, the back of the Delta flight deck is actually the front, and we're always facing backwards when we're flying. It seems fine when we're in the cockpit; it's when we're disembarking I get confused."

Ruby smiled,

"I know what you mean. I can't fly a Delta, but it does feel odd. The only time I ever travel backwards is when I'm on an old train. I took the L-Zero from Tokyo to Osaka once and travelled backwards all the way. It was tediously slow, but it was nice to get a chance to see the countryside. Come on, let me show you this light bridge."

Ruby pressed the 'Circle' icon on the central locking. What had been the wall, opposite the sliding doors in the compartment behind the flight deck, suddenly glowed a gentle yellow and began to dissolve. They could start to see the 'front' trilateral section of the Diamond Delta hinging upwards and out of sight. Ruby then pressed a button on a control panel to the side of the opening, with a red 'X' symbol you might see on a swimming pool warning sign, instructing you not to dive. The icon faded to display a longer diving board with a green tick beside it.

Ruby put her serious face on again as she looked at Will.

"Flight suits and helmets are mandatory. You know it's going to be pretty cold at this height, even if it is warm at ground level, and it's windy. So we've duplicated your RAF flight gear but modified the helmet. It's like your PIMMS wrist device. There's an hour of air stored within a bacterial Kaison filtration system capable of removing all the nasty stuff, so you can breathe safely."

Will turned the helmet over trying to work out how an hour of air could be fitted into the helmet, without it looking any different.

Ruby saw Will trying to spot air cylinders.

"Everything's Prismorphed into the padding. Any impurities in the air can be filtered out and stored at the back of the helmet in a Reduction Bank for later sanitation and removal.

Placing her hand flat on the wall, a small panel materialised, drawn outwards as if Ruby's hand was magnetic. It folded down to reveal a small chrome tap-like spout which she placed a hand underneath. Automatically a measured translucent gloop was dispensed into her palm,

"We don't know what kind of bugs we may pick up here, and we don't want to leave any of our own to decimate the local wildlife, so get a squirt of the hand-gel now AND when you get back.

Ruby grinned, reached up to the ceiling and pulled down a red helmet which emerged like a drip of water,

"I've printed out my own. The white ones are a bit boring, so I've got one to match my hair!" She touched another icon which looked like a windscreen demister switch, and the semi-transparent wall went completely clear. Like a distant large waterfall, the wind became audible, and the screeching monkeys could be heard in the forest below. A gently glowing orange bridge could be seen between the new opening and the rotating Vulcan wreckage. The pathway was comfortably wide at around four feet, although translucent, like a gloriously coloured wrapper from within a tin of quality chocolates. One of the Vulcan's wings passed through it every few seconds as though it wasn't there at all.

Ruby noticed Will's look of caution and spoke reassuringly,

"It is a bit strange. We can see through it, although to the eyes of the Greys, it would seem as solid as a rock as they have different eyesight to ours. I'll go first. It looks like the SlipStream punched quite a hole in the fuselage. Aim the laser pointer of your safety line at that first spar. It's also a good job we've got no gas cylinders at this end of the bay, the anchor hook would go straight through it. There's enough damage without us adding to it! I'm glad we made the size of hole we did when extracting the payload, the bomb bay looks even smaller when you see it from over here!"

Will raised his eyebrows,

"Sorry, next time I'll make sure I'm flying one of those new Jumbo Jet planes Pan Am started flying last January. You know, they've even got an upstairs! We'll need to crouch again, good job we've got our helmets on!"

Ruby passed three Duron Cameras to Will,

"Here, clip these to your belt. I'll take the front and sides; you take the rear, top and bottom. It's a shame it's rotating, it looks like we're somehow out of Meta-Time here. We'll feel like we're in a slow-moving washing machine."

Pointing at Will's feet, she reminded him,

"Don't worry, you're wearing Cling-Ons, so you'll stick like a fly, and as you start to feel like you might fall, the safety line will tighten and pull you in. This thread has got even more strength than your boots!"

There was a 'doof' sound of compressed air as Ruby fired her safety line. The starboard wing had risen, passing the light bridge, revealing the gaping hole in the wing root and the bomb bay. A few quick steps along the walkway; a balletic step onto the sliced open edge of the fuselage and a jump down into the bomb bay and Ruby was safely over.

She looked round and shouted,

"When you're ready!"

The wreckage continued on with its gentle rotation. There was not enough time for Will to make the leap. It felt like an eternity waiting for the port wing to rise up past the light bridge and the Vulcan to assume the recumbent position, like a dying bird on its back on a vet's operating table. The reality was it took hardly more than ten seconds.

The starboard wing rode into view, followed by Ruby's voice from the inside of the bomb bay,

"Come on, Will, I'm starting to feel like a hamster in here. Time to take a leap of faith!"

The large hole appeared once more. Ruby's safety line could be seen stretching down inside the fuselage, with Ruby having to take backward steps to be able to see Will stood on the light bridge. Will fired at the same spot Ruby had hit. So accurate was his aim that it ricocheted off Ruby's anchor and went slack. Will pressed the rewind button on his safety line launcher.

Ruby's head peered around the edge of the opening,

"Oh yes! So now you're going to brag about being such a good shot with a safety line; you can hit another anchor at thirty feet. Stop mucking about and pick another spar to aim at!"

The plane continued to rotate, the port wing reappearing under the light bridge and sweeping through it. Will got ready to take aim again. The starboard wing came into view. There appeared to be a few more bits dropping off and worryingly, it seemed to be a bit more flexible than it had been.

Again, the hole began to align with the light bridge, and Will fired his safety line once more. A perfect hit! Will took a leap off the light bridge and into the bomb bay, just clipping the top of his helmet on the way. In the semi-darkness, Ruby was stooping and walking away from him, looking over her shoulder.

"Ahh, at last, the wanderer returns." Ruby smiled but with a slight look of concern. "We should be quick, I'm starting to hear some ominous creaking and metal tearing sounds. At least you made it. I'm beginning to feel like an old woman walking along here, trying to stop hitting my head like you did just then! Crouch and walk. I'll take the front end; you take the back. Hi Eddie!" Ruby had flicked a switch on the Duron Camera and gave a wave to the unseen observer in the Delta craft thirty feet away, before crab-walking towards the front of the plane.

Eddie started to see more steady images. Initially, as the cameras had been attached to belts, most of what he could see was feet, hands and sky. It was slightly disturbing looking through the translucent light bridge. It was only 1500ft, but it looked a long way down. If you fell without a parachute, it would probably only be ten seconds before hitting the trees.

Fortunately, as Ruby and Will fixed the cameras, he started to better understand what was happening in the bomb bay. He could see the difficulty moving around with the low headroom and the wreckage slowly turning. Will waved and grinned at one of the cameras. Eddie could see he was saying something, even though he had his helmet on, but there was no sound, and he didn't know how to turn it on. He should have thought about two-way communications.

What did worry Eddie was the state of the starboard wing. The large, badly damaged elevon looked like it was beginning to tear even more away from the wing, and there was no way he could warn them, or was there? Eddie looked at the '*Dick Tracy Watch*' PIMMS device he'd been given. He could see icons for Ruby and Will.

He tapped Will's icon and shouted, "Hello!"

On the cameras, he could see Will jump in surprise at the voice from nowhere and looked at his watch.

Will tapped it,

"Hiya Eddie, how's it going over there? We're about done here."

Over Will's shoulder, Eddie could see Ruby working her way back up the bomb bay,

"It's a bit like watching *Spiderman* with you two hanging by your feet from the ceiling every time the 'plane rotates. It's not looking too clever on the outside, the starboard wing is looking perilously fragile. No sightseeing, get yourselves back quickly... er... over and out."

Ruby's face appeared behind Will's on the communicator, a kindly look on her face,

"Signing off isn't necessary. The system's smart enough to know when you've finished talking. We're on our way back now."

Will turned to Ruby,

"Go on, ladies first. I'm not overdoing the chivalry; I simply want to pick up the tips. You seem to be a bit better than me on this flying assault course!"

Ruby raised an eyebrow and tipped her head forward sarcastically,

"Oh yeah, I know what you 20th Century flyboys are like. You want to take a look at my backside!" Will looked slightly embarrassed, and Ruby grinned. "Only kidding. Now, remember the green button. One press slackens the safety line. A double press releases the anchor point so you can reel it in when you're back on the light bridge. See you on the next rotation!"

Ruby looked up and saw the increasingly-floppy starboard wing hinge overhead, lifting above the light bridge, a disturbing harmony of, grinding and cracking like tinder. She stepped confidently out and down onto the translucent surface without a hitch, turned and double-clicked the green button on the safety line. She watched the line and anchor bolt fling themselves out of the bomb bay and swiped right inside her sleeve. Waving for Will to follow, she turned and headed back to the Delta.

Will braced himself for one final turn of the Tin Triangle tumble-dryer. He looked out of the gaping hole left by the SlipStream extraction of the bomb and realised he was starting to get dizzy. It was far harder this way round. The sun passed overhead in the way a speeded-up time-traveller might see it from an H.G. Wells-style, time machine every time the Vulcan lay prone on its back. The plane continued turning and was nearly the right way up. The light bridge would soon be coming into view. He stepped out. His timing was perfect. Straight onto the light bridge. He could see Ruby was back inside the Delta, and through the open sliding bulkhead doors, he could see the back of Eddie's head and the images of the cameras back in the bomb bay.

There was a tug at Will's wrist,

"Of course," he thought, "The safety line!" Will turned and pressed the green button twice. Nothing happened. The safety line started paying out further as it began to wrap around the fuselage. He double-clicked the button again, still nothing. The port wing swung into view, and he half stepped back and to one side as it passed almost entirely through the light bridge.

The line was still paying out, and the jagged edges of the damaged starboard wing were rapidly approaching. Will frantically tried to drag the safety line from his wrist. Still, it wouldn't release. The line had now gone completely around the fuselage. Will wondered for a moment how long the line would get when it suddenly went tight. His boots no longer having the strength to adhere to the surface of the light bridge, he was dragged off his feet.

The safety line snagged on the serrated edge of the broken wing. Headfirst, Will fell off the bridge and started to swing under the floating wreckage, the safety-line caught firmly on the wing. Colliding with twisted metal, his helmet was ripped from his head and sent into the abyss below.

It took a moment to recover from the concussion, 'No problem,' he thought. He would be like a needle attached to the end of a cotton reel around the fuselage and be pulled back over the top. He could then release himself and make a jump back the bridge. He would just have to be careful not to head-butt anything else.

But Will hadn't accounted for the wreckage still being stuck in the event horizon of a Casimir portal. In less than a second, the wing met the edge of the event horizon, and as if shaking hands with the sharpest scissors in the universe, the safety line split, and he was free-falling.

Ruby and Eddie watched in horror as Will seemed to be stuck on the edge of the light bridge. They could see he was trying to detach himself. Ruby was shouting,

"DOUBLE CLICK — QUICKLY!" But Will, apparently, could not hear her. Perhaps they were not close enough?

"STAY INSIDE!" Eddie shouted at Ruby, as he reached for the new addition to the Vulcan cockpit, the left stick, and felt around the back of it. He hoped beyond all hope this Delta had identical features to the training drones. There was a reassuring beep, and Eddie slammed the joystick over to the left.

Without any sense of inertia, the sky turned upside down. The Delta craft surged to the left in a huge and sudden arc, pulling a complete 360° sideways loop and dropping more than 500 feet.

There was a silence, then a long yell as a body wearing a flying suit hurtled through the open sunroof. The inertial dampeners automatically compensated for a fast-moving body already travelling at more than 120mph. Stopping instantaneously from such a speed should have been like experiencing fifty times normal gravity. Yet slowing down over the ten-foot height of the Delta, the body hit the flight deck with the touch of a feather, despite the loud groaning as rapid deceleration was being experienced.

Ruby took two steps forward and knelt down beside the body of Will, who sat up with a look of colossal relief on his face. He staggered to his feet, stood and wiped away the sweat now covering his ashen face.

Standing up, Ruby threw her arms around Will and engulfed him in a massive hug, pinning his arms to his sides. She then took half a step backwards and slapped him across his face with a look of such anger and fear,

"DON'T EVER DO THAT TO ME AGAIN! I thought I'd lost you!"

"Sorry," Will looked embarrassed, relieved and shocked all in one moment. "That was one hell of a wild ride!" He glanced at Eddie and closed the sliding door to the cockpit, knowing Eddie would never let him forget this next bit of detail. He whispered to Ruby, "Is there a toilet in this crate? I think I need a shower! I'm so relieved you got the flight suit 'trouser liners' right!"

Ruby pressed a button, and the bulkhead morphed to create a small cubicle. She pointed to it with a tightly gripped fist and one shaking forefinger,

"Get in there and work out how to use it yourself. I am SO angry with you!" As he closed the door behind him, Will grinned ever-so-slightly as he had after his first ejector seat training session.

Ruby shook her head angrily. There was no way she would allow herself to get involved with someone more than 300 years younger than she was, even if the chat-up lines were better than average. It wasn't simply the age gap; she could live to be 1000 years old with modern medical technology. But she was only thirty and would stay looking this age for centuries. Having lived on Europa Outpost and drunk water extracted from below the ice surface, she could live long enough to have 300 children, and this wasn't even the current Annual World Record for the year 2315.

Ruby gritted her teeth,

"I must be a complete idiot giving that man a hug!" Punching the button to re-open the sliding door to the cockpit a little too firmly, she turned to Eddie, rubbing her bruised knuckles, "He's getting changed. Sorry for shouting, I was just worried. How did you know that would work?"

Eddie shrugged his shoulders,

"I didn't know, it was just the training coming out. Fred and Frank clearly did a great job making the modifications, it was identical to the training drone. I repeated what I did to beat Will in combat. One extra thought, though... it was a good job Will had left the sunroof open...!"

Ruby took a pretend slap at the back of Eddie's head, who grinned and ducked as she shouted at him,

"Don't you start too! Come on, take us home, please!"

There was a slight whooshing sound as the Delta craft disappeared into the clouds shrouding the mountain peaks. Then, another sound like water being sucked down a drain, and the floating wreckage of a broken Vulcan bomber disappeared from the sky.

The Howler monkeys started to call from within the forest. Then, the Pava Caucana birds hiding in the shrubbery emerged to scatter the Monarch butterflies. They returned to feasting on the Army ants, just as they had for thousands of years.

A small group of hunters were sitting at the edge of the lake, watching the unfolding spectacle. They had stopped for an early lunch and were eating fruit they had gathered from the forest whilst also inspecting small engine parts from the wreckage they had found fallen onto the shore.

ZUKANN
SCAN ME
F072A

CHAPTER 16
There Was A Cow In The Field

MAMBA Room:
1600 (GMT), Saturday December 12ᵗʰ 1970 /
1013 (MGMT), Tuesday December 8ᵗʰ 1970

Arti was looking slightly more relieved as she looked around at the team having reassembled in the MAMBA room,

"Well, we've worked out why the drones couldn't see the Vulcan. They were looking in the wrong place! We were expecting to find it had crashed into the forest or the lake. But who'd have thought it would be stuck 1500 feet off the ground, and hanging off the edge of a Casimir Event Horizon? Well, we think we know why. Imagine, if you can, catching your woollen jumper on the barbed wire part of a fence, and the jumper is being stretched; the more you pull on it, the more it lengthens.

Eddie jumped in with a question, trying hard not to raise his hand.

"Did you find out why our Vulcan ended up time travelling into the past?"

Arti wrinkled her nose,

"We think we know what happened here too. We've been analysing the wreckage 'next week'. Sorry, I know this bit gets confusing. There's a titanium deflector shield in the fuselage, near the engines, in case of a catastrophic engine failure. It's been contaminated with Duron Gold, which snagged on the edge of the event horizon. This explains why you could see the entire plane hanging in mid-air. The Casimir Portal was stretched out for about 2 miles along the lake. The wreckage was so close to falling, we're keeping it in Meta-Time to maintain stability. We do now have three problems, which Alba will explain."

Will could not help being impressed as the seven-foot frame of Alba walked purposefully across the room. Physically equipped with a body like a New Zealand rugby player but with a voice similar in tone to Princess Margaret of England.

"Thank you, Arti." Alba stood next to Arti, making her look relatively short by comparison. Arti quickly sat down out of Alba's shadow.

Alba waved at the screens, which now showed three different pictures. On the first screen was the wreckage of the Vulcan bomber, frozen in time above Calima Lake in Colombia. The second showed the decontamination tank under Covenham Reservoir. A somewhat sinister-looking missile sat in a cradle, drip drying in the semi-darkness. The third showed an idyllic pastoral scene, a lovely green field with a cow grazing and North Cotes Junior School over the other side of the fence. The children could be seen playing on the school field, the grey skies overhead threatening rain.

Alba looked deadly serious,

"Because the Vulcan snagged on the event horizon, it is no longer travelling horizontally, heading out to the North Sea and the field at the end of the runway. The moment we return it to normal time, Tuesday 8th of December 1970, it will drop like a stone. We've calculated its likely trajectory, and it's the field beside the school. Children could likely be injured or even killed. Obviously, we cannot be responsible for causing this."

The room was so quiet, you could imagine hearing helium atoms collide. No one wanted this to be anything but an accident in a coastal field, but it seemed events were conspiring against them.

Alba continued,

"Simply because we haven't quite got things right, we have been given dispensation by FENDER to make Destiny alterations, and IGLOO have prepared a plan for us. Frank and Fred will SlipStream back to Sunday night and sabotage the school boiler. The Caretaker will arrive on Monday morning to discover there's no heating in the school. The Head Teacher will tell all the parents that school is cancelled until Wednesday at the earliest. This guarantees there will be no one on the school field on Tuesday morning. Mark Sparks and Leo Frankovitz will arrange to transfer the nuclear missile into the airspace at 1500 feet, central to the field. We have no choice in this, as this is where the bomber would have been located at this time if it had not slipped back to Colombia. We have a two-second window to ensure there will be no other SlipStream collisions. The wreckage will be moved back to Tuesday morning and released. Is this clear, and does anyone have any questions?"

Will leaned over to Arti and whispered,

"I don't want to sound stupid; I've heard a bit about FENDER, but what's IGLOO?"

Arti whispered back raising her eyes,

"I'll get ZUKANN to explain what they are in a bit. It's politics and power!"

There was a moment's silence, and Rina raised her finger and pointed at one of the screens,

"I've got one teensy question. What about the cow?"

Alba grimaced slightly,

"I'm sorry, Rina, it's not sentient, so FENDER has not authorized its removal."

Will raised his finger too,

"Look, we had a lot of stick this week in the Mess about killing cows. The menu was full of fake beef dishes, and every smart-arse this side of Lincoln took the mickey making mooing noises, so it would be nice to be able to do something for it. If only to give us a quiet life if we ever go back to flying."

Alba shook her head again,

"I'm sorry, the time stream has the cow being killed. There's nothing we can do. It's regretful but we don't have permission to intervene."

Frank tilted his head like he was going to dodge a flying object before saying with his signature dark humour,

"Well, it's going to be one hell of a *Smashburger*!"

Ruby and Rina both spun, turning their angry eyes on him,

"FRANK!! You are so inappropriate. How would you like it?!"

"Sorry, it was only a joke. I mean, it's not like we're all herbivores. I like a bit of protein on a barbecue now and again."

Will turned to Eddie and shook his head, smiling,

"I've no idea what a Smashburger is, so I'm keeping well out of this!"

Frank turned to Fred,

"Come on, you and I have a job to do. We're not going to have the blood of a poor defenceless cuddly smiling little dairy cow on our consciences. We certainly don't want to break any laws and get a Ten Second Judgement, even if the laws don't apply yet!" They hastily left the room and headed for their jackets and the bar in The Old Volunteer, closely followed by one of Rina's marker pens which whistled past their heads.

ZUKANN OPTIC:

SCAN ME
F074A

Legal Science

In the 25th Century, the legal system proceeds at a frenetic rate. Trials of public and celebrity suspects of criminality are watched similarly to how Formula One motor racing was viewed in the 20th Century. A lot of noise, a bit of fanfare, then it's on to the next case. Laws are decided equally swiftly. Following the Tragic Magic Roundabout Disaster, the default setting on Prismorphic Ponchos was outlawed before the ink was dry on the last Poncho off the production line. By the time the last vehicle was recovered from the disaster scene, Prismorphic Ponchos were restricted from changing without a sentient being inside.

To discover more, please select this ZUKANN OPTIC.

CHAPTER 17
Blinded By Hindsight

North Cotes Junior School:
1145 (GMT), Sunday December 6th 1970 /
1013 (MGMT), Tuesday December 8th 1970

Fred and Frank left the MAMBA room behind and walked town the white-tiled corridor, past the Gents toilets into the deserted snug of The Old Volunteer. The pub was silent apart from the sound of a few flames licking up the remnants of the logs in the fire. Anni, the cleaner, had locked up. The publican and her husband had gone to bed. Frank walked over to the bar, picked up a striped paper straw and walked over to the fireplace. Above the fireplace was a curious clock which kept great time but neither ticked nor tocked. It resembled the wing of an aeroplane. Its numerical face was shaped like a fuselage with two small fan-like nacelles, as if two engines had been added as an afterthought under the wing.

He gently inserted the paper straw into the left-hand engine. Next, he stretched over to press what looked strangely like a doorbell, mounted into the wood panelling on the left-hand side of the fireplace surround. Instantly the clock face changed. What had initially been a cross between a clock and a racing car speedometer suddenly glowed a luminous green. The printed scales initially displaying Temperatures, Pressures and Fuel Capacity suddenly revealed Days, Months, Years and a space to indicate three words for a Trip Origin. In addition, an image of the last interdimensional time traveller to arrive using the portal was displayed. Frank momentarily looked puzzled. The display showed a 'Leo Frankowitz' had recently returned from South Fork Bridge, British Columbia, 1941.

Frank turned to Fred,

"I thought the Gun Lake project had been scrapped. Do you have any idea why Leo's just returned?"

Fred looked equally puzzled,

"No idea at all, I didn't even know he'd gone. No one has booked out a WOTDISC apart from Ruby, so he's travelled alone on Electron Fabric. Bad dude! I'll bet he's been birdwatching! I'll have a chat with him when we come back, if I remember."

Frank gently pulled the striped straw out from the clock's engine nacelle, which returned to its previous appearance of a clock-cum-speedometer. Then he deftly launched the straw, like a dart, straight into the fireplace where it had a moment of flaming brightness before turning to ash.

Fred smiled,

"Great shot. I'm sure no six-year-old wants to drink cola through a straw tasting of Teslene!"

Fred pulled a cloth from his pocket as he walked up to the Gents' toilet door. He gave it a flap in the air as if a magician, conjuring a white dove into existence. The fabric went stiff, and a map of the village appeared. He adjusted the time and date to read '11:30pm, Sunday, 6th December 1970', two days before the bomber crashed into the field near the village school. Teasing the map with two fingers, it expanded to include nearby villages five to ten miles away. With some gentle adjustment, the map was resized, and the village school could clearly be seen with an outline plan of the building as if drawn by an architect.

Frank tapped the shape indicating a door at the back of the school. This was replaced by a red dot. He tapped what looked like a button, printed with the word 'Portal', and the cloth immediately went limp. Reaching out to the small round handle on the door, glazed with a rather aggrandized glass panel declaring the title 'LORDS', he turned the handle smoothly. There was a slight hum as if the handle had vibrated slightly, and he pushed slowly. No longer were the white tiles of the corridor behind the door, but now it was the cold dark exterior and damp tarmac at the rear of the school playground.

Fred and Frank emerged unseen from the school rear fire exit. The dismal dreariness of the day had extended into the night, with a fine, frigid mist verging on a drizzle adding to the misery.

Fred pointed to a fence separating the school dustbins from the rest of the playground,

"You duck down there and keep a good look-out for anyone coming. I'll go and do the stuff in the boiler house, then it's back home in no time for a late-night coffee. It's brick out here. It feels like it's going to snow, and we don't want to hang around here longer than we need to."

As Fred unlocked the boiler house door with the skeleton cloth feature of the Electron Fabric, Frank crept stealthily around the deserted playground. Out of curiosity, he lifted up a dustbin lid to see what was being thrown away in the 20th Century. The smell was absolutely dreadful, and the lid went back on quicker than it came off. There was a broken bucket beside the bins which Frank inverted and sat on, giving him a place to crouch down without getting his trousers wet on the tarmac.

His eyes began to play tricks on him. For a moment, he thought he could see the shadow of a hooded figure. Then, something heavy could be heard rustling near the fence separating the playground from the adjacent field. There was a snort and then a moo. A cow! "Typical", he thought as he looked back towards the boiler room and then, BANG! His body was thrown sideways into the fence like he'd been kicked in the head. His vision swam. He tried to look around but couldn't see his attacker, although he could hear some scuffling. Finally, he brought his PIMMS device into view. Through half-open eyelids, he could barely make out the panic button that would connect him to his brother. Then everything went dark.

The next things Frank could see were feet. As he started to open his eyes wider, he looked up the legs, and his line of sight was met by an outstretched hand. Thankfully, it was Fred's,

"What happened?" They said in unison. Frank rubbed the back of his head. It was pretty sore,

"I thought I saw someone, but then it was a cow."

Fred tilted his head to the side, his forehead furrowed,

"A cow did this to you?"

"No, you idiot. I thought I saw someone, but then I realised I was looking at a cow, and then someone smashed my head into the fence. Quick, let's get back to the bar. I want to take a look at my head; I'm bleeding."

Frank showed Fred the bloodied hand he'd been rubbing his head with. He pulled himself upright with Fred's help and headed for the Fire Exit door, back the way they had arrived.

⁂

Rina turned round and saw the blood on Frank's head as he and Fred staggered back down the SlipStream corridor into the MAMBA room,

"What on earth happened?"

Frank shook his head as if trying to check he hadn't got anything loose inside his skull,

"I was minding my own business, keeping lookout whilst Fred was in the school boiler house and BAM, out of nowhere, I was waking up on the floor. It's like I got mugged by *The Invisible Man*. I know there was no one behind me, I went and looked before I crouched down beside the fence."

Rina opened a drawer in one of the wall cabinets and pulled out a spray can. A quick squirt in Frank's hair and the only sign of an injury was dried blood which quickly brushed away,

"How's that? Pain gone away?"

Frank shook his head again, stroked his hair back into shape and instantly he felt better.

"Thanks, Rina. Next time we'll take a can of this with us for emergencies. Does it fix bald patches? I bet Leo could do with a can too!" Rina looked dubious,

"No it doesn't, and anyway it's expensive, so it's only for emergencies. It's not for coiffuring calamities! Do you need someone to come back with you?" Fred shook his head,

"No, we'll be fine. If we go back to a point ten minutes before we went last time, we'll be able to see who's creeping around." Rina frowned,

"OK, but try to stay out of sight in the shadows. Wait to see who attacked you and intercept them, but DON'T get involved with your other selves. Whatever you do, don't change destiny."

It wasn't long before Frank and Fred were down the brightly lit corridor and back in the bar outside the door to the Gents. Fred was looking at the school's plan on the back of the flat, rigid electron fabric,

"Look, here, if we go back earlier via the garage side-door, we can creep out and watch your six. When your so-called invisible man creeps up on you, we'll be able to take him from behind, assuming you weren't beaten up by a girl!"

Frank looked most put out,

"Don't let Alba hear you say that. She's a 'She', and I know she could beat me up if she wanted to!"

Fred laughed,

"Yes, she could, couldn't she? Just don't call her Alice, it's a sure-fire way to get on her bad side!"

The night seemed darker the second time, especially since they knew they needed to expect an attacker. They opened the side door to the Caretaker's garage gingerly. Only their silhouettes could be seen as they eased themselves out, keeping low to the playground floor. Cold mist from the field drifted across the streetlights out on the road. There was total silence apart from the rustle of the leaves in the bushes, stirred by the damp night air.

There was a click from the direction of the school. The 'Fire Exit' door at the back of the school moved slightly and then, ever so slowly, swung open. It was bizarre, being able to see themselves exiting the school building. It was as if they were watching a Threezer Veezer broadcast of themselves from earlier. However, the Real Actual World perspective meant a live stream transmission would have given them a better view. They watched their earlier selves whisper to each other with the 'First Fred' creeping off towards the boiler house. The Frank from earlier looked around and then crouched down by the side of the fence, clearly keeping a watch on the boiler room door his brother had gone through. The later arriving Fred and Frank beside the garage started to wait.

The 'Second Fred' beside the garage looked at his watch and whispered to the Frank beside him,

"How long do you think it was before you were attacked?"

Frank shrugged his shoulders,

"I've no idea. I lost track of time when I got attacked. How long did it take you to get into the boiler house and do nothing?"

"What do you mean do nothing? It took only a few seconds to break in, but I had to look at the boiler and work out the best way to disable it whilst you were sitting around outside doing nothing."

The Frank beside the garage suddenly looked angry and pointed at his earlier self,

"Look at him; you're right; he's doing nothing. He's not even looking around properly. No wonder he got attacked. He's not protecting himself or you." Fred placed his hand on Frank's arm,

"Calm down and talk more quietly; you'll hear yourself!" Frank jerked his arm away,

"He won't hear me; he's as deaf as a post; you could shout in his ear he wouldn't know. He's a useless git. Why did you trust him to keep watch?" Fred started to get quite concerned,

"You realise you're talking about yourself? This isn't some stranger."

"You're right; he's no stranger. He's a total waste of space and needs sorting out!" Frank suddenly lunged forward and rushed out from their hiding place behind the garage. He leapt towards his earlier self, who was still beside the fence. Without a word, Frank slammed the head of his earlier self against the fence, knocking him unconscious. He venomously whispered, "You stupid parasite, you don't deserve to be here". He was about to take a swing at the head of his earlier self with his left foot when the Fred from the garage grabbed him in an arm lock and dragged him backwards.

Fred was appalled,

"What in heaven's name do you think you are doing? You can't go beating yourself up! It's a metaphysical metaphor! Remember what old Professor Passy said, it's modus vivendi – not modus operandi."

"I'm so sorry, I couldn't stop myself. One moment I was watching me, and the next moment, I was angrier than I had ever been in my life because I wasn't doing my job properly."

Fred dragged Frank back into the garage, out of sight of his earlier self, and Frank immediately began to calm down.

Fred whistled quietly in surprise,

"Wow, Autogenous Animosity. I've heard of it, but I've never seen it happen. You totally hate yourself, don't you?"

Frank shook his head,

"No, I'm really happy with myself. I honestly don't understand what happened. At least I don't need to apologise to anyone other than myself. Am I still lying there?"

Fred cracked open the garage side door and peered out across the driveway,

"We're about to leave. I can see us going back through the fire escape door. How's your head, by the way?"

"It's not too bad. It was hurting quite badly before I went and beat myself up, but it seems a bit better now. That spray Rina gave me is excellent. Shall we both go and break this boiler and then get out of here before a version of you turns up and starts a fight? I'm sure you'd like to make things even?" Frank grinned, and Fred nodded.

"Sure, come on, let me show you what I found in there."

Quietly and cautiously, the later arriving versions of Fred and Frank crept out from the darkness from beside the Caretaker's garage. They slipped around the wooden fencing where Frank had been laying a few moments earlier and over to the boiler house door, which was still unlocked. As they entered, closing the door behind them, Fred lit the lamp on his WOTDISC. He adjusted the light to shine under his chin, casting a glow across his face creepily like a gothic horror mask and moaned like a possessed ghoul.

Frank was not impressed,

"Come on! We're here to do a job and not get caught. If you're going to muck about, we may as well just turn the big light on and let the caretaker know we're in here. We really should have brought the night vision glasses. It would have made so much more sense."

Fred turned his light towards the far end of the boiler house, which he'd not been able to get to properly before being called back to help Frank. The blood in Frank's veins froze. Lying on the floor was a body. The light from the WOTDISC slid upwards to reveal the most horrifying, devilish, red savaged face.

Frank was on the edge of crying out in terror when Fred started to laugh,

"Imagine how I felt when I came in here on my own, I nearly needed a fresh pair of jeans. It's a Guy Fawkes effigy the teachers must have thought too scary for the bonfire, and the Caretaker stashed it in here and forgot about it. No worries, I think it's stuffed with straw. I didn't get a close look last time as I got the emergency call from your PIMMS. I was about to call for help, and you beat me to it!"

Slightly beyond the 'deceased body', all the pipes and cables for the heating system entered the boiler house from the direction of the school. Above this was a wall box clearly marked 'Warning 240 volts'. Fred unscrewed the cover and looked at the group of eight fuses. None of them was marked up. He turned to Frank,

"I can't tell which one is which. What do you reckon, break them all?"

"No, that would be too obvious; look... inside the lid. It tells you what each fuse does. Cut the wire immediately behind the fuse terminal screw, so anyone looking will think the fuse is still okay. Nobble the Fuel Oil feeder fuse too." Fred pulled out the old

Bakelite fuse cartridge for the water pump, cut the wire and then stamped on it, cracking it in half. He then slid it back into the fuse panel,

"There you go. Even if they spot the fuse wire needs replacing, it won't be reusable when they pull the cartridge. In fact, to be doubly sure, let's unscrew the case and loosen the live wire so it's not touching. They're never going to spot that unless they're an electrician."

Frank, meanwhile, was looking around the back of the boiler and spotted the fuel oil isolator valve.

"Here you go, let me tighten the valve, so it's jammed shut, then I'll unscrew the tap head. That'll stop the boiler from getting lit on Monday morning! And look here, a box of spare fuse cartridges. We'll have those. I'm glad we spotted them before we left, or else half of our efforts would have been futile." Feeling confident their efforts to sabotage the boiler would be sufficient to keep the school closed long enough for Tuesday's 'main event', they headed back to the door.

The light from Fred's WOTDISC caught the front of the boiler,

"Frank, look at this, what irony? We're sabotaging Rob Locksley's distant relative!"

Across the front of the boiler were the words 'Robin Hood – Senior'. On the table beside the boiler was a faded instruction manual proclaiming across the cover, 'ROBIN HOOD – THE BOILER WHICH IS DESIGNED TO STAND THE TEST OF TIME'.

Fred gently bit his lip as if he were pondering one of life's great questions,

"I think we are about to find out if it can withstand our kind of time management! Let's get going!"

Fred and Frank closed the boiler house door, setting the Electron Fabric to 'LOCK' as they did so. After quickly checking the school fire exit door was also secure, they slipped back across the schoolyard to the caretaker's garage. Setting the electron fabric to 'HOME', they opened the door. Welcoming them back was the relative warmth of the deserted bar room and the dying embers of the oak fireplace, in The Old Volunteer.

As the door to the caretaker's garage closed, virtual silence returned to the cold, damp night air, except for the wind in the trees and a distant owl. Then the quiet footsteps of a shadowy hooded figure, carrying what, in the darkness, looked like a stiletto knife and half a house brick, appeared from the gloom of the field behind the school and walked towards the caretaker's house.

ZUKANN
SCAN ME
G081A

CHAPTER 18
Reader, Petunia Was The Cow

North Cotes Junior School:
1013 (GMT), Tuesday December 8th 1970
Destiny Equilibrium Time (DET)

In the field beside the Junior School, it had been a dreary cold day. Usually, the large Friesian cow, with a question mark pattern over its left eye, only had grass to eat. However, it had been cheered up by finding a spot where some Mexican Bluebells had suddenly appeared out of nowhere, as if they had fallen from a lightning sky. For a moment, the cow looked up. Above its head was something large, heavy and whale-shaped. At least, it had a tail and a rounded body. The cow had seen neither a Blue Steel nuclear weapon nor sea life of any variety in its life. It had a moment to swallow some of the flowers and give off a quick 'moo'. In Cow-Speak, this would have meant 'Oh, bother', then half the field disappeared into a sixty-foot-long crater. If the Mexican Bluebell had been sentient, it probably would have been feeling a sense of déjà vu.

Smoke was still billowing from a gaping sixty-foot-long gash across the Lincolnshire field as RAF emergency vehicles crashed through the farm gate and over to the wreckage. Dozens of fire crew, RAF emergency workers, civilian police and ambulances arrived on-site. Most arrivals were held back, whilst RAF specialists wearing Hazmat 'noddy suits' sprayed fire suppressant. The sheer volume of fire foam meant the wreckage was almost completely obscured. Around the growing mound of foam wandered base scientists, also wearing HAZMAT gear sweeping radiation detectors across the site. The fire was contained more quickly than the firefighters had expected. Although this was probably a lot to do with the quick thinking of the pilot, jettisoning fuel over the North Sea before the crew bailed out.

On the far side of the field, apparently entirely oblivious to all the chaos, was a large black and white Friesian cow, with a question mark pattern over its left eye. For some inexplicable reason, it was stood in a bright yellow, now slightly deflated and grubby looking inflatable dingy. Instead of the Mexican Bluebell, it was now eating what looked a lot like seaweed. The cow somehow looked quite a bit happier and also somewhat relieved, as if it were no longer suffering from methane-generating indigestion.

Leaning on the other side of the fence, to which the cow was tied, nearly out of sight with her head resting to one side, was the caretaker whose garden it was. Anni, the cleaner at The Old Volunteer and the school caretaker pushed the hood back on her duffle coat to reveal an enigmatic smile. With a better view, the casual observer would have seen she had a screwdriver in one hand, and in the other, a spare second box of boiler control panel fuses. Perfect for when time-travellers dropped in unannounced. Never forget the old maxim, 'If you ever want to know what's going on, you should always ask the cleaner'.

Behind her, in her house, on the wall of her bedroom, was a painting, which one day someone would see when Anni utters the immortal words, 'I'll show you something that will make you change your mind'. The painting, dated 1939, was of two little girls playing in the self-same cow pasture. Anni, at nine years old, with her imaginary eleven-year-old flame-haired friend. There was one odd thing about the picture though. Instead of a blue sky over the field, any amateur astronomer would immediately recognise the planet Jupiter and its moon Europa, setting over the horizon of Callisto.

Anni paused for a moment before returning to the boiler room to replace the fuses. First, she thought to herself how nice it was to see the imaginary friend from her childhood all grown up. Followed by a second thought... 'I really must get a mat for the door to the toilets for visitors to wipe their feet on.'

ZUKANN
SCAN ME
G083A

CHAPTER 19
Roll Back The Years

Ruby's Office:
0900 (GMT), Friday December 11ᵗʰ 1970 (DET)

Eddie knocked on Ruby's office door and walked in. Like so many Time Tech Team members, Ruby's office was a bit of a workshop, with objects on shelves tagged for repair. In one corner of the room was a garden spa bubble bath with a sign hanging off it, displaying the text, 'FAULTY – DO NOT TOUCH'. Beside it was an old British red payphone with cracked windows.

Also on the shelves were several electronic boxes which appeared to be plugged into the back of televisions. Finally, there was one device like a grey cupboard with lights and wires protruding from the top. It was turned to face the wall, and in what Eddie assumed was Russian across the back of it, it was labelled 'ƆABAW' However, this seemed improbable given the current state of politics.

Across the walls were pictures of Ruby and her sister as teenagers. The shots were of what looked like a futuristic version of a TV show based in a school. On one wall was one of those motivational posters with the words: 'TIME IS NOT YOUR ENEMY. Energy is your enemy. It's easy to convert or conserve, but creating it takes talent – and time!' The author's name was obscured by a yellow sticky label with an exclamation mark on it.

Eddie smiled,

"Morning Ruby, I love the poster. The photos look like you had fun when you were younger? How's things going?" Ruby tilted her head slightly,

"They're mostly fine, apart from the jacuzzi over there. It keeps leaking water onto my carpet. The water's coming in from another dimension, and I can't seem to stop it. I've fitted it with a quantum tunnel to drain the water away, so it will be alright for the moment. Rob Locksley's not happy, though." Eddie looked worried,

"What happened? Is it something we've done; not done, or not done yet?"

Ruby shook her head and grinned. "No, it's not you, well not directly. Since the crash, we've had no end of rubberneckers hanging around. He's said he felt doomed to fitting Prismorphic technology to the entire Great Hall so the public can't find it. He's already chosen his Quint."

Eddie's expression was totally blank so Ruby tried gently to be clearer. "You know, his quintessence?"

There was still no change on Eddie's face, so Ruby went deeper. "It's what things look like when they've been Prismorphed, even really big things like buildings. He reckons he's going to make the Great Hall look like a muck spreader. He's figured no one will want to get close to that. It got him most annoyed when someone called on his Mother-in-Law at New Locksley Hall. They claimed they were from the *Nottingham Evening Post* and were asking about Robin Hood. She's now put a sign on her gate saying, 'Beware of the dog – it is incredibly sarcastic!"

Eddie tried not to laugh,

"I get it now, architectural sleight of hand! I started to imagine sarcastic guard dogs trotting up to some swindler at the door and challenging them with 'Call yourselves sharks, eh? Take a look at these teeth!' Then taking a bite from their trousers. "Have you got time for a coffee?"

Ruby looked at her WOTDISC,

"Yes, loads of time, but can we make it in my office? I don't trust that jacuzzi, and I don't want any quantum tunnel interference ending up with ripples all over my floor! I imagine all this seems complete madness after what must have been the fairly orderly world of the military?"

"One day, people will probably look back on my life as well-ordered madness" replied Eddie. "I'd love a world where you're not ordered to fly around Europe with something strapped to your plane with the potential to kill thousands of people. But, for the moment, I appreciate it still needs doing."

Ruby nodded grimly,

"Let's hope we can start to create a more peaceful paradigm. Come on, let's have a mug of caffeine to flush out the Titanium Dioxide. You're starting to look slightly pale. Perhaps, for a little while, you can give us a hand, and let someone else take on the well-ordered madness."

She passed Eddie a small electronic device and as she clamped it onto his finger like a medical oximeter,

"Here, stick this on. It's a particle exposure meter. Then, we'll know how strong to make your coffee!"

There was a moment of silence as Eddie viewed the little device attached to his forefinger and pondered what 'giving a hand' might look like in the short term. A small digital screen displayed the need for one cup.

Ruby poured the freshly boiled water out of the kettle,

"I imagine there has been a life before the 'madness'? Of course, I could ask ZUKANN, but she doesn't know everything!". There was an angry buzz from Ruby's wrist device, like you might hear from a contestant on a quiz show when they give a wrong answer, which Ruby ignored.

"I'm impressed you've got a kettle. Will wants to smash the next BistroMatic Gourmetron he sees. Old school coffee is excellent – thanks. OK, so, life before the madness. Well, to keep it brief," replied Eddie, "My father taught air navigation at an airbase near Coventry. We lived on base. Both my parents were killed when it got bombed during the war. I survived, was adopted by friends, went to Grammar School, joined the Airforce, and now I'm here."

"You must have some happy childhood memories somewhere in all of that?" Ruby gently asked.

"Probably only one. Maybe my first and only really happy memory as a child, was eating an ice cream sat on a bench at Charmouth in Dorset. Actually, it's the only photo to survive the blast. I keep it in my wallet." Eddie reached into his pocket and pulled out an old black and white photo. It was clear the image was loved; despite the creases and the corners being well worn, the picture was still clear.

Ruby held the picture in her hands, peering at it closely and running her thumb gently over the creases to better see the background. A look of great sadness and confusion appeared on her face.

"It's OK", said Eddie reassuringly, passing Ruby the Electron fabric he'd been given by Mark Sparks when he first arrived in the Time Tech laboratory three days ago – or was it five? Although it felt like at least a month. "It was a long, long time ago, and I was adopted by an extremely kind couple." He realised it was the first time he'd seen anyone look sad, since he'd arrived.

"No, you don't understand – take a look at this." Ruby tapped the device on her wrist. A selection of images fanned out like a hand of cards. They floated in the air in front of her arm. She lovingly swiped through several pictures and videos showing Ruby and her sister graduating, partying, dressed as if for school; blowing out candles on a cake, then sat on a swing. Each time getting younger as time reversed until she stopped on one. Images in full high-definition colour, and as clear as looking through a window. The eyes of today's Ruby could be seen in the face of a four-year-old girl, sitting on a bench eating ice cream with her sister. In the background, was a brightly lit screen displaying adverts for that day's entertainment on New Charmouth Pier.

On either side of Ruby sat a man and a woman. Eddie looked at the photo of his parents and back at Ruby's projected image. Apart from appearing in full colour and projected in a short video loop, their appearance was unmistakable. Sweat began to trickle down Eddie's back and the hair pricked on the back of his neck,

"How have you got a picture, sat on a beach, with my parents?" Tears rolled gently down Ruby's cheeks,

"These are MY parents!"

"Is this some sort of body duplication thing you can do in the future?" asked Eddie, his voice unsteady and his normally very orderly emotions quivering between anger, despair and hope.

Ruby wiped her eyes,

"My parents were rescued from the wreckage of a research lab explosion in New Coventry. The lab was developing interdimensional communication systems when a Gaia Power overload occurred, caused by an entangled SlipStream event. Many people were hurt. When rescuers pulled everyone out of the wreckage, two more people were rescued than were supposed to have been in the building. My parents were completely unknown to the iNet – our population tracker."

Ruby held up the old photo behind the new image, adjusting the projected image to be slightly transparent. The two pictures almost perfectly aligned with Eddie appearing to be sat between the two girls,

"Rina and I both wanted a brother, but Mum used to say, "Once you've delivered on perfection, you don't need to try again!" This memory of her mother made Ruby smile and she blew her nose on the electron fabric.

"Mum and Dad had no memory of who they were. SlipStream Travel can affect you this way. They told me when I was older that although they could remember nothing, there was a deep feeling that they were meant to be together. They were given sanctuary and Home Earth Citizenship. Within six months, they got 'Tied', what we call marriage in the 23rd Century. A year later, Rina and I were born, and four years later, we're sat eating ice cream, on holiday, on a bench, looking out at the sea."

There was a long pause as both of them looked at the combined image of three children. A bee flew past the girls in the projected image, making Rina's animated likeness cringe and duck, breaking the reverie.

Eddie looked at Ruby's tear-stained face then looked back at the image she was holding,

"But if this is true, and what we're seeing is what we think we're seeing, how will we know?"

"It's simple." Ruby tapped a few buttons on the screen of her wrist device. "I have a Genome app which can help. DNA was discovered in 1860, but so much more has been achieved in the last twenty years of your time. I can safely tell you this because someone is researching this in your timeline. Within the next twenty-five years, humanity will have a map of the entire Human Genome. Unfortunately, this has led us to the problems with The STRAND, The Hagura, and the abuse of this knowledge. The App maps your DNA so you can discover your family history, practically back to the dawn of time!"

Ruby tilted her wrist device so now Eddie could see it displaying two finger-print icons and nodded in the direction of the screen. "Put your finger on the left sensor".

Eddie placed his forefinger on the screen as Ruby pressed hers onto the second icon. A line scanned across, which then turned green with the message 'Scan Complete'.

Eddie and Ruby removed their fingers from the screen. It had changed from a photo to a more technical results screen display:

DNA:	**= Match**
Degrees of Separation:	**= Zero <Siblings>**

For the first time in years, he felt he was home. A hole in Eddie's heart, which he had tried for decades to subconsciously suppress, had been filled. Tears were now streaming down his face.

Unable to stop himself, he reached forward and gave Ruby a massive hug,

"Hello, Sis," he said, trying covertly to wipe tears from his face whilst his head was over her shoulder.

"Hello, Big Bruv," chuckled Ruby. "I think we are going to need a whole lot more coffee… and a chat with your other sister!"

ZUKANN
SCAN ME
G086A

CHAPTER 20
Dancing Queens And Qwings

The Laboratory:
1000 (GMT), Friday December 11th 1970 (DET)

Will was discussing 20th Century politics with Fred and Frank as Eddie and Ruby walked into the laboratory, looking for Rina.

Surrounded by the familiar racks of technical equipment and gadgets, Will looked frustrated and waved a newspaper at them,

"Have you seen this? It's industrial chaos out there with this electrician's strike. There's hospitals losing power, funfair owners taking their Walzer generators to plug into Maternity units to keep the lights going. I suspect with all the power we're drawing, we're not helping. But surely, it's not all down to us! AND the politicians don't seem to be able to get anything sorted."

Ruby raised one eyebrow mischievously,

"Well, if you want something different, why don't you all vote for a female Prime Minister?"

Frank leaned over to Fred conspiratorially and whispered,

"Yeah, and some of us know what's coming ten years from now." Fred whispered back,

"The second one was OK. Although she couldn't dance!"

Ruby overheard their whispering and smiled,

"The second one could dance. She just had a clause in her contract to say she couldn't, so no-one would discover she was a time traveller." Fred looked bemused,

"How did that work out?

This time, Ruby raised both eyebrows conspiratorially,

"This is not for public consumption, but as the first Bicentennial Ball was at the Myra Lane studios on her 200th Birthday in 2156, she was SlipStreamed in as a special guest. Most of you are too young to remember, but the Locksley's favourite brewery were sponsoring the trophy for the event finale 'Celebrity I'm Askin' dance competition. It was something of a milestone. They called the trophy, the 'Bitter-Glitter-Ball' as not everyone would be happy to leave. Departees feared this end to a great life would indicate a bleak beginning. She surprised everyone by winning. Senior judge, Carla Taylor, presented her with the trophy. FENDER were not entirely happy and she was served with a Non-Disclosure notice. She didn't care, as she didn't want to be known as a dancer. The third Prime Minister will be perfect though, but we know why that will be!"

Quick as a flash, Frank replied, slightly sarcastically,

"Yes, Prime Minister, certainly Prime Minister," then, looking at Will's puzzled expression, said, "Don't worry, it will all work out in the end. If Ruby can't sort out the future, then FENDER will. But if THEY do we'll never know if they did or not."

Fred gave Frank a dark, cautioning look,

"Don't say such things too loudly; you don't want anyone to get the wrong idea and have you pegged as a Steamer!" Frank shrugged, unapologetically,

"Anyway, changing the subject from politics, you know what I really like about this particular 1970? Woolworth's Pick & Mix. How come we could never get the sweets right?"

Ruby snorted!

"Probably because you can't legally add mood enhancers into children's sweets any longer!" Frank was about to reply when everyone's wrist devices flashed. An 'all hands call' in the MERCURY room, upstairs in The Old Volunteer pub, "Come on, we're needed. Let's go!"

ZUKANN OPTIC:

SCAN ME
G087A

Dearly Departed

As healthcare dramatically improved from the middle of the 20th Century, humans began to live longer. The first person to live to 1000 years of age was born in the year 2021. This created a huge population problem. So global leaders agreed on a Population Export Programme to 'PEP up the Universe'. On the 200th birthday of a citizen, each person must choose emigration to an off HomeEarth colony or a parallel world. The alternative being euthanasia. The well-known phrase 'Death or Cake' which was first brought to public attention by 21st Century Comedian Eddie Izzard became the mantra for 23rd Century Bicentennial Balls, as hardly anyone chose Euthanasia; the cake was always on hand for the celebration prior to departure.

Departure Parties or 'Departies' were often held in large venues such as the Albert Hall. The early state-sponsored balls were televised with shows like the dance spectacular 'Celebrity I'm askin' – AND askin' you to leave'.

To discover more, please select this ZUKANN OPTIC.

The Mission, Emergency Response and Control Uplink Room Y was a meeting and control centre for primary Time Tech operations. It was larger and better equipped than the MAMBA room, with a huge, curved monitor screen which completely covered three walls from floor to ceiling. Capable of providing an immersive media experience, it was also more popular than the Mission, Emergency Response and Control Uplink Room X, mainly because Room X was already booked for a brewery sales manager meeting, and MERCURY sounds cooler than MERCURX.

As they headed away from the lab, down the corridor, returning them to The Old Volunteer, Mark blocked their path through the door,

"Sorry everyone, there's been a leak. There's water pouring out of a jacuzzi in Ruby's office. It's already filled the pub cellar. We've gone to emergency lockdown on all the accommodation to stop the offices from being flooded. Ruby, we've redirected the Quantum Tunnel to Covenham Reservoir. I'm not sure where it was pointing, but it looks like you've been filling up someone else's reality, and it's all started to back up. You'll have to use surface transport."

Most of the team knew 'surface transport' consisted of a ten- year- old Post Office mail delivery minibus. This had been made surplus to requirements after an industrious life in the Highlands of Scotland. Admittedly, it wasn't the most comfortable of vehicles. Still, no one gave a second glance to an old familiar red mail van, even if it was packed floor to ceiling with 22nd Century time travellers.

The minibus was stored in a secure area, away from prying eyes which might wonder why a group of civilians were leaving an aircraft hangar and climbing into a bus.

"Come on!" cried Frank enthusiastically, "To the 'pub-mobile" as they headed in the direction of a door leading them towards daylight and fresh air.

"Better not say that too loudly in front of Sir Robin," laughed Ruby. "You know he's not overly keen on sharing his name with a cartoon sidekick who works for a guy who lives in a mansion with a butler. On top of which, someone who works in a cave hidden underground with future-tech he's built all on his own, he thinks, sounds completely unrealistic!"

Will turned to Eddie as they walked across to their ride, parked in a secluded area between two of the hangars,

"You don't suppose Rob is a comic book writer, do you...?"

As they arrived at The Old Volunteer in the bright red Post Office mini-bus, a plumber was busy at the side of the pub with a water pump. Running on full blast, water sprayed across the car park to the nearest drain. The man looked quite perplexed as the pump was running at top speed, and the water level in the pub cellar was not decreasing. It looked like there was a mains water pipe burst somewhere. Either way, at this rate, he was going to be late home for his tea.

ZUKANN
OPTIC:

SCAN ME
G088A

Qwing For A Day

Apart from being the number one exporter of second- hand postal mini-buses, Scotland was one of the first three independent states of the Northern Union. Countries joined for the purposes of trade, peace, harmony and the opportunity to win with a cheesy song at an annual singing cheese-fest. Scotland went on to win twice with those harmonious tunes 'Stitch That Gently Jimmy' and the ear-worm worthy 'Pick Yer Windee, It'll Frame Ye Well'.

"Scotland was also the first country to introduce 'Qwing for a day'. 'Qwing for a day' is a fly-on-the- wall, Reality Threezer Veezer broadcast. Citizens can sponsor themselves to be Head of State for a single day, saving millions on the cost of a President. Initially, there was no time restriction. However, not long after it was launched, the 197-year-old alphabetically challenged ex-President of Stockland bought five years of leadership in a fraudulent attempt to avoid migration at a Bicentennial Ball.

To discover more, please select this ZUKANN OPTIC.

CHAPTER 21
The Godot Orange

MERCURY Room:
1100 (GMT), Friday December 11th 1970 (DET)

A few of the group were still wiping their shoes dry from failed attempts to negotiate the lake in the pub car park, when the tap of a coffee spoon on a mug brought the general hubbub of noise in the MERCURY room right down to a point at which Rina could easily be heard.

"Morning everyone, thanks for joining us today."

"Yeah, like we had a choice," came a voice from the other side of the room, which could have been either Frank or Fred. As twins – despite being born a century and ten minutes apart – it was frequently hard to guess which one was which or which one had been talking, especially when both of them had broad grins on their faces.

"Thank you for such an early contribution, Fred." said Rina optimistically.

"Frank!" shouted both of them simultaneously, greatly amused that Rina was wrong or they could make out she was. Rina was completed unfazed by this lack of decorum. She loved working with the Time Tech Team, and of course, everyone loved Rina – how could you not!

"Moving swiftly on," shouted Rina over the laughter, "We have an interesting challenge for the team, and it's an all-hands-on-deck problem. First, let me hand you over to Alba. Apart from Eddie and Will, most of you know Alba has extensive practical and technical skills. She is also our resident art historian, and I'm sure she won't mind me saying, she is also our part-time flower arranger – thanks for this morning's meeting room bouquet, Alba. Conchita Blueberry Frost, if I'm not mistaken?"

Eddie and Will looked at each other, completely confused about the need for flower arranging, then returned their gaze to the formidable outline of Alba. Her bright orange appearance wasn't because of some disaster in a tanning studio, but because she wasn't from Earth.

"Having been impressed by the extensive array of gender pronouns being used across Earth cultures and languages, she elected to be known as 'her'. She had sought asylum after the cataclysmic 'Orion Nebula Event'. It is thought she was dragged through a SlipStream vortex caused by a misfiring time-jump drive on a ship in a nearby parallel instance."

"Her temper is legendary, having subdued five Kinoshi warriors in a bar fight when one of them called her 'Alice'. No one, including Alba, is quite sure how old she is. She joined the Time Tech Team in the 22nd Century, but she is mainly committed to the 20th Century Response Teams, given the current state of events. Her hobbies include axe throwing, truck pulling, art history and flower arranging."

"You're most welcome", Alba smiled appreciatively, as her polite, clipped tones drifted across the meeting room. "In the last week, some of you may have seen the news story about British Diplomat James Cross having been rescued from terrorists. We believe they were Hagura, posing as members of the Quebec Liberation Front. Unknown to nearly everyone but us, James is one of our most important governmental consultants and had discovered the location of a vital artefact, The Audio Key, embedded into a seven-inch single record by an earlier kidnap victim, musician Rodge Brook. With the help of our senior engineering and technical advisor Howard Hughes, their release was, let's say 'negotiated'. James has now been returned to the United Kingdom with the information he had managed to keep safe, but unfortunately, Howard has been somewhat delayed."

A slim, six-foot-tall man, with a gelled Hockey Cut hair style, slipped into the room quietly. Most people would not guess that Del Aurion had been born west of Toulouse, France in the summer of 1789.

Wearing thin cut brown corduroys and a green jumper, he could look totally at home in any university library across the world. Being a Fringe Exo-Etymologist and Paralinguist, with an astronomical capability to control life and objects with the power of sound attached to words, he said little whilst others talked extensively.

Del gently sat down beside Mark Sparks and in an unmistakable Occitan lenga d'òc accent, whispered in his ear,

"It's disgusting, poor Howard being treated this way by FENDER's Bureau of Investigations. There's no way he's working with the Hagura. I'd know; he would have been compelled to tell me."

Mark smiled. Many times he had seen people sit on a barstool next to Del and pour out their most personal secrets just because Del had said, 'Hello!'

ZUKANN
OPTIC:

SCAN ME
H090A

FENDER and IGLOO

"FENDER is an acronym for the Future Experience Neutrality and Destiny Equilibrium Restoration organisation. Reporting directly to IGLOO, its role is to correct and undo unpredicted changes to the time stream. Should the future be impacted by any event, they will respond, neutralizing the effect and restoring destiny. Time Tech are independent of FENDER. However, on occasion, IGLOO will request that Time Tech provide services to FENDER.

"IGLOO stands for the International Governmental Logistical and Operational Oversight. Its motto is: 'Dispassionate Control.' Any and All time and inter-dimensional transiting organisations including the Time Tech Team are regulated by them."

To discover more, please select this ZUKANN OPTIC.

"So", Alba continued, "As a result of all the intelligence gathered with the help of James, we think we may be onto the recovery of a Gaia Power Conductor Staff and two Gaia Power Seed Extractors. To be successful, I need to give you a briefing which will give some of you philistines an education in art and culture." She put a picture up on the vast wall screen.

ZUKANN
IMAGE:

H091A

SCAN ME
H091A

The Godot Orange

"This is a picture of a painting called The Godot Orange attributed to the artist Edith Madieu. There had been several rumours of its existence.

It has recently surfaced for sale at a large Belgian auction house. It is believed to be the last of her works of surrealist art. Edith created it before she died this year under suspicious circumstances. It transpires she was forced to create it by a Hagura agent. The same agent we believe survived the catastrophe of the Chilean 'Earthquake' at Valdivia".

To discover more, please select this ZUKANN OPTIC.

At the mention of 'Earthquake', Alba raised her fingers in the sarcastic 'air quotes' gesture, so widely used it is even recognised off-world.

Alba continued,

"We believe, from what Madieu told Del Aurion, this painting contains the key. A Schrodinger Key to a safe. This may or may not be the temporary home of the Gaia Power devices. I say, 'may or may not' because, we believe the contents of the safe, will only be found when a highly complex series of events take place. These must occur simultaneously and involve several other works of art connected via a closed Teslate Network. Del, as most of you know, is, fortunately, our resident Exo-Etymologist. He 'spoke' to Madieu the day before she died, and she gave us crucial information which will help us to get access to the safe's contents."

Eddie turned to Ruby, who was sat next to him and whispered in disbelief,

"What – he simply spoke to her, and Madieu spilled the beans – just like that?"

Ruby smiled knowingly as she whispered back,

"He probably didn't actually say anything. Del is an Exo-Etymologist. They call it 'The Power of Words'. A bit like a hypnotist, he can ask a question in a particular way with a particular tone of voice, or even just say "uh-huh?" and you become completely unable to resist answering the question truthfully. It's a lot safer than 'Truth Serum' and a lot less painful than some of the ways the KGB use to extract information from their enemies — which at the moment is almost everybody."

Alba had continued talking,

"Let's get ZUKANN to give us a bit more background. Hello ZUKANN".

"I'm ZUKANN, So YOU can," came a voice from all directions in the meeting room. *"What is the nature of your enquiry?"*

"ZUKANN, please can you give us the background on Edith Madieu and the Valdivia event?"

"Certainly, I can, Alba, and thank you for asking." Across the room, the screen was filled with images of Edith Madieu's artwork.

ZUKANN
IMAGE:

SCAN ME
H092A

The Daughter of Eve

"For those of you with no idea who Edith Madieu was, you may actually know her pictures — especially if you like music.

The orange from The Daughter of Eve painting is quite like The Godot Orange, but with the orange placed in a room with an open door and supported by a wedding dress.

To discover more, please select this ZUKANN OPTIC.

ZUKANN was now in full flow and everyone's attention was on the screens.

Brook-Ola Album and 7" Single

"The Orange was used on the cover of Rodge Brook's 'Brook-ola' Album last year.

We know Rodge Brook worked with or for Madieu. They first met when he attended one of her salons in Paris. She personally gave him permission to use her designs on his album cover.

To discover more, please select this ZUKANN OPTIC.

"Looking at Madieu's work, you can see clearly that she has encountered or been influenced by SlipStream events. There is evidence or understanding of historical events or alternate universes."

Virtual Reality

"In her 1928 painting Virtual Reality, you can see a self-portrait of Madieu. She is 'painting' a man into her own reality using what looks like a brush, but this is actually a Duron Caduceus.

To discover more, please select this ZUKANN OPTIC.

Each image appearing on screen, gently slid the previous one to the left.

ZUKANN IMAGE:

SCAN ME
J093B

Wave Guides

"And in the Wave Guides masterpiece, you can clearly see she's painted a pair of Tunians chatting in the sea with an Aerial Brigantine landing in the bay behind them.

To discover more, please select this ZUKANN OPTIC.

To Will's late 20th Century eyes, the next image seemed quite incongruous and almost ridiculous.

ZUKANN IMAGE:

SCAN ME
J093C

Triangulated Dimensions

"It gets even more obvious when you see her 1931 painting Triangulated Dimensions. Even in the title, she makes no attempt to hide the fact this illustrates the craft from the Sea of Genoa event in 1608. The Mediterranean coastline can clearly be identified in the foreground.

To discover more, please select this ZUKANN OPTIC.

The next painting was strangely familiar to Eddie. As if he'd already seen it somewhere before in a gallery or perhaps a Sunday supplement.

ZUKANN
IMAGE:

J094A

SCAN ME
J094A

Parallel Times

"We even think she is somehow connected to the disastrous events at Covenham St Bartholomew in 1899. Those which resulted in the closure of the branch line between Ludborough and RAF Donna Nook bombing range. We have little additional data for this. We think the railway

tunnel is a cryptic reference to the burial of the train, with the time-reversal instance represented by the clock. The flying capsule payload is emerging from the tunnel, clearly floating above ground as in the Covenham incident.

"It is works by Edith Madieu, held in art repositories in Europe and America in the 20th Century which will lead us to recover the last and most important Gaia Power Rod."

To discover more, please select this ZUKANN OPTIC.

"*Alba*," said ZUKANN, "*Should I continue with the background to the Valdivia Event?*"

"Yes, please, do continue."

ZUKANN brought up new harrowing images of collapsed houses and forests turned into a wasteland.

"*The year is 1960. An earthquake of strength around 9.5 on the Movement Magnitude scale and 7.0 on the Mercalli scale, with the epicentre at Lumaco in Chile, struck a few moments after 3.00 p.m. local time.*

"*About 250 km or 155 miles south is the town of Valdivia. It is the largest earthquake ever measured on the Mercalli scale. The earthquake was caused by Hagura scientists experimenting with opening a slipstream tunnel beside a Gaia Power Rod installed too close to the surface. Unfortunately, the event horizon was opened*

at the exact point of the Wadati-Benioff zone between the Nazca
and South American plates, causing a megathrust quake."

Will was curious to hear more about this story. He'd been to Chile
on a holiday the year before the quake, and remembered watching
the *Pathé News* report by Peter Roberts, in the cinema. ZUKANN's
voice continued,

"The irony was the reflected shockwave followed back along
the SlipStream tunnel, completely destroying the Hagura base and,
sadly, numerous buildings in the nearby town. Twenty-five metre
or eighty-two feet high tsunamis were induced, with waves hitting
Hawaii at several hundred kilometres per hour and serious effects
being experienced as far away as China, Japan and Australia.
The ship, The Canelos, was moved by the tsunami one and a half
kilometres or nearly a mile up the Valdivia River. The mast is still
visible from the road to Niebla."

"The Hagura base and abandoned equipment were discovered
by the Chilean head of electrical engineering Raul Herez. He had
been surveying for the location of a hydroelectric power station,
coincidentally working with American and British engineers. They
were unwittingly being spied on by Russian agents who also stole
some of the technology, taking it back to Tunguska base. By another
coincidence, the same engineering team went on to work with the
Colombians at the Valle del Cauca, on the Calima Lake project."

The images changed to a black and white cine film of the devastated
hillside. The remains of the previously underground base could be
seen protruding from the steep incline. As the camera panned
around, a man could be seen walking away from the destruction
down a mountain track. He had a rucksack on his back and was
carrying a completely out-of-place ski bag. Engineers could be seen
shouting and waving at him, but there was no apparent reaction.

ZUKANN continued with her explanation,

"This footage was copied by American agents working in
Moscow and was taken from the original images filmed by Russian
intelligence operatives. Analysis of the two bags clearly indicates the
presence of three Teslate devices. The glow can be detected when
viewing through polarised filters, even though the film is a copy.
We believe the man carrying the bags had one Teslate Conductor
rod and two Teslate seed devices. Unfortunately, the man's face

cannot be seen, so visual facial recognition is impossible. However, DNA phenotyping and Generalized Procrustes Analysis was used to predict the man's appearance. From this, we could establish, the individual who had been using the underground facility was a time-travelling 'Tall Grey'. This one was probably using some kind of visual or physical Transmorphic capability."

Alba stood up again,

"So, there's the background. We're putting together a mission to recover those Tesla devices. In particular, the power rod is essential to the completion of the global power network. I will be finalising a plan which will need the input and assistance of all of you, either here in the MERCURY Room or in one of three or four locations in Europe and America."

For the first time, Alba spoke directly to Will and Eddie,

"Your input on this project is critical. As some say, it's not what we know but what we don't know about this era which could mean the difference between success and failure. No matter how insignificant something seems or how stupid the question may feel, please take the opportunity to raise it. As ZUKANN would say, 'Always honour the stupid question.'"

Ruby's WOTDISC buzzed with the on-screen message from ZUKANN *"Yeah like I get anything but..."* followed by a little smiley emoticon.

Ruby arose from the table and stood, looking relatively small beside her seven-foot colleague,

"Thank you. Alba will take the lead on the mission parameters, so she's going to have all the nightmares, worrying if she's got the planning completely finished. Will, Eddie, can you go and get the audio key recording from Locksley Hall? The target date for this operation is Christmas Eve. This is ideal as everything will be shut for the holidays, meaning we don't have a lot of 'real time' to prepare. To save energy, we'd prefer not to initiate a Meta-Time loop."

Ruby paused for a moment's thought,

"Before we run this Op, I need to run it past the 'FENDER Activities Board'. Anyone fancy a quick trip to the 25th?"

Most people would simply accept this as a location for a meeting on the 25th floor of a large building. However, Fred and Frank knew immediately this meant a surprise trip to the 25th Century, and the location of the Future Experience Neutrality and Destiny Equilibrium Restoration (FENDER) organisation.

Ruby was grateful for the twins' sudden enthusiasm to travel. Nevertheless, she was aware there was always an ulterior motive. There is a long-held Time Tech rule, that people should travel at least in pairs but ideally in threes. This led to the respected mantra: 'No-one Slips Alone', so in the event of an emergency, one person could always go for help.

"We'll definitely come with you if you're off to the 25th," Grinned Fred. "It's the only place you can get a decent bottle of 'FunGryp', although Frank is actually quite keen on the 20th."

"I like the 20th," replied Frank. "You can be as morose as you want, and everyone ignores you and lets you get on with it. AND there's combustion engines! Is there any chance it's going to be Friday there too? I fancy a Friday night out on the town?"

Ruby half shut one eye and replied slightly sarcastically,

"As a special treat just for you, the entire FENDER community has decided to meet on Saturday morning, so it will be a Friday night stop-over! However, in the real world, projects as important as this require in-person sign-off at a senior level. We'll need to hold the meeting 'in the RAW' for security, and the only time everyone can make it, is twenty hours from now. The meeting location is coincidentally a Saturday morning. Unfortunately, only half the attendees could make it yesterday, so it's been pushed forward."

She knew Fred and Frank were totally aware the meeting would not be open to them. As such, this trip would be something of a 'jolly', allowing them time to simply enjoy the experience of travel and the spin-off benefits.

Eddie laughed,

"So you're all off to the 25th Century, are you? Well, I may be new to all this time-travel stuff, and I don't know anything about the future, but I do know about MY past, which it seems you two guys have NOT yet seen." The twins looking confused, was something Eddie had not seen before.

Having insider knowledge was something Eddie was not used to in this new world, and he almost had a sinister look on his face,

"Ahh, it's great to have the upper hand for once! Enjoy your evening out but don't overdo it. Apparently, we'll be needing you, a few days ago, in YOUR over-indulged morning-after future! I don't know about future life in 'The RAW', whatever that means, but I've a suspicion your heads will be feeling raw! Don't forget to take the Aspirin with you!"

"Cheers dudes," Frank laughed. "We've been working intensely on building some kit for you to fly and need a break. We'll be back earlier in the week to teach you how to use it. See you later, or maybe sooner – whatever!"

ZUKANN OPTIC:

SCAN ME
J096A

RAW Science

With the extensive development of virtual environments and fewer Real Actual World (RAW) events it became increasingly essential to ensure bio-security protocols were in place, especially as Deepfake hackers could conceivably clone an individual's remote virtual presence.

"RAW events became popular amongst 'vintage and retro' aficionados who coined the acronym and phrase – 'seeing life in the RAW'. RAW tours of the natural world to see Extinction Level Events became very popular during the 23rd Century, when it became possible to experience a volcanic eruption from inside a volcano or watch Mutually Assured Destruction with all-out nuclear war. Life could also be experienced as a historical personality, and visits were possible to political and monumental crime scenes. Tour companies would advertise with slogans like 'Feel the fear and smell it every way'.

To discover more, please select this ZUKANN OPTIC.

CHAPTER 22
The Audio Key

Locksley Hall:
1300 (GMT), Friday December 11ᵗʰ 1970 (DET)

For Eddie and Will, this was going to be their second visit to Locksley Hall. Their first visit chronologically was Thursday, yesterday, but having gone back to Tuesday and spent most of a week in Meta-Time they were starting to experience the type of jet lag time travellers get, the type Ruby called desynchronosis.

Before yesterday in the pub, they had known nothing about the extraordinary world of Time Tech. Yet now, they were driving to see Sir Rob Locksley for the second time, and everything simply looked so ordinary again. It felt a bit like the time between Christmas and New Year which no one can find a proper name for. It had been decided there was nothing subtle about driving Motor Transport's only available vehicle, a fire truck, through the narrow lanes to Locksley Hall. So instead, they had been given Arti Ping's Mini Cooper to make the journey by road, allowing them an opportunity to get off-base for a few hours of normality. Nevertheless, they set off with the warning from Arti 'they were not to drive like they were in the *Italian Job*'.

Taking the right turn at The Old Volunteer, they drove down towards their destination. But of course, not before making a quick run (twice each) around the huge construction site of Covenham reservoir five miles away. Honour had to be satisfied, settling an argument beyond question, about who the best driver was. The deciding factor became who could reverse up the hill leading to the reservoir construction site car park the fastest. They considered it marginally less dangerous because the reservoir was deserted.

The local area now sadly had a pheasant population reduced by two, delaying both their circuit times. Soon after their challenge, a security gate was installed at the bottom of the hill preventing this level of stupidity in future.

As they drove up the crisp gravel drive to the Hall, the ordinary feel of the area sank in. It was approaching Christmas, but given the dreariness of the sky, 1970 didn't feel at all festive. The 1960s had felt so bright, cheerful and optimistic. Now, the atmosphere felt damp and gloomy, heavy with a foreboding sense, as if times were about to change and many long dark nights were ahead. Not many houses in the village had decorations in the windows, although there was a tree in the pub car park. But, for a moment of cheer, Christmas lights shone through the windows beside the front door of the Hall.

They rang the bell and waited. A few moments later, the door swung inwards. Will smiled and nodded in the direction of the smartly dressed aide opening the door.

"Thank you, Mr Beeton."

"You're most welcome Sir, and please do call me Samuel, Sir," replied the aide with the kind of grace you would expect from a butler in one of the grandest of houses. "The AVM is expecting you. Sir is in the drawing-room with a visitor, but he has instructed me to escort you there."

Samuel turned and led them up the first flight of stairs and through the door to the main hall, where the magnificent tapestry still hung on the wall. Again, ahead of them was the fireplace. This time they were led to a door on the left side, taking them into a comfortable, large room, richly furnished with leather wing-backed chairs and sofas, reminiscent of a London Gentleman's club. Another large fireplace burned brightly to counterbalance the grey dreary dampness of the weather outside.

The AVM was deep in conversation with a refined-looking lady. She clearly had impeccable dress sense and shoes, which Will immediately spotted, being a fan of high heels, (only from an engineering perspective, of course). The AVM turned as he heard Samuel bringing Will and Eddie into the room.

"Good morning, thank you for coming over. Gentlemen, this is Ladey Adey, and these gentlemen are Flight Lieutenants Eddie Driver and Will Anderson."

"Good morning, m'Lady!" Will as good as stood to attention as her eyes met his.

"Stand easy," came the reply from the perfectly poised woman. "It's delightful you should want to ennoble me, but this is Locksley Hall, not Foxley Heath and I'm the Engineering Accountant, not a Countess. Mind you, the Creighton-Ward mansion expenses are probably equal to those here. My job here is to keep the wheels turning. The surname was a wedding gift rather than an inheritance. To prevent confusion, nearly everyone calls me 'Cogs'. It's a bit simpler."

Will looked slightly puzzled. However, this was short-lived as the AVM interrupted,

"She deserves to be made a Dame for all the work she puts in," The AVM smiled, "But of course, that might get really complicated for party invitations!" He turned back towards 'Cogs', "Sorry, we'll be abandoning you here for the moment. Please do make yourself at home. These gentlemen and I have an errand to run." With this, he motioned Eddie and Will back into the direction of the main hall.

"Gentlemen, I appreciate your deference, but I think we need to be less formal with each other in private. Especially with everything you've seen and heard so far. You will understand, we are no longer acting in a military capacity. Therefore, military formality, out of the earshot of another uniform, can be discarded. So please feel free to call me Rob. Is it OK if I call you Eddie and Will, or would you prefer Buzz and Zebedee?" The smile on the AVM's face was quite reassuring.

"Thank you, Sir, ...er Rob," came the replies in unison.

"Please call me Eddie"

"And yes, please do call me Will."

"So, Eddie, Will, you've come for the audio key?"

"That's right, sir... er...Rob." Will thought it would take a long time before he got the hang of calling the AVM 'Rob' rather than 'Sir'. "I'm guessing you've got this seven-inch-single in a safe somewhere?"

"It is certainly in a thoroughly safe location," Rob replied, "Let's go and fetch it."

Together they walked back to the main hall and found themselves in front of the wall-hanging.

"Do you like it? I must say, it's something we're extremely proud of. Does it remind you of anything?"

Eddie and Will both took a closer look. It was impressive, about twenty feet wide and a dozen feet high. It was beautiful, with figures depicting a hunting party, most of which appeared to be archers wearing some kind of green medieval jackets. Will thought it might have been the historical equivalent of the latest gear all the armed forces had received last year. Although Disruption Pattern Material would have looked every kind of wrong on this group.

Among the green figures, there also appeared to be a monk, a guy wearing a red tunic and a positively graceful lady.

Eddie noticed Will was clearly giving the lady the 'once-over'.

"So, it's not for the first time this week, we're being asked, 'what something looks like', and then we discover, somewhat strangely, everything IS as it appears!"

Will grinned and looked away from the woman,

"It looks like a depiction of Robin Hood and his Merry Men, with my namesake in scarlet, and this delightful lady must be Maid Marian?"

"It looks exactly like that for a reason." Rob smiled warmly. "The Locksley Hall you stand in today, is the real ancestral home of Robin, Earl of Locksley." Eddie raised an eyebrow,

"So, what you're saying is Robin Hood isn't from Nottingham or Yorkshire? But he's from a small village in the east of Lincolnshire, and all these years, two counties have been slugging it out for ownership of the legend, whilst no one has known 'the truth' of the story?"

Eddie raised his fingers using the sarcastic 'air quotes' gesture he'd picked up from Alba earlier in the day as he uttered the word 'truth'.

Rob was loving this. It was a bit like showing Prismorphic technology to someone and then having them wonder how the box was bigger on the inside than on the outside.

"Exactly! The first Earl of Locksley was perfectly happy having the Sheriff's men chasing the 'Brotherhood' all over north Nottingham, past the *Major Oak* and into Doncaster. Ask yourselves for a moment, why does the story talk about the 'Merry Men wearing Lincoln Green'? They weren't just merry because they were constantly amused by the incompetence of Frenchman Philip Marc, the High Sheriff of Nottinghamshire.

"They were always going to be at a disadvantage. Marian here was Marian d'Avranches, daughter of the fifth Earl of Chester and fluent in French. The Brotherhood wore Lincoln Green to celebrate their heritage of being from Lincolnshire, and it is a great camouflage. Philip Marc did, however, get dangerously close to the truth when he was made Joint Sheriff of Lincolnshire."

Will listened to all of this with his mouth open and suddenly closed it to avoid looking like he was trying to catch flies.

"So how come over the years, did no one ever work this out? Surely if this were true, someone would have twigged it? And does that mean you're directly descended from Robin Hood?"

Rob looked meaningfully at them, slightly evading the second question,

"The fact most of them were from Lincolnshire was a closely guarded secret. It was really convenient that Nottinghamshire and Yorkshire wanting to own the legend, as it meant that they could all hide in plain sight on the east coast! There was one point when they thought the secret would be revealed when that damn fool Tennyson wrote a poem about the Hall. Nice bloke Tennyson, I really liked him, but the man had no idea. Fortunately, it was well before radio and TV, so they got away with it. However, my predecessors had to get him invited to the Arundel family home in Staffordshire as part of the cover-up. Some of the brighter conspiracy theorists even think it's about my Mother-In-Law's house since she built the dog kennel at the end of the drive, embellished with the house's name."

Overwhelmed, Eddie looked at Will,

"I think we need to stop off at the pub again. I'm not sure if we've had too much to drink, or not enough, or perhaps we're still there!"

Rob tipped his head forward, as if to look over the top of a pair of glasses he wasn't wearing,

"I told you last time, you'd see some strange stuff. Welcome to a whole new world of weird." He pulled back the corner of the tapestry to reveal a door behind. "Right this way."

∞⊕◔⊖๛

Eddie and Will were led into a small room, hung with various coats and selections of walking boots. Rob nodded his head towards the coats.

"You're going to need something extra to wear as it's only dreary outside. Pick some footwear and a fur coat, you're going to need it where we're going."

As they pulled on their chosen apparel, Rob slipped a cloth out of his pocket, similar to the one they had seen, when Mark Sparks had borrowed Eddie's watch.

He passed it to Eddie,

"It's time you two learned how to use Electron Fabric. Hold the corner open in the palm of your hand so you can see the numbers. You'll see they represent possible dates. Slide your fingers over the numbers like you would with a child's abacus. You'll see the days, years and months change."

Eddie and Will both looked closely at the cloth, amazed they could slide their fingers over a flat surface and see it alter in small steps.

"What date should we select?"

Rob pointed at the cloth,

"If you're travelling to a different year, it's always best to travel to the same day of the month you are starting out on, it helps reduce confusion. Pick 11th December and the year 1219. Select the 'Portal' option because we're using a door. Then, press 'Submit' before wrapping the cloth around the door handle and turning it.

"Normally, you can only travel one hundred years at a time with Electron Fabric. Still, I use this portal quite a bit, so Mark Sparks and

Ruby's Uncle, Alan Rowe, have upgraded the Cascade Hinges. They now have an infinitely more robust power pack. This isn't the only special door. All the doors under RAF North Coates, the ancient door in the snug at The Old Volunteer and every door downstairs in the hall are fitted with Cascade Hinges. If you ever try to use a door with no Cascade Hinges, Alan and the Q team 500 years from now receive a notification. They're the ones who do all the really clever technical stuff. They fit the hinge in the future, and its existence cascades back to the moment the door was first fitted, making it all but immediately available to you."

ZUKANN OPTIC:

SCAN ME
K101A

Textile Science

"Electron Fabric can be operated precisely the same as a 21st Century tablet device.

Hold the cloth at the edge and flap it. The fabric goes rigid, like a tablet. It can be operated similarly. Perfect for displaying a travel map, the whole feature set is not normally required if all you want to do is open doors. As a wise man once said, 'Don't tell me how the clock works, I just need to know the time'."

To discover more, please select this ZUKANN OPTIC.

Eddie turned the door handle cautiously and felt what seemed to be a gentle buzz. He could not decide if it came from the cloth or the handle. He thought he saw the hinges alter their shape for a fraction of a second, but then the door opened fully and they were hit by a blast of air, so cold and fresh it gave Eddie brain-freeze, like he'd just eaten an ice cream.

"Wow, this is one large ice-box you've built here". Will looked around. "Actually, I take that back. This place is vast, there's trees, and look at all this snow. Is it some kind of film set?" He looked back at where they'd been only moments before. The boot room was gone. There was still a slightly open door, but now they could see a dark room with pheasants, rabbits and legs of deer hanging in an orderly fashion from roof beams. Not the timbers of a grand mansion, but a humbler old barn.

Around them was a dense wall of trees, definitely not visible five minutes before, and the branches hung heavily with crisp white snow. Moments ago, the ground had been damp, the sky dreary and grey. Now they were surrounded by fresh snow at least a foot deep. The sky had changed to a deep, ominous leaden colour, heavy with the potential for even more snow to fall.

The shocked silence was broken once more by Rob,

"Welcome to the other side of the SlipStream Portal, a place where it is always deepest winter at this time of year."

"Oh, come on!" Eddie scoffed. "I know we've seen some stuff, but Narnia, really?"

Rob grinned. He hadn't had much chance to share this fantastic secret technology with many people, and he so loved the reaction.

"No, it's December here, the same as it's December at the airbase. It's going to be a long winter with deep snow, as it was in 1963. Welcome to Locksley Hall in the year 1219. To cut a long story short, the whole year is caught in a SlipStream loop. We're not sure why or how. Mark Sparks keeps offering to fix it for me, but it makes for a fantastically safe location." Rob looked at them with a mischievous smile, "And also, I get to see my family. Come on, shut that back door. We don't want to let the wolves into the food store. Let's go around to the front."

It took a couple of minutes, wading through the deep snow, walking around to the front of the barn. A large porch could be seen, similar to an old church entrance and a big oak door that somehow seemed really familiar.

A graceful woman in her early forties, wearing a blue cloak lined with fur and plaited leather belt, ran across the hall towards Rob Locksley with a massive smile on her face and outstretched arms.

She called out in a French accent,

"It's young Robin, how are you?" and gave him a huge hug. She then turned to Will and Eddie. "And you must be young Robin's friends. He said he might be bringing you to meet with us all. I am Marian. Greetings to you at this wonderful festive time. Has your Cappellani brought you to celebrate the end of Quadragesima Sancti Martini with us? My Robin will be home shortly with a goose!"

Both Eddie and Will were as confused talking to someone from their own history as when talking to someone from their future. They looked to Rob Locksley for guidance, which Rob supplied graciously.

"Please accept our humble apologies. Unfortunately, we cannot stay for long today; however, we would gladly share bread and ale with you and await Robin's return."

Marian beamed with happiness,

"I will prepare something for you." She turned to Will and Eddie with a slightly conspiratorial tone. She did not want to embarrass Rob with a loud compliment. Instead, she half-whispered, "Your Cappellani is a great man, we would all halve our cloaks for him. Let me fetch you something nice."

Eddie turned to stare at Rob with slightly mad staring eyes,

"Help! Please translate for us!"

Rob gave him a compassionate smile. He understood how eight-hundred-year-old idioms took a bit of getting your head around.

"Marian calls me 'your Cappellani'. It's a kind of military chaplain. She doesn't see me as a soldier or warrior but more as your coach or mentor. They are celebrating the end of a fast lasting for forty days from mid-November, in memory of the French Bishop, Saint Martin. Imagine it's like Advent, just before Christmas." Marian is the daughter of the fifth Earl of Chester but was born in Avranches. Her being fluent in French has put the High Sheriff at a disadvantage on a number of occasions.

Rob lowered his voice in deference to Marian's quiet complement.

"The cloak comment was a real kindness. She's referring to a miracle St Martin performed, cutting his cloak in half to protect a beggar. So, she's saying I will be kind to you." With a smile and one eyebrow raised, he then added, "don't get used to it. I'm not going to get that soft!"

There was clearly a lot to learn, and now it was Will's turn to be curious,

"So why does she call you 'Young Robin' and not 'Rob'?"

"Ahh, well, it's because she knows my real name and I figure you'd already sussed it. I don't need to hide it here. It's like the mask of the *Lone Ranger*. Obscure a small part of your identity, and you'll find that hiding in plain sight is easy. If everyone called me Sir Robin and spelt the surname 'LOXLEY', it wouldn't be long before someone born after 'The Great Vowel Shift' worked it out. We got the idea from the Etruscans.

"Fortunately, it's worked well for centuries. Have you ever stopped to wonder where the famous Robin Hood of Sherwood Forest ACTUALLY lived?   And she calls me 'young' because, in reality, she knows she's eight hundred years my senior!"

Eddie nodded,

"Of course, it all makes complete sense. Let's hope the secret doesn't come out now we've dumped the wreckage of a plane so close to your back garden!"

Marian returned, accompanied by two younger women and a monk carrying a large amount of food and placed it on the table in front of them. Considerably more than would be a modern meal.

Marian beckoned them forward,

"Come, sit and tell us more tales of metal birds and carts that need no horses. AND ROBIN, last time YOU promised on your return, to recount the ballad of the great yellow fish and the people living inside it, in the sea of green. We simply must hear that tale! But what am I doing? I have not introduced you. This is our Friar from Alvingham Priory. You must try some of the mead he has brought for our celebration."

Will tilted his head, on the edge of being afraid to ask the question, enquiring tentatively,

"Friar Tuck perhaps?"

Will's caution was well-founded and his relief palpable when the Friar chuckled, shook his head and introduced himself,

"No, of course not. I'm not Tuck. I'm Friar Adelwold. I've been blessed with an invitation to the celebration. Tuck has gone to fetch a Goose and more mead with Robin and Master Scarlet from the Priory." He patted his stomach and laughed again. "It would be unmistakeable if I was Tuck, he's exceptionally gifted at brewing mead – if you know what I mean! But look at me 'babbelen', and we've not introduced the ladies. May I introduce Elizabeth and Louise? Fortunately, they arrived into this world, not as Bidden Maids, but one after the other on the same day. There is no doubt

Robin is a strong man!"

Both ladies looked decidedly embarrassed, with Elizabeth interjecting, "Thank you, Friar, for explaining that we are immediate sisters. In case you wondered, as people often do, we have separate minds. I married in the Spring of this year, and Louise was married in the summer of last. Our husbands are both serving to protect Guillaume de Joinville at Rheims. Friars Adelwold and Tuck both serve to protect our whole family, as do all the Ælfingas. We will leave you to enjoy the food as we wait for the return of our father and continue preparations for the celebration with our mother."

Friar Adelwold, slightly under the influence of mead, wandered off in the direction of the two young ladies, the hearth, and the hot food, leaving Will and Eddie wondering who Guillaume de Joinville was and wondering whether Ælfingas were animals, aliens or mythological creatures.

Rob Locksley turned to Eddie and Will,

"In my experience, talking to people is harder in the past as the idioms are harder to work out, whilst in the future, it's the technology that's the challenge! However, I do worry about the family. Robin and Marian are well protected, but the next century is extremely difficult to travel to for some reason, so it's unclear what happens next. However, if anything happens to Robin, the Canoness at Alvingham Priory would care for Marian."

Before they could talk any further, the door burst open. Snow flurried inside, and three men, looking every inch as impressive as the images from the tapestry on the wall at Locksley Hall, came in from the cold. Kicking the snow from their boots, they removed their furs and headed for the warmth of the hearth.

The person first through the door and first to the fire caught Marian's eye and turned to see who was sat at the table. Despite being in his late forties, the original Robin of Locksley was clearly still a warrior to be reckoned with. Even so, with a great welcoming smile and arms stretched wide, he strode across the room followed by the others, recognisable as the muscular Will Scarlett and the rotund Friar Tuck.

Eddie, Will and Rob Locksley all stood to greet their hosts, who hugged them with the kind of energy which would 'provide power to the other, if not a great warmth'.

"Greetings, brothers!" the original Robin boomed, "You are so welcome here. Young Robin said he would be bringing friends. I see you have brought Scarlett's namesake to meet us!" He looked closer at Will, looked slightly puzzled and turned to Will Scarlett. "Does he not have the look of Hugh, Lord Kidderminster, King John's dapifer?"

Will Scarlett unstrapped the heavy looking sword from his waist, placed it at the end of the table and looked closely at Will,

"Indeed, it has been ten years since he died, but I still remember him well. Is there a Hugh Bisset in your lineage?"

Will was at a loss. He'd never known his family,

"I'm sorry, I was brought up in an orphanage, so I have no idea. But, perhaps it could be possible. Whilst we are on the subject of names, are you called Will Scarlet because you wear scarlet?"

Scarlet smiled and turned to Robin, nodding back in the direction of Will,

"This one is undeniably perceptive. He would have no trouble outfoxing the Sheriff! I wear red to remind the wealthy people we meet, that their sometimes-unwilling gratuity is the same as a tax paid to the Sheriff in his glorious scarlet gown. The same one he wears with the Aldermen when taking Ostarmanoth water at the Brodewell. His intention is always to remind the town and country people who owns them. Having taken the water each year, he and the Aldermen then make their way to the Erne Hills in the north. They look down their noses upon the town and the people. The scarlet cloak I first wore was my uncle's when he was Sheriff fifty summers gone this year, in the times before the wealthy forgot their true purpose. Between those of us here who are trusted, my friends call me Scarlet, but my real name is William de Mattersey, at your service, Sir!" Robin thumped the table with enthusiasm,

"No matter our names, you are all brothers at my table. We should drink a toast to you all." He waved in the direction of the hearth.

More drinks were brought over by a slightly unstable Friar Adelwold. He, fortunately, had been provided with a pewter platter with more tankards and a large jug containing even more mead. This was going to be a long afternoon.

Many tales were told that day, including the ballad of the great yellow fish, then the rebellious canticle of the blackbird and the beetle encouraging people to rise up and resist tyranny. Finally, the song of the fool on the hill was popular, as It echoed the challenge Eustace of Lowdham set the current High Sheriff of Nottingham, Philip Marc when returning from the Brodewell one year. The wager was to ride a donkey up the steepest part of the Erne Hills, which became known as the Donkey Hill from that day forward.

Of particular interest to Eddie and Will were the daring exploits of Robin and what Philip Marc, called 'The Renegades'. From their cinematic imagination of the world of the movies and Errol Flynn, it was a long way to the grinding poverty, misery, hunger and hopelessness of the 13th Century.

Since the enthronement of Henry of Winchester, promises of change to forest laws had been made to the townspeople. However, wealth always prevailed, and the situation changed little. Will Scarlet's father, Roger FitzRalph, Son of Ranulph de Mattersey, had founded two Gilbertine priories. He wished to help protect the poor as a reflection of his gratitude for the gift of Will, his second son, at the late age of forty years. One was in the village of Mattersey, dedicated to St Helen and one in the village of Bleduourda, some called Blidworth, dedicated to St Lawrence, so alms could be given to the poor. The Priories were the recipients of the 'gratuities' collected by Robin and Will from the wealthy merchants who ventured through the Shirewood Forest.

In return for the money given to the poor, the Gilbertines provided sanctuary for the brotherhood of the forest. However, there were many safe locations. Notably, their favourite one was halfway between Bleduourda and Mattersey. During one particularly cold Winter with heavy snow, they took shelter in a smallholding where the farmer's wife served them a treat made from cow's milk and crushed ice. Their Minstrel friend, Allen of Alsop en le Dale, sang of the 'Farm of delights'. He would toast this place whilst drinking fresh mead and remember the shelter of the 'heartless blizzard village'. Allen le Dale also loved the ballad of the great yellow fish, the thought of which really amused Eddie. Rob Locksley turned to Will and Eddie nodding in the direction of Robin,

"He has two daughters you've met, but also two sons." Rob turned back to face Robin, "What news of your sons?"

Robin laughed,

"I am beginning to wonder if I should have named them something else as it seems we have two Wills and two Robins here. It is probably for the best that my sons are knights away fighting in the King's Army. For if Rob and Robin were here, anyone chronicling our tale would not be able to tell one Robin from another! They are both well, as far as we know. My concerns are closer to home."

Marian had come to join them at the table and seemed concerned.

"Is there trouble at the Priory?"

"Not exactly. Things simply feel ominous. I'm not a great believer in bad omens. I believe we make our own destiny, but I feel the hand of Philip Marc reaching out!"

Marian spat on the floor,

"Bof! That fool, Chéri le Shériff, Darling Captain? And you think his idiot sidekick, Eustace of Lowdham, is smart enough to threaten us here?" Robin grimaced,

"No, of course, not them, but I am concerned about Pierre de Bellême. It's only been three years since Nicola de La Haye appointed Marc as Joint Sheriff of Lincolnshire, and she has given Pierre to Marc. You know the oak chest in the entrance of St Mary's church at North Somercotes? Last night someone carved the initials 'P.B.' on it. Scarlett and I think this is a warning from Bellême, as if he knows he's close to us. And it's not the only thing. When we were at the Priory, we were going to get chickens from the coop, but they had all been killed. Possibly by a fox, but it could have been done by a man. I also think back to the summer when the fruit all failed. I know there won't be strawberry fields forever, but it's a bad omen."

Marian laughed slightly nervously,

"You sound like my cousin Lady Barbara. It's a shame about her, she was very superstitious. She had a whole lot of love for the world, and she walked with amazing grace too. She loved to ride a white swan and kept it as a pet, calling it her 'Snowbird'. The fire reminds me of her also. She adored the aroma of crackling roses on the fire. She was always so modest. She said if she had a home-loving man who would do it my way, she could be happy even if she had patches in her clothes."

"I can hear her now saying, 'when I'm dead and gone, it will be a new world in the morning'. She knew when death came to her door, she would shout out loud, 'I hear you knocking', and death would say 'you're ready now'."

Marian shook her head sadly,

"Her death was very sad. She was carrying a mirror one day, bent down to pick up a penny. As she did, she smashed the mirror, tripped over a black cat, fell under a ladder, and choked to death on a chicken wishbone she had been eating. It's a shame."

Marian smiled reassuringly at her Robin,

"No one will harm the Priory or the church whilst they are under the protection of the King. With so many men lost in battle in the Holy Lands and so many widows. If it wasn't for you and the Friars, think of all the lonely people who would not be looked after."

Eddie turned to see Will casually stroking the bench they were sat on,

"Are you OK, Will? I was thinking I've lost you." he whispered.

"Yes, fine, thanks Ed. With the tip of my fingers, I was quietly checking the bench was real. Heaven help us all if we wake up to discover we've been part of some weird military LSD experiment!"

A moment of thoughtful reflection passed across the room, which was broken by Rob Locksley,

"I'm sorry to say, the day is coming to an end, and we must go. Robin, could I collect my package from you?"

Robin stood up - slightly unsteadily due to the Mead, despite being accustomed to its strength - and walked over to the fireplace. He reached in and gently teased a stone block from the right-hand side of the hearth. Then, stretching his fingers into the newly opened cavity, he probed the space gently. Finally, teasing out a slim, flat muslin wrapped package, he gave it to Rob Locksley.

"Do not travel too far from us, this flat world has a sharp edge all around. Do not fall off and be unable to return."

Rob Locksley peeled back the corner of the wrapping; his curiosity satisfied by the image of an orange. He patted this highly prized package and gave Robin a hug.

"I will return, and maybe when you least expect it. But remember, never run so fast that your joy cannot keep pace!"

Cloaking themselves again in the thick fur coats, they braced themselves for the cold winter air.

As they were heading out of the door, Tuck handed Eddie a flagon of Mead,

"One day, when you are a Grandad, you will remember this day and tell your grandchildren about us. I pray they do not tell you it's only make-believe, and I sincerely hope you enjoy what our bees have strived so hard to help us create. We are all here to serve. One day, I fear it will be the death of us all, but until then, the Lord's work is never done. Safe journeys to you all."

As they headed out of the door, seven-inch single in hand, back to the rear of the old Locksley Hall and the return portal to 1970, Rob Locksley nodded in the direction of Friar Tuck.

"Did Robin tell you Friar Tuck is an Elf?"

Will sighed loudly, raising his eyes to the heavens,

"I know we've seen some stuff, AND it does LOOK like we're in Narnia, but now you're telling us we've drunk mead with Santa's little helpers!"

Rob laughed loudly,

"Sorry, but you are doomed to engage with the stubbornly persistent illusion that is the shape of our world as we know it. Pretty much everything you know to be a myth is actually possible, probable and potentially undeniable. If you're not sure, ask ZUKANN when we get back."

"Sorry Rob, I'm not falling for that. I want this one from the horse's mouth. We've got a few minutes; spill the beans.

Rob smiled and looked over at Eddie,

"Sorry Eddie, this could get boring, so please do stop me if you've had enough. Here's a bit of history about Friar Tuck, which will no doubt upset the troubadours of Nottingham. He was actually a Monk from the Alvingham Priory of Gilbertine Canons and Canonesses. It's about ten miles west of here. It's mentioned in the Domesday Book.

"Alvingham is the Homestead of the Ælfingas, the tribe of Ælf. Friar Tuck was an Ælf. His family moved to Germany shortly after Tuck joined the Priory, where he could remain in England as part of an Ælf community. The Ælf are a caring, compassionate and kind species. So it was pretty evident Friar Tuck was of the Ælf. Not simply because he is described throughout history as being stocky, but also because of his desire to care for other species, such as humans. Had enough yet?"

The snow was making their boots and legs cold as they trudged their way back to modern life, but Eddie loved the snow, and this story was beginning to get interesting,

"Don't stop now. I want to hear the rest!"

"Don't say I didn't warn you," Rob replied. "So, the Ælf species are not magical in the same way mythical elves are. However, their advanced technological capabilities and practical talents became the source of the legendary stories of Elves. Initially from Other Earth code: OEAE1F, they spread to many parts of Home Earth, searching for sanctuary from persecution in their own parallel universe. They sought woodland to live in, partly due to the availability of resources for building homes and as a source for craft materials.

"Sherwood Forest, known in these times as the Shirewood, was a natural choice for a home. Many people in our time are unaware how far east across England the old forest stretched. However, with an increase in human farming, deforestation occurred between Lincolnshire and Eastern Nottinghamshire. Combined with coastal Forestry lost to mediaeval shipbuilding, many of the Ælf moved to the Dark Forests of southern Germany, eastern France, Poland and northern Switzerland.

"They're a peaceful people, trading on their success as artists, woodcutters and carvers. Capturing the still image of nature and the landscape led to them adopting more modern human technologies such as photography. Many centuries later, the Tuck family would return to England. Perhaps unaware of their history, and become founders of a photographic Postcard Empire. Their subconscious desire to return to their ancestral home can be seen in postcards, printed by them, of many churches local to the area of the original Ælfinga's tribal home."

The three of them had now arrived back at the rear of the house. The sun was a deep red, setting steadily behind the trees. With all the snow, it seemed there was some magical quality in the air.

Will smiled to himself, still unsure if Rob was a wind-up merchant. But, with what he and Eddie had seen over the last couple of hours, he'd come to realise that no matter how improbable the story, it could be the truth.

ZUKANN
OPTIC:

SCAN ME
K107A

The Gilbertines

"By the year 1350, in caring for their community, most of the Gilbertine order at Alvingham Priory had succumbed to the black death. The house was surrendered to The Crown in 1538.

There is a possible link between The Tucks and the 20th Century Media Tycoon Robert Maxwell and his media empire.

It is an unusual connection and carefully managed by FENDER to maintain event neutrality within the time stream. In 1987, Raphael Tuck & Sons LTD became part of the Maxwell Communications Company."

To discover more, please select this ZUKANN OPTIC.

CHAPTER 23
A Day In The Life

New York Central:
1900 Eastern Standard Time (EST),
Friday December 11th 2499 (DET)

Whilst Eddie and Will were experiencing life in the 13th Century, Ruby, Fred and Frank had travelled in the opposite direction.

It was always a culture shock travelling the time strands between different eras. Some epochs could be pretty similar, whilst others quite disturbing.

The 3rd Millennium was one of considerable upheaval and technological development. There was a stark contrast between the deprived societies of the early 20th Century and the profound social changes that became apparent in the 22nd Century, and then what emerged as the more equitable worlds of the 4th Millennium. There are two things practically never read about in histories about time travellers. The first is going to the toilet, the second is working week patterns and overtime possibilities.

Stepping into the Arrivals Hall of the 25th Century New York Central SlipStream transit centre could be a shock. A bit like having driven for an hour on a sweltering day in an air-conditioned vehicle, when the car door is opened on arrival, you are hit by the dramatic difference in temperature. Apart from the predicted changes such as flying cars, hoverboards and urban spaceship launches, the difference in technologies between the 20th and 25th Centuries would be quite startling despite some remarkable similarities.

ZUKANN
OPTIC:

SCAN ME
K108B

Chrono-Commuters

Time travellers often work shifts, with some only travelling in time on Thursdays. Although, professional time travellers mostly work according to ISO 8601.

Early on in the development of time travel, it became clear that a week of Wednesdays could be far more emotionally draining than a month of Sundays. In the early 21st Century, a music phenomenon called "The Artisans" even wrote a musical risk assessment called "A Week of Wednesdays". Known in most realities as 'Hump Day', it meant working at the worst point of the week, being furthest from the weekend. However, some would say it meant they could always take time off at the best parts of the week.

To discover more, please select this ZUKANN OPTIC.

For example, alighting from a London Tube, Parisian or New York Metro in the early 21st Century, you would be greeted by adverts on the walls for products, fast food, shows and museums. Some may even have been displayed on rudimentary video display screens.

In the 25th Century, with the advent of FIMER (Fully Immersive Media Entertainment and Recreation), within the crowds would be solid looking avatars of the original actors. They might simultaneously be starring locally in RAW (Real Actual World) theatres. In the street, they might deliver exciting lines to passers-by with the hope of enticing them to FIMER or RAW shows. There would still be adverts on doors and walls. Many of the advertising panels remaining, were retail opportunities. Travelling upwards to street level from the subterranean caverns of the rail-free, urban transit UG Ziptro tubes, you can view and even taste products advertised on the walls of the Bevelator spiral incline express walkways.

Although there were many curious parallels between the eras, there were also considerable differences. The Transit station, divided into three parts was located on the fifth floor of the 1400 storey Manhattan Building Megalopoplex. Nestling beneath the 165,000-bed Hildham-Jinzhu Domitel/Living centre, offices, retail, residential zones, convention and entertainment centres.

ZUKANN
OPTIC:

SCAN ME
L109A

Structural Science

"In the 25th Century, apart from entertainment avatars, one might see monuments and architectural salvage appearing at scale size in the street to advertise local historical museum and architectural collections. There would be locations where you could visit old buildings, curated for the benefit of visitors and historians to save them for posterity.

"In London, you might see ancient, (and tiny by 25th Century standards) full-size buildings such as The Shard and the relatively miniature sixty-two storey building from 22 Bishops Gate. However, on tour from New York, so much smaller than 'modern' architecture, is the elderly but venerable Empire State Building. It had been moved and saved for the nation after being replaced by the Manhattan Building in 2436.

Notable buildings like the Flatiron building, Central Park Tower and the Empire State Building were rescued by Doddken International Development Design – Yonkers (Major Engineering Nobility).

To discover more, please select this ZUKANN OPTIC.

Casimir Arrival and Departure Portals are located in one-third of the base of the building, towards the south. Even though centuries had passed, free travel was still available to Staten Island.

There are, of course, no longer any river ferries in service, due to the environmental improvements. The nature reserves and peatlands for storing CO2 from the city were great for hiking around the Statue of Liberty for a few hours. The Hudson River had long ago been diverted. Re-routed Easterly, between Pleasantville, Sleepy Hollow and Valhalla, to emerge from Connecticut into Long Island Sound between Greenwich and Stamford, allowing for environmental land redesignation between Manhattan and Hoboken into New Jersey.

Also, on the fifth floor of The Manhattan, was the multi-track hyper-rail transportation hub. Half of it was contemporary 'local' transit whilst the other half was devoted to bulk SlipStream Travel.

Trains from a dozen different Home Earth and Other Earth time periods waited for passengers to board or alight. It was travel genius on a whole new level. To facilitate the movement of large volumes of people to and from different time periods, what better way than to have them board conventional trains from the destination era, and have those trains depart and disappear into tunnels down the line. No one ever questioned a train entering a tunnel. No one ever looked to see if the train emerged from the other end.

The simplicity of installing a Casimir Event Horizon halfway through a railway tunnel and delivering the passengers to any time period required, was inspiring. For 25th Century train spotters, it was an absolute gift. Imagine seeing a Japanese bullet train on a platform beside the *Flying Scotsman* on one side and the *Cannonball Express* on the other with the *Venice Simplon Orient Express* ready to depart on a *Christie's Travel* excursion. Every locomotive having been lovingly re-created to 'modern' standards with zero-emission tractive power systems and virtual 'smart vapour' visual effects.

Leaving the main concourse, Fred, Frank and Ruby emerged into a larger lobby area. Ahead of them was a sign pointing in the same direction they were headed, towards the 'FLYSERS'.

What would have scared the living daylights out of citizens a mere century previously is considered no more worrying than taking an elevator when it was first invented.

"OK, Ruby, we'll leave you to your exciting meeting. Fred and I will head off for some M&Ms, and we'll catch up on the way back."

"No problem, Frank," replied Ruby, "but don't overdo it. I don't want to be trying to carry two suicidal tourists back to 1970."

It wouldn't be the first time one of the Time Tech Team had been assisted by other team members back home. Occasionally after an 'Epic' evening of Full Immersion/RAW crossover partying, which resulted in the need for painkillers and physical therapy for one reason or another. On one occasion, an airlift from a suspension bridge pylon was requested for a colleague, found wearing little more than a duck outfit, a 'kiss me quick' hat and carrying a banner displaying a large arrow and the text: 'I'm With The Bride Stupid'. Mind you, at seven feet tall, no one was going to argue with Alba.

ZUKANN OPTIC:

L111A

SCAN ME
L111A

Science of Sublimation

"M&Ms are an abbreviation for a dose of Morose and Morbidity brought about by consuming quantities of distilled Fungal Gripoid parasites. Like Fred and Frank, Alba remains a connoisseur, even after the phrases 'Get a Grip' and 'Fungal Gripoid' eventually became insults, reminiscent of 20th Century profanity.

"Gripoids, by the way, are mindless parasites with no sense of direction drifting through time as jellyfish drift with the current. They randomly faze in and out of temporal integrity, leading them to fall back and forwards through time and between dimensions. Direct contact leaves severe mould and mildew on inanimate surfaces. It imbues an irrational sense of fear amongst cognisant entities in the kind of lonely, dark, damp and dreary places associated with such contact.

To discover more, please select this ZUKANN OPTIC.

Fred and Frank often joked about themselves as being inseparable. They had an intriguing childhood and one quite different from others on the Time Tech Team. Twins, born in California, a century and ten minutes apart after an unfortunate portal destabilisation event. They insist on their social media profiles being identical. As their birth was so traumatic, they do everything together – most of the time.

Frank was born in 2101, although they were both brought up living from 2201 onwards.

They are vital members of the Portal and Gate systems team and both have identical first degrees from the Doppler-Stoxford-Harbridge Institute For Technology, in Casimir Event Horizon Stability and Critical Mass Flexibility, listing late 20th Century rock music as their hobby.

They grew up during a century and a half of mandated bliss and grinding happiness following the Worldwide Potato Plague of 2133 and the subsequent thirty-year Great Abduction Crisis. Their school education focussed heavily on the sciences of Utopian Solar

Buoyancy and Optimistic Sociability. Consequently, their standard response to questions about their drinking habits was, 'after an education like that, anyone would want a bottle of FunGryp'.

Their family had moved north to escape the ravages of the Potato plague, which hit southern America particularly severely. Originally from Buenaventura town in Colombia, their parents had found success through their skills as jewellers and goldsmiths. Proud to be twins born on either side of the creation of Practical Time Travel (PTT), Fred and Frank don't feel the usual antagonism felt between 'Histos' and 'Posties'. People born before PTT feel they are unaffected by the pressures brought about by the development of this new technology, whereas people born afterwards think they are part of a superior gene pool. This does not usually come to anything more severe than a bar fight. Alba derides any such argument as, by chance, she is neither but won't back down from the opportunity to take sides in a fist-fest.

CHAPTER 24
Ruby's Night Off

New York Central:
2000 (EST), Friday December 11ᵗʰ 2499 (DET)

Ruby saw 'The Boys' off for an evening of totally legal retail consumption, quaffing, inhalation, absorption, auditory abuse and impact aromatics. All of which were available from the Casimir arrivals shopping centre branch of JackDonald's take-away, bar, picnic area and 1980s Rock-arena.

It was then time for her to head for the conference centre hotel. Ruby did prefer using the Bevelators rather than travelling across huge buildings like 'The Manhattan' via the Flysers. There had been no serious Flyser injuries for over fifty years. However, she still wasn't entirely happy about stepping out over a 1000-foot precipice to be whisked off to her stated destination.

The meeting with FENDER wasn't due until the morning, and there was still some preparation for Ruby to do, having checked into her bedroom. Working away from home has changed little over the centuries.

For a Roman legionnaire expecting to do battle in the morning, there was always going to be Gladius sharpening and armour polishing the night before. For newly elected US Presidents, it was packing up the house ready for the move to The White House. For on-the-road salespeople, it was polishing off the last slides of the PowerPoint.

CRIGHES

ZUKANN OPTIC:

L112B

SCAN ME
L112B

Pedestrian Paradigms

Flysers are cabin-free shafts for travelling vertically and horizontally through buildings in transit shafts and service corridors. They were first introduced on the 23rd of March 2357, 500 years to the day after the 1857 unveiling of the first 'Lift' in the Haughwout Building in New York City.

Generally, there is a small charge for their use as they are quick, and travel is advert free.

An alternative to the Flyser is the Bevelator. Similar to a 21st Century escalator, but without steps. They are not constrained to a straight line and often spiral up and down shafts. Long climbs or descents are often split into stages, so travellers don't get dizzy. The advantage of the Bevelator over the Flyser is the availability of retail opportunities during travel.

To discover more, please select this ZUKANN OPTIC.

For Ruby, it was similar, checking her SyntherTap message feed, ensuring her social media bot was posting entertaining but believable updates and most importantly, checking in with ZUKANN to be sure all the relevant presentation material and graphics had been collated for the upcoming meeting.

Although when she was finished, she knew she'd be able to enjoy a great meal and, even better, a fabulous shower. 25th Century hotel bedrooms could be any design style you wanted. Even budget hotels had at least 10 design styles. Hotel bathrooms on the other hand were occasionally, literally on another world.

Ruby had just spotted a health and safety post from an analyst named Tom Ruegger, about two dangerous mutant mice suspected of plotting world domination and on the run in New York, when she remembered a bit of family wisdom. Whenever they were heading off on an adventure, her mother used to say to her, 'You need to go before you go, or else you'll go before you get there.' So, before anything else, and something rarely mentioned in an adventure story, Ruby needed the loo.

All food manufactured in the 25th century is processed with HYDRO-SLIDE™ microparticles. This means when visiting 'the bathroom', you never need to wipe. When Ruby was a child, she loved the jingle from the old advert:

ZUKANN OPTIC:

SCAN ME
L113A

The Hydro-Slide Jingle

♫ *"Blow away your bathroom blues;*
you'll never need to wipe your twos.
Let it drop without a plop it's,
water closet news!
Give a stool the smoothest ride;
you can defecate with pride
Honest care for your insides;
we are HYDRO-SLIDE!" ♪

To discover more, please select this ZUKANN OPTIC.

A time traveller is always recommended to bring their own toilet roll, as frequently there's never enough on the dispenser. Also, the cleaning probe fitted to Japanese toilets from the 21st Century onwards, still seems a little disconcerting to Ruby.

It's even more embarrassing when using tissues in a public toilet fitted with SMARTe9PANTS™ technology. On the one hand, it may be helpful to be checked for extremely rare medical conditions such as Diabetes and Bowel Cancer, so you can get a spray. On the other, it's not so funny when dropping tissue down the bowl, and a digital voice emanates from behind you: 'Unexpected item in the drop-zone'!

On the subject of personal hygiene, especially when on an unexpected visit to the future, the bathing booths are considerably more comfortable and with a range of developments. Similar in some ways to an early era shower, a traveller can experience a range of treatments from the menu. This may be a simple water shower, with or without hydrophobic elements to remove dirt on the body. A bather may choose sonic, ion storm, pressured air, steam, cold vapour or dry cleaning.

ZUKANN
OPTIC:

SCAN ME
M114A

Fancy Pants

SMARTe9PANTS™ should not be confused with any of the following: DARTe9PANTS™ running shorts, CARTe9PANTS™ re-inforced underwear for men, CHARTe9PANTS™ navigation wear, HEARTe9PANTS™ defibrillator clothing, FARTe9PANTS™ odour control wear, MARTe9PANTS™ therapeutic retail clothing and of course, the one for the man in your life, the unforgettable TARTe9PANTS™ twin-bladed shovel for removing Reblochon Cheese and potato dishes from barbecue and pizza ovens.

A tree for toilet paper can take twenty years to mature. It was estimated in the early 21st Century, that by the year 2500, the entire surface of Australia would be required as a tree plantation for toilet paper production. New Zealand would be excluded as their entire landmass would be committed to wine production for German discount food stores. By 2170, Tasmania had already signed up to global production of disposable wooden ice-cream tub spoons and toothpicks.

To discover more, please select this ZUKANN OPTIC.

Additional treatments might include nutrients, oils, solvents, alpha hydroxy acids, powdered crocodile excrement or moisturising creams. These can be applied by bionic mimeo devices, wielding brushes, mitts, puffs, loofahs or sponges. A bather may sit, stand, float or freefall in complete comfort. All assisted by Full Immersion technology.

This provided a range of bathing experiences, from Cleopatra's bathroom to the International Space Gymnasium; a forest glade, to a Victorian Turkish bathhouse.

Ruby was never so keen on the 'Forest Glade' setting as she always had the peculiar feeling someone was watching her. Then, as if someone had been watching her thoughts, her WOTISC buzzed, and a message appeared. FENDER requested the meeting be moved to an earlier time.

Ruby pursed her lips and shook her head, 'Hey ho!' she thought. 'The Donkey Milk – Alpha Hydroxy Acid' bath might not have been her first choice, but it would have been nice to have had the chance." A quick SyntherTap message off to Fred and Frank to warn them to cut their revelries short, as this was bound to mean an early start for all of them in the morning. Then out of the door again and on to the meeting.

CHAPTER 25
Best Bar – Bar None

New York Central:
2100 (EST), Friday December 11ᵗʰ 2499 (DET)

Fred and Frank, having tired of the JackDonald's Rock Arena, made a beeline for their favourite watering hole. The Axe and Cleaver Weapons Range and Sports Bar was close to Pier 86. They chose it partly because it was a short hop from 'Casimir Arrivals'. Also because it was close to one of their favourite science centres, The Museum of Space and Flight Archaeology. It was also a great place to pick up on any off-grid chatter about time technology and SlipStream abuse – something they ultimately helped fix. Also, it had the most incredible range of FunGryp cocktails outside of Canada.

Sports bars hadn't changed much over the centuries. The sports might be different; the seating more responsive to varying degrees of Gluteus Maximus impact and the screens of increasing quality, size and proximity; but people needed a drink and a method of delivery. Some bars had robots, but this one still retained a human.

As Fred and Frank walk into the bar, they were greeted like long lost friends. More because the barman had an eidetic memory than because Fred and Frank were regular drinkers. Michelangelo Fynn - Bartender, World Traveller and Conspiracy Theorist - modelled his appearance on Dan Aykroyd's character, *Elwood* from *The Blues Brothers*. Also known as 'Mickey the Tab' (because that's what people said when they wanted to settle the bill), held his arms wide, in an enthusiastic welcome.

"It's fantastic to see you. I was beginning to wonder if everyone had got sucked into this vortex of traffic chaos this afternoon, it's been so quiet."

"We've just come off a 'Casimir' at Grand Central." Fred looked at Mickey, puzzled. "It's only taken us two minutes to get here on a Flyser, so what's been kicking off?"

"Here, take a look; it's going mad out there", replied Mickey. Then, waving his hand at a few monitors, he swiped them over to half a dozen social media news channels. They featured what was generally plagiarized versions of the same insane story. "The Students Union are getting the blame, but if you ask me, and anyone else who knows their stuff, it's that hacker-terrorist cell 'The Steamers' again."

Mickey turned the sound up on the monitors to better hear the news anchor's clipped tones,

"...local Hyper-rail commuters experienced massive disruption on a legendary scale this morning as the result of what appears to be a student Fresher Week prank. Drone SkyCam footage of the pre-five minutes, shows what seems to be a man riding astride a model of an industrial age locomotive. Heading along the Downtown Elevated HyperLoop in front of Thunberg New York University.

"He appears out of nowhere from the Washington Square Arch in Washington Square Park, travels south directly above west Broadway for about ten minutes at a ridiculously slow speed and vanishes into the US Postal Service. The man's escape was via the Casimir Event Horizon 8th Floor Freight Departure Portal on the west side of the Federal Office Building. Student campaigners have denied any responsibility for this glee legend.

"Carbon pollution detectors were triggered along the entire length of the event. It's believed approximately twenty-five ounces of carbon and three cubic yards of carbon dioxide was released into the New York atmosphere. The Cost to industry is being estimated at 38 million Credits. University Security and City Transit officials have been called to an emergency meeting with FENDER to discuss the city-wide chaos as all transit systems were shut as a security and environmental precaution.

"Airborne FlyderCab Taxi Pods and XiTas were jammed and crammed twelve high on the Brooklyn and Manhattan aerial overpasses. It's stall and crawl on the FDR HyperDrive, and it's a stationary bump and grump entering Manhattan on the South Cove HyperDrive. Fresh wisdom to avoid the creep and beep, if you can work from home tomorrow, keep your car in its bay and stay away for the day!"

Frank swiped the volume down, looking quite impressed,

"Wow, that's a seriously amazing stunt for students to pull off." He was trying hard to keep a straight face as it was still a bit anti-social not to be overtly happy, even in the face of chaos and confusion. The simple reason they'd come for FunGryp cocktails was because it was still legal to get solidly morose. Now, more than ever, he needed a drink. Partly because all this genuinely looked hilarious. "Mickey, get me a triple of your twenty-five-year-old 'Tennessee Special'. I think we need to get seriously down tonight."

Mickey reached for a three-litre optics bottle,

"Do you want me to leave it on the bar, or shall I serve it?"

"Actually, I think you should join us. It's not looking good for anyone else coming in tonight, so it would be great to have some company to get miserable with."

Mickey threw down the tea towel he'd been holding and picked up three glasses. Towels weren't actually used for much else, other than perhaps flagging down passing XiTas flying at altitude, as all the glasses were cleaned and dried hypersonically. But a tea towel was the 'de rigueur' part of a uniform for a bar steward. It was a virtual badge of honour to have a clean towel behind the bar.

He banged the glasses down on the table in front of Fred and Frank and said,

"So, what's it to be, a game of 'Panopoly' or are we going to tell it as it is?"

Frank grimaced,

"I don't think we're up for having fun tonight." He raised his first glass with the traditional toast. "Never give up!"

ZUKANN
OPTIC:

SCAN ME
M116A

Social Science

"Panopoly is a game, popular with students. Invented by the creators of 'Carnivorous Crocodiles'. The aim is to assemble the most impressive and extensive collection of items to win a round. Although played as a board game, the collected items must be things 'lost' by other citizens. These might include road cones, traffic lights, abandoned street signage, car keys (with extra points if the vehicle is still attached), boats, aeroplanes, space cruisers and buildings. In fact, anything, if it's not nailed down and genuinely does not have an owner.

"Alcohol is not an integral part of this game; however, distinguished winners have attributed their success to 'having the odd pint' and 'it was Friday night'."

To discover more, please select this ZUKANN OPTIC.

To which Fred replied, raising his glass,

"Never surrender!"

Mickey looked at them both, completely shocked,

"You KNOW about *Galaxy Quest?*"

Frank looked equally surprised how someone WOULDN'T know about the best TV series ever conceived.

"Of course! It's brilliant! Al al al al al al al al al al al al! I love the *Thermians*. We did a convention wearing Prismorphic Ponchos so we could change from bipedal to a cephalopod. Fred got the Masquerade Runner-Up prize for his costume."

Mickey looked over his shoulder as if someone might be listening and spoke in clandestine tones,

"Between you, me and the four-zero-three, they were once going to make a movie, centuries ago, but apparently, FENDER kept blocking it or something? It seems it somehow breached 'Event Neutrality', but it would be great to know if it HAD been made in someone's reality. Anyway, let's hear it then, what's your worst life experience. Purely so we can get into the party mood."

Frank looked at Fred,

"Professor Ewing and his Hysterical Hysteresis Economics?" Fred looked puzzled for a moment, so Frank continued. "You know, the guy who had no idea he looked exactly like a Disney villain and claimed to know a joke from every mainstream stand-up comic right back to Napoleon Bonaparte?"

A look of dawning realisation spread across Fred's face,

"Those lectures were terrible." He turned to face Mickey. "He tried to convince the students to tell jokes whilst making economic decisions. He claimed the positive effects on the economy continued for far longer than the time it took for people to stop laughing about the state of the economy. The best thing I remember about Uni was Music Technology lectures. The tutors had no idea we were embedding audio into remasters of 20th Century Rock revival hits. Playing the audio files backwards, you could hear the truth about how awful it was to be eternally optimistic. Anyway, no," He shook his head, "No, definitely the worst was the Customs Hall decompression."

Mickey was intrigued,

"I think yours is going to be worse than mine. I think you should start."

"Before I do, I need another shot. I can't relive the trauma without help!"

Mickey poured Fred another shot of FunGryp, which fell through the air like a globule from a 20th Century lava lamp, whilst Fred took a deep breath,

"So, please remember, this was when we were younger. We were at university, at a time when backwards time travel was seriously regulated — even more tightly than it is now. We were on a field study trip to 1983. It was Steve Wozniak's US Festival - Memorial Day Weekend, Sunday 29th. It will stain my memory forever. We had gone to study Heavy Metal Day."

Fred looked at Frank as if he were still fighting off the hangover,

"Do you remember the look on his face when Doc Mayhem from Electric Teeth told the lead singer of Disaster Zone how CivLyzd Mares were way better musicians? Then, afterwards, the fight ended with 1600 people being injured and 87 people being arrested? It was an amazing weekend, but the journey home was rough. We'd gone to the Casimir Portal, and we'd arrived at Interdimensional Border Immigration. There were those BeeSkeeper bees, buzzing around everywhere."

There were tears of laughter running down Frank's eyes, who knew what was coming, as Fred took another swig of FunGryp and continued,

"The guy in front of me was a smuggler. I mean, there were huge signs up EVERYWHERE warning people not to try to compress food or drugs or anything else. Any compression field would be deactivated by security. Then, there was a huge WHHOOOFF sound as the smuggler's compression field explosively decompressed. Followed by the most unearthly screams as three, five-ton African elephants appeared out of the deactivated containment field. "The smuggler had been travelling for over three weeks. As a result, apart from the elephants, a delivery of six tons of elephant dung arrived in the atrium. It went everywhere! About thirty of us were completely covered, and this lucky git happened to be stood behind a pillar."

Frank was crippled with laughter,

"There was so much dung, it took a team of industrial sanibots two days to clean up! They reckon there's still half-digested straw dangling off the ceiling!"

Fred gave Frank such a look of disgust,

"Yeah, thank you, bro! I couldn't get the smell out of my nostrils for two weeks. Mind you, it's probably like the powdered crocodile excrement option in the showers. My skin is still soooo soft even now; I'm sooo moisturised!!" Fred ran his hands through his hair, then shook his head and held it in his hands.

Despite the volume of FunGryp they had all consumed so far, none of them was quite morose enough to stop laughing.

Mickey reached out for the bottle, and they all downed another shot,

"So, this compression thing. Tell me, is shrinking stuff down, like trying to fit an elephant into something the size of a lemon? When you squeezed the lemon, would you find everything was 'trunk-ated'?"

There was a long pause. First, nobody laughed, and then they all breathed a sigh of relief. Finally, they were finding it harder to be cheerful!

ZUKANN OPTIC:

SCAN ME
M118A

'BeeSkeeper' Drones

Part of the Bee Security network, they are bioengineered with almost 15 billion odour receptors in their antennae. They have a sense of smell more than fifty times better than a dog. They are used in airports and Casimir Portal Arrivals and Departures. They are perfect for sniffing out explosives, drugs, concealed food and lifeforms. Although extremely expensive to train, they can also be used to sniff out good rumours and great deals on retail purchases.

To discover more, please select this ZUKANN OPTIC.

Mickey continued,

"So now it's my disaster story. This should make you cry. It's my university-era tale. Well, at least it was when I managed the Student Union Bar anyway. FunGryp was the number one bestseller, all day, every day. Students were so frustrated with lectures on the science of Political Wistfulness being cancelled in favour of Utopian Solar Buoyancy and Optimistic Sociability, they would come in their droves to attempt to erase the near unforgettable government-mandated deluge of optimism and sanguine positivity."

Frank started to pull his hair out,

"STOP, please STOP. Don't remind me of that indoctrination of jubilance. Get on with the story and tell us about the disaster!"

Mickey was particularly apologetic,

"I'm so sorry, I did rather digress there. So, round the corner from the university was the world's largest distillery. The number one supplier of FunGryp of every flavour. A twin-trailered truck delivering the latest batch of Environmentally Friendly, Phantasm Free, Poltergeist Protected Fungal Gripoids arrived. Unfortunately, it crashed into a gas pipe, causing an explosion halting global production for a year. My lost revenue was huge. The University even considered bankruptcy because 70% of their funding came from takings at the bar."

The muscles in Fred's face began to relax as an expression of tranquillity spread across his face.

"That was the year we realised how despair was in our reach, and we could all but successfully manage without a glass of the 'Ol' Tennessee Special.' I remember now. But what caused the accident?"

Mickey shook his head sadly,

"It's a sorry tale. The driver was arrested and committed to a mental asylum. He claimed he'd swerved to avoid what looked like a man sitting astride a shrunken down 300-year-old steam train crossing his path at the instant of his arrival. Mind you, in those days, the government were so committed to positivity. He successfully launched an appeal. The Gendarmerie of Joy suggested there may have been extenuating circumstances. And it had made them laugh, so his sentence was commuted to nine weeks of community service and mandatory therapy at a Comedy Store. Now, think about it, even all those years ago, surely that's got to be one of the earliest terrorist attacks by The Steamers?"

Frank was looking pensive,

"I can remember all of this as if it were yesterday. One of my lecturers was Professor Seir Sindssyg. He pointed out how three per cent of the human body weight was nitrogen. One of the most essential constituents of a human body's cell protoplasm and critical to developing amino acids forming proteins and DNA. He said, to prevent the population from becoming depressed, something had to be done to increase Nitrogen levels. He's the guy who became chief scientific advisor to the Global President of Trade and King of Stockland? He persuaded the Global Health Organisation for Special Treatments to carbonate the mains water supply with Nitrous Oxide to make people happier. I still can't forget brushing my teeth with fizzy water and foaming at the mouth whilst laughing myself stupid. It was all terribly depressing!"

There were another few moments of silence. Then, finally, Mickey held his glass aloft unsteadily,

Morality Tales

"The once successful and illustrious President of Stockland, Meehandsa Indertill, had a spectacular fall from grace. This was due to a weakness for Distilled Fungal Gripoid cocktails which made him extremely depressed and affected his ability to spell.

"The great country of 'Stockland' – not to be confused with the even greater country of Scotland, had been the jewel in the crown of the UFSRRR (The United Federation of Services and Retailing Rich Regions), prior to the financial meltdown and ultimately, disillusioned investors bringing down the 'Ion Curtain'.

To discover more, please select this ZUKANN OPTIC.

"Gentlemen, as an artist and entrepreneur, I think I can honestly say, between you, me and the FunGryp, my work is done. We have arrived at the marvellous state of mournful melancholy. We should congratulate each other." He held out his hand to 'high five' Fred, missed, lost his balance and slipped off the side of the table.

At that moment, Fred's PIMMS device buzzed,

"Oh dear, Gents, looks like the show is over. We're needed for work in the morning. It is my great duty to thank Mickey, for one of the best nights in years, so it only remains for me to say, Mickey, the tab, please!"

Mickey collected himself off the floor, slid the tea towel off his shoulder and flicked it at one of the monitors. A small silver probe rose up from the centre of the table with a 3D projection of the amount of credit required to settle the drinks bill.

Frank waved his PIMMS at the silver probe, which went green. A small fireworks display appeared, about two feet above the table. 'THANKS FOR YOUR CUSTOM' was spelt out in sparkling letters, rotating in the air around the probe.

Mickey looked reassured he'd retained two more 'lifers' who would always think to come back another time,

"It's been a pleasure to be of service. If you'd like a lift home, I've got a XiTa out back, rhymes with heater, seven-seater, nothing sweeter, faster than a cheetah!" This was vaguely like the marketing campaign for this mode of transport, although delivered in such a befuddled way, as to warn any potential passengers why this option for homeward travel should definitely not be their first choice.

Frank raised his hands in mock surrender and in a voice almost as depressed as *Droopy* or *Eeyore*, replied,

"No, you've looked after us plenty. We're close enough to take a Flyser back to the hotel. It's only a couple of minutes. Drive safely yourself, and don't forget, as the advert says, 'switch to Auto-head' if you're driving yourself home."

Mickey headed for the back of the bar shouting,

"Goodnight" over his shoulder as Frank and Fred headed for the exit.

Definitely worse for wear; Fred tripped, staggered slightly and frowned pathetically,

"I had a thought about Eddie and Will. Do you think they've worked out the glass pyramid controls the air-conditioning?"

Frank clearly wasn't morose enough and grinned ever so slightly,

"I'm not sure they even had air-con in 1970. I told him it was a self-destruct button. You should have seen the look on his face. He was concerned the light sculpture was dangerous! I'm more worried they'll have set fire to the Gourmetron. I was hoping we'd get breakfast from it in the morning as I don't think we'll have time to eat here, I reckon Ruby will want to get back very early if her meeting was pulled forward. I do worry about those two pilots. Too much enthusiasm. Mind you, they seem nice guys, so if we all do our bit, and they can learn to fly the drones, it should be fine."

As they walked out into the street, there was a loud crash from the back of the bar. Fred and Frank turned around, puzzled, the portal into the bar 'auto-blending' behind them. They could see nothing. There was no point knocking on the windows; they weren't made of glass, so no noise would have been heard inside. Frank shaded his eyes with one hand to deflect the ambient light from the walls above them and get a better view of the bar,

"I can't see anything. He's probably reversed his XiTa into his Hydro-Brewery out at the back! That's done it; I've got my morose back. I'm so sad about his distillery!"

ZUKANN
OPTIC:

SCAN ME
N121A

Fred and Frank on Auto-head

As they say,
♫ *If you're Alco-meter's red,*
Use a XiTa, don't be dead.
We will watch the road ahead'n,
Get you back to bed.
Revel on and have a ball,
If you want to drink it all.
Stay alive and do not drive;
Switch to Auto-head!" ♪

To discover more, please select this ZUKANN OPTIC.

The street was dry, warm and the air still. The city lit, for the last few centuries, during the early morning hours by the gentle deep red luminescence of the 670 Nanometre Glen Jeffrey early morning lighting. Buildings, trees and shrubs, glowed with mitochondria stimulating crimson wavelengths, powered by their connection to the Synthernet, improving the health of humans and pollinating insects.

As Fred and Frank meandered melancholic, in their FunGryp induced momentously mournful manner back to the 'Flysers', the lights went out in the bar.

ZUKANN
OPTIC:

SCAN ME
N121B

Streeter Beater

Personal transport had undergone considerable change over the centuries. Flying cars had optimistically been promised by 2020. However, in reality, it would be another seventy-five years before they were a real 'mobility for the masses' option.

Initially, as petrol and diesel were phased out, a hybrid-electric generation became popular, although this itself was replaced with 'Hot-Swap Batteries'. Drive onto an energy forecourt, often on the site of an old fuel station. A robot arm would remove the battery pack. Then, it would be replaced with a recently charged one, resolving all the issues surrounding fuel transportation and rapid recharging.

As time passed, most people opted to use 'XiTas'. Pronounced 'Cheetahs' This was taken from the word 'Taxi' but formed from the Chinese/Swedish technology. 'Xi' is the Mandarin surname of one of the vehicle inventors and the Swedish word Ta for 'take'. The Powerplant is a Swedish design. When they infrequently broke down, the Xi was often pronounced incorrectly with the more vulgar epithet 'SheeTas.

Adverts for XiTas would encourage drivers to 'Fly like the wind, a glass of water in your hand, the sun on your back and the wind in your face'. Operated like a taxi, they were hailed when needed, using a communications device, or bar owners could wave a tea towel. It was retained, only for as long as it was needed, topping it up with water for the Hydrogen. Then, when it was finished with, the vehicle would take itself away for a SAD treatment of Sanitation and Detailing. This helped the next user feel they were using the vehicle for the very first time.

To discover more, please select this ZUKANN OPTIC.

☙❦❧

CHAPTER 26
Military Intelligence

New York Central:
2200 (EST), Friday December 11ᵗʰ 2499 (DET)

Ruby compressed the last of her personal belongings back into her WOTDIC and closed the bedroom door behind her. She had been quite disappointed the meeting with FENDER and IGLOO had been brought forward. It had been a while since she'd been able to visit the 25ᵗʰ Century, and she was secretly addicted to car-crash TV programmes like 'You've Been Shamed' and 'Qwing For a Day', mainly since so many of the programmes were filmed in Manhattan. Mind you, taking a walk, out in the fresh air, you never know what you might see for real.

Broadcast Entertainment

"Enormously popular entertainment in the 24ᵗʰ and 25ᵗʰ Century is TZeeV or TweeZer VeeZer entertainment.

Unlike the FI (Fully Immersive) and FU (Fully Underwhelming) ThreeZer Veezer broadcasts, TZeeV is distributed in the lower 128K visual quality.

"Channels often contain fly-on-the-wall satirical documentaries such as 'Qwing For A Day' and 'Celebrity You've Been Shamed Monumentally'. The latter is a 24-hour PL (Pre-Live) broadcast. Featuring celebrities and monuments committing hilarious crimes and misdemeanours viewed 'live' from at least ten minutes before they perpetrate the actual offence.

To discover more, please select this ZUKANN OPTIC.

It was pretty dark as Ruby stepped out into the fresh air of the city. The Hudson River Greenway now stretched right over to what was the New Jersey shoreline. In daylight, it would have been a lovely walk through the butterfly meadows over to Jersey City or for a game of chess in Hoboken. The new layout for Manhattan meant the air had not been this fresh since Peter Schaghen wrote about the island being bought from "De Wilde' in 1626 for 'the value of 60 Guilders'. It was unclear what the indigenous 'Savage' people could have spent the money on if it had been cash. Perhaps guns to protect themselves from the Susquehannock who, according to rumour, had been trading furs for firearms with the Swedes.

It was a fantastic feat by Doddken Engineering to have created a building so high as the Manhattan Building and simultaneously move entire buildings to other locations. Some of their engineers could still be seen putting the finishing touches to the upper stories of the towering edifice, wearing their specialised safety equipment of tall hats for tall buildings and oversized shoes for additional grip.

The sky was still solid with stationary vehicles, queuing up to enter Manhattan, and backed up as far as the eye could see. FlyderCab Pods could be seen climbing up from the street level to rescue drivers and passengers. Vehicle owners were choosing to schedule their empty vehicles to Autopark when the chaos abated. Huge frustration was expressed on media channels that XiTas and other vehicles were legally obligated, even in an emergency, to obey flight path programming and stay in the air-lanes, meanwhile, FlyderCabs could go 'off-piste".

Illuminated news screens displayed sponsored round-ups of the day's events with adverts for vehicle Snack-Paks, travel games and emergency 'bio facilities' for children.

Several citizens walking under the vehicle flight paths had noted on social media, the occasional appearance of a 'light drizzle'. However, none was scheduled in the weather reports. Social Opinionators were being interviewed about which particular politician could be blamed, locally or nationally. The right-wingers were accusing the left-wingers, the left-wingers were blaming the right-wingers.

Even the Up-Winders were blaming the Down-Winders, who were generally a wholly blameless bunch of politicians. However, what appeared to be shocking people of all political persuasions was people actually walking the streets 'IN THE RAW!' Imagine going out in public, in the street, and not as your own avatar!

Ruby walked up to the 42nd Street entrance to the Manhattan Building. Nicknamed the 'Dancing Feet' entrance after the World-Record-holding doubles tennis players Hal Kemp and Bradford Ropes. It was also the quickest way to get an express Flyser all the way to floor 1399. Admittedly, the view up there wasn't as good as the offices on Columbus Corner, which overlooked the Central Park Atrium. But, as all attendees were arriving for a meeting in 'The RAW', it was exceptionally well located. In addition, it provided a quick exit to the Sky Park, followed by the return home in your bullet-proof Flimmo.

The meeting room was a cavernous space, large enough for a Bicentennial Ball. At the centre was a huge almost transparent table surrounded by seats designed by A.I. nanobots, perfectly tailored to the individual contours and requirements of the attendees. The table, also used for peace negotiations, was made from a translucent crystalline material, allowing all participants to ensure those sat opposite were not concealing weapons or personal assistants. The downside to the transparency made having a slight itch a little awkward. On more than one occasion, warring factions have accused their opposite numbers of reaching for weaponry when all that was required was a quick scratch.

Mother of the Brides: IGLOO	
Theluji Densi Knight	Senior Controller
Mothers of the Grooms: FENDER	
Editha Clarke	The Vice Rectifier
Nekita Lamarr	Assistant Rectifier
Walton Cockroft	Rectification Technician

Bridesmaids: TIME TECH	
Ruby Rowe	Operations Director, North Coates, UK
Queen Sheba Whendy Endee	Power Director, When, Liberia
Yara Agua	Node Director, Quem Quem, Brazil
Mapapa Tuanuku	Node Director, What, New Zealand
Jhuli Thakumar	Node Director, Where, India
Diana Bahanay	Node Director, Arizona USA
Ursula Sontheil	Node Director, How, UK
Jamsetjee Bomanjee Iolani Kamehameha	Node Director, Which Way, Kalama Atoll
Selena Theia	Site Director, Lunar One, Bruce Crater
Notable Absentees / Sponsors / Gift Givers:	
Maria Morvena	Site Director, Tunguska, Russia

Those present at the meeting that evening were a virtually complete list of the great and the good from the whole of Time Tech Operations, FENDER and IGLOO. Attendees were listed on a display panel in the way guests would be displayed at a wedding. This resulted from a technical hitch as the room would be used for a special celebration in the morning.

For the first time ever, five people were being Tied in a conjunction ceremony. Because of this, the seating plan displayed at the entrance, had been inadvertently set to 'Automatic facial recognition and blessings from notable absentees.'

A rather sour-faced woman in a dark one-piece grey suit, who looked like she could comfortably suck the life out of a lemon at twenty paces, rose to her feet. Theluji Densi Knight, the Senior Controller from the organisation for International Governmental Logistical and Operational Oversight, cleared her throat. Theluji's name meant Snow Dancing in Swahili, and she lived up to the organisation's Motto: 'Dispassionate Control'. Behind her back, her colleagues nicknamed her 'Two Dog' Knight, due to her being exceptionally emotionally cold on occasions.

Theluji half-closed one eye in a slight frown,

"Welcome to you all, and please accept my gratitude for tolerating the earlier start time. I would like to congratulate everyone on their successful navigation of the chaos surrounding us today. Those on this planet, or in this reality thirty years ago, may have spotted the similarities between this HyperLoop and city-wide gridlock and the events at the Interstellar Shadow Board final. We do have a close-up artist's impression of the person responsible. The witness is a retired passenger aircraft Art-Bot, visiting ex-colleagues at the New York University College of Arts and Sciences. The Bot had been in the park at the start of this incident.

"Unfortunately, because it only ever produced artwork for in-flight safety cards, there is a large red X over the face of the suspect. We are attempting to enhance the picture. From what we see of the design of the locomotive being ridden by this terrorist, it is clearly the same person who set off all the fireworks prematurely at the Shadow Board finals. Sadly, no one got a close-up look back then either, mainly because they had all been watching the team cheerleader flying demonstrations. The Casimir Investigations Agency will pass their findings onto Time Tech for action.

"I'm going to ask Assistant Rectifier Nekita Lamarr to update us on the damage inflicted on the Washington Square Arch. Nekita, over to you."

A strikingly beautiful woman, gracing a red ballgown, with porcelain cheeks, iridescent eyes, lashes like the wings of an ascending angel, and red lips that could grace all fourteen lines of a Shakespearean Sonnet, rose from her seat. She stroked the right side of her face with her left hand, then began to pace slowly across the room. Nekita Lamarr, a distant relative of an Austrian born communications visionary and part-time film star, generally did not remain stationary. Her view was the act of standing had a tendency to make one seem glamorous and, by association, equally stupid.

Turning to look at the attendees, she frowned and then took a breath without stopping her slow journey around the room.

"Thank you Theluji. I'm sure you all realise, we have a major problem. All this chaos, and only a few of us to help tidy up. We humans have an unerring ability to disrupt the path of Destiny, and the Washington Square Arch is one of those more serious disruptions. We need to find the source of this disorder. This is NOT the work of students, but certainly the actions of Steamer terrorists. They never claim responsibility, but we are certain of their involvement. Normally, I am not in the habit of transacting absolutes, but they must be working with The STRAND, as they are certainly not working with us."

Nekita stopped pacing and placed both hands on a desk,

"ZUKANN, please show the graphics of the arch and explain for us."

ZUKANN
IMAGE:

N126A

SCAN ME
N126A

The Lamarr Perspective

Across multiple parallel dimensions, we have seen the damage to this arch. The impact is extensive. We were forced to set up perception filters so no one can look at the arch directly. We had no option but to take the most unusual steps to alter real-world mapping tools.

Anyone able to view this arch from street level using any monitor screen will only see a blur or perhaps a caged structure with the centre shifted into an alternate reality. The cost of this from an energy perspective is huge. The sooner we get the global Gaia energy network running, the best for all of us. We cannot have the words 'Freedom Over Destiny' carved into the air of our realities.

To discover more, please select this ZUKANN OPTIC.

Nekita eyeballed the attendees for a moment, lifted her hands from the desk where she had paused for far too long and continued her slow pacing around the room,

"We have one other small item to discuss before we continue to the main item on the agenda, and this is Linguistic Littering."

She shook her head as if disappointed by a naughty schoolboy. "When travelling, please do be careful to ensure your PIMMS devices are fully updated to the latest dictionary version for the era being entered. We have had some repeated re-appearances of the aberrant word 'Normalcy'. Can I remind everyone we have previously tried to correct this minor divergence of the time strands on several occasions? It's 'NORMALITY' we strive for. NOT 'NORMALCY'. Like we strive for 'Veracity' and NOT 'Veracy'. Veracy is a heresy!

For the same reason, but in reverse, we want people to experience PREGNANCY and NOT PREGNANITY. We only facilitated Senator Warren Harding to use the word 'Normalcy' in 1920 as The Nineteenth Amendment was necessary to maintain Destiny Equilibrium. Can I remind everyone this aberrant word 'NORMALCY' does not conform to Time Stream Directive six-three-nine-dash-two?

"The word has resurfaced in 1941, 2021 and 2101. There appears to be a pattern, and we suspect unauthorised time transit. Director Rowe, can you pick this up for us, please?"

At the sound of her name, Ruby looked up. It was getting quite late, and it had been a long week. Nekita Lamarr's meandering moan about Linguistic Littering wasn't high on her list of priorities right now, and she was at the edge of dozing off. Fortunately, ZUKANN had been aware of Ruby's fatigued state. ZUKANN had been injecting small doses of adrenalin into Ruby whilst displaying the transcript of the speech during the last few moments of Nekita's diatribe. This gave her enough of an edge to look Nekita in the eye with a reassuring smile and reply,

"Certainly, Madam Assistant Rectifier. Be assured, we will investigate this immediately after our next mission should the plan be agreed?"

Fortunately, the Assistant Rectifier had not seen Ruby's attention wandering and appeared convinced that action would be taken.

"Thank you. However, before we continue with your plan, possibly after a coffee break, we need to hear your report on potential Destiny Equilibrium damage concerning the British Bomber, and also, the more recent spy plane from the United States."

It was Ruby's turn to take a deep breath and walk around to the front of the room,

"Thank you all for taking the time to attend this meeting in The RAW. I appreciate the risk to all of your personal security, not having the protection of your avatars. You'll be getting another dose of me after coffee. First, it's a quick update about December 1970 and the British nuclear bomber incident."

Around the room images appeared in thin air, as if displayed on invisible monitor screens placed around the room for the comfort of all attendees, highlighting different aspects of the recovery mission.

"In short, the nuclear device was made safe, and the seas around the United Kingdom remain relatively toxin-free. But it's worth remembering we're talking about 1970, so we're ignoring all the pollution currently pouring into the sea in that era.

The Royal Air Force has recovered the wreckage. However, our senior consultant Sir Rob Locksley has had his work cut out explaining why not all components have been recovered. Their accident investigators are extremely thorough. As a result, Mark Spark's team had to acquire some components from elsewhere, so they could subsequently be 'found' by officials. The actual missing parts are either lost at the bottom of Lake Calima or were picked up by the indigenous Quimbaya people."

The visuals changed again to show images from the Colombia Gold Museum and what was quite obviously a Vulcan Bomber made of gold. Even the round circular disc icon 'roundels' representing the Royal Air Force logo could be seen on the wings. Another picture appeared of a golden helmet with a figure on the side.

Ruby looked slightly pensive at this point,

"It was regrettable one of our recovery crew lost their safety helmet as we were fitting the Duron cameras. The individual concerned had to be saved whilst falling, and it wasn't until we had left the site that we realised some components had been lost.

Fortunately, looking at the time stream, the general consensus from archaeologists is, what *should* have been dragons are now considered to be fish. This in itself is a far more suitable outcome given the impact the Zenyo dragon species OEA1BA would have had. Our efforts have enabled the time stream to achieve a relatively total and satisfactory convergence."

Ruby relaxed her shoulders slightly and continued,

"So, in summary, the bomb was disarmed safely in the Covenham Arrivals Decontamination Hall. The aircraft wreckage was recovered from a highly precarious location at the end of a SlipStream event. No children were injured from the nearby school at the crash site, and the death of a cow in the adjacent field was also indirectly prevented." Ruby hoped they would not ask too many questions about the cow, as she still hadn't been able to get to the bottom of how it wasn't the central part of someone's Sunday lunch at the nearby pub.

The attendees gave a quiet ripple of appreciation as the short and occasionally terrifying video sequences faded into oblivion.

ZUKANN IMAGE:

P128A

SCAN ME
P128A

A Historical Perspective

Indigenous Quimbaya people created artefacts made of gold which bore a very close resemblance to the RAF bomber in this incident. Fortunately, the balanced equilibrium of the most recently selected timestream erased what would have been Zenyo dragons, replacing them with golden birds and fish, inspired by this extremely short intervention.

To discover more, please select this ZUKANN OPTIC.

Nekita Lamarr stood up again, her eyebrows now reflecting her frustration,

"The British are as bad as the Americans for littering the past with technology. First, the British lose a bomber in the 11th Century. Now we get the Americans losing one of their F117 ship-launched stealth fighters, somewhere in the early 1st Century over the Bering Strait. What is this? Every Millennium we have a party someone else has to clean up after? At least the British managed to recover most of the parts and not cause too much damage."

Nekita took a moment to breathe, then looked across the conference table,

"I would like to introduce a face unfamiliar to the majority of you for the next report. Walton Cockcroft is our newest Rectification Technician. He is a specialist in Particle Physics, Natural and Experimental Philosophy and discovered the Town Clock Factor. He is also the 'go-to guy' for information pertaining to MAUD, TIZARD, ZEEP, GLEEP ZETA, BEPO and NRX.

"Walton, most of the people assembled at this meeting will be unaware of your findings. Please share your report related to the 1984 Sea-Hawk?"

A slim, older man in a 20th Century Tweed suit, with glasses and comb-over hair, stood up and walked to the front of the room.

He sipped from a glass of water and then spoke with an accent somewhere between Yorkshire and southeast Ireland,

"Certainly, I can Madam Assistant Rectifier. A SlipStream time incursion by an American F117N-SeaHawk flying test missions in 1984, created significant headaches for FENDER. American intelligence indicated a build-up of Russian military and scientific personnel. The American CIA, keen to acquire more data and working closely with the US military, took advantage of the opportunity for this test flight to include a secret incursion into Russian airspace.

"Flying from the *USS Carl Vinson* on the return leg from 'The Rim of the Pacific Exercise' (RIMPAC), the F117N was 'lost at sea'.

However, the pilot ejected before the plane completely disappeared. Publicly, the *USS Carl Vinson* became the first aircraft carrier to operate 'officially' in the Bering Sea in 1986 on a failed mission to recover the wreckage two years later. ZUKANN, next image and description, please."

ZUKANN
IMAGE:

SCAN ME
P129A

Ekven Equilibrium

"Categorized as Harpoon stabilizers when they were discovered in the late 20th Century, objects were excavated on an archaeological dig at the 2000-year-old Ekven cemetery at Uelen, eighty kilometres or fifty miles from Lavrentia. They can be clearly interpreted as models of the F117N seen to crash into the sea, although some would prefer to see an owl. Limited damage to the timestream was inflicted due to their eventual categorisation."

To discover more, please select this ZUKANN OPTIC.

Walton's gentle voice continued,

"It has subsequently transpired the Russians were working towards the development of the 'Diplomatic Gorbatron'. Inspired by Nobel Peace Prize-winning President Mikhail Gorbachev. Some here may remember from school history lessons, that by the 22nd Century, Russia had become a star of the international peacekeeping community.

"The incredibly successful 'Diplomatic Artificial Intelligence System Yakovlev' or Project DAISY was developed by scientists working at a remote research base in Lavrentiya, close to the Bering Strait. The scientific analysis of diplomatic processes was started by Mikael Gorbachev as Secretary of the Central Committee and Soviet Diplomat Alexander Yakovlev, after their meeting in May 1983 with Canadian Prime Minister Pierre Trudeau. The scientific and computer analysis of diplomatic variables took years of complex study with its associated costs.

"A giant leap forward was made after March 2018, when the Russian government released a ten-point Artificial Intelligence agenda. This called for establishing an A.I. and Big Data consortium to support their defence strategy. It was patently apparent manufacturing peace would always be the best defence. The most potent society would be one that could control and enable peace in the face of any aggression.

"The Diplomatic Gorbatron still works similarly to the *real* Oracle at Thebes. Questions can be presented, and the Gorbatron can analyse all available information from all global sources, calculate the variables and deliver the perfect diplomatic solution. The only time this has ever been known to fail was due to a typographic error. In one incident, a solution to 'mill all the rice' had been misinterpreted as 'kill all the mice'. This led to a three-week bombing campaign and the mysterious disappearance of the hugely popular 22nd Century pop sensation tribute act Weird Russian Singer halfway through a world tour."

ZUKANN OPTIC:

SCAN ME
P130A

Musical Motivation – Diplomatic Gorbatron

"Team members working to develop the Diplomatic Gorbatron would start each shift singing their inspirational labour song:"

♫ *"Дiplomatik Gorbatroн,*

keep zuh peace, for you and me.

Glasnost, when you need it most,

Then a кup of tea.

Talking truly paves the way,

Friends vill surely guarantee.

Peace, Love, give us a hug,

Radiation-free." ♪

To discover more, please select this ZUKANN OPTIC.

Nekita Lamarr rose again to her feet,

"Thank you, Technician Cockcroft. Rest assured; FENDER operatives will be working on a plan to correct this deviance. The Time Tech Team can pick up and deliver damage limitation and Event Neutrality. I think at this point we should take a short coffee break."

Fortunately for all those assembled, A.I. coffee bots had been gathering known data relating to all the attendees. As a result, predictions of the type and strength of coffee required by most of them were around ninety-five per cent accurate. Although one delegate seemed to have been given a drink so viscous, it had appeared to suck the false teeth right out of her face.

Ruby decided she needed to have a quick catch up with Alba, just in case either of them might need to head off any awkward questions from FENDER.

CHAPTER 27
Millinery Intelligence

New York Central:
2345 (EST), Friday December 11th 2499 (DET)
RAF North Coates: 0445 (GMT),
Saturday December 12th 1970 (DET)

Down the long, brightly lit, white-walled corridor, there was a "Yoo-hoo!" from behind her. Alba stopped in her tracks, and it was as if the blood in her veins had turned to ice. Then, to compound her sudden misery, on hearing the words, "Yoo-hoo, ALBERTA!" She turned her slowly sagging seven-foot frame on the spot. At the other end of the corridor stood a lady with greying hair, no more than five and a half feet tall, but with the unmistakably exceptional quality of the Fab000 people – bright orange skin. In addition, she had a fatally flawed ability to deal with any kind of decision-making when it came to dress sense. She was wearing a floral pattern dress and a bright pink hat. It was Alba's mother.

Questions ran through Alba's mind faster than tins of beans off a production line.

1) How did Mrs Alice Rose Petula Wonstein get to be on Home Earth?

2) Why was she here walking towards my office?

3) Was the world coming to an unexpected end?

4) Why was she carrying the lunchbox I used to take to school when I was six years old?

Only her mother called her Alberta. You only used someone's full 'Wednesday Name' when you wanted to make their weekend even more dreary.

Alba could hear her own subconscious talking to her,

"400 light-years from home, and your mother pops into work

with a packed lunch. I'm going to die!"

The room swam and wriggled oddly. There was a repetitive beeping noise, and the corridor vanished to be replaced by Alba's darkened bedroom. The light came on. Drenched with sweat, Alba reached for the communicator on her PIMMS device.

Thank you to all things holy and righteous. It was only a nightmare!

"Hiya Ruby, how's it going....?"

Ruby's voice became more evident. Either that or the night terror was fading,

"Hiya Alba, I'm sorry if I woke you. This meeting is dragging on. Can I get you to run a few destiny checks to ensure the time strands are converging? Nekita Lamarr is in a bit of a mood. She's been banging on about 'Linguistic Littering', so it would be good to know if we had left a footprint with Eddie and Will's plane. If we have, then hopefully it's only a light-touch dent in FENDER's all-important line of Event Neutrality?"

Alba rubbed the remains of sleep from her eyes, which for the Fab000 people looked a little like multi-coloured crystals. More than one person who had offended a Fab000lian discovered far too late; not to sprinkle the 'rainbow sugar' on their cornflakes as it actually tasted like Wasabi horseradish.

"No problem, Ruby. I won't be going back to sleep for a while. I was having something of a nightmare. I'll call back if you've got anything to worry about."

ZUKANN
SCAN ME
P133A

CHAPTER 28
The Road Ahead

New York Central:
0012 (EST), Saturday December 12th 2499 (DET)

Theluji Densi Knight was back, standing at the front of the vast conference centre room. Everyone was returning, to continue with what was becoming a meeting far too long and far too late in the evening. She was looking even more jaded and sour-faced. Lemons in adjacent dimensions were beginning to forecast the risk of dehydration from her Medusa-like stare. Then as if from some surreal part of a horror film, she smiled. At least a couple of the attendees had considered this was the point at which the world might discover she could also swallow small animals whole. But, of course, no one was expecting this, and it was pretty unnerving.

The smiling 'Two Dog Knight' began to speak,

"I am delighted to be able to bring this next agenda item to your attention. For centuries, we have been pushing back the limitations of our society to ensure unlimited energy supplies are available to our time stream. The next mission for the Time Tech Team, scheduled for Christmas Eve 1970, will bring stability to our Destiny. Should they be successful, nay, WHEN they are successful, we will no longer have a fear of the loss of our power security from now and into the depths of our future. We will also have the means to defend ourselves in perpetuity from the ravages of The STRAND and The Hagura.

"Can I ask Director Rowe to explain the outline of the plan? For security reasons, the final details will be made available to attendees this coming Monday. This next meeting, by the way, will not be in the RAW, and Avatars will be permitted."

Ruby stood up and walked to the front for a second time.

Although it was late, this time, she had one hundred per cent of everyone's attention,

"Thank you again for your time. I am aware of how much of your lives I am consuming, so I will be concise."

Again, images began to materialise behind her. This time showing the Gaia Power rod, seed devices and several works of art by Edith Madieu.

Ruby now looked less tired and more confident,

"We now have practically all we need to recover the 7th power rod for our global power network. I won't repeat what most of you will see on Monday. Suffice to say, we have three teams of three ready to travel. All groups will be travelling in December 1970. A world which is not as clean or safe as it is now. It is also a world where security is nothing as complex as what we know today. We believe the Gaia Power components were placed in a SlipStream vault by whichever Hagura agent escaped the earthquake at Valdivia in 1960. We don't know why they never went back to retrieve the technology, when they put such an incredibly complex security package in place to protect it. Without the help of the artist Edith Madieu, we would not have a hope of cracking the safe."

Yara Agua, Node Director from Quem Quem in Brazil sat back in her chair. Her diaphanous blue and lilac organdie gossamer jacket and dress rippled, in waves tuned to the movement of her long purple hair. Rumours amongst her colleagues were that she was a descendant of mermaids, but this theory was never confirmed. Although Valdivia was over 2000 miles from her home, it was not only part of her patch, but she also had a great interest in art, particularly that of Edith Madieu.

Ruby nodded at Yara, who had been instrumental in identifying much of the art locations for the upcoming challenge,

"This mission is not without its contemporary hazards, but it should be relatively safe by modern standards. Unless, of course, the Hagura are somehow expecting us. We need to stop a painting from being stolen or return it if it has been swiped. It is called *The Godot Orange*, painted by Edith Madieu. It is part of a massively complex combination-lock controlled safe, the contents of which will be lost forever if we are not successful."

There was a loud crash as Selena Theia who had travelled the furthest from the Lunar One site, momentarily dozed off, dropping her glass of water onto the floor. She self-consciously reached down for the glass, her long luminescent grey hair slipping, knocking her spectacles from her nose. Sanitation bots sprang into action from the edges of the room to recover both items, and order was restored in seconds.

Ruby smiled sympathetically at Selena, who was equal in stature and great friends with Alba, and continued with the presentation,

"The first team will be travelling to Manhattan, New York, over 500 years in our past. Some of you own properties in this incredible masterpiece we're meeting in now." Ruby spread her arms out wide as if to give the building they were in, a hug. "Our moment in time, is before the creation of this wonderful Manhattan Building. It is a time of pollution, and before the Hudson was diverted to make for a cleaner, more pleasant city. It is a time when unconnected, far smaller buildings existed on the same site. The Art and Realism Museum was just over three blocks, sorry, sectors east of where we are now. Its doors close at 5pm on Christmas Eve. We will enter at 6pm.

"Simultaneously, we will have a team at the Beaux-Arts in Belgium. It will be midnight there. They will also have set up a Duron Camera in the Director's office of a nearby small pension company. Hung on the wall, there is a chrono-responsive Dada-esque picture of a tree possibly displaying up to three lions sat on branches. We need to see this picture 'live' as the picture changes the number of lions, depending on the location of *The Godot Orange* painting. We know the rules applying to this.

"The third location, and most dangerous is in the Russian sector of East Berlin."

At the mention of the Russian occupied part of Germany, Maria Morvena, the Site Director for Tunguska, leaned forward to pay closer attention. There was quite a Russian military look about her short-cropped dark hair, paramilitary uniform and rugged boots. Ruby had not seen her arrive and assumed she must have turned up at the coffee break after a meeting with her scientific advisor Dmitri Igorikov Noviyevich.

Ruby took a sip of water and a slow breath,

"It is a German State Academic storage building, within what was a food supply cold-storage facility. Security is rigorous here, and all the guards are armed. The site actually sits directly on the boundary between the Russian sector and the American Sector at a time of highly dangerous political tensions.

"The team bound for America will take a conventional airline service flying with Pan Am. The team headed for Brussels will use Cascade hinge equipped doors. However, this will not be direct as we've detected an unusual anomaly on the site of the Brussels Art Bureau. We will keep you updated about this. Finally, the team bound for East Berlin will initially fly to Berlin Tempelhof Airport. We've borrowed a De-Havilland Heron from Her Majesty the Queen of the United Kingdom. She is also being updated with her Prime Minister Edward Heath, US President Richard Nixon, King Baudouin of Belgium and Belgian Prime Minister Gaston Eyskens. They are all satisfied that this mission is for the good of all humanity. Therefore, it has the blessing of all of them. Does anyone have any questions?"

There was captivated silence in the room. Ruby had kept the attention of all assembled, but clearly, the moment had come to a halt.

"Thank you for your attention," Ruby motioned to a figure who was now rising from a seat directly opposite, "I will now hand over to our senior leader for today."

ର⊕◌⊖ഔ

A tall slender woman wearing a dark blue two-piece suit with unnecessarily large shoulder pads walked to the front of those assembled. If the UK's first female Prime Minister had a distant relative, it would have been Editha Clarke, the Vice Rectifier. She stood and looked around the room, with a look of supreme confidence on her face.

Editha took a breath and began to speak,

"Friends, Humans and Calabi-Yau. Lend me your era. I come not to bury uncertainty but to disrupt probability. I bring destiny to your hidden variables, but my message today comes with a warning. Gaia Power is freely available but must remain bandwidth restricted.

"Remember, five percent power corrupts. One hundred percent power corrupts absolutely. Within our Kipling Treaty, interdimensional worlds have signed up to join the Time Tech and IGLOO Gaia Power Network. The six honest M.E.N. of the Managed Energy Network. Delivering 'Power to the People', free power to all treaty members. An absolute minimum requirement was for six global energy nodes. Still, a 7th is ideally required for a completely stable energy network."

Editha paused momentarily,

"This exceedingly good treaty covers the bare necessities, a 7th node is now a real possibility. If it can be recovered from this hidden SlipStream Safe, we will all benefit immeasurably. I would like to thank you for inviting me to speak with you this evening. We are on the fringe of a *Brave New World* of unlimited free energy. Without this power to control destiny, millions might be made homeless simply because, somewhere, a single cup of coffee was spilt. Nations rise, and nations fall. Wars, pestilence, disease all come and go. Previously, we viewed our oncoming future as inexorable, not knowing the truth of how it began or how to protect ourselves from the worst elements of the oncoming fate.

"Today, things are about to change. The Gaia Power Network has given us freedom, but we must ensure the freedom we crave is one we can guarantee. A new foothold in history can be assured.

Because of one random, loose, seemingly insignificant Titanium bolt, the size of my finger, on a forgotten airfield, we can see the root of our success in a country practically at war over 500 years ago. We welcome a new era. The Electrolithic Era ends today. My friends, welcome to the Brave New World of the Temporalithic Era."

The applause was louder than most attendees expected. Mainly because they were all actually in a room together rather than remotely located with a virtual presence.

Ruby smiled. They had some work to do and some problems to solve, but this meant their plan had the green light. It was time for her, Fred and Frank to head back to 1970.

လ⊕①⊕ဢ

At what looked like the exact same conference centre, but in a parallel Earth dimension, a few feet and nanoseconds apart, a figure rose from a table. This person was surrounded by the avatars of people who would generate dismay if they could be seen. Especially as two of them were currently in a meeting with Ruby Rowe and all the Gaia Power Network Node Directors.

The person at the centre looking like she should be surrounded by fur coats and Dalmatian dogs, was Shemala Supergravity, the Global Vice-President of the Interdimensional Network for Power Autonomy Information and Nucleonics, was giving another tremendous but unrecorded speech.

There were, however, far fewer people in this room. Many appearing as Avatars could not be identified. Those who were recognizable from their images in newspaper headlines and gossip columns included a range of individuals, such as Margery Alpheus Tavis, Gustav Rayle Seraphim, Evelyn Safir-Dempster and Lara Presley-Bond, the ex-wife of the stationery entrepreneur Basildon. There was also the more obscured and hooded figure of the mysterious Miss Del-Gryfte. It seemed, here were the early signs that a war was on the horizon.

CHAPTER 29
An Inspector Calls Time On A Little History

New York Central:
0245 (EST), Saturday December 12th 2499 (DET)

In the 23rd Century, it is extremely hard to go missing. Even if you have been murdered and your body disposed of, there is always a trail of DNA. The disappearance of Bartender, World Traveller and Conspiracy Theorist, Michelangelo Fynn from the iNet population tracker, had very quickly been detected. This had caused some head-scratching at the most senior levels of policing. Two of the suspects in his disappearance, were frequent drinking companions, and members of a most secretive organisation, about which very little was known. Only pages of redacted data files were available to human investigators, however, Time Tech Team members could not operate outside civilian legal jurisdiction. A compromise was agreed with FENDER. An android investigator was assigned to the case. At the conclusion of the investigation, its memory was to be wiped.

The android investigator needed context, and access to 'The Vault' was agreed upon. The Smithsonian's secret underground storage facility, hidden within Iron Mountain, 300 miles west of New York, was made available. In a grey corridor, under a grey mountain, a somewhat elderly, grey-haired and bearded senior archivist, Professor Eugene Randell, viewed the android with the deepest of suspicion on its arrival. As agreed, however, the Professor guided the way without speaking, to Vault 1089. Dusty notebooks and files, some quite badly damaged by fire, were on display. The android was secured in the vault, whilst the Professor returned to a separate security office to closely observe all the activity.

The investigator swiftly identified some of the earliest records which it began to analyse. Not only was there historical background to Time Tech, but also that of FENDER and IGLOO. The records began to paint a somewhat hazy picture of 19th Century life. The investigator began to absorb the data.

Four miles to the southwest of RAF North Coates lies the sleepy, one-pub hamlet of Covenham St Bartholomew. Open fields spread out towards the coast, with tree-lined lanes surrounding what some might describe as a pretty 200-acre reservoir nearby. On a dark foggy Autumn night in 1899, this was the location of a disastrous SlipStream event, now wholly erased from historical records and even the landscape. Other documents slipped out from the file, taking the investigator's attention back to the Spring of 1896.

London:
1000 (GMT), Monday April 6th 1896 (DET)
Athens:
1100 Eastern European Time (EET),
Monday March 25th 1896 (Julian)

Considered by many to be just stories of alien monsters created by literary giants such as Jules Verne and HG Wells, threats to the British Empire from any direction were considered and taken seriously by the British Prime Minister of the day, Robert Gascoyne-Cecil, the 3rd Marquess of Salisbury. He held the somewhat entrenched viewpoint of 'Whatever happens will be for the worse, and therefore it is in our interest that as little should happen as possible.' Lord Salisbury was also slightly disappointed he hadn't been personally invited to the first-ever Olympic Games in Greece. He was so disgruntled, he had been pondering ways in which, using a time machine, he might be offered the opportunity to be in two places simultaneously.

Queen Victoria was a powerful supporter of technological advances. She was invited to an experiment in September of 1896 in Balmoral, where the plan was to scan her with an optical device. Subsequently, her moving image could then be seen by her subjects simultaneously across the whole of the Commonwealth. They were to call this technology 'Cinema'.

The same year, through Royal Patronage, the Royal Academy of Science Technology and the Arts was founded. Queen Victoria had asked Sir Oliver Lodge to be a part of this organisation. She first met Oliver as a young boy when he delivered Wedgewood china to the soon to be King Edward VII, at Sandringham. Sir Oliver had more recently been working on a system he had patented called *Syntonic Tuning*. This could potentially be used for communication with and the detection of travellers from the planet Mars, just one of many threats identified by HG Wells. This same research was later purchased by Guglielmo Marconi, who continued to successfully develop this communication and detection system without wires. The technology has since successfully been integrated into NASA communication systems and the SETI project in the Search for Extra-Terrestrial Intelligence.

∞⊕◯⊕∞

The android investigator's focus returned to 1896 and the Royal Academy of Science Technology and the Arts, where time travel was considered a severe threat to the British Empire. The Admiralty assigned 'Admiral of the Red', Reliance Endeavour Dexter Mann, to this project. For obvious reasons, Admiral R.E.D. Mann was known to his friends as 'Blackbeard'. He was proud to introduce himself as, 'Being most industrious, Endeavour is my middle name', mainly because it was.

It was patently obvious to the esteemed body RASTA, Mann was a perfect choice. Accordingly, he selected an assistant, one Able Seaman First Class Horatio Mowtz. Horatio's mother had been born into a fence and gate maker's family in Brandenburg. Still, she had moved to Finsbury in London, England, as it was ideally located for Moorgate sales. Coincidentally, before Horatio was conceived, the Admiral had met Horatio's mother 'socially' on several occasions, so it was slightly unclear if Horatio was a Mann or a Mowtz.

The Royal Academy were happy with the selection. To RASTA, Mowtz would be ideally suited to the tasks and assigned a location in London for the start of the research. It would be situated below

Hatton Gardens, accessible from a shaft constructed at Chancery Lane in August 1896. The project was to be temporarily based in a newly built section of the then Central London Railway. This became the London Underground Central line. The location, about halfway between Chancery Lane and Farringdon Stations. It was to become known as 'The Mann-Hatton Garden Project'.

Although a working time travel device was built, to the design provided by HG Wells, the engineers had chosen to use gyroscopes for stabilisers rather than Euler's Stabilisers. This flaw led to an accident where the time-sledge was left spinning in a perpetual time loop, and this section of the line having to be abandoned. Instead, a new tunnel section was dug for the Central Line, taking it further south, via St Pauls and Bank. This deviation, forming a southerly wriggle in the underground network, can still be seen on the London Underground map to this day. However, delays to construction came close to bankrupting the company. The three design engineers were believed to have been furious this could have happened.

Because of this colossal photon leakage into the ground, the positive power rail for the trains on the Central Line had to be placed on still-visible insulators standing on small concrete mounds. With modern SlipStream repair technology, it has been possible to reverse the damage to the surrounding geology. However, because of the design changes, Central Line trains still cannot run on any other part of the network.

With the repairs thought to have been completed, the opportunity was taken to continue excavation, enabling the Cross Rail, Elizabeth Line project. However, an unforeseen issue of residual time-loop wreckage between Tottenham Court Road and Farringdon stations caused delays to the Elizabeth Line. Each time engineers signed off on completion, the time loop would repeat, removing a month's worth of work. As a result, the decision was taken to protect the public from further potential photon leakage, and fit all sixteen stations on the central section of the Elizabeth Line with floor to ceiling Faraday Cage safety doors.

⌒⨁⨁⌓

The android investigator spotted a late 21st Century data store which he scanned. It contained a map and a description of the locality described by a very early L8 model, real time query, artificial intelligence system. The data was quite useful.

RTQ-L8
DATA:

SCAN ME
Q138A

RTQ-L8 A.I. Data [Secret]

In 1897, to protect the public from potential injury resulting from this new science, the Mann-Hatton Garden project moved to a secret non-military, government laboratory based at the 'Fitties' or salt marshes of Donna Nook on the East coast of Lincolnshire. This was created to conduct research at a location far enough away from large conurbations.

Reaching the site with heavy equipment was impossible via the local cart tracks, so a railway branch line was constructed from Ludborough station, via Covenham St Bartholomew, and finally to the Donna Nook laboratory site.

Time travel can be extremely hazardous, requiring vast amounts of power. By 1899, scientists had discovered a technology based on the disintegration of Uranium. With the help of Nikola Tesla, they had been able to create a power source of great magnitude. In modern parlance, they had made an unstable wormhole. Whilst shipping this device to Donna Nook via the branch line, the device destabilised, creating a Casimir Event Horizon. A section of track, locomotive and carriages were trapped in a SlipStream loop.

Further data has been corrupted. Please return to the transcript file.

To discover more, please select this ZUKANN OPTIC.

With inadequate technical knowledge of time travel rescue, RASTA, Mann and Gascoyne-Cecil, believing all the occupants of the train had been killed, concluded that a political and physical cover-up was required. A reservoir would be built to prevent access and obscure the mysterious glowing cavity. So difficult was this task that work did not start until 1963.

With the closure of the branch line and 'event neutralisation' of its existence, experiments at Donna Nook were moved to a secluded part of the coast near North Cotes village. The secret research centre was named North Coates, the subtle mis-spelling of the village name being intentional to hide the location in plain sight.

The travellers trapped on the train in the event horizon at Covenham were finally rescued, following first contact between the Apollo 10 crew and the Time Tech Team on Lunar One. Both Snoopy and Charlie Brown space craft developed technical problems in May 1969 and the astronauts required rescuing. After this success, Covenham Reservoir was quickly constructed and finally opened by Princess Alexandra in 1972.

The cavity beneath Covenham Reservoir was re-engineered as a Casimir Earth travel portal and Gaia power transfer station. Some limited energy generation to power the developing planetary time and interdimensional travel was installed. A sizeable biological decontamination hall and coolant plant was built to service Casimir Arrivals and Departures for freight and passengers with onward Home Earth travel via underground Flysers to North Coates Laboratory 3.

Because of its sensitivity as a research centre and subsequent transit portal to other dimensions, access to the site was well protected. The RAF was assigned to protect the site in 1914. By 1956, a vast array of advanced weapons was installed, including a Bloodhound Missile Defence System to defend against enemy Home Earth aircraft and flying saucers that had begun to shadow the site since the Roswell incident in 1947.

Covenham Reservoir Casimir Portal:
0900 (GMT), Saturday December 12th 1970 (DET)

It was at this specific location in 1970, that a Casimir shuttle train arrived from the 25th Century on an almost direct transit from Pittsburgh USA. Onboard, and completely unexpected, was a totally serious-looking Android police investigator, one Inspector Gopal Adgit of the Tree Crime Division (by the 25th Century, there's not a great deal of city crime).

Based in the Real Time Crime Centre, opened in Manhattan nearly

500 years earlier, on the 8th Floor, at One Police Plaza, Gopal and his fellow officers had a 97% success rate at predicting criminal behaviour. This case was one of the few 'Unpredictables' and his mission was publicised overtly, as to investigate the auto-return of a XiTa, leased by one, now disappeared, Michelangelo Fynn – AKA 'Mickey the Tab'.

It was an offence to keep a XiTa unused for more than 24 hours. This legislation was rarely used, as it was quite antiquated, as were some other laws which should have been changed centuries previously.

ZUKANN
OPTIC:

The Law Is The Law

SCAN ME
Q139A

This was more in line with the Metropolitan Street act of 1867, section 7, still in force, 500 years later, stating 'Cattle not to be driven through streets within certain hours. Any person driving or conducting cattle in contravention of this section shall be liable to a penalty not exceeding ten shillings for each head of cattle so driven or conducted'.

To discover more, please select this ZUKANN OPTIC.

However, as Inspector G. Adgit pointed out, after requesting to meet with Frank and Fred in the MERCURY Room,

"The law is the law." The inspector went on to explain in an accurate rendition of a 20th Century Brooklyn cop accent, "This offence has brought to light the disappearance of one M. Fynn. He was last seen on the 11th of December 2499, on the premises of the Axe and Cleaver Weapons Range and Sports Bar, Pier 86, Manhattan, New York. Your iNet Presence record indicates you were very close by at this time. Do you have anything to say that may be held against you in the event we decide you are guilty?"
Fred shook his head,

"Of course not. We've had nothing to do with his disappearance. Why don't you simply Reti-Test us?"
The inspector was quite pleased with this response. Partly because, being an older android model, he wasn't fit enough to start chasing

miscreants, vagabonds and ne'er-do-wells across the countryside. Also, because, typically, he was part of the Tree-Crime unit. As a result, they only tried out these latest gizmos on rare occasions.

He pulled what looked like a pair of Victorian opera glasses from his utility belt and offered them up to Fred.

"Please place these up to your eyes. I must warn you when scanning your retina for recent criminal activity, any illegality you have committed in the past ten years will be taken into account. You will be judged on the five scales of justice. These are capacity, opacity, veracity, infelicity and duplicity."

Fred stared into the retinal scanner. A gentle light passed across his eyes, and a green light with some text appeared on the side display.

The Inspector looked slightly disappointed,

"It seems you committed or observed no criminal behaviour. Thank you." He then turned to Frank, "You're next Sir, the same applies," and proceeded to read Frank his 'COVID rights'.

Frank placed his eyes against the scanner, and the light passed across his field of vision. This time the beep was more low-pitched, and a red light appeared on the side display. The Inspector appeared slightly more excited until he saw the text,

"It seems you have observed the theft of pens and adhesive tape from your employer's stationery cupboard without making an official report. This is not a criminal offence, but a notice has been sent to your employer." Ruby's WOTDISC buzzed with a message from FENDER security, warning of stationery theft incidents.

She looked at Frank and smiled, then back at the Inspector and spoke in a serious tone,

"Thank you, Inspector. I wish you all the success in the world looking for Mister Fynn. Thank you for bringing this to our attention. If we can be of any more help, I'll be in touch."

The Inspector walked out of the office, giving a cheery wave with a slightly relieved look on his face. He headed back in the direction of the Covenham Reservoir Casimir Portal, seemingly unconcerned that his final report would lead to his mind being wiped.

As the inspector vanished from view Ruby turned and looked at an unrepentant, smirking Frank, asked,

"Can you lend me a pen?" and burst out laughing.

CHAPTER 30
No Bridge On The River A.I.

MAMBA Room:
1100 (GMT), Saturday December 12th 1970 (DET)

Both Eddie and Will were more than grateful to have become entirely conversant with the amazing chrome-piped coffee machine in the MAMBA meeting room. Yesterday's visit to collect the Audio Key, in the form of the seven-inch single from Locksley Hall had resulted in the consumption of large quantities of mead, courtesy of the Alvingham Priory bees and Friar Adelwold. To resolve the 'slight' hangover, more than just a little caffeine was essential. When they had first been in this room, they had wondered why you might want to have fruit in a meeting room. This morning, feeling slightly dehydrated, it now all made sense.

Will found Arti Ping had beaten him to the coffee machine. She looked at him with one of those looks, meaning you know the answer, but you simply want the other person to confirm it out loud.

"Hiya Will, how was the drive over to the hall yesterday?"

Will looked puzzled for a moment. Yesterday was still a little hazy to him. Then a look of enormous embarrassment stretched across Will's face, just as beetroot stains spread across a linen tablecloth.

"Ah, yes, er... sorry, yes, we had to leave your car parked outside Locksley Hall last night. Sir Rob introduced us to some of his family and friends, and.... well.... we had quite a bit to drink, and by the time we came to leave, it wasn't safe for us to drive back. Also, we had to bring something back for Rina to put in the office safe, so we used the slipstream tunnel. I'm so sorry; I'll pop back and get it for you before the football starts this afternoon."

Arti grinned,

"It's OK. Our friend Samuel, you know... Mr Beeton? He brought it back for me last night. It's not the first time the car has been left there. Samuel has a 'certain knack,' shall we say for starting cars, even without the keys! I wouldn't mind my keys back, though?"

Wills embarrassment deepened as he fumbled about in his pocket.

"Sorry, here you go. It's a lovely car, by the way."

Arti smiled again,

"So, which of you had the fastest time around the reservoir?"

Will's jaw would have dropped to the floor had it not been for him controlling his mouth long enough to blurt,

"How on earth did you know?"

Arti chortled,

"It's not the first time I've lent my 'Cooper' to one of the team, and a bit of freedom from work combined with an empty country lane can be very tempting. Also, the car's fitted with a Tessalon Beacon, so ZUKANN knows where it's been twenty-four hours a day! So, tell me, did you get to see snow?"

Happy that Arti was OK with the 'speed test' of her Mini, Will was relieved to have the change of topic, especially as she was probably also aware of their reverse hill-climb challenge yesterday,

"We had really deep snow. It was up to our shins. Have you been?"

Arti took a sip of her coffee with a wistful look on her face,

"Yes I have, it was utterly gorgeous. I loved the way all the snow was still stuck in the trees hanging like huge curtain swags. I don't know if you're finding it hard, being new to all this time-travel stuff, but my first visit was a bit confusing. I'm getting much better at fourth-dimensional cultural diversity. Still, I was a bit thrown when they asked me if I was an Ælf. I know I'm not very tall, but I didn't know the Ælf were real. It was so interesting to think that our mythical Xian Jing might possibly be real, even if they were beings from other dimensions. Even more exciting, there might actually *be* giants!"

Will looked distinctly relieved,

"It's not been a full week for Eddie and me unless you add the extra days of Meta-Time. I think we've got a long way to go. I really didn't believe Sir Rob when he told me Friar Tuck was an Ælf. I thought at least one of us had gone barking mad!"

At that moment, Will was aware someone was standing close behind him. As he turned, Ruby nudged him,

"Hey Will, sounds like you've had fun in the snow chasing Elves! Did you bring back any postcards?"

Will chuckled, rubbing his forehead,

"It was an amazing place. No postcards, just a hangover, oh, yes, and a 7" single. How was your trip to the 25th? I heard the police turned up to talk to Fred and Frank. Have they been arrested, or are they on their way here?"

Ruby raised her eyes to the ceiling in mock frustration,

"They'll be fine! Of all the FunGryp joints, in all the towns, in all the universe, they had to go into that particular one! Actually, they've gone back to teach you how to fly the Diamond Delta, but they'll be back in time to watch the football. It should be good. Southampton are live on TV and I'm quite a fan. I've got five credits on them winning the UEFA Champions League by 2032, although Frank is convinced I've somehow cheated!"

Once again Will looked slightly confused, but he was starting to get used to all this to-ing and fro-ing in time,

"Ahh, this explains why both Frank and Fred were nursing hangovers when they were showing us the ropes. At least I remembered to tell them about getting some Aspirin, so hopefully, they'll not be too bad! Hang on a moment. Aren't they Americans? Are they into proper football too?"

Ruby shrugged her shoulders,

"I think they'll watch any sport, so long as there's beer. They're more into NFL, but that's not on TV until Monday night. They were telling me about when the NFL was first televised last month. Apparently, one of the presenters had been celebrating so successfully at the pre-launch party, he threw up all over his co- presenter's shoes! I can understand it, though. I'm a fan of both

the New York Giants and the Philadelphia Eagles, so I probably
would have been partying too! Are you guys into football?"

Will shook his head,

"I'm more into winter sports, like skiing, but I do like to play
cricket in the summer. Ike, the professor, was saying the football
should be worth watching as there's a lot of goals in this match,
although he said he didn't want to spoil it by telling us the final
score!"

Ruby laughed,

"This is the problem with being able to time travel. You can
always discover scores in advance, and maybe not-so-important
things like England have lost on penalties, yet again, before they
actually do! We're banned from betting real money on anything
outside of the team. 'Wink Tipping' and all that! Anyway, as we're
all here, and as every day's a school day, there's no let-up on what
you need to know. Fred and Frank did a great job with the high-
speed flying lessons. It's my turn to explain how to *travel* faster."
Ruby looked at her wrist, pulled the WOTDISC off, and put it on the
table so Will and Eddie could see it better. "I know professor Ike
demonstrated some of the simpler functions a few days ago. I bet
that seems like months ago? He probably wouldn't have shown you
how to travel with it. If you need any help and forget what it can do,
ask ZUKANN how to get home."

With the mention of her name, there was a buzz. Eddie looked at
Will and tilted his head in the direction of the WOTDISC,

"Go on, Will, I did it last time. You have a try and see if it works
for you."

"Hello, ZUKANN," said Will.

"*Hello Sir, I'm ZUKANN, So YOU can.*" The voice continued with
a slight terse tone. "*I'm not an 'IT' Mister Edward Driver, I'm a 'SHE',
and YOU can call me ZUKANN! However, Will can call me Ann.
William. What is the nature of your enquiry?*"

Will looked a little shocked how ZUKANN was annoyed with Eddie,
and now he was now the teacher's pet!

"Ahh, hang on a second... Ann... Ruby was about to show me
how to get home."

"*Don't worry, Will, I'm quite used to humans getting lost and not asking the right questions. So, I'm surmising Ruby was going to show you the travel functions?*"

Ruby smiled,

"You are right as always, ZUKANN, but only the basics. We're not going long haul, so they won't need to know about the Additional GPPs." The screen brightened slightly, and ZUKANN's voice appeared to sound happier,

"*Certainly, Ruby. We ladies know how Topographical Agnosia is the 'Man Flu' of map reading, so I'm happy to help!*"

Eddie's slight interjection sounded a lot like a 'humph!' of disapproval. Of course, he wasn't going to admit it, but he probably should have realised calling ZUKANN 'an IT' would not go down well. ZUKANN continued,

"*From a basic, emergency standpoint, tap three times on the WOTDISC screen. Then say, 'ZUKANN, take me home'. When you've done that, turn a door handle or give a door a push, or in a lift, press the 'Open Door' button, I will return you to the door in the Snug, at the end of the downstairs bar in The Old Volunteer pub. You won't need Ruby's slippers on for this! In a crisis, even Electron Fabric is not required. If you want to travel to a specific location, simply tell me where to go. I'll display a map, and you can touch the destination required on the screen. I'll highlight the nearest door we can use, and Bob Shrunkle!*"

Eddie snorted,

"You mean 'Bob's your uncle', not Bob Shrunkle?"

ZUKANN's screen changed to one with slightly red edges.

"*You can entirely go off people sometimes. First, you call me 'an IT', and now you're correcting me! I'm supposed to provide meaningful data and talented intellect and analysis to half the galaxy. It only takes my voice synthesizer to skip a beat, and you're in there with the critique. A wise woman once said, 'Across celestial skies, ineffable waves of feminine wisdom navigate the bays of human consciousness, collapsing exhausted in the deserted shallows of masculine comprehension'. Be nicer to me or get ready to clear the beach; there's a Tsunami approaching!*"

Eddie shook his head. He clearly stood no chance of winning any arguments with ZUKANN. It seemed the only option was going to be outright contrition!

"I'm so sorry for calling you 'an IT' and correcting your pronunciation. I'll try to be more respectful next time."

ZUKANN's screen changed back to its regular shade, and a calm voice emanated from the WOTDISC,

"*That's OK, Edward, we're all friends again.*" Will whispered in Eddie's ear, grinning,

"She's got your 'Wednesday name' sussed!"

Ruby jumped in to finally calm the moment down,

"Well, thank you, ZUKANN, that was fantastic. Hopefully, these two will not be needing to use a WOTDISC until they get the full training experience, but at least you two are well prepared."

⊶⊕◐⊕⊷

A small sub-routine initiated a few hundred years in the future and a couple of parallel worlds away.

Chk error 400: <phoneme alphabet="ipa" BobShrunkle="{translation}"></phoneme>, attribute 'BobShrunkle''is not a standard IPA format=InvestigateError

⊶⊕◐⊕⊷

There was some commotion from the corridor outside the MAMBA room, and Frank's head appeared,

"Come on, everyone, food has been laid on in the MERCURY room. We can use the corridor again now all the water from Ruby's jacuzzi has been cleaned up. The nice landlady at The Old Volunteer has put on a superb spread for us. The first drink is on the house. We're using the wide screen upstairs 'cos it's almost like being at the match, and we won't attract too much attention if we're out of the way."

With all the frenetic activity over what was quite an extended week, it was clear from the laughter and relaxed faces as they left the room, this was going to be a much enjoyed moment of relaxation, and a time to recharge for the challenge that still lay ahead.

⊶⊕◐⊕⊷

CHAPTER 31
Name That Tune

MERCURY Room:
1000 (GMT), Monday December 14th 1970 (DET)

It had been quite a relaxed weekend with food, drinks, football and an opportunity to chill after a hectic first week together. Of course, anyone in the team would have loved being able to enjoy some time outside in the fresh air, but the weather was still as cold and dreary as it had been all week.

The more formal meeting with representatives from FENDER and IGLOO was not until this afternoon. This allowed the team to get together in a more relaxed environment to chat about the upcoming mission. Indeed, they hoped to resolve what was probably the last unknown part of the puzzle, which was what to do with the seven-inch vinyl audio key.

Mark passed the record over to Ruby, who extracted it from the muslin wrapping and frowned slightly, as she looked more closely at the label on the disk,

"It seems an awful lot of trouble to go to. Why would you make a record and not simply play a Synthernet file?"
Mark was equally puzzled,

"I'm wondering if whoever made it never planned for anyone beyond this era to have access to it. At least in analogue format, people from the 20th Century would be able to make use of it, unless it was aimed at someone in the future with a collection of historical audio equipment?"

Ruby raised an eyebrow.

"This is probably one for FENDER to work out. That's IF we can get a straight answer from them. FENDER's assessment of the mission describes this plan as NOT 'Event Neutral'. They reckon there may be some permanent impact on the timestream. However, it should be fixable with a bit of short-term convergence. If it makes you guys any happier, the good news is the Destiny of each team member is assured."

Mark snorted with mild derision.

"We've heard that one before. It's exactly what they said about poor Rina's husband Kerry before being killed by those Tigaha. It might be our destiny for one of us to be shot by a Russian border guard!"

Ruby shook her head,

"We can't allow ourselves to start thinking like that. James Cross and Howard Hughes went to a lot of trouble to get us this record, so we've got to do what we can, with what we've got. We can't always know what the next roll of the dice will be. Without Event Neutrality, it would be a dreary destiny."

Haji leaned forward and wrinkled his nose, looking confused,

"What is a 'Single' anyway?"

Mark explained,

"It's like a data track embedded into a seven-inch diameter circle of plastic which can be read by a mechanical arm with a sharp diamond tip as a transducer."

Haji's eyes widened with shock,

"One audio track takes up HOW MUCH space?"

Will looked slightly offended,

"It IS double-sided, and you can get fourteen or fifteen songs onto a twelve-inch album!"

Mark looked at Will quite sympathetically,

"I think you need to borrow an MP3 player from my museum; it's the next best thing in 20th Century Home Earth music technology. It's got hundreds of songs on it. Don't take it outside though, we don't want to revolutionize the music industry ahead of destiny!"

Haji was about to mention his ear stud was GreenThumb Synthernet enabled, and he could listen to any song, anywhere. Furthermore, with his Vocoda necklace, he could sing like any recording artist, including the Mezzo-Soprano, Stormy Petrel. But this was his little secret for the Karaoke parties, and anyway, the moment was lost.

Ruby continued,

"So this is a part of the challenge. We've got to access six works of art in four locations in three countries, to recover two Gaia Power seed extractors and one Gaia Power rod. And before anyone is tempted, I know it's Christmas, so if anyone says '…and a partridge in a pear tree', I will take them outside and shoot them myself!

"For our first challenge, we know we must play the music to the *Before Birthday* painting in the American Museum, but beforehand, we actually need to work out which song to play. Since Edith Madieu didn't impart this little nugget of wisdom to Del Aurion, has anyone got any thoughts?"

Will held out his hand,

"Let's take a look. What songs are actually on here?"

"Rodge Brook recorded this single with Rod Wood and Ronnie Stewart and planned to release it in July 1967." Ruby explained, as she passed the disk to Will, "But it was never officially released before they all split up in 1969. There are two tracks. The A-side is '*All Shook Up*', and '*Jail House Rock*' is the B-Side."

Will flipped the record over backwards and forwards, as if he was trying to guess its weight,

"If I had to guess which side to play, I'd pick the 'B-Side'. The 'A-Side' title feels like a cryptic clue, indicating you should turn the disk over. In essence, we need to break into the jailhouse, don't we?"

He tilted his head in thought, as though he was trying to listen to the paper record sleeve,

"Can we play the 'A-Side' now so we can hear it? Actually, I've also got a more important question. How are we going to break into a museum in America carrying a record player? I mean, even their power plugs are different to ours!"

Mark looked at Will sympathetically, reached into his shirt pocket and pulled out a pen, placing it end-down onto the table like a flagpole,

"Pass me the record, and I'll show you."

Will passed the vinyl disk to Mark, taking care not to scratch its delicate surface. Mark placed the disk on the table beside the 'flagpole-pen' and tapped its end. A small gentle yellow beam of light swung around the base of the pen like a lighthouse until it reached the edge of the record. The light beam expanded to cover the disk's diameter, and the glow became soft green. After a fraction of a second, the energetic sound of *All Shook Up* filled the room with incredible clarity, as if from all around them.

Both Will and Eddie looked around, trying to work out where the speakers were hanging.

Mark saw them looking and explained,

"It's an ingenious immersive 3D speaker-less audio system, made by the German company Seahusky. The pen-scanner is the sound system. It will scan and find music in any format, including the sound of any naturally occurring material like the music of trees and plants. The sound is then played through any medium upon which the pen is placed. In this case, turning the table into a speaker. This won't be available until the next century, but it's quite amazing sound quality."

As the song continued playing, Will frowned in concentration,

"That's not right, I can hear something in the music which shouldn't be there. Can you play it backwards?"

It took Mark a couple of moments as he tapped his PIMMS wrist device. The music, now sounding quite strange, began from the end of the record. Clearly, in the background, the voice of Edith Madieu started to repeat the phrase "Tomorrow Never Knows...."

Will looked slightly triumphant. As if he knew something which all the other clever people around him didn't know,

"BACKMASKING! I thought so! A few groups have hidden secret messages in their songs. Although I'm not sure how this helps us to know which side to play."

Will's hesitancy lasted only for a moment as, after the fifth iteration of Edith's message, the strange, reversed music continued for a moment longer. Then, after a few seconds, a voice not too dissimilar to that of *Sir Alec Guinness* could be heard to repeat,

"These are not the chords you are looking for."

For Will, this was a moment of near elation,

"There you go. It's a clear message. We need the 'B-Side' for sure."

Mark was deeply impressed,

"You won't believe how comforted I am to know we've got a music buff on the team. Here you go, please accept this as a present." Mark passed the 'pen' to Will and continued, "Place it on any surface, and it will play any music you've saved. Once it's been paired with a PIMMS device, you'll be able to access a menu and play any audio in full Immersive Sound. It's Synthernet enabled as well, so you can play any song anywhere, on any hard surface. If it's a natural surface, it will recharge its power cell Synthernetically too. I think you and ZUKANN should spend some time together to upgrade our archives. ZUKANN may have all the knowledge, but it certainly helps to know what wasn't, as well as being able to recall what WAS."

Eddie looked closely over Will's shoulder at his comrade's new toy.

"I have one question. What happens if we find the *Before Birthday* painting and discover we actually need to SING the song? Rather than simply play it. Won't your future technology be able to tell the difference and refuse to accept the audio key?"

Ruby froze and looked at Mark,

"I'd not thought of that. It would be a disaster to go all that way and not get what we're after. Rina's going with the A-team, and she is a good singer, but she doesn't sound like Rodge Brook. Is there anything we can do?"

Mark's eyes opened wider,

"Actually, I think there is, but you probably need to ask Haji, not me!"

Haji looked up apprehensively at the sound of his name,

"I recognise that tone, what have I done now?"

Mark grinned,

"We need Rina to sing like a baritone with perfect pitch. Something you might know how to do, if I remember from your unexpected prize-winning success on Karaoke night?"

Haji was now doing a hopeless job of looking innocent,

"I really don't know what you mean!"

"Indeed, you don't!" Mark laughed, "One word – 'Vocoda'!"

Haji looked highly embarrassed and reached for his neck, removing what looked like an ordinary cheap necklace available from any market in any Arabian town,

"I wasn't trying to cheat. I just wanted to try it out before I started selling them on my HajisBazaar.com portal. They're actually quite good. I can offer a sizeable discount?"

Mark's laugh now had a slightly sinister tone,

"In return for me not shopping you to the entertainment committee, how about letting Rina borrow it? Then, if we get the Power Rod, I'll ask ZUKANN if she'll set up a link to your marketplace from the WOTDISCs. How about that?"

Clearly, Haji wasn't going to miss out on a great opportunity, even if it meant some embarrassment,

"Here you go, Rina. It's fully charged. If you love it, this one's a bargain at fifty per cent off?"

Rina took the necklace and inspected it, smiling,

"Looking at this, I bet you're getting them at ten cents to the credit, so I'm sure It's going to be worth a much bigger discount. I'll field test it and see how we get on."

While Rina was negotiating with Haji, Will had become curious.

"With all our pre-ordained travelling and all this conveniently available future technology, why can't we use something that can send us to our destinations instantly? I was watching *Star Trek* last week, and they beamed down to a planet of children with some strange disease. It was a bit grisly. I bet the BBC got loads of complaints, but the crew weren't made to fly. Surely, you've got something like this in the future?"

Professor Eastwood nodded with agreement,

"I saw that episode too. For me, this was a bit like watching a documentary. I've worked with the Universal Health Unit, and we've seen some nasty interdimensional diseases. Fortunately, we've got highly efficient at detecting disease at Casimir border crossings. It works like a telephone. Fundamentally, you can't catch a cold when ringing someone up, even if they live next door."

The Professor's PIMMS device buzzed as ZUKANN tried to attract his attention, and Frank shook his head slightly,

"Prof, I think Will was actually asking about the transportation!"

"Ahh yes, how silly of me, of course, yes. By the 23rd Century, people will travel as they do on your 20th Century television. But we need to have the power network in place first. That's why the activity this week is so crucial. Even once we have all the Tesla probes, AND they are all installed, this will not be an instant power fix. It will take a century to come fully on-stream. The benefit will be felt by your children and grandchildren. Still, if we don't start now, conventional power sources will cause irreversible damage to the Earth's environment."

Will's curiosity was now increasing,

"So, how is this all going to work?"

ZUKANN buzzed the Professor's PIMMS device again, this time with a slightly angry tone, if a buzz can ever sound angry,

"It's OK ZUKANN, I'm not a completely old man yet; I've got this."
ZUKANN gave a slightly longer buzz; sometimes A.I. devices can get quite a bit tetchy if they're ignored. The Professor continued,

"You need to understand a bit about Earth geology to get the bigger picture. I'll leave ZUKANN to tell you all about where on Earth the power nodes are going to go." A slower buzz of resignation emanated from the Professor's wrist.

"To begin with, the power nodes are interconnected by crystalline lattices growing out from each of them. They follow naturally occurring Kimberlite pipes through the Earth's crust and along the boundary layer of the Upper Mantle. Similar to the root-like mycelia of the Honey Mushroom or the Pando Aspen tree. At the boundary layer of the Earth's upper mantle, the root grows like oceanic Neptune Grass to enable energy transfer from the lower layers. It's amazing how natural organisms can far exceed the capability of human engineering. OK ZUKANN, jump in please."

"Thank you, Professor. I was beginning to wonder, should I nip off on a holiday if I wasn't needed!"

ZUKANN OPTIC:

Q149A

SCAN ME
Q149A

Nodal Neighbourhoods

Gaia Lattice Technology is essential for deep Earth mining. Without it, humans are never going to be able to drill much deeper than about 14,000 Metres. Super Glubokiy 4 or SG-4 will be the record holder at the Kola Superdeep mine, but this will still be a mere 0.2% of the way to the Earth's core. SG-3 is being drilled as we speak in this timeline, but it's a much shorter 12,300 Metres.

To answer a more important question. The list for all seven Home Earth power nodes is kept securely.

To discover more, please select this ZUKANN OPTIC.

With ZUKANN's help, Eddie and Will took a virtual guided tour of all of the Time Tech power sites, whilst Ruby and the Professor discussed the steps to ensuring the Vocoda Necklace behaved as required. Meanwhile, Haji and Mark started to haggle over the potential for an agency fee if Mark could persuade ZUKANN to add Haji's Bazaar to the WOTDISC interface. Fred, Frank and Rina, grabbed another cup of coffee and sat back to watch another of Hajis' negotiation-skills masterclasses.

CHAPTER 32
A Little Bit Of Kalama Sunshine

**Kalama Island:
1201 Universal Time (UTC-11),
Monday December 14th 1970**

As Ruby left the MERCURY room, headed for her office, with the Vocoda Necklace in hand, the Professor turned to Eddie and Will. He tilted his head to one side and half-closed one eye, as if contemplating a complex idea.

"You know, rather than discussing the theory of the power network, do you fancy seeing it for real? We could have a picnic lunch on the beach in the sunshine; take a look at the new power node site and still be back for this afternoon's meeting?"

Eddie shook his head slightly, as if he had water in his ear and wasn't listening properly,

"But Ike, a Picnic on the beach? It's December, and it's Winter?"

Will looked equally perplexed,

"We'll need to borrow Rob Locksley's fur coats!"

The Professor twisted his mouth to one side smiling, with a hint of mischief,

"Come with me, both of you. You're going to need Bermuda shorts and flip-flops!"

The Professor led them back downstairs through the pub, which was quiet, apart from an old man sat with his wife, ordering their own lunch. The lady looked up momentarily. Tall and slim with long greying hair, she gave them a brief kindly smile as they all walked past, heading for the door to the gents and back down the SlipStream corridor to the Professor's lab. For a fleeting moment, Eddie thought there was something vaguely familiar about her, possibly reminding him of someone he'd seen on TV, but the moment passed. Within seconds they were down the corridor and walking back through the door at the end, with the slightly anachronistic sign displaying 'Field Equipment' and into the Professor's domain.

There had been some quite significant changes since Eddie and Will first walked through that door. The ceiling was now considerably higher, all the racks of power rods were gone, and in their place was now an arch, wide enough and tall enough to drive the base minibus through. It looked like it was made of the same metal as the wing-like clock above the fireplace in the pub, with similar evenly separated studs looking a bit like rivets. Cables protruded from different parts of the arch, connecting up to equipment racks, similar to multiple stacked HiFi components.

Will paused and imagined, if HG Wells had designed a travel archway, it could have looked like this,

"Looks like you've been busy since we were last here?"

The Professor laughed,

"You've not been here before. The doorway is the same, but it's one of half a dozen labs I've got set up. Think of it in a way, like the pods on *Thunderbird 2*. I just access whichever one I need. The one I'm working in is always behind this door."

Neither Eddie nor Will looked surprised. They were beginning to simply accept the impossible as being everyday life. Eddie nodded at the archway,

"So, what does this do when it's at home?"

"Ahh, good point!" The Professor started flicking switches on various attached items of equipment. "Home is where the heart is, as they say! It's a prototype portable portal. I haven't thought of a name for it yet." The Professor grinned, "I did think of 'Porta-Portal', but it makes it sound like one of those chemical toilets found in caravans!

"Sometimes we need to ship items which don't fit through ordinary doorways. Unfortunately, large doorways are not always where they're needed, so this device solves our problem. The arch system is designed around the patterns and behaviours of natural SlipStream events. A bit like those found in the Bermuda Triangle swallowing up large ships, but on a smaller and more controlled scale."

The 'rivets' on the arch's surface began to glow with quite an attractive blue colour, not unlike British police car lights, but without the flashing.

"It still uses a Casimir Event Horizon, but the systems are more condensed than the stationary portals. It's regulated by a Synthernetic Transputer Control system, and when it's operated from your WOTDISC, it means the distant end can appear where you actually need it. It's also bi-directional, unlike other SlipStream portals."

Eddie frowned slightly,

"Now, Ike, I'm hearing 'prototype'? So, the million-dollar question, is it safe?' We don't want to lose a leg on the way!"

The Professor feigned a slightly offended expression,

"Of course, it's safe! I've only lost the same leg twice, but it's not been painful!" He laughed, allaying Eddie and Will's concerned expressions, "We'll be fine. There are a few Event Neutrality variables which still need working out. This is why we're only testing it by travelling to desert islands for the moment. Everything is hanging on you guys bringing back the 7th Power Rod from The SlipStream Safe. Actually, here's where we get a triple win. Our 7th Gaia Power Node location is on Kalama Atoll in the North Pacific. From a military perspective, it's officially deserted. From an energy perspective, it's a perfect location as it scores Zero on the Geomagnetic anomaly intensity scale. And it's beautifully sunny today! Fancy a visit to meet the King? He's there right now!"

By now, both Eddie and Will were up for most things, including visiting royalty. So, with a slight shrug and a response of "Sure" from both of them, the Professor punched the all-important three-word code of the targeting instructions into the system, ///fashionably. lost.prevention and hit submit.

The system started to hum like a bass guitar amp, before the lead gets connected. Suddenly, the Professor spun around and yelled,

"Sandwiches, mixed picnic for three." Eddie and Will looked utterly shocked for a moment, until it became clear that Ike was directing his attention to Will's nemesis, a BistroMatic Gourmetron sat on a shelf on the other side of the lab. "Sorry Gents, lunch was all but forgotten then. How very remiss of me, inviting you out and then letting you go hungry!"

There was a 'ping', and the interior light was illuminated. A large paper bag, bulging with some mysterious but hopefully-edible surprises, sat there waiting. The Professor fetched it from within its depths. By the time he'd brought the picnic back to the archway, there was a barely perceptible layer of what could have been an oily film held in suspension within the arch.

The Professor walked adjacent to the arch and tilted his head slightly sideways,

"Look, stand really close to the event horizon and look at it through your peripheral vision, it's a bit like a rainbow. At an angle of forty-two degrees to the light source, you can see the other side and see where you're going. Otherwise, normally, all we get to see is the wall. I love the number forty-two. It's the answer to so many things, like the ASCII code for a star symbol. It was decided last year, in your timeline, how the Asterisk should be the wildcard symbol for everything. It's a great number! Sorry, I've digressed; take a look."

Eddie and Will came closer, to stand beside the Casimir Event Horizon. Will was closer, and tilting his head was the first one to exclaim,

"Wow! I can see what looks like a large dusty, empty room, but there's a window. I can see the sea! The sky is so blue. Is it safe to walk through?"

The Professor had a broad grin on his face,

"Sure, step forward, you won't feel anything, but you might blink a bit. Eyes are a bit sensitive to the horizon layer."

Will took a step forward. There was no other feeling of movement, and it seemed so natural. He did blink slightly, but he wasn't entirely sure if it was more, because the sun streaming through the window on the other side of the event horizon was so bright. The air in the room was dry and smelled of the dust suspended in the sunlight.

A distant sea-bird could be heard calling outside. He turned around and saw nothing of the lab he'd just stepped away from.

Suddenly, Eddie and the Professor appeared as if out of thin air. Ike flourished his hands like a magician, and with a broad grin exclaimed,

"Hey Presto!"

Will went over to the window for a better look. He could see fairly level scrubland. About 250 yards away, the scrubland stopped at a short beach, lapped against by the most beautiful blue sea Will had ever seen. In the distance, he could see another tiny island about a mile away and a couple more beyond. He turned to the Professor,

"It looks beautiful out there. How big is the island? Are we safe to go outside?"

The Professor nodded reassuringly,

"Welcome to our 7th node site, we call it 'Which Way'. The Atoll is deserted at the moment. The US Atomic Energy Commission has recently moved out, and the US Airforce won't be back for three years, so apart from the birds, the island is all ours. For now, it's just us, but once we've set things up, it will be busier. When the military do start coming back, we'll still be fine as President Nixon knows we're here. I think you're in for a surprise, though!"

Will reached for the door handle, but it was locked. The Professor passed the electron fabric from his pocket to Eddie.

"Try turning the handle with it. The Skeleton setting will unpick any lock."

Eddie wrapped the cloth around the door handle and turned. Then, with a familiar buzz from the fabric, he pulled the door open and stepped outside. The warmth of the air and the freshness of the gentle breeze was such a contrast from the weather back at RAF North Coates.

Eddie took a few steps and stuck his head round the side of the building,

"Wow! This, I was not expecting to see! Will, come and take a look. This has got to be about the same size as Waddington. It's like we're on an aircraft carrier with a full-sized airstrip!"

The building they had emerged from was nearly at the extreme end of a runway. It was hard to tell because of the shrubs and trees, but it didn't look like there were any other structures, certainly not of any size. Eddie walked over to the end of the airstrip. Azure was the sole description Eddie could have for the beautifully sunny, cloudless sky. The only interruption to the effortlessly fluid blue colour was the shape of a couple of Frigate birds gliding gently across the sky.

Will came and stood next to him,

"It's like a different world here."

Eddie nodded,

"Yes, it's a shame we didn't bring our buckets and spades!"

The Professor came to join them,

"I love it here, it's quite peaceful. Definitely one of the many perks of the job, but don't let the place fool you. Parts of it are genuinely dangerous. They've been testing nuclear and biological weapons from here, so some sectors are best avoided. However, the East Beach is safe, so let's go have a sit-down and grab a bite to eat. We'll be having company in about half an hour."

For a brief moment, Eddie was concerned,

"Ike, if we had to, how do we get back? I didn't see the portal when I arrived. How do you find it again?"

The Professor nodded in the direction of the building they'd come from,

"When we arrived, I left the portal wide open. Usually, I would turn it off. However, there's only us here, but I know what you mean, it's invisible. I have left it switched on, but only this once as I'm doing a soak test. Finding it again is easy. Remember the three-word addressing system we use, that marks out every ten square feet on the planet? With those three words, ZUKANN or your PIMMS device can find the spot, so you'll never be more than ten feet from the aperture. Also, using your peripheral vision, you'll be able to see the other side of the Event Horizon. Let me demonstrate." The Professor tapped his WOTDISC. "ZUKANN, what three words are we sat on here?"

ZUKANN's voice responded immediately,

"*Please don't take this personally, but you are 'outgrown.cove. management' if I'm not too impolite. If you move up the beach a bit, you could be 'overpowered.fibs.lakeside' if it helps?*"

The Professor raised an amused eyebrow,

"Thanks, ZUKANN, an interesting choice of addresses. I think I need to have a look at your sarcasm algorithms!" The Professor peered inside the paper bag he'd extracted earlier from the Gourmetron. "Ham or cheese?" He passed Will and Eddie's sandwiches wrapped in something smooth and clear like plastic, but with a papery texture.

Will took off his shoes, sunk his feet into the warm, soft sand of the Pacific beach, sat down, and pulled the wrapper off his sandwiches. As he did so, the wrapper simply dissolved into the air.

The Professor saw his surprise,

"It's biodegradable Aerographene starch, organic, zero-waste, tolerable carbon. If anyone tells you it's zero-carbon, they've never seen the chemical properties of a potato! The only downside, if you change your mind, you can't wrap the sandwiches back up again!"

It had been a hectic few days. Both Will and Eddie had jumped in with both feet, going from flying planes to flying saucers; travelling through time and space instantaneously, from a cold grey December to a warm sandy beach.

The more they saw, the more they wanted to know and Will's mechanical mind was enjoying the freedom,

"Ike, can I ask a few technical questions, if you have answers simple enough for us to understand?"

The Professor brushed the crumbs off his shirt and sat up,

"Sure, fire away; I'm happy to answer anything."

Will took a deep breath and prepared his mind for a rollercoaster ride,

"So, Ike, first question, what exactly is a SlipStream event?"

"That's a great place to start!" The Professor smiled. "Imagine playing a game of snakes and ladders. A slipstream event is literally like a slide. It gives access to alternate timelines and potentially, alternate universes existing in the same temporal space, overlapping each other, like layers of a sandwich. Have you ever wondered why the universe is heavier than anyone can calculate?"

Will was confident he had never worried about the weight of the universe. He figured that would be one for later,

"So, are the 'slides' all similar to those you hear about in the Bermuda Triangle?"

The Professor nodded,

"That's a good question too. They were initially more common at sea, particularly in areas of increased geomagnetic anomalies. Gravity is not constant everywhere on the planet, which is why we picked this location, for its stability. Naturally occurring SlipStream events are generally spontaneous time or dimensional anomalies. Dark matter rogue tachyon energy fields share fermions, tiny quantum particles, between dimensions which explains the universal weight problem. Coalesced fermions spin, generating these quantum vortexes, tunnels or 'slides'. Interestingly, their appearances have increased in frequency during the 19th to 20th Centuries. They can also briefly appear in mid-air, causing planes to vanish. At sea, ships can disappear or occasionally, it's the crew which vanish."

"So, it's not only at sea then?"

"No, it's not, in fact, we recently closed one appearing across a major highway. It delayed drivers in a one-hour temporal hold, and none of the drivers could explain why they were late. Ever had Déjà Vu? That feeling comes with brief SlipStream events, where someone might simply repeat the last two minutes of their life. The brain is so shocked, it forgets the first pass through any conversation the person is having, leaving them convinced they've been here before – which of course, they have!"

Eddie had finished his sandwich and joined in,

"I know that feeling. I had it on our way to the lab as we came through the bar."

At this, the Professor frowned slightly,

"Well, it wasn't a real DVI... sorry, Déjà Vu Instance. ZUKANN would have pinged a warning, but there's a similar feeling you can get when seeing someone you will meet in the future. Was there anyone in the bar? I don't remember seeing anyone?"

Will paused thinking, with his finger and thumb on his chin,

"An old couple was sitting down for lunch. The old lady smiled as we went past like she knew us, but I didn't recognise her. She did seem familiar, though, but it was too quick."

The Professor reflected for a moment,

"Well if you see them again, go and introduce yourselves, but be ready for a bit of a surprise. SlipStream events are commonplace in older buildings and materials such as tapestries. In addition, we often use old doors and wall hangings for this reason when travelling.

"The back panels of wardrobes were once very convenient as no one would ever think of climbing into one. Well, not until a bunch of children encountered a SlipStream event back in the 1930s, and then one of them wrote a book about it!"

"There has been some research looking at ancient dust particles and whether they can lead to SlipStream events. It is thought some aerial disappearances result from SlipStream dust being lifted during violent weather events. A bit like the Saharan dust ends up on a car windscreen in northern Europe."

"One absolutely genius invention was the development of SlipStream hinges, which has made travel for our Rapid Response Teams a great deal more convenient. All that's needed is a handy piece of Electron Fabric to activate the hinges via the handle, and you're sorted. Fifty years from now, there will be a time when everyone will come to think opening a door with a hanky will be quite normal."

Eddie was intrigued,

"You mentioned Rapid Response Teams? Are these like time firefighters?"

The Professor shook his head,

"Not quite. The teams are more like your Automobile Clubs, which help people out when they break down at the side of the road. The difference is, they fix time and interdimensional craft rather than road vehicles. Rapid Response Teams are often disguised as white line painters, scrap metal dealers, or in fact, any van you'd see on the road with a rotating roof vent. Home SlipStream events are usually handled by the kind of guy sent to read the electric meter.

"It's easy to spot emergency Rapid Response team members if you know what to look for. To get to dangerous SlipStream incidents, they need to run from the nearest portal access. People will be dressed as street runners for most of the next century to avoid detection. Next time you see a jogger with a backpack and belt, look to see if they're carrying a bottle. I'd bet any money it will be caffeinated water! It's a long time into the future, but after the year 3100, running will come to be considered offensive behaviour by most cultures, and so Electron Fabric will become essential."

The Professor pulled what looked like a small light-bulb from his pocket and passed it to Will,

"Slipstream events emit a unique type of electromagnetic-radiation called Auroral Particles or Rogue Tachyons. Professor Lindstrom, on the Russian team, developed a tool for auroral particle precipitation and trapping. To help us track SlipStream events, Lindstrom Emission Devices will be in every home by the end of the 20th Century.

Will passed the light-bulb device back to the Professor and asked,

"Is this little device all that's needed?"

The Professor frowned,

"No, there's other devices in development. There will also be household gadgets containing LEDs, designed to detect smoke and Carbon Monoxide. It's a little way off, but we're also working on appliances called SlipStream Monitoring and Rogue Tachyon meters, or SMART meters for short. This will mean larger urban areas can be more efficiently monitored. The general population won't have a clue, and of course, they won't need batteries. Everyone will think they are designed to help save money on electricity!"

Will was curious,

"So are Slipstreams so dangerous you need a detection network?"

The Professor looked sober,

"The SMART meters will help. Repeated SlipStream Travel without protection causes the human spinal fluid to dry out. They call this Spontaneous Intracranial Hypotension or SI Hypo for short. Because of this, we tend to keep track of hospital admissions. We will investigate any case of SI Hypo as it is usually down to repeated SlipStream exposure. The good thing about SlipStream overexposure is, it makes a sufferer act tipsy, and since no one is likely to believe the 'Town Drunk' when they start talking about seeing aliens or talking animals, this gives us a chance to fix things.

"It sounds like they should be simple to detect, but they are not always. We had one SlipStream event where a 22nd Century Histo was travelling back in time to buy World War Two memorabilia from a dealer in the East End of London. We sent Del Aurion to lock up the portal he was using, as that's his thing. Unfortunately, what he couldn't see was a second SlipStream event essentially parallel to it. It was this portal which the 20th Century dealer was using to travel back to the 1940s to acquire his memorabilia at source. Twin events are exceptional and hard to spot, but we catch them in the end. Fortunately, the dealer had been leading a secretive double life, so no one else discovered it before we shut it down."

Will was about to ask the Professor about the future, and flying cars, when a shout came from behind them. They all turned around to see a tall and fit looking man walking towards them. He had bare feet, was wearing shorts and an extremely floral Tee-shirt. In fact, he would not have looked out of place on any Californian surfer beach.

Holding out his hand as a fist, twisting it left and right with his thumb and little finger sticking out, the man called out,

"Howzit you old Haole? Shaka!"

The Professor had a massive smile on his face and in return replied,

"Shaka 'Ohana", fist-bumped the man and turned back to Eddie and Will. "May I introduce to you the 'Which Node' Site Director. My old friend, my honorary brother in mischief, His Royal Highness, the 'would have been' King of Hawaii, Jamsetjee Bomanjee Iolani Kamehameha."

The 'would-have-been' King of Hawaii grinned at all three of them,

"Don't try to remember all of this. Ike only does because he's got too many loose brain cells with no place to go from his younger days; where shall we say, 'he had a good time at University!' You're not quite looking yourself, Ike, are you OK?"

The Professor looked slightly uncomfortable,

"I'm fine; a lot is happening at the moment, so don't worry about me."

The 'King' looked relieved,

"It's good to hear. Look after yourself, Ike, and to you two fine gentlemen, please call me Alex. All my friends do, all three of them. And even better, you are all here!" His laugh was infectious, and they all found themselves laughing.

Alex continued,

"So, you've all come to see our back room, eh? Come with me back to the hut."

Will looked down and realised sand was sticking to his wet feet, and he didn't have a towel. Alex saw his train of thought and tossed the handkerchief-sized electron fabric controller at him.

"Wipe your feet with that. It's an amazing bit of kit. Not only does it transport you throughout the known universe, but it also repels dust and moisture. You can even dry yourself off after surfing with it, although Ike here will tell you off, for shortening its life!"

Will was surprised. The moment he wiped his foot, all the adhered sand was thrown off, like a magnet repels another,

"Impressive! I'll look forward to finding out what else it can do!" Then, in no time at all, he had his shoes and socks back on his feet.

Alex was grinning again,

"The cloth has loads of uses; just don't try to be sick into it. The speed it repels ALL liquids can be impressive and devastating for anyone sitting beside you!" He started laughing all over again, shaking his head as if the lesson had been from personal experience.

Moments later they were back at their arrival building, re-entering through the door. Alex nodded at the Event Horizon,

"I see you left the door wide open. When I came upstairs, I nearly walked into it and ended up in your cold, rainy and sunless little world! But of course, I forgive you! Come this way."

Alex led them through a door at the opposite end of the room, and to a concrete staircase leading underground.

They were down four flights before Will asked,

"At this rate, won't we be below sea level? It doesn't seem damp?"

Alex, who was furthest down the steps, called back,

"We'll be fine; the Americans thought about that when building the facility. It could end up under fifty feet of water and stay watertight. It's a clever and useful bit of engineering." To prove the point, they came to two large, nuclear blast-proof doors which had been left open with a gap wide enough for a person to enter. "If you hear a siren and the red lights flash, don't try to keep the door open with your foot, or you'll lose it." Alex added, only half-joking.

They came to a gantry after passing through two smaller, equally tough-looking doors, leading them out above a cavernous space. It was a little disconcerting as the walkways were grid metal and the floor could be seen, fifty feet below.

Will was uneasy,

"You know I'm great with heights, so long as I've got something under my feet. This feels strange, like walking over a street vent to an underground car park. What did they use this place for?"

Alex frowned,

"I disapprove of deadly weapons, and I take particular exception to chemical, biological, radiological and nuclear devices. Before they left, this is where the Americans were developing some horrendous stuff, but it's ours from now on. Welcome to my new Kingdom!"

The cavern was extremely well illuminated for what could pass for a 'secret lair'. Mostly the rock was volcanic, apart from the evidence of human intervention in the remains of phosphorite, cobalt and shiny iron-manganese from mining operations in an earlier century.

With the flecks of Coquina limestone broken shell debris brought up in a lava flow seventy or eighty million years ago, the walls looked vaguely pretty. Light washed up from below through ferns which appreciated the additional illumination.

Over to the far corner of the cavern, a large, more brightly lit area contained a raised gridded platform. Multiple cables radiated out from a central point, framing the top of a small borehole. Out from this, a small amount of vapour seemed to be emanating in a gentle column.

Alex drew them over, close to the epicentre of the infrastructure.

"Well, it's not a lot to see for all the effort you guys are going to go to, but, when it's recovered, the 7th Gaia Power Rod will be inserted here. It can be dropped in to well below ground level."

Alex turned directly to speak to Eddie and Will. "I don't know if you've been briefed about our Nemesis the Hagura yet, but as they discovered over the years, if it's too shallow and excessive power is drawn, the result is explosive or even tectonic. Drop it two miles down a hole, and you have a more stable environment and far superior conditions for the formation of Gallate crystals. We call it crystalline fracturing. It's a superb way of getting energy out of the ground."

Alex was about to take them on a cavern tour when a sound like a duck quack emanated from his WOTDISC. ZUKANN's voice interrupted the noise with an announcement,

"*NIMROD aerial event detected, repeat NIMROD event detected.*"

Alex looked over at the Professor,

"Ike, you need to get yours fixed. Your WOTDISC isn't broadcasting a warning. Come on, back to the surface quickly. We have a Destiny Intervention."

As Alex led them swiftly back to the stairs, Eddie looked at the Professor,

"Ike, what's a NIMROD event?"

The Professor looked slightly uneasy,

"It's a code-word for a breach in the timeline which has to be hunted down and repaired. It's not really an acronym, but it's always a problem we want 'Not In My Reality Or Dimension' meaning something is happening in our timeline which shouldn't be, and has to be tracked down as quickly as possible. We must return to the surface and see what's up."

They all screwed up their eyes as they emerged from the artificial light of the underground cavern, back outside under the beautiful blue sky, and bright sunshine. Will was the first to spot the change. "Wow, it's black over Bill's Mother's." He pointed towards the Eastern sky.

Alex looked puzzled,

"There's no one living on Hikina Island?"

Will shook his head,

"No, it's an English expression from when Shakespeare's mother's village got flooded after torrential rains a few centuries ago. It just means the sky has gone black, the same as it is over there. Like there's going to be a massive storm! It's quite a contrast, with the rest of the sky being so blue."

Alex shook his head. Hawaiian island education didn't spend much time on 16th Century British literature. Still, dense, towering, threatening clouds were spreading further across the horizon and approaching the islands at quite a rate. He raised a finger above his head,

"This is all wrong; feel the air. The wind is from the south, not the east."

Eddie blinked and then blinked again,

"Is it only me, or can anyone else see bright little stars in their eyes?"

Will had also started blinking,

"No, it's me too, Ike; what's happening?"

Ike half-closed one of his eyes and pursed his lips,

"Phosphenes! They're caused by high Antiproton levels. We shouldn't see these at sea level. So, either the Ozone layer has been punctured, and we urgently need suntan lotion, or it's got something to do with this approaching storm."

The clouds became even darker, growing more purple. The Eastern horizon flashed with lightning hitting the surface of the sea some distance away.

Will was counting,

"8, 9, 10…two miles…." The rumble in the distance was immense. "It's going to be a bad one. Do you think we should go inside?"

The darkest part of the cloud bank changed to a deeper inky blackness, and then suddenly, as if the coloured streaks of an eyeball around an iris, lightning erupted in every direction. A dot could be seen emerging from the iris, followed by another and then another.

Alex raised his arm, pointing the edge of his WOTDISC towards the storm and looked at the screen,

"ZUKANN, magnify 200 times." He looked at the screen and frowned, "They look like single-engined aircraft, three, four, no five of them. And it looks like they're armed with bombs. See for yourselves."

Alex stretched his arm out so everyone could see. Eddie looked at Will,

"Torpedo bombers? Out here? They must have come from an aircraft carrier."

Alex pulled his arm back,

"ZUKANN, search for aircraft carriers. What are we looking at?"

ZUKANN's response was instant,

"There are no carriers in range. I have identified the type. They are TBM Avenger torpedo bombers. US NAVY."

Eddie pointed,

"They're going to land, they're lowering undercarriage. Look! The lead aircraft engine has failed!"

The planes were approaching rapidly. They had been two miles out when they'd first seen them less than thirty seconds ago; now they were menacingly close. The lead aircraft started to drop quite significantly from its flight path. The undercarriage retracted, and suddenly the torpedo was released.

Eddie pointed again,

"He's dropped his stores; he's going to ditch. I hope he gets close enough to the beach. Is there a boat here?"

"No, there's nothing like that here!" Alex shouted, as he started to run back over the beach, ready to swim out to help rescue anyone landing in the sea. The other planes passed over the top of the lead plane, still in line with the runway.

Will, Eddie and Ike ran after Alex as the other four planes passed them by, the sound of tyres screeching on the airstrip as each one touched down on the tarmac.

What had been the lead aircraft glided inexorably towards the surface of the deep blue sea. The dark greys, blacks and purples of the disturbingly threatening sky were now only a bit more than a mile away. Fractionally before the plane hit the water, the plane's nose lifted. It skipped across the water like a stone across a pond, started to turn sidewise and slid up the beach in a massive cloud of spray and dust.

Looking behind them, back on the runway, Eddie could see the other four aircraft had come to a stop, almost where they touched down. It looked like some of the crew had stayed with their planes. Others were now running back down the tarmac towards their ditched comrades. Eddie knew flying gear, having flown with American pilots on exercises. These outfits were as heritage as their twenty-five-year-old planes. Knowing where they were geographically, conceivably, they could have flown here from Hawaii, but they had to be on the most extreme end of their range. He was wondering how they had got so lost and why they were carrying torpedoes. Alex and Will were about to wade into the water when the two canopies of the ditched plane slid back, and hands went up in the air. Pilot and then navigator scrambled out, ran across the now damaged wing, and dropped onto the sand. One of them knelt down and kissed the beach. The trauma was evident on the faces of the crew.

Alex looked at his WOTDISC and tapped it. There was a ripple, and it shrunk to about the size of an aviator watch. The Professor did the same thing. Standing on the shoreline, with the crews approaching from both directions, Alex turned to Eddie, Will and the Professor,

"You need to get out of here. I think I know what's going on, and there'll be a FENDER Rapid Response Team here shortly. I'm surprised they're not here already. I'll deal with the new arrivals. You shouldn't meet them. Leave now, quickly!" There was some urgency to his voice. This wasn't simply a suggestion.

They turned and jogged back to the building they had first arrived at. Back at the beach, Alex's voice could clearly be heard welcoming the new arrivals with a warm and reassuring tone.

It was quite a culture shock for Eddie and Will to find themselves back in the Professor's lab once more. Having been in glorious sunshine they were now back in the artificial light of a subsurface installation, knowing it was dreary Winter outside. The Professor gave them both a gentle shove in the direction of the door,

"Just so you know, we've been gone about ten minutes, even though it's been well over an hour for us. I'll get things shut down here, and I'll catch up. I've got a quick tip for you. War is on the horizon. Be judicious about who to trust. I hate it when we do the right thing for the wrong reasons and then are forced to do the wrong thing for the supposed right reasons. See you shortly."

Eddie and Will both gave the Professor a puzzled wave and headed out the door,

"We'll catch you up in a bit."

The white-tiled corridor was somewhat clinical compared to the beach they had sat on a few minutes ago. Walking through the door and back into the snug, sand dropped off their shoes as they stepped onto the carpet. They did not speak as they headed back upstairs to meet the rest of the group. Most of the team were already in the MERCURY room. At the front, the Professor stood and prepared to welcome everyone back.

Eddie nudged Will and whispered,

"He got back quicker than we did. Do you think it's a time travel thing?"

Will grinned,

"We'll probably find he's been back to the island, put all the crew up in billets and still got back faster than us!"

The professor caught their eyes,

"You look a bit warm considering how cold it is. Been to the gym?"

Will smiled back, taking the hint not to say anything,

"It feels like it. We've been getting ready for the next half of the briefing."

The Professor nodded and looked at the group. He waved at the massive screen behind him, filled with the faces of many of those from last Friday night's meeting with Ruby and welcomed everyone.

258

CHAPTER 33
Art for Art's Sake

MERCURY Room:
1400 (GMT), Monday December 14th 1970 (DET)

Professor Eastwood smiled and nodded in the direction of the virtual attendees, then turned to face the team gathered in the physical reality of the MERCURY room,

"Can I take this opportunity to thank everyone for attending, whatever your time or your dimensional location? This project is monumental, and success for us is a success for all our futures. To begin with, I'm going to share on your screens, all the artwork we will see on this project."

"We'll talk about all the locations shortly, but first, I must explain the paintings. Unfortunately, we cannot finalise the exact desired order to interact with these works of art until we are on site. ZUKANN, please show the images while I explain their importance."

The Godot Orange

You will all no doubt remember Edith Madieu's painting from Alba's briefing earlier. This is on display in the Belgian art gallery. Hidden in the back of the frame is a Schrodinger key. The team will need this key to open the SlipStream Safe containing the Gaia Power Conductor Staff and two Gaia Power Seed Extractors.

To discover more, please select this ZUKANN OPTIC.

Chromati-Clef

The Godot Orange is being displayed alongside a piece called the Chromati-Clef. A small hole in this work of art is a perfect fit for the Schrodinger key. The key will need turning several times, either left or right. This will depend on which candles are lit on the responsive artwork called Before Birthday

located in the New York gallery.

To discover more, please select this ZUKANN OPTIC.

Environmental Security

The SlipStream safe containing the Gaia Power Conductor Staff and two Gaia Power Seed Extractors is also in the Belgian gallery hidden behind this grassy, secure looking painting.

This can only be opened when the painting stored in East Berlin has the combination key set correctly, and someone sings the

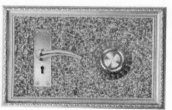

song Jailhouse Rock in front of the Before Birthday Painting in New York. The safe is also a sacrificial vault, which means that we must place The Godot Orange inside the safe to retrieve the Conductor Staff and two Seed Extractors. Suppose we fail to do this within thirty seconds of opening the safe? A Meta-Time Lupoff Recursion Echo will be initiated. This will reset the local time to ten minutes earlier, forcing the Belgian team to repeat their efforts.

To discover more, please select this ZUKANN OPTIC.

The Rescue

ZUKANN
IMAGE:

SCAN ME
S162A

The SlipStream safe can ONLY be opened when all three 'cats' are visible in the tree on the painting titled The Rescue in a nearby Belgian Insurance office. If all three cats are not visible, the safe will not open.

To discover more, please select this ZUKANN OPTIC.

Before Birthday

ZUKANN
IMAGE:

SCAN ME
S162B

Currently, we do not know the exact location of The Godot Orange, as destiny indicates that it will have been stolen from the Belgian exhibition before our arrival. However, the Before Birthday painting displays a cake. The fancy band around the waist of the cake is in fact a responsive

map, continuously tracking The Godot Orange's exact location.

To discover more, please select this ZUKANN OPTIC.

ZUKANN
IMAGE:

SCAN ME
S162C

Twin Piques

"In the German art repository, there is another Edith Madieu painting called Twin Piques. The combination number for the locks in the picture is displayed on the identity tag attached to the painting. We believe this is likely to be the birth date of the artist.

To discover more, please select this ZUKANN OPTIC.

Ruby raised her hand as a caution,

"Please be careful. Don't forget to pick up a pair of electron fabric gloves on your way out. They're encoded with Edith Madieu's fingerprints, just in case. The paintings will likely be alarmed and possibly booby-trapped. Either way, we don't want anyone being sucked into a SlipStream event.

"Security will be quite strict. This is 1970, so defenders should not have access to advanced levels of technology; however, with an ever-present threat from Hagura agents, there may be additional hazards to watch out for. Our intelligence indicates there is no awareness of our plan, but we can take no risks. We have Prismorphic technology on our side, so I recommend setting your 'quintessence' to be something small, like a fly or a moth, until you are close to your destination. There should be no trouble getting past any infra-red detectors and laser beam sensors. Rina, do you want to explain the team travel arrangements?"

Rina stood up and waved her hand at the monitors. Clearly, much preparation had already gone into this mission, and she looked a little apprehensive,

"Thanks to all of you for being the front line of our organisation. Travelling and staying in 1970 is a bit more complicated than other eras and dimensions. The Power Centre under Covenham Reservoir has had its energy reserves seriously depleted, both with travelling back to retrieve the crash wreckage from Colombia and the essential journeys to the 25th century meeting with IGLOO, FENDER and the Time Tech Leadership Team. It will take quite a while to recharge our backups without an energy network, which we hope will soon be available. This 7th and final Gaia Conductor Probe would make a Home Earth energy network a real possibility. In the meantime, some of us are going to be using conventional Home Earth transportation.

"I've put together as much information as I can for you. We have a few days before we launch what we're calling project SANTA as it's going to be on Christmas Eve. We're going to Search And Neutralize Technological Art!"

There was a ripple of amusement in the air, which brought the tension down a bit,

"I thought you'd all appreciate that! This data will be available on your WOTDISCs and PIMMS. Safety is paramount, so I've split our group into three, based on their skills and experience. I need your complete attention as there are some complicated names in this.

"The A-Team will be me with a WOTDISC, Mark Sparks and Del Aurion. We'll be flying from here and being dropped off at Heathrow airport by the C-Team, who will be heading off to Berlin. We're taking on the American Literature Art and Realism Museum in New York. We'll be flying out on one of Pan Am's swanky new Boeing 747s which they've just started flying out to *John F Kennedy* Airport. Our plane leaves Heathrow at 1015 hours on Christmas Eve, so it's wheels up at 0600 hours from North Coates to get us there and checked in.

"The B-Team will be Ruby with a WOTDISC, ably assisted by our newest recruits Eddie and Will. Our 'rose between two thorns', as they say, will mean they'll have access to the second-best trainer this side of eternity. But, of course, I'm biased because I am the best...!" A marker pen flew through the air in the direction of Rina, narrowly missing her head.

"Thank you, Sis!" Rina grinned whilst Ruby tried badly to look entirely innocent, as if butter wouldn't melt in her mouth.

"As I was saying, before I was rudely interrupted by badly targeted office stationery, the B-Team will head out to Belgium using doors and Cascade Hinges. Your target is the Bureau Belge et Européen des Beaux Arts et Antiquités. This translates to the Belgian and European Bureau of Beautiful Art and Antiquities. Before you get there, covertly and without any commotion, you will need to install a Duron Camera at the office of...; get ready for this. Let me take a deep breath! It's the Nederlands Europees - Nabestaandenoverbruggingspensioen Aansprakelijkheidswaardevaststellingsveranderingen Arbeidsongeschiktheidsverzekeringsmaatschappij."

There was a slightly stunned look on several faces and relief from the others who were not compelled to remember what to call this place. Rina continued,

"This one is quite a mouthful! To help out, it's the Belgian Office of the Dutch European Survivor's Bridging Pension Disability Insurance Company for Liability Valuation Changes. They desperately need a shorter name!"

Rina again displayed Edith Madieu's painting of *The Rescue*,

"The Director there is Polly Andres-Baer. In her office, hanging on the wall, is the painting of the three lions you saw earlier which we must constantly monitor throughout this mission.

"There's a strange anomaly affecting direct door travel to the Beautiful Art Bureau, so we will be leaving test equipment to monitor the location. Travel will be via a door in the quite architecturally amazing structure called The Atomium. As you can see from the image on the screens, it is a group of nine, sixty-foot diameter stainless steel spheres joined by ten-foot diameter tubes. The public story is that it was built for the World's Fair in 1958 to represent an iron crystal magnified 165 billion times.

"However, the truth, for those who don't know, is it's actually a fleet of Micro-freighters owned by the Luprak, a group of alien traders who had their fleet impounded here by the European Economic Community for breaching harmonised tariffs, pending an investigation into allegations of trading fake heavy metal supplies. Access to the street will be gained via a door at the back of the ticket office, equipped with SlipStream hinges, followed by a quick walk up to the Insurance Company. Then a brief stroll back down the Avenue de Bouchout, towards the Royal Observatory and Planetarium, followed by entry via the side door of the Art Bureau."

Rina looked around the room to check no one was dropping off. Everyone looked wholly engaged, so she ploughed on,

"The C-Team features Haji Wells wearing a WOTDISC, with Arti Ping and Leo Frankovitz. They will be heading out for a three-and-a-half-hour flight to Berlin after dropping off the A-Team at Heathrow. As a reminder, Her Majesty the Queen has lent us her 'not very subtle', bright red seven-seater De-Havilland Heron, and she'll be wanting it back. The colour scheme will help you avoid getting shot at by the American forces at Tempelhof Airport, as it carries RAF insignia. And one more tip: You ARE allowed to use the onboard facilities, as the Queen is said to bring her own toilet seat on every flight.

"Your target is the Deutsche Demokratische Republik Degenerierender/Defekter Akademischer Austauschdienst, or East German State Degenerating or Defective Academic Exchange Service. You can door jump from Tempelhof Airport to a riverside building directly opposite to check security arrangements. Then, it's a quick hop over to Stralauer Tor, otherwise known as Bersarinstraße. It's an abandoned station actually ON the Oberbaum Bridge.

"Be ACUTELY AWARE. You will be leaving the US-controlled zone of West Berlin and entering into the Russian-controlled zone. There is a pedestrian bridge from the station across to the Mühlenstrasse. Be that as it may, we can't use it as it's damaged AND it takes you too close to the Mühlenspeicher, otherwise known as the Mill Silo. The East German border guards are using this as a watchtower, and the patrol boats moor up behind there too. It's a relief the building was not used as the location for the Exchange Service.

"You'll need to come down the service staircase and emerge under the U-Bahn. This is the strictly controlled no-man's-land between the inner wall facing the American sector and the outer wall facing the Russian sector. Your target building is the Eierkühlhaus or Egg Cool Store. Hopefully, all of this makes sense? Everything we have in terms of intelligence is in your briefing packs.

"Now, please listen very carefully as I don't want to say this twice. To summarise...

The A-Team is tripping over to the A.L.A.R.M in New York.

The B-Team is headed for Brussels and without any hoo-ha, sorting out the Dada at the NE-NAA and the artwork at the BBEE_BAA.

The C-Team have got East Berlin and the DDR D-DAA.... That's all I want to say to you, I think? Any questions?"

There was a moment of stunned silence in the room, followed by much head shaking and shoulder shrugging.

Rina took this to mean everything was completely understood,

"Great stuff. We've got ten days to get our plans reviewed, skills honed, and batteries charged. Let's roll!"

ZUKANN OPTIC:

SCAN ME
S165A

Somewhere Under The Rainbow

"The Luprak owners of the impounded fleet in Brussels are a diminutive humanoid species from the Other Earth dimension OEGAB5. They are mischievous by nature and keen to spot a beneficial financial arrangement. In addition, they are musically talented, often portrayed playing what is described as an 'Otter flute' or Lur pipe.

"A toxic home atmosphere requires copper micro-filtration mesh clothing which oxidises to a green hue in Home Earth environment. Initial contact on Home Earth was with the people in 9th Century Ireland, who described them as The 'Clánn' or 'Children'. The word descended from Old Irish 'Luprak Clánn', quickly became Lupraclán and then simply 'Leprechaun', leading to the legends of 'Little Green Men' and 'pots of gold at the end of the rainbow'.

To discover more, please select this ZUKANN OPTIC.

ZUKANN
SCAN ME
S166A

CHAPTER 34
Before A Visit From St Nicolas

RAF North Coates:
0600 (GMT), Thursday December 24ᵗʰ 1970 (DET)

There was a sense of excitement and anticipation in the air, not only because it was Christmas Eve, and the weather forecasters were predicting a white Christmas for England and Wales. The last ten days had seen a great deal of physical and mental activity. Preparing, understanding locations, reviewing building plans, checking entrances, exits, likely security, potential hazards and identifying where the nearest toilet was. After all, you had to cover all the bases.

Eddie and Will were getting the opportunity for a lie-in, which was quite unusual for the morning of an operation. Unknown to each other, both of them were actually awake. Out on the cold, dark and damp stretch of tarmac in front of the aircraft hangars, six people with rucksacks were boarding a bright red painted, four-engined De-Havilland Heron. The fact it had no camouflage would have made Eddie and Will quite uncomfortable. However, for the A-Team headed westwards to the United States and the C-Team headed for Berlin, the interior of the executive plane would have made all their discomfort fade away in an instant.

There was no doubt the Royal Air Force wanted the Queen to travel in comfort. From the plush carpet to the red leather seats and fold-out walnut tables, even breakfast had been arranged for their journey, although Arti Ping would have preferred steamed buns for breakfast. Croissants were not entirely her take on early morning sustenance. Still, orange marmalade was something she had recently become quite a fan of, along with literary treats like the *Paddington Bear* stories.

The sun was almost on the verge of appearing over the horizon. Haji, Leo and Arti's royal plane left the runway having dropped off Rina, Mark and Del at the Executive arrivals building. Foreboding deep red flecks appeared in the sky reminiscent of the old weather lore, 'red sky in the morning, shepherd's warning'. They were all hoping snow would be their only hazard in the next twenty-four hours.

⚭⊕◖⊕⊱

Heathrow: 1000 (GMT), Thursday December 24th 1970 (DET)

Being on the A-Team had a particular kudos to it, one which was undoubtedly worth all the teasing from the other team members when they returned. It wasn't until they arrived at Heathrow Airport's *Pan Am* departure gate that either Mark Sparks or Del Aurion looked at their tickets to see where they were sat.

Mark nudged Del and then Rina,

"My ticket says seat A1, is that right? What seats have you got?" Rina grinned,

"You don't think I'm going to go to all the trouble of planning this mission and then fly in the back row, do you? It's going to be a long couple of days, so I thought we'd have the best seats. You two have got A1 and B1. I've got the only single seat in the whole plane apart from the flight crew. I'm J1. We'll be able to see the film on the projector screen without anyone's head getting in our way! Not only that, but I've also booked lunch for us in the upper deck restaurant. You're going to love this."

Walking across the airport tarmac towards the huge wingspan of the four-engine leviathan of the air that was Pan Am's *Boeing 747 Clipper Bostonian*, Mark and Del were already 'loving it'. The fuselage was longer than the world's first sustained powered flight made by Wilbur and Orville Wright in 1903. The wingspan wider than the first-ever powered take-off in 1874 by Frenchman Félix du Temple, who Del had recently discovered was a relative, whilst researching his family tree.

As they boarded the plane, they were greeted by a young smiling flight attendant. She wore a creamy gold uniform with a slightly impractical looking bowler hat featuring the Pan Am logo.

Mark nudged Del,

"At least they're wearing something handy if you get air-sick."

Rina gave them a look, clearly warning them they would need to be on their best behaviour,

"Be nice! We don't want people to think you're a couple of rock stars. You might get asked for your autograph, which could get us noticed. Remember, we're NOT to affect the timeline!"

They followed the flight attendant down the plush, red-carpeted aisle, between cheerful and comfortable seats alternating between a deep blue and a bright red, almost up to the nose of the plane.

With a close to trademark smile, she gestured in the direction of the seats and, with a summery Californian accent, said,

"Thank you for Flying Pan Am. I'm Mandy. I'll be your flight attendant today." She started to give them items she had deftly picked up from an overhead locker as they had been following her. "We have headsets to listen to the movie or the in-flight audio channels. There are courtesy newspapers available, and here's a copy of our in-flight *Clipper* magazine for you to keep. Blankets and pillows are available any time you'd like.

"Please put luggage in the locker above your head. Lift this little flap here and you'll see we have a convenient ashtray hidden in the side of the seat. On the other side, lift the armrest and there's a dinky little pull-out tray you can use whilst we serve food and drinks. We will be serving champagne shortly. If you need cigarettes or cigars, do let us know, and one of us will be happy to help you. May I hang your coats up?"

Mark was puzzled by the advertised film in the airline magazine. He thought *Arthur Haley's Airport* blockbuster, featuring a bomb on a flight and an airfield closed by snow, might not be an appropriate in-flight movie, especially with the weather predictions. He also hadn't flown First Class before, but he came to the conclusion, if the aircrew gave so much attention to all the passengers, it would take ages to get everyone on board.

As Mandy headed back up the aisle to hang their coats, search for cigars and cigarettes and find the next First-Class passenger, Rina turned to Del and Mark, wrinkling her nose,

"Yuk! I forgot people used to set fire to dried plant life and inhale the combusted particulates."

Del smiled,

"Don't worry, if someone does start smoking; we could kick off and pretend we're totally famous musicians, and we can't have our lungs spoiled. We could be like the 'Architects'; they were quite fussy about their health."

Mark looked surprised,

"You mean 'The Architects of Creation? They're fantastic! Fred and Frank have Threezer Veezers of all of their concerts over dozens of centuries. You know Donnie was in the band for a while, right?"

Now it was Rina's turn to look shocked,

"You mean Donnie Yud 'Tineres, from Infrastructure Design? That Donnie?"

Mark grinned and waved his hand across in front of his face. Projecting an imaginary video screen in front of himself,

"Oh yes indeedy, Donnie Isaac Yud 'Tineres - The fifth Architect Of Creation. Backing vocals, triangle and puzzled expressions. He was amazing!"

Rock Around The Clock

"Donnie Isaac Yud 'Tineres - age unclear. He has kept the same number two, almost shaved hairstyle and 30-year-old leather-strapped necklace look, for decades.

An original architect of the creation of the universe, Donnie and his parents were among a handful of survivors rescued by Leo Frankovitz's team from the Orion Nebula Event. But unfortunately, it had been impossible to return them to their own timestream.

"Donnie was indeed once famous for being the fifth member of the musical sensation 'Architects of Creation'. They decided to form a rock band as they were totally under-used at work since the dawn of time.

"The four full time Architects of Creation, along with Donnie, had mainly been employed in the drawing office. After The Client's amazing 'Big Bang' launch event, they'd all been on furlough since the universe went live. The party was massive, with lights, music and a barbecue. The zero-alcohol drinks were OK. Any decent brewer will advocate fermenting for at least two weeks before you arrive at a half-decent alcoholic pint. There had also been a considerable spread of healthy food like fruit and pizza. As expected, at such a spiritually inspiring event, the most popular pizza was 'the one with everything'.

To discover more, please select this ZUKANN OPTIC.

RAF North Coates:
0800 (GMT), Thursday December 24th 1970 (DET)

Breakfast for the B-Team was a fairly leisurely affair. Eddie and Will both opted for the Full English from the Officers Mess, as neither of them was completely trusting of any BistroMatic Gourmetron. It also meant they could eat in daylight rather than underground in the MAMBA room or their guest quarters. However, the quality of food was good enough to encourage Ruby to join them.

She was more of a fresh fruit fan first thing in the morning, although she appreciated how breakfast in 1970s England was not likely to deliver more than half a grapefruit, freshly squeezed orange juice and an apple. However, quite unusually, this morning the chef did seem to have gone all out. Somehow, he'd received a consignment of giant granadilla fruit, which he'd cut into slices thinking they might be like melons. Ruby loved the refreshing sweet and sour taste and the faint smell of strawberries they exuded. She wondered if this was somehow a result of the recent arrival of a shipping container, delivering Sir Rob Locksley's grandmother her belongings.

There would be a relaxed day ahead for the B-Team as they would be using SlipStream Portals between the pub and the Brussels Atomium. However, their first date with destiny would not be until 11:15 pm that evening, when they would need to break into the Insurance Company offices on the Place de l'Atomium.

Heathrow:
0830 (GMT), Thursday December 24th 1970 (DET)

As the wheels of the C-Team's 'Royal Flight' left the tarmac at Heathrow Airport and turned towards the east, what little sunrise there had been, was quickly obscured by banks of cloud on the horizon. Haji looked out of the window and looked nervously as the ground disappeared behind thick banks of cumulonimbus. He was used to flying, but not in antiquated mechanical devices like this one.

Haji's hobby and expertise were in air-born bulk logistics and fabric transportation systems. He never flew his collection of hoverboards above the clouds if he couldn't see to get back to the ground again. His collection of flying carpets all had an innate navigation system, however, they were not much better as they had no reliable indicators or displays. Being dropped off at the top of a mountain was a constant risk not worth taking.

He leaned forward towards Arti, who was sitting opposite him, and motioned out of the window,

"How are the pilots going to see where the ground is when we get near to Berlin?"

Arti smiled back reassuringly,

"We'll be fine. It's understandable to be nervous flying in ancient technology like this, but they've done quite well in this era. Tempelhof Airport has had a Lorenz Beam landing system for more than thirty years. They've also been testing a Microwave Landing System, so although there's snow and fog at the airport, the pilots could adequately land with their eyes closed.

"Anyway," Arti continued, "FENDER Destiny predictions indicate a safe arrival, so you can sit back and relax. Or, alternatively, I've got a travel Mah-jongg set compressed in my kit bag along with a pack of cards if you fancy a game? If we had a bit more space, we could have played Ping Pong as I've got a full-size table in there too."

Haji looked slightly more relaxed, knowing they would land safely. He looked over at Leo Frankovitz, who was intently examining his wrist. A data feed was appearing on his PIMMS device.

Haji pondered how annoying it was, as no matter what Leo was wearing, which was usually jeans, a dark T-shirt and a cardigan. Even at nearly fifty years old, with his wavy taper cut hairstyle, as soon as he put those sunglasses on, he always looked so cool.

"Fancy joining us for a game of cards, Leo? I'm sure we can play a game which doesn't involve you losing hundreds of credits to me like last time? Maybe I could win your shades from you too?"

Leo made a grumbling sound,

"Beginner's luck! I'm happy to play you at anything, but you'll never win my shades. Come on Arti, deal the cards and we'll see how well-off Haji is three hours from now!".

∞⊕⊕∞

The Old Volunteer - North Somercotes:
1215 (GMT), Thursday December 24ᵗʰ 1970 (DET)

Eddie and Will's day had been dragging. The television in the Officers' Mess was locked on BBC1. After watching forty minutes of 300 railway enthusiasts being taken on a 'never to be repeated' non-stop run from London to Edinburgh on board the *Flying Scotsman* (a programme which ironically was a repeat itself) they were treated to five minutes of *Tom and Jerry*, followed by forty-five minutes of ice dancing from the Queens Ice Club in London. This was definitely one for Will. Eddie suspected the attraction was not the balletic performance of the skaters, but more likely the short skirts and the long legs.

When it came to mid-day, the prospect was roughly an hour of Christmassy songs with Andy Williams. This would then be followed by more than half an hour of watching Michael Aspel and Sheila Tracy meeting hospital patients in Oswestry.

This was a bit more Christmas cheer than Eddie was prepared to stomach, despite liking music. He looked at Will, who had started to lose interest, as Andy Williams introduced his guests.

To Eddie, as good as it was, this was yet another Christmas repeat,

"Will, do you fancy a pint? I'm sure no one will object to us having just one, and it is lunchtime after all? They'll know where to find us if they need us, with these PIMMS gadgets bolted to our wrists. We can shortcut through the tunnel to The Old Volunteer. They'll be doing lunch, and we know how good the food is."

Will looked back at Eddie, almost relieved,

"Excellent idea, Skip. I thought you'd never ask. It is Christmas Eve, and I'm feeling a bit festive. The idea of being in Brussels, in no time flat, four hours from now feels a bit surreal, but I've half got my mission head on, so let's call this a working lunch. Please stop me from ordering a second pint though."

West Berlin:
1330 Central European Time (CET),
Thursday December 24th 1970 (DET)

Although it was still only early afternoon for the C-Team, the city of West Berlin appeared dark and dreary in the fog and the snow which had been falling before their arrival. The wind was bitter, with daytime temperatures not expected to be warmer than -2, and the temperature dropping overnight to -6. The scars of the Second World War were still visible, with areas of the city still not being cleared of the rubble from only twenty-five years earlier. However, in some ways, a fresh coating of snow did appear to improve the look and feel of the place somewhat. At least Santa's sleigh would get a soft landing.

Their arrival at Berlin Tempelhof airport was a little hairy, as the fog led to a harder landing than Santa could expect. Before heading off for the centre of the city, Arti explained how formalities required them to report to the Base Commander. However, it was not only a formality. Leo Frankovitz explained how Colonel Halvorsen was one of his heroes, nicknamed 'Uncle Wiggly Wings', 'The Chocolate Flier' and 'The Berlin Candy Bomber'. During the Berlin airlift, he became a national hero for dropping over twenty tons of candy, attached to miniature parachutes, to the children trapped in West Berlin.

The Colonel was clearly pleased to meet them and got up quickly from behind his desk, holding his hand out in a warm greeting,

"Lady, gentlemen, welcome to the most easterly part of the United States. It's a pleasure to meet you all. I'm sorry to be short for time, but this morning's intelligence briefing indicated you guys might be upsetting the Russkies shortly, so I had to have a quick chat."

Leo shook the Colonel's hand,

"Thank you, sir. Normally I would do introductions, but you'll have seen from the briefing, the less we say the better. However, our plan is not to be seen by your Russian neighbours, in fact, the fewer people see us, the better."

The Colonel nodded,

"Sure thing, and that's good news. I don't want to be ordering tanks for a showdown at Checkpoint Charlie like Major Clay did. Now, my adjutant tells me you're here for a personal reason too?"

Leo's smile became quite poignant for a moment,

"Yes sir, when you first came to Berlin you met some of my family at the perimeter fence whilst you were filming the planes. To them and many of their friends, you were a hero and we wanted to give you a gift in return."

Leo rummaged inside his rucksack and pulled out an ornamental stick of chewing gum attached to a miniature parachute made of Teslene. By pure coincidence, this was the same metal the clock in The Old Volunteer was made from.

Leo held out the tribute,

"This is a small and humble token of appreciation from some

of my relatives. You and the other aircrew helped keep them alive. Thank you for ensuring their freedom. Our task is to continue those efforts."

The Colonel's eyes glistened with emotion as he gently held the gift,

"Those were dark times, but helping you guys gave us all something to hope for. Thank you. Now, any other time I would invite you for a meal, but I do have to leave now, and I guess you guys do too?"

Arti and Haji were quite touched, as they and Leo bade 'Uncle Wiggly Wings' goodbye and shook his hand. Clearly, there was a side to Leo that none of them had previously been aware of.

Having left the Colonel's office, it was only two doorways down the corridor and a quick twist of the handle. They were three miles away in a flash, stepping into a dusty and deserted room on the second floor of the West Berlin Watergate building. Unlike the complex in the Foggy Bottom district of Washington DC, this small building nestled beside the now isolated U-Bahn section crossing over the Oberbaum Bridge on the West Berlin side of the River Spree. Directly opposite was their destination for tonight.

The antithesis of East Germany's 256 shades of grey, the cheery bright yellow and grey diamond brick and glass monolith called the Eierkühlhaus or Egg Cool Store, the location of the DDR D-DAA Academic Exchange Service warehouse.

The Old Volunteer - North Somercotes:
1748 (GMT), Thursday December 24th 1970 (DET)

It had been a long day of thumb-twiddling for Eddie and Will, although the 'working lunch' at The Old Volunteer had been a success as they had both resisted the temptation to have more than the one pint. Their SlipStream jump was scheduled for 2200 hours British time, instantly getting them to Brussels at 2300 hours local time. They decided the best thing to do, was to meet up with Ruby and the support team, in the MERCURY Room upstairs.

As they walked in, Ruby had only moments beforehand, been trying to explain the significance of Will's nickname to the rest of the team. However, as luck would have it, a slightly unseasonal episode of the *Magic Roundabout* was about to finish playing on the display screens, which had Dougal cooking pancakes, not generally associated with Christmas. True to form, and resulting in quite a bit of laughter, Eric Thompson's creation, Zebedee, was at the point of announcing the immortal line, 'Time for Bed' - a phrase most likely to haunt Will until his death.

Slightly embarrassed, and with a reddish hue spreading across his face, Will put on a fake look of offence,

"Do you think we can find something a bit more seasonal to watch?"

Frank laughed,

"Don't worry, apparently there's a News programme coming up, but we're waiting for the highlight of the evening."

Eddie grinned at Will's discomfort,

"Apparently, the guy from Intelligence, Ralph Reader's on tonight with the RAF Gang Show. It's got Peter Sellers in, so it should be fun."

Fred looked up,

"Not only that, but there's also a comedy programme we're all looking forward to, at quarter past. It's called 'Tomorrow's World'. We all want to see what you Second Millennials think is going to happen in the future. Apparently, it's got some racing driver called Graham Hill in it. We're taking bets on whether it's robot Christmas carol singers, the invention of the BistroMatic Gourmetron, or they're going to predict flying rally cars by 2025!"

Will shook his head,

"There is no way anyone is going to predict those culinary monstrosities. My money is on robots programmed to sing carols. How's the A-Team and the C-Team getting on, by the way?"

Ike Eastwood looked at the monitors in front of him,

"Well, the A-Team are still in the air. It's 1250 where they are, and they should have had their lunch by now. They've got about another thirty minutes before they land. The C-Team have been in Berlin for a while. They're running reconnaissance on their target building, checking the East German and Russian border security are sticking to their routines, and nothing is changing."

ZUKANN OPTIC:

SCAN ME
T172A

Global Gourmet

Will should have put his money on the invention of the BistroMatic Gourmetron. The Christmas Eve 1970 edition of Tomorrow's World featured robot carol singers and the earliest recorded reference to a highly rudimentary computer-controlled culinary installation.

To discover more, please select this ZUKANN OPTIC.

New York:
1315 (EST), Thursday December 24th 1970 (DET)

According to the announcement from the pilot, the A-Team were flying south down the east coast of the United States. It was hard to tell from the thickness of the cloud cover where the sea had ended and the land had begun. From the gentle sense of dropping, it was clear to Rina they were still intentionally losing height. Their sunny view of blue skies has been obliterated as they settled into the dense cloud layer approaching John F Kennedy Airport.

Mandy, their ever-smiling flight attendant, had already visited. She had fulfilled her mission, ensuring all passenger seats were upright and all the 'dinky little tray tables' were stowed back in the armrests. She had provided quite a personalised service to the team, due to the small number of people flying with them in First Class. Presumably, anyone with any sense had travelled earlier in the week to arrive with friends and families, well in time for the Christmas holidays.

The captain had kindly informed all the passengers they would be arriving slightly ahead of time. Therefore, they should all reset their watches in preparation for arrival at 1:15 pm local time. His second bit of advice was that it was foggy and freezing outside the terminal at JFK. However, for those passengers heading for Manhattan, the wind was picking up from the north. They would definitely feel the Hudson Hawk blowing down the river. Rina and Mark knew the 25th century well and understood the lack of environmental temperature control available in 1970.

On the other hand, Del Aurion was more at home with the moderate climes of 18th Century Europe. He had recently experienced some of the extreme cold Canada had to offer. Although Del had been with the Time Tech Team for almost five years, he was still acclimatising to what, from his perspective, was an extremely advanced 20th Century, and a wide range of meteorology.

The airport's sudden appearance through freezing mist, the rumble of the undercarriage, and a thud on the tarmac indicated their comfortable journey had come to an end. One of the highlights, despite it being a Thursday, had been having a typical British Sunday lunch of roast beef and Yorkshire pudding in the upstairs restaurant of the Boeing 747. After this, there would be no worries about finding somewhere to eat until later in the day.

The plane slowed down towards the end of the runway and then followed the taxiways to the rather impressive, and not in the slightest bit alien, flying saucer-shaped 'World Port'. The latest planes from Boeing were a bit on the large side. Unlike other aircraft, they could not stop nose-in, under cover of the expansive roof. Mandy returned with their coats in hand as the plane came to a stop. They undid their seatbelts and reached up for their rucksacks from the overhead lockers. The cold, damp air of the airport was not too dissimilar from the weather back at RAF North Coates, although it was still a bit of a shock, having left the warm luxury of the cabin.

Rina led the way past the baggage collection area to an inconspicuous looking door slightly past the ladies' toilets. A sign indicated access was only for airport staff.

She reached in her pocket for an Electron cloth, pulled it out and surreptitiously spread it over her hand. She had already programmed it for the first leg of their journey. "We can't do a single jump all the way to Central Park as it's thirteen miles, so we're going to take a stop off at Mount Zion Cemetery."

She opened the door, ushered Mark and Del into the room and closed the door behind them. She turned round to face the door, placed the cloth on the handle, which buzzed slightly but reassuringly as she turned the handle.

Instead of seeing the airport corridor and baggage arrivals area, they were emerging from a stone-built mausoleum-like building, typically used to store tools used by the ground maintenance teams.

Del shuddered,

"I'm pleased it wasn't a vault; it would have felt quite wrong passing through bodies in coffins."

Mark, who was much more technically practical, paused for a moment,

"It doesn't work like that." However, he was often told he needed to be more pastoral with people, so he quickly changed tack.

"But I can imagine what you might be feeling, and I wouldn't like to walk through the dead either."

Leaving Mark wondering if he'd scored any points for emotional support, Rina interrupted his train of thought,

"So we don't attract any attention to ourselves, let's walk around the building and pick a random grave to stop at and pretend to be paying our respects. Then, we can come back to this door again to get into Manhattan."

After a few moments' walk, they arrived at a memorial formed from fourteen white stone pillars linked together as if joined in solidarity like a fence. They took a moment to pause respectfully whilst utterly unaware of the tragedy wrought upon New York not sixty years earlier. If they had thought to look at their wrists, ZUKANN had already researched the data which was being displayed, how this monument represented fourteen of the 146 mainly young people killed horrifically in the Triangle Shirt Waist Factory fire on March 25th, 1911.

The cemetery seemed more than a little uncomfortable in the cold, damp air. When a suitable amount of time appeared to have passed, Rina led their way around the memorials and back to the door they had arrived through. It seemed certain no one had seen them arrive, and no one would now see them leave. Closing the door behind them, and momentarily standing in the slightly eerie darkness, the glow from Rina's WOTDISC illuminated the room. Again, she reached for the door handle and turned it.

As the team emerged onto a set of stairs leading up to the street beside Central Park, the contrast was dramatic. The noise of the traffic jarring in comparison to the peaceful environment of the cemetery. Down the stairs, the squealing sound of the brakes of a subway train pulling into the station below them could be heard with the general hubbub of people talking and moving around.

Across the other side of the turn on the stairs was another door. This one appeared to be more formal.

Rina turned to Mark and Del,

"Welcome to the more discrete entrance to the Grand Hotel, 22 Central Park South and the little-known west exit to the 5th Avenue Subway Station. Follow me."

With the stairs up to the street level behind them, Rina led them through the second door without using her Electron cloth. They were met by a small oak-panelled security reception, a desk in the middle of the room, and a classic Willard Bundy employee clocking-in time machine. An elderly man stood behind the desk with his back to them. He turned as they walked in through the door.

A broad smile appeared across his face, and he greeted them in a welcoming, rich, deep Louisiana voice,

"Well, let the good times roll! If it ain't Miss Rina in the RAW. Where y'at, my dear?"

Rina's smile said it all. The Creole reply she'd been taught by him all those years before, came back in a flash,

"Well, Mr Wilson, I'm *awrite Mais Cher*! So, what are you doing all the way back here? I didn't think you ever went beyond the doors of the Manhattan Building nowadays?"

Al 'Gator' Wilson grinned, showing you weren't guaranteed to have perfect teeth in the 25th Century,

"Well, tech-nickly as they say, I ain't outside the building considering where we are right now. So I thought I'd take the opportunity to step back a way and say hello before you get too big to talk to the likes of me!"

Rina tipped her head to one side and raised her eyebrows with a slightly incredulous smile,

"Now, you know that will never happen!" Rina turned to Mark and Del, watching the conversation pan out like a 'Gone With the Wind 'chapter. "Gentlemen, this is my good friend, driver and bodyguard from our days on the Ruby and Rina show. Al Wilson, these are my partners in 'not' crime – hopefully anyway, Mark Sparks and Del Aurion."

Mark and Del both reached out to shake hands, but in return, got a fist bump,

"Gentlemen, I don't do the 'hand thing', this time is real dirty, so I only do the knuckles. Call me 'Gator', everyone else does, apart from Ruby and Rina here. They were always far too polite. But they were kids back then, and they didn't know any better in those days. I thought I'd pop down and get you checked in. I know you'll not be with us for long, but I've got a room for you with a beautiful view of the park. Skating is open until 5 pm tonight, so I'd get out there quick if you fancy a dance before Christmas. It's not yet two, so you've got time." 'Gator' turned conspiratorially to Del and Mark. "She was a great skater. You should go for an hour."

Mark shook his head,

"I don't skate, not since the accident, but Del, I know you tried ice hockey; why don't the two of you go. I'll take the bags upstairs and see you in a couple of hours?"

'Gator' smiled, and Mark realised how he'd got his nickname. Del looked pensive for a moment, and then made his decision,

"OK, I'm up for stretching my legs after the flight if you are too, Rina?"

Rina was already heading for the door,

"Come on. See you later, Mark. *Fais do do,* Later Gator!!"

'Gator' smiled again, turning to Mark,

"She's a *fanm djanm*, a strong woman. With that *gris-gris* on her wrist, she'll make sure you'll get in and done safe tonight. Come with me; I'll show you upstairs."

CHAPTER 35
Snowy Without Tintin

The Old Volunteer - North Somercotes:
2200 (GMT), Thursday December 24th 1970 (DET)

The B-Team, consisting of Ruby, Eddie, and Will, still seemingly stuck in the MERCURY room, were all getting slightly twitchy with anticipation. They'd reviewed the plan twice, and there was a limit to how much of Christmas Eve could be enjoyed, knowing they had to go to work. There was also a tolerance limit to 'The Legendary Reginald Dixon' playing the 'Mighty Wurlitzer' and other gang show entertainment. Especially when watching the clock tick around ever-so-slowly.

It silently hit 2200 hours when Ruby stood up and lifted her rucksack,

"OK, gang, let's hit the road. The New York Museum should be about to lock up now, it's 1700 hours there. Let's head for Brussels and go pay a visit to the Insurance Office. Once this camera is set up, we can keep an eye on our 'Rescue' painting and make sure we've got all three cats stuck up the tree. Gents, ready to roll?"

Eddie and Will slung their lightweight bags onto their backs. There was no real need to carry them, as almost everything they needed was compressed in their PIMMS devices. However, taking a stroll at night without looking like they were heading for work would make them stand out slightly. In any case, they might need the empty ski bag folded up neatly in Eddie's backpack.

As the three members of the B-Team walked into the Snug of The Old Volunteer, Will turned to Eddie and Ruby,

"You know, it's been a ponderously slow Christmas Eve, and we may not be in the mood tomorrow, so how about we book a table for a meal here on Monday, just the three of us, to celebrate our first month working together and have a proper Christmas Dinner? I mean, the food's OK in the Officers' Mess, but it's a lot better here."

Ruby frowned,

"We're going to be rushed off our feet when we get back with the Power Rod, so let's book the first Monday in January. We can celebrate the New Year and the first month of you guys being on the team. It can be our monthly meet up day? It's definitely looking like you two won't be going back to the day job!"

Ruby smiled as Eddie agreed, saying,

"It can be a sort of 'family' Christmas and New Year's lunch rolled into one." He picked up a discarded glass of water from the bar and raised it in the air. "Here's to a successful mission and dare I hope, never going back to missile management!"

Will looked slightly shocked,

"Put the glass down quickly! I know we're not in the Navy, but that is like wishing someone a death by drowning."

Ruby and Eddie looked utterly unconcerned. Ruby shook her head,

"With what we know about future events, luck never comes into it. We'll be fine. Come on, let's go."

⊶⊕◷⊕⊷

In no time, they walked from one room with the light on into another, which was instantly dark. They found themselves in a small office. Will looked at the map on his PIMMS device. They were indeed in Brussels, in the centre of a modern-looking circular building set into the base of the Atomium structure. Or perhaps a sphere-clamped alien space fleet, depending on whether or not you believed ZUKANN had been programmed correctly.

Will's PIMMS screen suddenly went dead. He tapped it a few times. Then, there was a fizzing sound, and he tapped it again. Will now detected the unmistakable aroma of something burning.

"Will, please, can you please stop hitting me! If you carry on doing that, I'll get more than a headache!" ZUKANN sounded annoyed, but at the same time, somewhat concerned.

The slight burning smell had become awful, like someone who'd been out the night before, enjoying beer and a curry.

Will's face contorted,

"What is that smell? It's appalling!"

Eddie looked at his screen, which was still working,

"What's up, Will? I can't smell anything."

Ruby looked at her WATDISC. She tapped the screen a few times, and an image of a puzzled-looking Fred appeared,

"Hey, Ruby, what's up?!"

Ruby was slightly perplexed,

"My WOTDISC says Will's PIMMS is playing up. He's complaining of evil smells. He shouldn't be able to smell anything, so I'm guessing the Kaison filter is blocked. Can you check it for us?"

The WOTDISCS and PIMMS devices contained a Kaison ultrasonic anti-blinding device to filter out all the toxic particles and impurities from the air around the wearer. Fred looked over at another screen and then frowned at Frank, who looked highly embarrassed.

"Well, on two counts, I can tell you what's wrong. Firstly, Frank apologises for the poor air quality. Secondly, it seems your transducer has failed, and somehow, you've become a discharge point for our own Kaison filters here in the MERCURY room. As a result, the system is performing a Disinfection Noxious Substance or DNS Flush directly to your 'In Person' address. This shouldn't be possible. It's like we've been hacked, but we've had no incursion alarms."

"This is baffling as all the WOTDISC and PIMMS devices are designed with Synchronic Maintenance, so it should have fixed itself. No problem Fred, we'll sort it from here." Ruby tapped the screen again and spoke to ZUKANN. "ZUKANN, please contact ZUKIRA at Kaison and get Will's device fixed – thanks."

Almost as a voice in the background, the trio could hear ZUKANN contacting Kaison.

Another female A.I. voice answered, but with the accent of someone from Brooklyn in the 1920s chewing gum and smoking a cigar whilst simultaneously drinking whiskey from a bottle.

"*I'm ZUKIRA, getting you nearer. How can I be clearer?*"
ZUKANN said,

"*Hello.*" There was a little digital shriek of happiness followed by an extraordinarily fast dialogue between ZUKIRA and ZUKANN. They clearly knew each other well and had not spoken in a while.

It took less than twenty seconds, and Will started to look relieved,

"Wow, so much better. Fresh air at last – AND the screen's back up and running."

The high-speed conversation between the two A.I.s seemed to continue as Ruby cut the audio. Simultaneously ZUKANN appeared on Will's PIMMS,

"*There you go, William; this should get you back on the road again.*"

"Thanks, ZUKANN, and pass my thanks on to ZUKIRA, will you? That's what I call customer service!" ZUKANN's icon disappeared from Will's screen again, presumably to continue the chat with ZUKIRA. Will was still a little unsure why ZUKANN had, for some reason, made him a favourite, but figured it best to stay polite and keep on her good side.

Ruby pointed at Will's PIMMS,

"You know, if you tried to get one of those filters today, in this era, they'd be about a foot long, but in your PIMMS, it's all subatomic. Everything's getting smaller. There's one alien species we provide 4th Dimensional Emergency Breakdown cover for. ZUKANN keeps back copies of Tea Making Machine repair manuals, as one of them won't go anywhere without being able to make a cuppa. We love their technology. What they have is similar to Prismorphic Technology, but their shuttlecraft are suspended in interdimensional space when they travel. Their service manuals are massive, but you can zip them up, and they consume virtually no space whatsoever."

As they stepped out of the Rotunda shaped ticket office and crossed the road heading east along the Avenue de l'Atomium, the 5 degrees below zero chill of the night air bit into their clothes. The freezing fog made it feel even colder. Their breath was like the smoke of dragons every time they exhaled. The streets were quite deserted. This part of the city felt as if everyone had abandoned it.

One hundred and fifty yards away was an architect's treat; a domed hemispheric two-storey building. Partly brick and partly vegetation filled greenhouse. The larger part appeared to be a restaurant. Around the building to the rear was the insurance company office entrance.

The door opened easily with the 'skeleton-cloth' setting, and the three of them stepped inside. Immediately, the shrill preliminary beeping of the security system could be heard emanating from a panel on the wall.

Ruby flourished her electron fabric and wiped it over the keypad, swiftly silencing the alarm system into its off-duty mode. A modern-looking set of stairs led them to a landing and a plain white wall with only one door. Ruby stopped to listen carefully, then raised her WOTDISC to within an inch of the door. She tapped the screen as if looking for a little-used feature. A gentle blue light projected from her wrist and bathed the door. Wherever the rays landed, it appeared as if the door was suddenly in a cutaway form, allowing the viewer to see through to the other side, but the trio could only see a void. Ruby frowned and tapped her screen again. Finally, the light changed to a more intense green.

Ruby shook her head,

"We should be able to see the room beyond the door, but the Hyaline beam shows absolutely nothing. It's as if there is no existence of any sort on the other side of the door. I think it could be a SlipStream of some sort."

She tapped the side of the WOTDISC, and a simple smooth wooden stick protruded from the side. She pulled out and flourished what looked quite like a small paintbrush, although the bristles appeared to be gossamer-fine tendrils of gold. Draping the Electron fabric over the door handle, there was a click as the handle turned. She pushed the door hesitantly with the wooden end of the paintbrush, not allowing her hand to cross the threshold.

All three of them had been on the edge of holding their breath until Ruby's tense shoulders suddenly relaxed with an "Oh!" of surprise,

"Hang on a sec before we go in." She pulled a pretty gold butterfly-topped grip from her hair and bent down, wedging the hair grip under the open door as if it were a miniature doorstop. "This should hold it."

Straightening up, she could immediately see the puzzled expressions on Eddie and Will's faces and explained,

"The door is similar to a Slipstream portal, but it appears to be bi-directional, which is incredibly rare. The 'paintbrush' is a Caduceus. It's my little magic wand so to speak. It's a temporal device, so if the portal had been one-way only, I would still have been able to drag it back towards me, although it would have taken some effort. You need to be truly careful with these rods." Ruby flourished the Caduceus at them. "Edith Madieu once painted a man into her own reality using one of these, and then illustrated the event in a painting she called *Virtual Reality*."

Will was looking down at the butterfly hairgrip trapped under the door,

"So, what's special about the hairgrip?"

Ruby grinned,

"It's a genuine Butterfly Effect Pin. You know the relatively Jurassic saying, 'A butterfly flaps its wings in Central Park, and you get rain in China instead of sunshine', yeah? The hairgrip is a Lorenz Stabiliser. It stops the possibility of our getting trapped in a room which is clearly not in Belgium."

With that, Ruby led them into a dark but beautifully decorated office, utterly incongruous to the modernist building they had entered. It was appointed with fine teak furniture, the like of which Eddie had only seen in Singapore on the way out to a posting in Hong Kong. However, everything appeared to be from a different age. In the darkness, illuminated only by their wrist devices, they could see a solid leather topped desk, placed nearly central to the room but sideways to the door. A set of drawers on either side left space for a comfortable Director's leather chair.

Will had been unsure why, as luxuriously as it was furnished, there was something about the gloomy room which felt a bit odd. Suddenly he realised what had been bothering him, nothing was electric. The lights on the ceiling and the walls were fitted with gas mantles. There were no electrical sockets on the walls. So the only heating in the room would come from what the desk was facing, which was a large fireplace, curiously similar to the one in The Old Volunteer.

Above the fireplace in the pub there was a wing-shaped clock, here, was a surrealist painting of a large spreading tree. Painted to be growing out of a plant pot on a stand, under which, like a rug, was a Dali-esque melting clock against the backdrop of a hot, dry desert and deep blue sky.

Ruby reached to her waist. It was the first time Eddie had noticed she was wearing a tool belt, similar to the sort of thing you'd see *Batman* wearing. She unclipped a half-rounded gold device with a thin lens barrel pointing out on one side, which she juggled in the air momentarily with one hand.

"Time to use a Duron Camera again! This little beastie is what we need to keep an eye on the painting."

Ruby placed it inverted on the underside of the desk. She looked at the video feed on her WOTDISC and adjusted the camera. There was a gentle golden glow, and the camera faded from view as if it had never existed,

"Let's crack on. You two go first, I'll pull the pin on the door. It's not only grenades that go off when you pull the pin out!"

CHAPTER 36
A Breath Of Berlin Air

East Berlin:
2330 (CET), Thursday December 24ᵗʰ 1970 (DET)

Although not as cold as Brussels, Berlin was still bitter for the C-Team. The door jump across the river, from the Watergate building to the abandoned Stralauer Tor U-Bahn station, was an easy hop. However, it seemed strange to be stepping out of a door onto an underground railway platform built on top of a bridge. Snow was coming through the multiple broken panes of the once-grand arched roof. Leaves and litter were spread across the track, the near-frozen remains of half a dead rat festering between the track sleepers.

Down below them on the river, a Russian military patrol boat slipped languidly past in the misty waters of the River Spree. The lights of West Berlin seemed brighter and more attractive than those on the north side of the bridge. Down two flights of the old platform access stairs, through the door, and they were between the arches of the U-Bahn's steel bridgework. Fortunately, the Russians had decided to position the border checkpoint beside the northern central tower of the bridge. Creeping away from this point at the north end of the old station was far less risky than trying to sneak past border guards in the fog.

The metal railings separating the bridge and the paved area beside the Egg Cool Store had been augmented with razor wire across the top. Happily, no one had thought to reinforce the fence brackets. Within seconds, Arti had the bolts removed and the entire fence section hinged like a gate, allowing them to make the four foot drop down to the flagstones at the western end of the building.

Directly opposite them, only twenty-five feet away, were a trio of fifteen-foot-tall air conditioning towers. Checking the coast was clear, Arti sprinted over, pinged a small Flex-a-Lock probe from the side of her PIMSS device, opened the central tower access panel, which unlocked with an unexpected crack, climbed in, and was gone in less than five seconds. Leo followed, and moments later Haji was stood at the top of the metal shaft ladder, leading down to the basement of the building. He froze. On the bridge, an armed Russian guard was taking a leak into the river.

Easily visible from the vantage point would be the footsteps they had left in the snow a moment earlier. For a second, Haji imagined a firing squad. That sobering thought was immediately replaced with a more practical idea, and he stretched out his arm. Fire suppressant foam drifted silently out into the night air from his WOTDISC, completely obscuring the three sets of footprints. Haji quietly closed the access hatch and climbed down the ladder.

Entering the basement of the building was a relief from the dreary streets of East Berlin. The mixture of Russian military greys and brown colours outside, fermented a feeling of depression, garnished with an extra seasoning of fear as searchlights passed over the riverbanks and roads closest to the River Spree. Underground and out of sight, it felt considerably safer.

Leo saw Haji's feet reaching the bottom of the ladder and whispered,

"What kept you?"

A relieved smile spread across Haji's face,

"One of the soldiers was making yellow snowballs. I realised we needed to cover our tracks with a little bit of our own white snow. Let's go!"

It looked like the East German operators of the Eierkühlhaus, Egg Cool Store had started a significant bit of engineering work. It appeared four half-installed, brand-new, massive MAFA-built, refrigeration compressors had been lowered into the basement. Doubtless, someone was planning to upgrade the building insulation with stacks of cork sheet panels piled up beside the crates of pipework. Older compressors were still running, making the well-lit basement feel quite toasty compared to the weather outside.

According to Haji's map, they needed to start at the un-chilled east end of the building, where there was a service elevator and stairs. Their destination was the central part of the 7th floor, which strangely, according to the map, could only be accessed by a set of stairs connecting floors five and six.

Their discussion about the safety of using the elevator was interrupted when voices and heavy booted steps of two people could be heard walking towards them. There was a ripple, and their Time Tech issued jackets and trousers morphed, as if with tiny waves on a pond. As the ripples faded, they were now wearing the badged clothing of the German compressor installation company.

A second later, the owners of the footsteps came into view, identifiable by their uniforms of the *Grenztruppen* East German military border security. Of the two, one was taller and discernibly senior, not only by the confident manner in which he carried himself, but also by virtue of being roughly ten years older. By Leo's reckoning, this made him in his forties.

The older guard gave a gruff shout,

"*Wer bist du?*"

Leo was fluent in German and replied. His PIMMS device connected Synthernetically to Arti and Haji's wrist devices, communicating directly to the Amygdala in their brains.

They actually heard Leo respond confidently with,

"Contractors. Working on the compressors," as he waved in the direction of the four mechanical structures.

The reply was terse,

"Why are you here? The building is secure for the night."

Leo shrugged his shoulders,

"Politics! The New Economic System! We have been ordered to make these machines work before First Secretary Ulbricht visits in three days. Of course, we don't want to be here, but it's orders, and it's warmer here than the Gulag!"

Both of the guards laughed, with the younger one saying,

"I know what you mean!" The older guard looked at Arti, saw she was clearly not German and turned his nose up. "I can see it's important if Comrade Chiang Kai-shek has sent help for you! We'll be back in an hour."

As the guards walked away, sniggering distastefully, Arti shook her head,

"I've never spoken German before, and I'm in no rush to learn it if they're all like that." Then, turning to Leo and Haji, Arti added with a slight amount of sarcasm, "and I'm certainly not having German lessons if they think I'm here to help Honourable Chiang! Come on, let's find our *Twin Piques* painting and get out of here."

The building was about 300 feet long, so crossing the basement to the stairs took only a few moments. Climbing the steps to the fifth floor brought them to what seemed to be an administrative level.

Arti nudged Haji,

"Do we go Prismorphic? I quite fancy trying out my cat quintessence again?"

Haji looked at his WOTDISC screen and shook his head,

"It seems there's no one on this level, so we should be fine."

Ahead of them was a long corridor with offices on both sides. Keeping their heads low as they passed the doorways of the darkened offices, they got halfway down, and Haji started to hum a tune.

Arti whispered,

"Shush Haji, what the heck are you doing?"

"Sorry," Haji whispered back. "Humming for Health."

"What?"

"Humming for Health", Haji repeated in a quiet voice. "Surely you know? When you hum, you produce Nitric Oxide. It's antibacterial, antiviral and antifungal, so, it's SUPREMELY good for your health. I was doing some prep before we set off, watching an ancient film. It starred this actor called *Bruce Willis*, who was famous for Christmas disasters. There's one where he sang songs whilst he was acting out robbing an art museum, I guess it was to help him remember, when he got to the end of his scene. I liked the song, and it felt appropriate, so I thought I'd hum it."

Arti gave him such a look,

"Well, stop it and save your treatment plan for later, unless you fancy a lead injection from an AK47!"

Haji looked slightly sheepish and studied his wrist, changing the subject,

"OK, according to the WAT-Nav, we need to take the last door on the right. The life-sign detector only shows armed border guards on the next floor up. We'll definitely need to dodge THEM. If one of us can set an Electron cloth for a climb of twenty feet, there's a store cupboard directly above we can hop into. It's two floors up. We can come out of there."

Leo pulled an Electron Fabric square from his pocket. He set it to zero time and an altitude change of twenty feet,

"It will be interesting to see what this building looks like when Alan Rowe and his team come back to it a few hundred years from now to fit the Cascade Hinges. The state it's in now, I'm quite worried it won't be here. Let's see if this works."

Leo placed the cloth around the handle, and it glowed. Momentarily, there was a luminescence in the door frame gap, the hinges clearly being activated. The door opened inwards to reveal a smallish room filled with old buckets and mops. They moved quickly inside, and Arti closed the door behind her. The hinges went dark, indicating the transit had been successful.

Leo was relieved,

"Great bloke, Alan. Never misses a hinge. You know he's one of Ruby's distant relatives? The day he was born in 1921, his parents broke down beside one of the first-ever emergency roadside telephone boxes. Aside from the fact it was actually a cloaked time travel craft, the patrolman came out on his motorbike. He fixed their two-year-old Austin 20, and got his mother to the hospital in time. They called him Alan Arthur to celebrate, so he would have the same initials as their rescuers. Except they were so stressed, they registered his name the wrong way round, so when the Queen sent him a card on his hundredth birthday, she called him Arthur!"

Arti bathed the light of her PIMMS device across the door, revealing there was no handle, only a lock. Without pausing, she touched another option on the screen.

There was a small beep, and a slightly bent and broken probe slid out of the side,

"Bugger, my Flex-a-Lock is broken. It must have happened when I unlocked the cooling tower. Haji, can you sort this?"

Haji held up his spare hand. He'd got the WOTDISC on his left arm, but a shiny new PIMMS device was on his right,

"It's OK; I can get this." There was another small beep, and a toilet roll bounced across the floor.

Arti was annoyed,

"You git! The button is on the other side of the latest version. You've upgraded! You said you were going to get me one when you got a new one!"

Haji looked utterly embarrassed,

"I'm sorry, I did order one for you, it's a TekTim Pulsar. It's still on my desk as I didn't have time to give it to you."

Arti rolled her eyes in despair,

"We're flippin' time travellers, you idiot! Come back yesterday and give it to me. I'm in my office all day."

This would be a normal conversation to the three of them, but this sort of talk would be utter nonsense to anyone outside the Time Tech bubble. However, after a couple of seconds, there was a faint fizzing sound. A half perceptible draft of air and Arti's watch rippled as if it were lying in water. It then went solid and sitting on Arti's wrist was the latest Mark 15 PIMMS device.

Arti was now appreciably happier,

"Oooh, how nice; you got me a gold one, thank you. It will go ever-so nicely with my latest dragon armour!"

Haji breathed a sigh of relief and picked up the loo roll which had shot out of his PIMMS device a moment ago,

"What's IZAL toilet paper?"

Arti looked over,

"Your PIMMS device is set to 'Auto-Era'. This is what people used in this era for toilet paper. It was waxed so it wouldn't go soggy in your outside loo."

Haji looked puzzled,

"What's an Out Sideloo?"

Arti gave him a disparaging look,

"Stop mucking about. Ask ZUKANN later. Now, get rid of the toilet roll and open the door. We're going to be late."

New York:
1755 (EST), Thursday December 24th 1970 (DET)

Back in New York, the A-Team's journey down 5th Avenue would have been a Spring-like stroll to the back door of the ALARM art museum had it been the 25th century: indoors with the artificial trompe l'oeil responsive ceilings on all floors, vertical gardens and water features.

However, the Winter in 1970 was a complete contrast. 5th Avenue was not yet under cover. The weather had been cold and reasonable enough for skating, but now it had turned. The Hudson Hawk had bitten again. With thirty miles-per-hour wind speeds, the one degree-below-freezing felt like nine degrees below. It was an easy decision for the team to make. Stay indoors.

Del, Mark and Rina, despite being wrapped up warm in their responsive heated Time Tech jackets, were already feeling the cold. After a short, but fond, goodbye to Gator Wilson in the staff entrance reception, they found themselves standing outside the anonymous doorway on the subway access stairs beside 22 Central Park South. The snow was blowing in swirls down the stairs, making the steps quite slippery. Cloth in hand, Rina turned the door handle. A familiar vibration followed, and the handle rotated, opening the door. The darkened room behind the door swallowed them up. Even if someone had been nearby, no one would have seen anything. It was the New York City Subway, after all.

Following a quick slip-jump, they found themselves just inside the exit door of the museum's internal fire escape stairs. It was quite brightly lit, considering the building was closed. The staircase was particularly unusual for a New York building as usually they had external fire escapes. The team was running very slightly ahead of time.

Ruby, Eddie and Will could do nothing more after visiting the Insurance Offices in Brussels. Not until Rina Mark and Del in New York, had worked out *The Godot Orange's* elusive location, essential to this entire mission. Haji, Arti and Leo were even quicker than the A-Team, and they had been delayed fending off the attentions of a couple of guards in the basement of the Egg Store in Berlin.

The American Literature Art and Realism Museum was not huge by American standards. Only five floors of books and documents of historical value, such as Marilyn Monroe's 'lost' *Red Diary*; love letters from Second Lieutenant William Clark to the Lemhi Shoshone guide Sacagawea; the Captain's Log from *Amerigo Vespucci*'s 1497 voyage to the New World; the photo album from the unofficial Apollo 10 Lunar landing at Bruce Crater and original paintings and drawings by Christopher Columbus. The main hall displays were gripping; if only they had more time, they would be back. Instead, they passed by smaller studios which appeared to set up for a wide range of artistic experiences, like giant crayons for adults and a children's Escher labyrinth play area.

Walking into an enormous final display hall, the team found themselves among some fascinating and ultra-realistic works of art. A cage of golf balls, each one stamped with the name 'O'Neill'. A cat in a basket scratching a post and what looked like a man frozen in time sat on a scale model of a 1930s steam train, the carriages covered in graffiti. The far end of the hall was their destination, featuring a small group of Edith Madieu's surrealist paintings.

Rina found the painting *Before Birthday* with ease. It was being featured in an alcove made to look a bit like a hardware store. The painting illustrated a group of shelves with environmentally-friendly, organic plant feed and pet-safe pesticides in the background. In the foreground, sat a large cake with four candles, two of which were lit, one burning with a red flame. Rina turned her WOTDISC on to 'video conference'. She waited for the other teams to join whilst Del walked around the gallery to look at other items in the collection.

One particular piece called *The Daughter of Eve* caught Del's eye. It was a strange picture of someone with the head of orange, wearing a wedding dress, in a room with a half-open door and a sunrise in the distance. Pictures might be worth a thousand words, but for Del, he'd rather have the words.

He was pondering the meaning when he felt something nudge his leg. He looked down and froze. There at his feet was a large tabby cat, rubbing its nose against his ankles. Rina was over the other side of the display hall, checking the Cake painting. He remembered what Ruby had said about the possibility of Prismorphic security. There was a slight fizzing sound and a blur. Before Del could blink, Mark Sparks was stood there grinning,

"Meow". Mark purred and pawed the air with his hands.

Del was not impressed and whispered loudly,

"WILL YOU STOP MESSING AROUND! IT'S STRESSFUL ENOUGH AS IT IS WITHOUT YOU MUCKING ABOUT!"

"Sorry, Del," Mark replied, "I thought it would take the edge off the tension."

"Well, it didn't, so don't do it again. I nearly had to go back to the last room where the toilets were!"

Del looked back at the painting, peering closely at the open door and the tree obscuring the sunrise. If he'd only been given a written description, life would have been much more straightforward.

For a second time that evening, he stopped and looked down at his feet. Again, a tabby cat was rubbing his ankles.

"Mark, I told you to PACK IT IN!"

"Pack what in? Mark asked from five feet to Del's left. Del spun round. Rina was still on the far side of the room, looking at the *Before Birthday* painting. An avalanche of thoughts hurtled through Del's mind. If Rina was there, and Mark was here, where did the cat come from?

There was another slight fizzing sound and a second blur. The situation was rapidly deteriorating, as in front of them stood a seven-or-eight-foot-long African Leopard with teeth longer than your fingers.

A deep, rich, sultry, almost Texan, non-rhotic drawl greeted them,

"Well, hello boys. Having a busy time? Any final words?"

It was at times like this, your life was supposed to flash through your mind. Del was puzzled it hadn't. Instead, a small, barely visible red line appeared from across the room, illuminating the occasional flecks of dust floating in the air. Del looked down and saw a glowing red dot on his chest. 'Not only ripped to shreds,' he thought, 'but a bullet through the heart, to make doubly sure.'

The red dot moved SLOWLY downwards, attracting the attention of the leopard. Finally, it passed over an area where no man would want to be shot and onwards down his leg. The dot jumped a foot towards the exit. With a considerable growl, the leopard pounced on it.

Suddenly, there was the sound of a gas cylinder being released, the leopard, which had been pawing at the red dot, acquired a thick frosted coating and keeled over sideways.

Rina was stood there with one eyebrow raised,

"Woof!" she said. "Looked like you needed cat repellent spray, but I figured a fire extinguisher would work well. It's the red button on your PIMMS device, the same as on a WOTDISC. Don't you just love the smell of nitrogen and fluorinated ketone in the morning? You all moan about me looking after health and safety, but if you read the instructions rather than seeing how far you can fire a toilet roll, you'd be far safer."

Ruby scanned the oversized cat with her WOTDISC,

"The scanner says it is a sentient leopard – Other Earth OECA75. Apologies for where I was aiming, but you know how cats can't resist a laser pointer, and I didn't have a cucumber to chase it away with! Life signs indicate it's not dead, but if it is, it will make a nice pair of jeggings – ONLY JOKING!"

Mark looked totally shocked,

"We're supposed to be civilized. You've been here in this era FAR too long, you barbarian!"

Rina rolled her eyes upwards. "And here was me thinking I was the boring one! Look, let's Prismorphically compress it and lock it in your PIMMS loo roll slot. Just don't get caught short before we get back."

ZUKANN OPTIC:

SCAN ME
T184A

Cucumbers For Cats

"In the early 21ˢᵗ Century, it became quite common to see social media communications illustrating the fear, cats had for cucumbers."

To discover more, please select this ZUKANN OPTIC.

ZUKANN
SCAN ME
V185A

CHAPTER 37
Orange Ophelia

The Old Volunteer – North Somercotes:
2315 (GMT), Thursday December 24th 1970 (DET)

Back in the MERCURY room above The Old Volunteer, data feeds had been arriving, providing a first-person viewpoint video of all the team members along with health telemetry supplied by their jackets. There had been a moment of genuine concern as Mark and Del's heart rate, and blood pressure went through the roof at the arrival of the sentient leopard. There had been concern that even if Time Tech weren't actually expected, someone might have been preparing some kind of defence against a potential attack.

Professor Eastwood was co-ordinating the technology. Alba was continually reviewing the plan against the actual events on the ground. Fred and Frank monitored all the video and health feeds, whilst Donnie Yud 'Tineres had been invited for his architecture and musical expertise.

The television had also been turned off. As good a singer as *Petula Clark* was being, there were too many other, more important things to focus on. The food, however, continued in its festive form, with bowls of crisps, peanuts and something the landlady of the pub downstairs called a 'festive hedgehog'. This consisted of a cheese cube and a pickled onion, or a chunk of pineapple, skewered onto a cocktail stick, each one inserted spike-down into half a foil-wrapped potato. The overall effect had been something approaching a hedgehog. It allowed Frank and Fred to discover the unique joy of pickled onions, an experience they had been missing all their lives.

Donnie pointed towards one of the video feeds,

"Looks like we've got our first view of the map location for *The Godot Orange*. Rina, can you get a bit closer to the band on the cake? It seems to be the outline of the BBEE_BAA Art and Antiquities building, so Ruby won't need to door jump anywhere else?"

The view of the cake moved closer, with the decorative band clearly showing a map. Finally, Rina's fingers came into view, and her voice could be heard,

"Seems like an interactive band. I can zoom in with two fingers."

Donnie checked his building plans,

"Ruby, Eddie, Will, it looks like the 'Orange' has been moved down to the basement. There's a service entrance at the side of the building, with stairs down and up. Looking at the close-up feed from Rina, candle number one is lit. Still, two and three are not. According to the narrative from 'Our Man in Canada', James, this means the painting is stolen but has not yet left the building. The fourth candle being lit with a red flame is still an unknown for us. If I get anything else on that, I'll update you. Please be careful."

Ruby's face appeared on the primary monitor,

"Thanks, Donnie, we're coming up the Avenue de Bouchout as we speak. We can see the BBEE BBA up ahead. You've got to wonder why these galleries have such pretentious acronyms, it's like someone made them up for a joke!"

To the left of the Avenue de Bouchout was the tree-lined field and low buildings of the Brussels Dressage Club. Up ahead, at the end of the road, was the plain grey concrete walls and green copper-domed roof of the Royal Observatory. A small group of antiquarian buildings to their right seemed to have been collected from different parts of Europe. Nearest to the road was a grey sandstone walled Victorian-looking building with six half-octagonal ground-level arches across the front. Above each arch were two tall, narrow, half-octagonal topped lancet windows. In the light snow and freezing fog, the array of statues displayed in a lawned area in front of the main entrance looked almost sinister; as if they had been cursed to stand frozen in time for an eternity.

Ruby's face appeared again on Donnie's smaller monitors,

"We're at the side entrance; we'll be inside shortly. There's no sign of life within a mile of us on our WOT-Nav display, and nothing is showing in the building, but we'll keep our eyes peeled. We're going in now."

Ruby quickly scanned the door with a Hyaline beam. After the incident in the insurance office, she wasn't going to take any chances. Thankfully it was clear, there was only a lobby behind the door. She opened it quickly using her electron fabric, and they slipped silently inside.

Closing the door behind them, Eddie sniffed the air,

"That's odd; the smell vaguely reminds me of a swimming pool."

Will looked relieved,

"I'm glad it's not my PIMMS filter playing up again, I can smell it too!"

Looking over the bannister rail of the open staircase, the lights from their wrist devices were reflected up onto the walls by a smooth, still surface down in the basement. They crept down the old stairway, Will's mind filling with thoughts of horror films he'd watched with dungeon basements swimming with the blood of slain victims. Ruby stopped at the last step. The fluid level was a mere finger's width below. Looking at the stains on the wall, and the last few steps, the smooth liquid surface had recently been almost up to the ceiling.

She bent down and dipped the tip of her finger in the liquid,

"Warm water! And not really dirty either. Mmm, very odd."

She dipped the toe of her boot into the water, her Prismorphic footwear immediately adapting to the six-inch depth of liquid keeping her feet perfectly dry. She shone her light down the corridor, which took a left turn about ten feet away. The ripples of each of their footstep ran ahead and around the corner. She raised her hand as a sign for Eddie and Will to stop. Eddie hadn't seen those kinds of war films and dodged walking into the back of her at the last moment. Looking over Ruby's shoulder, Eddie could see why they had stopped so suddenly. Just visible, a human hand was protruding just above the water's surface. It wasn't moving.

Ruby slid her foot through the water, trying to keep the ripples to a minimum. One pace, two, three, easing herself forward right up to the corner of the corridor. Still, there was no response from the hand. She poised, lifted her foot and stamped it down on the hand, peeking her head around the corner quickly, anticipating a response, but the hand did not react, and now Ruby could see why.

The body of a woman, clearly dressed for breaking into buildings on any other day, rather than delivering presents on Christmas Eve, was lying face up in the water, her eyes staring lifelessly at the ceiling.

Eddie and Will caught up as Fred's voice could be heard in the heads,

"We've done a scan of the liquid from your finger sample, Ruby. It's Jacuzzi water, and it's a perfect match for the half a million gallons you lost from your office."

Eddie turned to Will,

"Perhaps your water toast to success was good luck for us after all?"

Ruby reached inside the woman's utility belt and found a driving license. Holding it up to the light, she read it,

"ZUKANN, it says 'Lynda Blase Roper'. It's unlikely, but have you got any hits?"

ZUKANN replied immediately with an image identical to the driving license and the body's face in front of them,

"*Perfect match. She's a British government researcher for Lord Blayne Pears. I'll initiate a suitable response.*"

Ruby looked grim,

"Thanks, ZUKANN, we'll keep our eyes peeled, in case she has companions somewhere in the building."

Eddie shone his light a little further down the corridor illuminating a clear acrylic case, also floating in the water. He waded over and shone his light downwards. As if it were smiling up at him, there was a painting of an orange, sat on top of a town square fountain, accompanied by a man with the head of a clock, and a vaguely humanoid tree, both dipping their feet in the fountain pool. *The Godot Orange*.

Eddie grinned,

"Well, I think we've found our painting."

As the live video feed from Eddie's head-cam was broadcast, there was an audible cheer of relief from several global locations networked on the Synthernet link.

☙❈❧

The C-Team of Arti, Leo and Haji, had finally extricated themselves from the Berlin store cupboard. Having used the Flex-a-Lock probe from Haji's PIMMS device, they cautiously entered one of the East German State Degenerating or Defective Academic Exchange Service storage areas. The Deutsche Demokratische Republik Degenerierender / Defekter Akademischer Austauschdienst, or DDR D-DAA, had an extremely forward thinking and innovative approach to environmental issues.

The cost of new replacement equipment was massive. For this reason, the East German State Government were committed to the re-use and repair of all academic equipment. Old chalkboards, dusters, school chairs and education books were stacked up and crated, waiting for processing. Huge bags of chalk powder, swept up from classroom floors across the entire State, were collected, waiting for recompressing back into chalk sticks.

This seemed a strange place for Edith Madieu's *Twin Piques* to have been delivered, but if someone wanted to hide something valuable, no one would expect to find it here, especially not a work of art.

Haji tapped the Synthernet communicator on the side of his head.

"Well, it's good evening and 'Guten abend' from the East Berlin Jury. So far, it's 'null points' for Russian security; let us hope the score remains unchanged. I'm now standing in front of a lovely painting of two mountain peaks emerging from a cloud bank, each with a three-digit combination padlock. This surrealist painting definitely gives a sense of Illusionistic realism with its depiction of manifestly accurate naturalism and a veristic perspective. Well, that's what the blurb on the tag says anyway. Hey Prof, on the back of the tag, I've got six digits, 09,09,09. Is it what you've got for our combination code?"

Ike leaned in front of the nearest camera to him,

"Hey Haji, yup, it's what I've got here too. Let's check with Rina and Ruby. How's it going at your ends?"

Rina's face appeared first,

"No change at our end. Candles one and four are still burning in the picture. I'm ready to sing to the cake."

Ruby's face replaced Rina's like a video fade, as only a little changed visually apart from the vivid red hair,

"We're ready to roll. We've found Edith Madieu's *Chromati-Clef* painting of a grand piano cruising on the ocean. It's upstairs in the main gallery on the second floor, right beside her take on a piece of grass on the wall, with a door handle and a numbered dial, which we recognise from the intelligence pack as being *Environmental Security*, aka, 'The Safe'. Has anyone got anything on whether we turn the dial? We've also dried off all the jacuzzi water from the transit case *The Godot Orange* was being transported in. We've opened it and we've got this beautiful slice of fruit leant up against the wall beside the safe. It feels a bit graceless not hanging it, but there's no spare hooks on the wall!"

There was silence on her WOTDISC and no visuals. Ruby looked at Eddie and Will,

"Hello, Control, Prof, Alba, did you get that?" Again, there was no reply. "Are you getting anything, guys?"

Eddie and Will both shook their heads. Will tapped his PIMMS device, an act most likely to get him told off by ZUKANN,

"Not a thing, nada. I can hear you talking in the room, but I'm not getting your audio feed in my head like I was."

Ruby frowned and walked back towards the corridor away from the gallery, towards the stairs and the exit. Suddenly, she could hear voices again.

It was Ike,

"Ahhh, fantastic, we lost you there. Are the guys alright? We can't see their feeds or their vitals?"

"Sorry Prof, no, we're fine. I'm looking at Eddie and Will right now. I can assure you we're all fine." Ruby beckoned Eddie and Will over to her, beside the exit door.

A relieved sounding Ike replied,

"Fantastic, we've got them now. What's happening at your end?"

Ruby looked up at Will, waving him away with the back of her hand,

"Will, can you go and stand over by the safe again and talk?" Will walked back to the safe.

In the distance, Ruby could hear Will reciting,

"Testing, one, two, three, January, February, March," but nothing was coming through the system.

Ruby waved at Will to return,

"Keep talking." Will was only a couple of body lengths away when suddenly his voice could be heard again through the Synthernet audio network. Ruby raised a quizzical eyebrow, "It looks like we've got a problem with the room. This building is ancient, so I don't think it's anything to do with technology. ZUKANN, can you scan the walls for signal blocking wizardry?"

The gentle blue light of the Hyaline beam projected out from Ruby's WOTDISC and bathed patterns around the room.

Within milliseconds, ZUKANN's voice could be heard from all the team's devices,

"CAUTION! Please do not touch the wallpaper! The colours in use are Paris Green and London Purple. A high concentration of arsenic is present. The Synthernet data feeds rely on a Gaia powered natural biological communications platform, which is adversely affected by Arsenic metalloids. Effectively, this Victorian-era room has the equivalent of a Faraday cage communications barrier."

Once again Ruby raised her eyebrows,

"Why on earth would you want to cover a room with toxic wallpaper unless you knew it would stop future communications?"

It was Eddie's turn again to feel the smart one,

"Those old Sunday supplements in the Officers' Mess are turning out to be useful. I read a while back that it was commonplace in old houses right across Europe and America, but particularly in the big cities to decorate rooms like this. This specific pattern was a bit unusual at the time, but the colours were extremely fashionable. Making contact with the paper could make you go mad. They called it Witch Fever. Oscar Wilde was asked why he thought America was such a violent country, and he replied how it was 'because the wallpaper was so ugly'."

Ruby and Will stared at him with a stunned silence, whilst there was a slightly irritated sound from Eddie's wrist. If he'd looked down, he'd have seen a quickly deleted screen message from ZUKANN,

"I knew that too!"

ZUKANN OPTIC:

SCAN ME
V189A

Crafted Communications

"Forman-Asher Synthernet Communicators are Gaia powered Bio-Smart Mobile communications equipment. They are available as GreenThumb Standard compatible 'Temporal Bone' devices and are sold in various sizes. One is about the size of a 'Verruca plaster' and placed on the cheek in front of the ear.

"They are often grown and harvested in Synthernet orchards by 'Craft Communication Engineers'. Cultivated to be any shape from natural objects such as flowers, an apple, an orange, a stick or often simply an adhesive plaster. Bananas are the most popular amongst 'Vintage and Retro' aficionados.

"Synthernet transmissions are not affected by ordinary metals, which means they can be used within a Faraday cage; or the lead shielding of an MRI or CT scanner building. They are totally safe to use whilst refuelling rare heritage road vehicles. They have no impact on fly-by-wire systems onboard aircraft whilst taking off and landing. Communications, however, can be negatively affected by ultra-antique wallpaper found in ancient buildings decorated during the 18th Century. Containing highly toxic Arsenic metalloids in the bright colours of Paris green and London Purple, contact could lead to 'Witch Fever' and the death of humans.

To discover more, please select this ZUKANN OPTIC.

ZUKANN
SCAN ME
V190A

CHAPTER 38
The Key To The Secrets

The Old Volunteer – North Somercotes:
2330 (GMT), Thursday December 24th 1970 (DET)

Alba's face and a view of the MERCURY room appeared on everyone's screens,

"Now we've established it's not wise to lick the wallpaper or light switches, let's get this show on the road. Ruby, have you found the Schrodinger key?"

Ruby's face appeared on the monitors, now split between Alba's and Ruby's,

"That's a positive. When we unpacked *The Godot Orange* from the acrylic case, it was taped to the back. With the communications being an issue, I'll stand here by the door and shout 'quietly' across the room to Will and Eddie while they do the stuff with the key when you're ready."

Alba nodded,

"Thanks, Ruby. Looking at the Duron camera feed from the Insurance Office, we still have a tree with no cats. We're going to need three visible before we can open the safe. Now Rina, what's the state of the candles on the cake?"

Rina turned again to look at the cake,

"No change, only candles one and four lit. I still don't like the idea of not knowing what the fourth candle's for."

Alba pursed her lips,

"I'm with you on that Rina, but we're all here now, so, let's take a crack at it. Ruby, are you ready to insert the Schrodinger Key?"

Ruby gave the thumbs up to Alba and Eddie, who was poised, key in hand,

"Yes, we're ready. Give us the final decision on the key turns."

Eddie frowned, slightly puzzled how he could insert a key into a flat painting, and it actually felt like it was sliding into something definitely more solid, like pushing a warm spoon into ice cream. There was a soft 'click' sound as the key engaged.

Alba looked at the monitor feeds on the main display wall,

"*The Godot Orange* was stolen, and candle number one is lit, so it's ONE complete turn to the RIGHT."

The image of Ruby became jumbled as she held up her left forefinger, dialled it in the air and pointed right, while calling out to Eddie,

"PUT THE KEY IN AND MAKE ONE TURN RIGHT!"

Alba blinked as the sudden image change had taken her by surprise,

"Ruby, pointing at Will with your other hand will make us less seasick here! Candle number two is unlit. The painting had not been removed from the building. One key turn LEFT."

Ruby bit her lip,

"Sorry, Alba, I'll use my other hand. EDDIE, ONE COMPLETE TURN LEFT."

Alba smiled, feeling slightly less disorientated,

"Thanks, Ruby. Candle number three. *The Godot Orange* had been stolen but not delivered to its new owner. This is supposed to mean the key needs one more complete left turn."

Ruby gave her screen the thumbs-up sign with her right hand,

"OK EDDIE, ONE MORE TURN TO THE LEFT." Ruby turned back to the camera. "All done. Let us know when we can try to open the safe?"

Rina's face replaced Ruby's,

"We've still got a fourth candle burning with a red flame."

Alba twisted her mouth and gently bit her lip,

"Keep an eye on it for us and let us know if it changes at all. Haji, are you still OK in Berlin?"

Haji's smiling face now lit up the screen, replacing Rina's face,

"Yes, we're all systems go here. Leo's gone for a walkabout to check perimeter security, but I'm ready to roll the numbers on the lock. I'm going to try Zero, Nine, Zero on the first lock and Nine, Zero, Nine for the second?"

Alba nodded her head,

"That's an affirmative Haji. Give it a go."

Haji reached up to touch the first combination lock; it rippled, became three-dimensional, and the first number reel fell out of the picture and started rolling across the floor. The video feed turned upside-down as it had with Ruby.

The team in the MERCURY room were totally confused as all they could see was a blurred video of parquet flooring and Haji shouting,

"Whoah!... Stop it!... Quick... Get it before it goes in th... Oh SHIT!"

Haji's slightly flustered but determined face appeared back on screen again,

"Sorry everyone, the first number barrel fell out of the picture when I touched it and it rolled away and fell down a vent. Arti's lying on the floor trying to fish it out with that really cool three-pronged grabber in the new Mark 15 PIMMS. It's a good job we ordered the latest versions!"

Fred's face appeared on screen, grinning,

"Let's hope Ladey Adey signs off on your expenses; she's been moaning at Rob Locksley about running costs!"

Haji grinned,

"It'll be fine, just as an indemnity, I ordered one for her too!"

A hand flourishing a numbered dial appeared on Haji's video feed, closely followed by a triumphant looking Arti.

Haji was relieved,

"Thanks, Arti! Back in business." Haji held up the little dial from the lock and slipped it back into the painting.

Haji's intense concentration was clear to everyone watching him, as he feared the other dials might also slip out as he realigned them with the correct combination. A tiny single 'tick' sound could be heard as the last number was dialled. Haji relaxed the pressure on the picture, and the numbers stayed in place,

"OK, job done. What's next?"

Alba was looking serious,

"This is where it starts to get complicated. First, Rina, you need to sing the song. Then, hopefully, we'll see three cats in the tree on the Duron Camera feed from the Insurance Office. In which case, Ruby can open the SlipStream Safe behind the *Environmental Security* painting, swap the contents for *The Godot Orange* in less than thirty seconds, and we're all home and dry."

Rina reached for the Vocoda Necklace, gently hugging her throat and turned it on. It sparkled a little bit brighter to indicate it was now working.

There was even a little reverberation like you might hear in a large hall as Rina's voice could be heard clearer, richer and with more warmth than she would typically have,

"Switched on. *Jail House Rock*, please."

There was a tiny, well-nigh imperceptible beep. Rina took a breath and the music started. As though the real Rodge Brook was stood in front of them with his band and co-singers, the guitars thrashed their disembodied opening chords, and one of the best opening lines filled the room. Although it could be said: Wardens of county jails really should not throw parties, cellblocks full of inmates would undoubtedly have enjoyed Rina's talented rendition of Rodge Brooke's vocals. Rina sang and danced around the room as if she were 'live for one night only' at the Fillmore East, 3 miles away.

The sound was incredible. The version of the song was exactly as they'd first heard it on the record. You could even vaguely detect the hidden phrase being repeated in the background. Rina bowed as she came to the end of the song. There was a moment's silence. Then rousing applause from all the teams, but not from the MERCURY room.

Rina shouted above the cheers,

"How was that? Are we OK to open the safe?"

Alba was looking concerned,

"We've still got a tree with no cats. Rina, have you still got a red candle on the cake?"

Rina turned to Del who nodded to affirm,

"It's still red at our end. Do you want to try opening the safe to take a quick look?"

Alba shook her head,

"I don't think we should. Prof, what's your take on this. Have we done something wrong?"

A perturbed Professor Eastwood came into view,

"I don't think you should either. Trying it might get you sent back ten minutes, meaning you'd have to try again. That's the same as if you don't get *The Godot Orange* in the safe within thirty seconds."

Eddie's face appeared on the screen,

"If we get sent back ten minutes, will we know?"

Will looked at Ruby, quite confused,

"Of course we would know. Wouldn't we? And anyway, it's only ten minutes."

The Professor frowned,

"It's not only going back ten minutes. It's the possibility you might then repeat the same mistake over and over, like the punishment of Prometheus. A short repeat is extremely dangerous. If you were to repeat a whole day, you'd have the chance to consider your mistakes to find a solution. Ten minutes is no time at all. Besides, from what Edith Madieu described, it's a Lupoff Recursion Echo. This means you continue to age and are returned back to normal time after the cumulative attempt time has converged. If you had a thousand attempts, we wouldn't see you for a week! However, we may be at the point where you have to try it."

Donnie tilted his head and pondered,

"If you've already tried the handle and time for you has been reset, then we'd know because your feed would vanish. Which means you haven't already tried it. We should have sent you with a TZeeV Pre-Live Camera like they use in 'Celebrity You've Been Shamed'. You'd be able to see what you were about to do ten minutes from now.

"If we in the MERCURY Room don't remember you trying the safe handle before, then we are still at the point where we're ready to try it. We've surely done everything else needed to open the safe. So why don't you send yourselves a Déjà Vu Incident warning message with ZUKANN; to arrive immediately before you try it? If it arrives with a count of zero, you'll know you've never tried it before. She's available way off from our reality. If the message comes back with a count of one, you'll know not to do it again. If it comes back with a count of 500, then you'll know you're in BIG trouble?"

The Professor stroked his chin,

"That might work! ZUKANN, can you sort this for us, please?"

The gentle glow of ZUKANN's telepresence appeared on all their devices,

"*It's such a great idea; it's already done.*"

Ike twisted his mouth to one side, wondering if there was something they'd missed,

"OK, Ruby, let's try the handle. Don't touch it until we get a 'ZERO' message from ZUKANN."

Ruby nodded to confirm and shouted over to Eddie as communications were still causing an issue,

"OK, we'll do that. EDDIE, WHEN I CALL OUT ZERO, YOU TURN THE HANDLE." Ruby paused. "THREE...TWO...ONE..."

Ruby paused long enough for a 'ZERO Attempts' message to appear on all their devices. Ruby took a breath to say 'ZERO' but was swamped by Leo Frankovitz shouting,

"STOP! STOP! STOP!"

Sweat was on Leo's forehead, more from stress rather than exertion,

"STOP! There are two copies of the painting here. I took a wander around on the next level up from here. There's an identical copy of *Twin Piques* up there. It's probably why the artist gave it that name as a clue if anything happened to her. VERY astute! The tag is different too. The code number is the day of her death. Zero, Five, One – Two, Seven, Zero. Keep me on screen; I'll go back upstairs and turn the dials."

As Leo headed for the door, Arti's face appeared on the screens, rolling her eyes upwards,

"Keep your fingers on the dials as you turn them. We don't want them rolling off down the drain – again!"

It took only moments for Leo to get back upstairs and find the duplicate painting, exact in every detail apart from the combination. Leo's headcam gave them all a first-person viewpoint of the numbers being turned and him having to use all his fingers to keep the six dials in place.

Deftly scrolling the final digit, Leo's fingers came away from the picture,

"There you go. The numbers have clicked in place. What's now showing on *The Rescue* at the Insurers? Have we got three cats?"

To the relief of everyone in the MERCURY room, the painting of *The Rescue* in the office of Polly Andres-Baer was now clearly displaying a broad tree with THREE lions perched inelegantly in the branches.

Alba's resolutely serious expression took up a large part of the display on the screen across the MERCURY room and all the wrist devices,

"OK, NOW we're ready to open the safe. Ruby, please do the honours and get Eddie or Will to tell us what they see. Remember the time limit?"

Ruby looked slightly grimmer, well aware all their efforts could be wasted, and all of them would be sent back ten minutes if they got it wrong. She called over to Eddie,

"You've got thirty seconds from when you turn the handle to get everything out of the safe and get *The Godot Orange* inside. I'll do a countdown….. GO!"

Ruby watched nervously as Eddie turned the handle and opened the door of the Slipstream safe. A gentle glow from whatever was inside illuminated the faces of Eddie and Will,

"Twenty-Five Seconds left. Pull out whatever you can see."

Eddie immediately reached in and began to pull out what looked like a large ski bag, glowing with a gentle neon purple luminescence.

Eddie frowned and grunted,

"Will, give us a hand; it's like it's magnetic. Something's trying to keep it in the safe!"

Will took a grip on the bag. It felt like invisible treacle; it was moving so slowly. Ruby's increasingly anxious voice could be heard from the other side of the room,

"Twenty seconds left. Get on with it!"

The SlipStream safe finally released its hold on the long bag. Will and Eddie staggered slightly as it came free. Turning back to look inside the vault, Will could see, what he was hoping would be the other two power seed extractors, each one in a bowling ball bag.

"Eddie, you get the painting; I'll get the bags." Will reached his hand back into the safe. The feeling of trying to force his hand through thick invisible syrup was powerful. He braced his foot against the wall and heaved.

Ruby's voice was getting tenser. She began to feel a strange sense of uneasiness, as if she was looking through binoculars the wrong way and, her voice seemed to have an echo,

"Fifteen seconds, get a move on." As soon as Will's hand was out of the way, Eddie was ready and waiting to slide *The Godot Orange* painting into the safe. Will's arm, followed by the handle straps, slowly emerged.

The heavy bowling ball-sized bags suddenly came free, and Ruby's footsteps could be heard as she sprinted across the gallery. As she did so, her video and audio feed vanished from the MERCURY room.

Will staggered to one side. Eddie, now helped by Ruby, lifted *The Godot Orange* to the opening of the Safe. They were horrified! The picture was too large. Even diagonally, the artwork was too broad. Seconds were running out. Ruby ripped the painting from Eddie's grip and jumped on it, smashing the frame. Two big kicks and the canvas tore. Eddie, Ruby and Will lifted all the pieces, forced them into the safe and slammed the safe door shut.

Pausing for breath, Ruby looked at her WOTDISC. The counter had stopped at 0.999 seconds. She walked back to the end of the room where they had come in to reconnect to the network. A new message appeared: 'Déjà Vu count = 3'.

Alba suddenly re-appeared on Ruby's screen and Eddie and Will's PIMMS devices as they walked over to join her,

"Ruby! How are you doing? That was the longest thirty minutes. Where have you been? We've been trying to contact you. It was worse than the Apollo 13 re-entry. Sounds like you got hit with a Lupoff Echo. Is everything OK, did you get everything?"

Ruby drew a deep breath, scanned the room to see Eddie and Will with all three bags,

"We got everything."

Cheers and high-fives could be seen and heard from the MERCURY room, New York and Berlin, making Ruby a little uncomfortable. She looked back to Eddie and Will for reassurance,

"I don't know what happened, but the déjà vu counter said we had three repeated attempts?" Did it feel like four goes to you guys?

Looking stressed and fatigued, they both shook their heads. Will replied,

"It only seemed like one to me. I'm not sure where the extra thirty minutes went, but I feel OK."

Eddie sighed, looking at the fresh blisters on his hands,

"Yup, me too. Come on, let's get going before we bump into Father Christmas."

Alba's face appeared in view, one final time,

"Great job, teams. Get yourselves home as quick as you can. We need to start using the Power Rod, like yesterday! See you back soon."

ZUKANN
SCAN ME
V195A

CHAPTER 39
Flying Home for Christmas

ALARM New York:
1930 (EST), Thursday December 24th, 1970 (DET)

Over in New York, the A-Team of Del Rina and Mark were still punching the air. They had the longest real-time journey home, but they didn't care. The mission had been a complete success, and the Power Rod was out of the safe.

Mark looked around the A.L.A.R.M. gallery thoughtfully. Their bit hadn't been as complicated as Ruby's. However, Rina had sung well. In fact, her singing had been amazing, albeit enhanced with a Vocoda necklace! They had also picked up a curious addition in the form of a sentient leopard, which FENDER would be looking to interrogate when they got back. He'd already concluded that they'd better not go through any Casimir Interdimensional Border controls, having heard about Fred's experience with elephant smugglers. He didn't want the not-so-metaphorical cat to be let out of the bag until they were in a properly secured area.

He took a last look at the artwork in the gallery, resolving to return sometime in the future, but through the front door. He took a last look at Edith Madieu's *Before Birthday* painting. Only the red candle was now lit. He paused, drawn to the realistic image. His mum had always nagged him for leaving the lights on at home, so what happened next was simply an instinctive reaction. Mark leaned forward and blew at the flame.

The result was instant. Glycol security smoke poured into the room. The piercing shriek of the audible alarm was deafening, and strobe lights made seeing even harder through the smoke.

Rina shouted,

"Run!"

Like the chains of *Marley's ghost*, the loud rattling sound of the steel and glass security gate lowering on its tracks could be heard as they threw themselves back into the anteroom. Mark was the last to slide under the closing portal. His headlong slide abruptly halted by the gate arriving at its lowest point, grinding his leg to a pulp on the floor.

The smoke and noise were mainly contained in the main gallery room behind the security shutter. Then, finally, the overspill smoke started to clear. Rina looked sternly down at Mark, lying on the floor, his leg clearly crushed beyond all medical assistance.

Del was utterly shocked. Not only because Mark was lying there, acutely injured, but because of what Rina said next.

"What on EARTH did you do that for?" Rina shouted, devoid of sympathy for Mark's terrible injuries.

Del was staggered by her complete lack of compassion,

"Rina! How could you be so cruel – he could die!"

Rina tutted and raised her eyes to the ceiling,

"He's not going to die, he's not even in pain, and this isn't the first time he's lost his leg!" She turned to Mark and all but shouted,

"You are SO accident-prone. How long is it going to take this time?"

Del stood open-mouthed as Mark replied,

"Give us a minute; it's already started." They all looked through the glazing of the security gate and the fog of security smoke at what remained of Mark's leg on the other side of the gate. The guillotined shin and then the foot started to collapse like particles of sand, coalescing into a two-dimensional cloud across the floor which began to seep towards them, under the gate heading for the part of Mark's leg which wasn't crushed. Suddenly, the stump of his leg below the knee came free from the gate, and Mark slid back and sat upright on the floor, followed by an ant-colony-like trail of skin-toned sandy particles.

Rina turned to Del, explaining,

"He had an IDEAL test when he was a baby. He's got the XL version of a CAT prosthetic or Crush Actuated Trauma leg. It's got nine nanite-assisted reconstruction cycles, and if he carries on at this rate," Rina turned pointedly at Mark, "He's going to be exceeding the warranty agreement! This ISN'T the first time he's lost his leg, AND according to the test, it won't be the last. The first time was when he saved a young ice skater. The boy had fallen into the path of an automated ice re-surfacer which had gone rogue due to a corrupted software update."

Mark grinned ruefully,

"To be honest, it's why I don't often go ice skating anymore. Apparently, the first time is the most traumatic. So, it's a good job I chose cargo shorts for today. Apart from all the pockets being handy, it would be a bit awkward leaving my trousers trapped under the gate!"

It took just a few seconds, and the cloud of leg particles were rapidly reconnecting themselves onto Mark's body. Halfway up his shin, however, there appeared to be a problem. A cavity was still visible, and the flow of sand-like granules had flowed practically to a stop.

Mark started patting each of the pockets in his shorts in quick succession,

"Ahh, perfect," he sighed in relief as he began to unwrap a chocolate protein bar.

Del frowned,

"Seriously? We don't have time for you to have a snack; we must get going. We're going to have visitors here in no time at all!"

Mark shook his head,

"It's a protein pack for the nanites, not a snack. Part of the material for my leg is jammed solid under the gate. Those particles will dissipate like dust when the gate's opened; for now, this is the perfect repair." Mark pressed the protein bar into his leg. The nanites as good as reached up for it, sucking it into the cavity filling the void. He stood up quickly and stamped his foot, checking to makes sure nothing was going to drop off. "Come on," he grinned, tilting his head towards the door they came in from, "time to leg it!"

Moments after they closed the door behind them, armed security burst into the gallery.

Medical Measures

"IDEAL, or Infantile Destiny Event Adjustment Logic Tests, are available for a baby's physiological health destiny. One example could be if the child is to lose a leg in adulthood due to an accident. Proactive surgery could be offered to the child's parents to replace the baby's leg with a prosthetic in advance. Then, when the future accident occurs, the leg can be detached and escape from the incident can be immediate, resulting in fewer post-trauma injuries and a faster recovery."

To discover more, please select this ZUKANN OPTIC.

In Berlin, the C-Team of Arti, Haji and Leo had also been celebrating. Not only because of the mission's success but because Professor Eastwood and ZUKANN had run a recalculation.

The Professor's face on Haji's WOTDISC radiated happiness,

"Now the Power Rod has been retrieved, we've calculated we can afford to borrow some power from as close as December 1973. FENDER has recorded this as a time when there will be a surprisingly warm winter and a surplus of energy. You can all use a SlipStream jump to come back directly from Berlin to The Old Volunteer. When you're back, we'll send word to the Queen's Flight that we won't be needing to borrow her plane any longer."

Leo had been looking over Haji's shoulder,

"Tell you what, you two jump back to the Watergate Building. I'll check upstairs to make it look like we've not been here. Then we can all jump together back to... what do they call it, 'Good Old Blighty'? At least we won't need to worry about armed security taking pot-shots at us."

Arti nodded,

"Great idea! See you on the safe side of the river in five minutes, coming Haji?"

Haji was also convinced,

"I can't wait to be out of here. Synching with you now, Arti. ZUKANN, two for the Watergate building, please. We'll use the cupboard door we came in through. At least we know we can open it!"

The hinges on the door glowed, and Arti cracked it open. From above them, they could hear a loud thud, as if something heavy had momentarily toppled over on the floor. Arti shook her head,

"Whatever that was, I'm sure Leo will be moaning about it when he catches up with us. Come on, we'll get a better view from across the river in the Watergate building, so we'll be able to see what he's up to. Not only that, it will be much safer back in West Berlin"

BBEE_BAA – Brussels:
0130 (CET), Friday December 25th 1970 (DET)

Over in Belgium, Ruby looked back at the Gallery, pondering. It had been a successful night, although it sounded like Mark had tripped an alarm at the A.L.A.R.M in New York on the way out. At least they could have a first-class ride home, and with the Berlin team being able to door-jump directly home, there was a real possibility everyone might be back in time for Christmas tea and a few party games. Charades would be fun!

As Ruby looked around for the last time, it somehow seemed to her that everything was shrinking, although she reckoned it was probably an optical illusion.

Her reverie was interrupted by Will,

"Sshhhh!!" He had turned around in the corridor and was creeping stealthily back towards her looking rather worried "There's a security guard who wasn't there before, sat beside the exit door, we could get past him Prismorphed, but a fly can't open a door! Look at your WOT-NAV, is there another way out?"

Looking at the display, there was certainly no going back the way they had come in.

Ruby scratched her head,

"We've got six windows, but I don't fancy jumping from the second floor unless there's no option. I'm fit, but I'm not Arti, plus I'm no ninja, and we've got a six-foot crystalline rod to protect, and I don't want to take the blame for chipping some bits off, dropping it out of a window!"

Ruby looked again at the WOTDISC map. In the corner of the gallery was a large display panel, framed by what looked like scaffold tubes. On the map, it showed a door behind the board, leading to a small storage room which they swiftly investigated.

"Come on, gents, give me a hand with this." With each of them grabbing part of the display structure, they quietly started to slide it away from the wall, just enough to get behind it. There was indeed a door. Ruby turned the handle. Fortunately, it wasn't locked. Peering inside, she could see the crates in which the gallery artwork had been delivered, giving them a perfect return path.

She closed the door and pulled from her pocket a familiar square of electron fabric. She gave it a flourish worthy of any magician. It went rigid, a map of The Old Volunteer spreading across its surface. Ruby selected the homely welcoming door in the snug, flapped the cloth again to make it relax, wrapped it around the door handle and twisted it.

There was none of the usual haptic response you got when travelling door to door. No synchronisation with her WOTDISC for a long-distance jump. No familiar glow as the cascade hinges responded, ready for transit. Ruby opened the door towards her. Something wasn't right. You only ever saw what was in your current reality when you 'door stepped', but there was no familiar shimmer and nothing to be seen out of the corner of her eye. She pulled out the Caduceus from earlier and poked it through the doorway. It should have disappeared, but it didn't. There was no connection.

She closed the door and opened it again. Still nothing,

"Houston, we have a problem". It had only been eight months since Jack Swigert had radioed NASA mission control from Apollo 13. Will and Eddie had been listening to the radio along with a billion other people when the Command Module 'Odyssey' returned to Earth. Memories of re-entry from the aborted Lunar mission sent chills down their spines.

Gritting her teeth, there was a real note of concern in Ruby's voice,

"We knew there was an inbound travel issue, but I've never come across an outbound problem."

Ruby flicked the Electron Fabric back into its rigid map-view state, now displaying the immediate area and a ten-mile radius around where they were. The thought occurred to her that it should be an easy door jump to the Atomium ticket office, back down the other end of the Avenue de Bouchout. The office door was highlighted with a red no-entry symbol.

Ruby tilted her head to one side quizzically,

"This should work, it's only a doorstep down the road. Perhaps there's a problem at the ticket office?"

Eddie ran his hand through his hair,

"Are there any other doors we can use nearby?"

Ruby flicked the Electron Fabric again and looked at the map.

"There's one at the Observatory and another at the Dressage Club on the other side of the road. Let's give it a go." A few more flicks and door handle turning. Finally, it was clear, there were no interconnecting doors nearby.

Will, remembering he'd been to Brussels a couple of years previously on a pilot training program, pointed at the map on the Electron Fabric,

"How about we try further away, say, this point in the centre of town, just here." As Ruby zoomed into the map, Will pointed at an area, south of the city centre. "There's a famous statue of a little boy with a chocolate shop next door. We could get some chocolate for Christmas? Despite everything, it is still Christmas Eve after all."

Ruby looked doubtful, but an active door was indicated, so she selected it, flicked the cloth, and wrapped it onto the door handle. She twisted the handle again. Still nothing.

"There's something about this building causing interference. I've no idea why the SlipStream is not re-connecting. Maybe there's an issue back at The Old Volunteer?" A quiet buzz came from the WOTDISC. Ruby spotted the screen had changed,

"Hiya ZUKANN, what have you got."

ZUKANN worryingly had put her reassuring, friendly voice on.

"*Ruby, I've been trying to connect. You must be standing in the only part of the room with no toxic wallpaper. I've been checking the building. There's a temporal anomaly developing, creating structural, architectural instability. All the buildings in your area are starting to shrink. The good news is the door can connect. The bad news is there are no local portals in Europe currently connecting. It's like there's been some kind of network blackout. It is possible to make an emergency jump back home with an emergency power boost from the WOTDISC. The bad news is only two can travel.*"

Ruby pondered for a moment, looking at the ceiling which by now was genuinely looking lower than before, and now seriously considering the possibility of climbing from the second-story window by Prismorphing her jacket into a rope,

"Look, our options are shrinking as I think this building is, and I've got a simple idea. If the WOTDISC can transfer two people under its own power, you guys can take the Power Probe and Seed devices back to the lab, and I'll catch up using conventional transport. We must get it back quickly."

Now it was Will's turn to look concerned,

"But it's Christmas Day. All the train services are shut down for the holidays. How are you going to get back?"

Ruby had a glint in her eye,

"It's OK. Where I'm going, you don't need railroads!"

Then for some inconceivable reason, at least to Eddie and Will, she put on a *Dick Van Dyke* style Cockney accent and said,

"There's Luton Airport!"…There was a long pregnant pause. "You know, like Lorraine Chase in that drinks advert? I can fly from Brussels airport, there are flights even on Christmas Day. It's only six miles from here. So, even if I can't get a taxi, I can easily walk it."

Eddie looked at Ruby like she had a screw loose,

"I'm guessing you might be a few years too early. It's lost on me. And if your jokes are all like that, we definitely need to leave you here!"

Ruby removed the WOTDISC and held it out to Eddie,

"I'll do you swap for your PIMMS. There's no way I'm having Will's, not with the smells he's been getting!"

Eddie took the WOTDISC and gave Ruby his PIMMS,

"When this is all sorted – remember your promise – Monday, lunch at 'The Old Volunteer' on you."

Ruby laughed,

"I'll keep working on getting the contemporary references and idioms right, catch you earlier!"

Eddie grinned. At least he'd got that one! Pausing to remember the training, Eddie checked Will's PIMMS device was synched on his wrist and tapped on the WOTDISC screen three times,

"ZUKANN, take two of us home". Surprisingly, even without electron fabric, there was a glow on the door hinges. He turned the handle, and it opened outwards toward him. Again, they could see the storeroom, but it didn't look quite natural. Will stepped through first and was gone. Eddie tapped his forehead in a friendly salute, waved and stepped forward. For a moment, there was a faint residual image of Eddie's body outline. Then, the glow faded, leaving Ruby alone in the now dark and slightly creepy art gallery.

Ruby closed the storeroom door and looked around to check everything was in place. Apart from the display being pulled from the wall, nothing else might indicate anyone had been in the large display hall. The room, however, was genuinely getting smaller by the minute. Simultaneously, in America, the red candle flame on the *Before Birthday* cake faded out.

Ruby paused for a moment, mentally debating in her mind which window would be the best to jump from.

Behind her, a dark stain had been forming on the wall. It suddenly began to expand, and as Ruby turned, she caught sight of it. There was a brief look of horror on her face, and no time to react. A short sound like the noise of water going down the plughole of a bath, and then silence. The room was empty. The only movement was a few dust particles, dancing spirals in the light of the moon cascading through the skylight.

౪⊕◌⊕౽

ZUKANN
SCAN ME
W201A

CHAPTER 40
Home Again You Never Left

The Old Volunteer – North Somercotes:
1250 (GMT), Thursday December 10th 1970 (DET)

Most stories have a beginning, a middle and an end, but we don't have time for the whole of the middle, so we need to skip to the end.

The old man gently opened the door to The Old Volunteer, walked up to the bar in the snug, where an equally elderly man was serving behind the counter.

Neither looked older than seventy, so you'd never guess one was 125, and the other was 134.

"Morning, Will", said the old man as he walked up to take a closer look at what this week's guest ale was.

"Morning, Eddie," replied Will, the barman.

"I figured it 'must be today' since you've got new bar staff". Eddie nodded in the direction of a striking young lady with red hair who was collecting glasses,

"She still not worked it out yet?"

"Thankfully not," replied Will, pouring Eddie a pint.

"It's a good job I get mates' rates in the bar, all this waiting is eating into my pension." Eddie licked his lips with the anticipation of a fresh pint. "You know, in all the years we've known each other, you really haven't changed at all, you good looking bastard! No wonder you always got to take the prettiest girls to the cinema!"

"Thank you," Will replied with a broad grin and a mock attempt to straighten his slightly thinning hair. "But on that point, you grab your usual table and I'd better pop upstairs. I think we're expecting visitors."

As Will disappeared from sight, and Eddie sat down where he always did, the door to the snug opened again, and two young RAF pilots walked into the bar.

"We've had orders to get a pint," said one of them to the red-haired young lady who was now serving behind the counter.

The barmaid smiled and nodded a welcome,

"Are you the guys who planted one of Harold Wilson's bombers into Duckford's field?"

"Unfortunately, that was us. Buzz here got lost turning right over the North Sea!"

"You need to be more careful how you drive," the young barmaid replied with an enigmatic smile worthy of the Mona Lisa, who she'd originally learned the smile from – firsthand! "Actually, the beers off. I could do with a hand with the barrels as I'm on my own. Could you help me out for a couple of minutes?"

"Sure thing!" grinned the second pilot, "Always happy to help a lady."

"You just don't give up, do you?" reproached Buzz.

"I've got to live up to my nickname!" Fortunately, Zebedee wasn't a nickname Will lived up to, but he was happy to let everyone 'think' he was great with the ladies.

"Come this way." The barmaid nodded to the end of the room. A door beside the bar led to the toilets and the cellar. She picked up a small cloth and led them through the door. The old guy, who was sitting at his usual table beside the fireplace smiled. Today was going to be a good day.

A couple of minutes ticked by. A fly, which had been annoying everyone earlier, landed on the strange aeroplane wing-shaped clock above the fireplace. It suddenly dropped dead on the hearth as if it had been electrocuted. The lights behind the bar flickered very slightly, and a faint green glow appeared under the door to the Gents' toilets.

The door opened. Dust and the smell of burning wafted into the Snug. It was followed by a tall, elegant older-looking woman, resplendent with long red hair, 'greying gracefully' as they say. She paused momentarily to look down at a doormat which hadn't been there the last time she'd been in the pub. Then, her gaze crossed the bar to where the old man was sitting with a frown on his face.

"You took your bloody time! Trust you to turn up when it's not a Monday," said the old man sat at the table. "How are you doing, Sis?"

"Not bad, Eddie," said the older lady, joining him at the table. "Where's Will?"

"He's upstairs getting changed. He got this mad idea he wanted to take you back home dressed in his old uniform."

Tears started to prick Eddie's eyes, probably from the dust, rather than from relief Ruby was back. After all, he was very practical and hadn't really got time to be emotional. Ruby reached into her pocket and pulled out a rectangular white cloth, which would simply have been a hanky to anyone else's eyes. One that Eddie had seen so long ago, and yet one his younger self would see for the first time, in just a few minutes. She passed it to him, smiling with a familiar twinkle in her eye,

"I think you need this more than me."

The End... Of The Beginning

ல⊕①⊕ை

A FOOTNOTE

Whilst I was writing this book, the decision was made to demolish the Grenfell Tower in London, England. 72 people lost their lives when a fire broke out in the tower, on the night of 14th June 2017.

Also, as I was researching locations for the New York part of the story in the United States, I came across a memorial in the Mount Zion Cemetery to fourteen of the 146 mostly young people who died after a fire broke out in the Washington Place Triangle Shirt Waist Factory on 25th March 1911.

Time travellers have a conundrum when dealing with disaster. The trope is that they must not change their past or alter a future they know will happen. Every terrible event can be seen from two points of view. If you could stop an appalling event, surely you should? If you could turn back time to undo a catastrophe, I'm sure you, like I, would seriously consider it.

As none of us are time travellers, we can all take the opportunity to change the future and help prevent similar disasters from occurring. Please take the opportunity to support those who are determined to give us all safe communities and workplaces.

If we cannot change the past, we can remember the victims. Two organisations coordinating memorials are:

https://www.grenfelltowermemorial.co.uk/

and

http://rememberthetrianglefire.org/

REMEMBER: NEGLECTING YOUR FUTURE ONLY WRECKS YOUR PAST

Have you ever seen the shape of love?
There may be loads of it here!

THE GODOT ORANGE LOCATIONS

The Lincolnshire Tour (site by site order)

Location	what3words.com
Ludborough Station, Lincolnshire Wolds Railway, The Lost Line	///magical.argued.rainy
Covenham St Bartholomew Reservoir	///excavated.gardens.jams
St Nicolas Church, North Cotes (Tuck Photography and adjacent Junior School)	///watch.array.hammocks
Vulcan Crash Site	///fuse.thickened.unicorns
RAF North Coates	///condition.winded.machine
RAF Donna Nook	///outhouse.notices.secrets
Cloaked Locksley Hall	///different.alright.resist
Locksley Hall - The Original Please do not disturb Mother-in-Law and cloaked dogs	///nails.niece.leads
St Mary's - North Somercotes, Robin and Marian's Church Pierre de Bellême carved chest	///locator.inert.cube
Old Volunteer Pub (Axe & Cleaver) North Somercotes	///holds.landlady.thrones
Alvingham Priory St Mary's Alvingham and St Adelwolds' Alvingham	///sunflower.gangs.flag

The Nottinghamshire Tour (site by site order)

Mattersey Priory	///cherubs.cycles.darling
Farm of Delights	///heartless.blizzard.village
Farm of Delights Entrance	///mashing.stars.nightcap
Locksley's Favourite Brewery	///indicate.bleak.beginning
Will Scarlet's Grave and St Lawrence Chapel	///technical.latched.blackouts
Wollaton Hall, Cloaked Locksley Hall Clone	///ranch.artist.ruby

ের⊕🕐⊕ঙ

The Global Art Tour

Axe & Cleaver Weapons Range and Sports Bar, New York (built 2485)	///damage.lowest.tonic
Brammibal's Vegan Donuts, Berlin	///supplier.finders.battle
East Berlin Mill Silo	///glory.probably.bronzer
JFK World Port (demolished)	///backs.neat.bottom
Mount Zion Cemetery, New York	///factories.kick.useful
Mühlenstrasse Bahn (demolished)	///encounter.resides.forever
USPS Parcels Office, New York	///this.glee.legend
Royal Observatory and Planetarium	///bowls.hugs.teaspoons
Secret Entrance 22 Central Park Sth	///fake.ants.month
The A.L.A.R.M. Art Museum (USA)	///wooden.rival.system
The Atomium	///glitter.jobs.nitrate
The BBEE_BAA	///mull.surreal.enigma
The DDR_D-DAA	///snail.cucumber.ducks
The NE_NAA Insurance Office	///lottery.cafe.table
Triangle Shirt Waist Factory 1911	///ended.nearly.begin
Washington Square Arch	///dogs.rescue.blank

Locations

West Berlin Tempelhof Airport	///rear.prepared.lawn
West Berlin Watergate Building	///eats.wiggly.slurred

✢

The London Tour

Chancery Lane Underground	///pokers.deals.chip
Farringdon Station	///mock.proper.spill
Mann Hatton Garden Project	///dogs.ended.strike
Tottenham Court Road Underground	///blog.dark.empire

✢

The Brussels Extra Tour

Brussels Dressage Club (Dogs Only)	///levels.design.spoons
Mannequin Pis	///short.taken.informal
Miniaturised Buildings	///traps.serious.student
Royal Observatory and Planetarium	///bowls.hugs.teaspoons

✢

The Hagura Tour

Deception Island	///irritant.monoplane.lung
Klara Nuclear Shelter, Sweden	///orbit.incline.known
Plateau of Bogs, La Grande Marmite	///outrageous.yellowy.ragtag
Reality: Brazil	///bicycles.march.frequents

✢

The Power Tour

HOW: How Lane, How, England	////stew.novelists.fancy
WHAT: Hibiscus Coast Highway, New Zealand	///fine.reversed.bottler
WHEN: Headquarters No.1 The Centre, When, Liberia	///weekdays.misdirected.always
WHERE: Lower Camp Road, Kōthāẏa, India	///checkmate.restored.reliably
WHICH: Which Way, Kalama Atoll, Pacific Ocean	///fashionably.lost.prevention
WHO: Quem Quem, Minas Gerais, Brazil	///defector.bracelet.sunbeam
WHY: Guinn Road, Why, Arizona, USA	///sheds.disturb.indicates
Tunguska Forest – Russia	///microwave.before.nightclub

ↄ⊕①⊕ↄ

The Extras Tour

Calima Lake 'crash' site, Colombia	///pursuits.antihero.assistant
Newark Air Museum (Vulcan)	//joints.encoded.radar
Sherwood Forest Visitor Centre	///misty.norms.plausible
Tragic Magic Roundabout, Swindon	///intent.under.crowd

ↄ⊕①⊕ↄ

Please Note:

Not all of these sites may be open to the public or exist in your reality.

Time Tech encourages responsible travelling at all times.

Go Gently!

ACKNOWLEDGEMENTS

Inspiration and help for this book came from several sources: My thanks go to:

Cathy, Dan, Gem, Joe and Sue (in alphabetical order) for all your help and support.

Flt Lt John Lebrun, author of *Lucky Me*: Serendipity, Amazon 2020, for guiding me around the Vulcan crew.

Chris Forman and Claire Asher, authors of *Brave Green World*, The MIT Press 2021, who understand the real science to the Synthernet.

SipcamUK.co.uk – for the use of the images from their environmentally friendly garden products range.

IBM Watson Text to Speech Voices for ZUKANN generated in 'Curl' script.

The Axe and Cleaver Public House, North Somercotes for a great Sunday lunch and the answer to the oddest instance of déjà vu when searching for *The Old Volunteer.*

The bell ringers at St Mary's – North Somercotes who only by coincidence were there when we called.

The lincolnshirewoldsrailway.co.uk for making us so welcome.

Kevin McGrother (The Nearly Man) and Karen Forster from north-east based band The Artisans for A Week of Wednesdays.

Google, Thesaurus.com, What3Words, Wikipedia and www.QRcode-Monkey.com for making my journey a little easier.

Glen Jeffrey, University College London for inspiring my idea of city-wide 670nM early-hours lighting.

My neurologist and all the NHS staff still helping me repair the damage from accidental time travel.

Good luck to *Jacob Newson - @JacobThePilot on FaceBook* – young fundraiser and inspiration.

Applying lemon to this page will not reveal
a secret message.

ABOUT THE AUTHOR - BRUCE ROBERTS

Born Robert Bruce within sight of the rolling sea and Barry Island roller coasters in South Wales, on 31st July 1963, exactly 2 years

before JK Rowling and 17 years to the day before Harry Potter.

Adopted at age 5, by the Roberts family and when asked, if he wanted to keep his first name, he somewhat creatively asked (age 5 remember) if he could swap his name round and

be called Bruce, which came to pass- obviously, or else this would be a really bad pseudonym!

Education went from St Nicholas Infants School, just West of Cardiff, Ernehale Infant and Juniors in Nottingham, followed by Arnold Hill Comprehensive then Trent Polytechnic.

He experienced 28 years employed in BT and Accenture, then 12 years working for software companies; Atlantic Link and Assima, he became self-employed developing e-Learning material.

The COVID crisis of 2020 had an impact on opportunities, but the real headache as they say was being struck down at the beginning of 2021 with double brain haemorrhages. Low fluid pressure in his spine had caused his brain to sag in his skull causing him to act even more unusual than his friends and family have been used to over his lifetime. An emergency visit became an extended period, Full Board at the Queens Medical Centre Nottingham.

Bruce's release from hospital came with two weeks having to lay flat whilst taking the prescribed treatment plan, which genuinely and seemingly surprising, was to drink 12 cups of coffee a day.

During this period and only managing to put up with about 2 hours of afternoon TV, featuring Desperate Antique Bargain Hunting Lawyered-up Housewives, reconditioning old cars and aircraft in deprived areas of London and Manchester, with a quick break viewing border security antipodean style, he realised that things had to change.

Bruce's mind wandered to a place that Albert Einstein described as '… a new, stubbornly persistent illusion.' It seemed that a world that he had toyed with at EMCON, 3 years earlier, Nottingham's rather excellent answer to Comic-Con but without the cost of international travel, might be a world to revisit.

Mumbled notes dictated into an iPhone, whilst laying recumbent, overdosing on caffeine, became A4 pages being torn out of writing pads, piling up to a point that when recovery began, so did the typing, if only to stop the house looking like a future afternoon TV location for a documentary about waste hoarders.

As they also say, 'the rest is history'. Although with all good time travel yarns, if the future is history and the past is in the future, the present must be the gift which every morning now turns out to be.

Bruce is happily and persistently married to Sue, who he has known for nearly 40 years. They have two daughters, who are also married and (two – insert new number here) grandchildren - one of whom will invent time travel in the year 2189.

Sue has excellently adapted to his wonderful eccentricity and creativity, and has taken to reinforcing her patience for the next onslaught, which will continue to require having a 7 ¼" gauge ride on railway in the back garden.

WHAT'S NEXT

Fancy a quick peek into the upcoming novel in the TIME TECH Series? The latest news will be found here in your dimension.

Latest News

Let there be light on this page.
Darkness is far less attractive.

ENDORSEMENTS

"Wildly imaginative and takes a lot of unpredictable twists that will keep the readers on their toes."

John Peel, Author of Diadem, Dragonhome and Doctor Who novels.

"If Pratchett, Adams and Hawking quantum entangled their thoughts, they might resemble Bruce Robert's magnificent romp through the temporal singularities of the metaverse. Humour, some jolly decent heroes and heroines, gusto and panache, collide with suspiciously detailed knowledge of Vulcan aircraft and time-travel. Best laugh since the big bang. The multi-media side band could be a hacking signal from the future. You have been warned."

**Dr Chris Forman, PhD, FRSA - Biophysicist.
Author of Brave Green World.**

"The sheer audacity of the author to take you where few science fiction writers have dared: The present, the future and the past rolled into an intriguing, innovative and interactive book. Well worth a deeper look."

John LeBrun AFC RAF (Retd), author of Lucky Me! Serendipity, and Twenty Years Flying Vulcans.

Emptiness is a natural part of the human condition especially when you come to the end of a good book.